Also by Denise Ryan

The Hit
Dead Keen
Betrayed

Backlash

Denise Ryan

ꏍ *Visit the Piatkus website!*

Piatkus publishes a wide range of bestselling fiction and non-fiction, including books on health, mind, body & spirit, sex, self-help, cookery, biography and the paranormal.

If you want to:
- read descriptions of our popular titles
- buy our books over the internet
- take advantage of our special offers
- enter our monthly competition
- learn more about your favourite Piatkus authors

VISIT OUR WEBSITE AT: www.piatkus.co.uk

Copyright © 2003 by Denise Ryan

First published in Great Britain in 2003 by
Judy Piatkus (Publishers) Ltd of
5 Windmill Street, London W1T 2JA
email: info@piatkus.co.uk

This edition published 2003

The moral right of the author has been asserted

*A catalogue record for this book is available
from the British Library*

ISBN 0 7499 3372 0

Set in Times by Phoenix Photosetting, Chatham, Kent

Printed and bound in Great Britain by
Mackays of Chatham Ltd, Chatham, Kent

Acknowledgements

I owe a big thank you to Pearson Fielding Solicitors, Liverpool. In particular, Andrew Pearson and Kieran Fielding for being kind enough to allow me to spend time there, Graham Polson for putting up with me tagging along, answering my questions and telling me alternately funny and hair-curling stories, and last but definitely not least, the lovely Sue Meacher-Jones. Without them this novel would not have been the same (?!)

Michael, thanks very much for finding out and explaining to me about crushers!

My thanks also to Gillian Green, Senior Fiction Editor at Piatkus.

To Peter, Mum, Michael, Elizabeth and Jerome & family,
David, Nuria, Marc and Martin.

Also to Sigrid, Kai, José & Kees, Margaret & Francis,
Famke, Panasse, Corina.

PART ONE

Chapter One

How much did it cost to get your future ex's paedo old
man stiffed?
More than you think
Ms Hot Bitch Criminal Lawyer!

Shannon Flinder gasped as she stared at the note thrust into
her hand by one of the black-gowned court ushers. Shock
punched her in the stomach; she went weak at the knees and
felt herself blanch. The voices, instant coffee smell and
bustle of Liverpool's Dale Street Magistrates' Court receded
as the words, handwritten in royal blue ink on a sheet of
smooth, ivory-tinted, A4 writing paper, leapt up at her. The
matching envelope had been tied with pink satin ribbon, the
kind little girls stitched on to their ballet shoes. It looked like
an old-fashioned love letter. Except that this was about hate.

She turned cold, started to tremble. Who the *hell*...?
Shannon didn't recognise the looped, sprawling handwriting, but that meant sod all. Who wrote by hand these
days, especially with what looked like a fountain pen?
Ministers signing treaties, maybe. And none of them would
write to her. 'Bloody hell,' she whispered, crumpling paper,
envelope and ribbon in one hand. 'I don't need this now.'

'I can't fix a new date yet to give evidence against your
no-show client.' The boy police officer strolled back. 'Our
answering machine's on. That sounds ... usual.'

3

'"Welcome to Merseyside Police,"' Shanon intoned. '"If you are being assaulted, press one. If you are being burgled, press two."' *If you are being threatened...?* She hitched up her bag and bundle of blue cardboard files.

He grinned. 'I'll radio in, ask for a talk-through. What's that?' He nodded at the crumpled paper and dangling ribbon. 'A cheesy lust letter from a perv who wants you to dress in black rubber and make all his wet dreams come true?'

Shannon frowned. 'I wish it was that simple.'

'Cheer up, love, it's not from me. I'm into necrophilia, not sad old rubber.'

'Really? Oh well, yeah. Look on the bright side, eh?'

He laughed. 'I'll get back to you about that new court date. See you, Shannon.'

'Okay.' He walked off and she glanced around the high-ceilinged lobby lit by pale sunshine. Rows of bored defendants and witnesses sat waiting to be called. A knot of solicitors and policemen were gathered around the WRVS coffee kiosk to her right. She sprinted after the usher and caught him as he pushed his way through swing doors into Court No. 7.

'Who gave you this?' She held up the note.

'One of the WRVS ladies, Mrs Flinder,' he smiled. 'She found it.'

'Thanks.' Shannon turned and hurried back. 'Did you see who left this note?' she asked the middle-aged, overalled lady serving tea, coffee and snacks.

'Sorry, darlin'. Haven't a clue.' The woman passed a frothy cappucino to a skinny youth in a navy tracksuit. 'I was pouring a cup of tea, then I turned and saw it lying on the counter. Whoever it was must have walked off and forgotten.' She paused. 'You all right? You look like you need a double shot of espresso.'

Shannon forced a smile. 'Not just now, thanks.' Her heart was pumping fast enough already. 'I'm fine.' She turned to the men standing around sipping tea and coffee. 'Did anyone see who left this?' They shrugged, shook their heads, answered in the negative.

She swept another glance around the lobby, scanning faces in the crowd. Was the mystery author still around? Watching maybe, enjoying her shock? A man in a leather jacket stared at her slim legs, encased in opaque black tights and black, polished, knee-length boots on this chilly March morning.

'Shannon!' a female voice shrieked, startling her. She turned and recognised her friend and ex-colleague, Jenny Fong. Jenny wore a white shirt and black trouser suit, her dumpy figure half hidden by the stack of files she carried. Shannon shoved letter, envelope and ribbon into her jacket pocket.

'How the hell are *you*?' Jenny dumped the files on the ground and grabbed her in a bear hug. 'Great to see you back. But are you sure it's not too soon after. . .?'

Car crash, miscarriage and impending *d-i-v-o-r-c-e* were the words Jenny needed to complete the sentence, but could not bring herself to speak. And thank goodness for that. They drew apart, studying one another.

'I've been off for nearly three months,' Shannon said. 'I was going mental sitting around that apartment staring out at the Mersey. How many ships, cranes and leisure developments can a girl count? Besides, I've got to keep my impending ex in the style to which he's become accustomed, haven't I?'

'You what?' Jenny's sallow skin turned pink. 'You're not still going to give him a lump sum as well as half of whatever you get for the house?'

'Yeah, well.' Shannon shrugged. 'It's not about justice.'

It wasn't Rob's fault that he'd freaked after discovering his father was a paedophile who had murdered several young girls. That was enough to make anyone fall apart big time. Although it didn't give him the right to beat her up, desert her and cheat on her with some WPC. Shannon flinched and caught her breath as the flashbacks hit. Now

5

that Rob's parents were dead he had inherited their big posh house in Woolton, plus all the money. His salary as a CID detective was well above the minimum wage. And they had no kids. Rob certainly wouldn't be short of a quid or two after this divorce. But Shannon didn't care about the money.

'I want this done fast, Jenny,' she said. 'A clean break. If I throw him more than he's entitled to, he can't argue or delay things.' Would Rob write that note? she wondered. He didn't hate her that much. Did he?

'Does he still pester you to go back to him?'

'No.' Shannon wiped her sweaty palms on her skirt. 'Can we get off the subject?'

'Sorry. Me and my big gob.' Jenny smiled at her. 'You look beautiful as ever. Bitch!' she joked. 'I love the black suit and red lipstick, very elegant. It's amazing, you'd never guess. I mean–' She broke off, blushing. 'Oh, shit!'

'I know. I don't look like I've been through hell. You're not the first to remark on it, and I'm bored in advance to know you won't be the last.'

'Oh, Shannon!' Jenny's eyes filled with tears. 'You *have* been through hell.'

'Hey, stop it. Whinging's my prerogative.'

Jenny hugged her again and Shannon started to feel faint. She wanted work, routine, laughter, even boredom. Anything but weeping, bleeding emotion. Brooding over the past and feeling terrified of the future. 'Don't be the next git to tell me how lucky I am,' she muttered. 'Or you'll be eating hospital food for lunch.'

'I wouldn't dream of it.' Jenny let go of her and wiped her eyes. 'How's your arm?' she asked. 'How many operations did it take to repair that artery?'

'Three. The pain and swelling's gone, but it still aches a bit now and then. The physio taught me some exercises which help.'

'You're left-handed too, aren't you? My God! Thank goodness you didn't lose the arm like the surgeon was afraid–'

'Yeah. Thank goodness.'

'Oh, Shannon, I'm sorry. There I go again. Excuse me while I shoot myself.'

'Forget it. When are you coming to work for me, Khalida and Mi-Hae?' Shannon asked, desperate to deflect Jenny from all things painful before she lost it and ran sobbing out of the building. Jenny meant well – everyone did – but questions and comments hit her like bricks. She was too raw, too fragile. Why couldn't people just shut the fuck up about her calamities? Confession wasn't always good for the soul.

'I'll throw in my lot with Kam Flinder Najeba when you get some big-time lowlife to defend,' Jenny grinned. 'That's what brings in the bucks, innit? Use your charm and wild blonde beauty, Shannon. Reel those suckers in.'

'Not all big-time lowlife are straight males, you cynical, politically incorrect little critter.'

'Come on. The vast majority of them are.'

'In that case, wouldn't an element of sexism form part of the stereotype profile? What makes you think they'd want me rather than a geezer in a sharp suit?'

'Because you're good. And it's politically correct to get a woman to defend you. Especially on a rape rap.'

'Rapists aren't generally big time. But okay, fine. I'll call you.'

'How's Finbar?' Jenny's blush crept back as she visualised the tall, gorgeous, dark-haired Irishman. 'I'm so glad you've got him now.'

'Finbar's fine, thanks.' He wasn't, but that was another calamity Shannon couldn't talk about. She recalled him lying in bed that morning, silently watching her as she got dressed, scrunched her hair dry and brushed some colour on her cheekbones, his green eyes brooding. Had he gone to India Buildings this morning, or the air cargo office at John Lennon airport? The club, maybe. He was supposed to be interviewing prospective new managers. She jumped as Jenny grasped her left hand and studied the diamond glittering on her third finger.

'At least you can wear your engagement ring again. It's fabulous,' she breathed. 'Must have cost a fortune. I can see blue fire twisting in the depths – like it's got magic powers!'

Shannon felt a twinge of guilt. She was pushing Finbar away, hurting him. But she couldn't think what to do. It took all her strength to crawl out of bed each morning and face the cold world. Now there was this bloody anonymous letter. How much did the bastard know, what did he or she want? Money, revenge?

Revenge for what? Not Bernard Flinder, surely. The scandal of the respected headmaster exposed as a murderous paedophile and blown up by a car bomb might have been booted off the front pages by the latest terrorist outrage, but it was still going strong. A lot of people knew Shannon had been his daughter-in-law; it wasn't inconceivable that she'd attract the attention of some nut job in need of mega doses of anti-psychotic medication. Or a crank driven to legal and clinical insanity by daytime telly. As she herself almost had been these past three months.

I had to have him killed, Shannon thought, breaking out in a sweat. He raped and murdered those girls. No one believed me. I was in terrible danger. She felt suffocated as she fought back panic. The bastard destroyed my marriage, he tried to murder me. The crash almost finished the job. I lost my baby! Haven't I been punished enough?

'Shannon, are you okay?' Jenny laid one hand on her shoulder. 'You look pale. Why don't you go home and rest? It's going to take a lot longer than three months to get over what you've been through.'

'Jenny, I'm fine. Please don't worry.' Shannon pushed back her hair, took a breath and glanced at her watch. 'I'm sorry, but I have to run. Got a client waiting.'

'Well, take care, okay? Let's meet for lunch or a drink soon.'

'That'd be great. E-mail me.'

'I will. See you, Shannon.'

Jenny frowned as she watched her friend rush off.

8

Shannon talked the same, looked the same. But some piece of her was missing. What was that look in her dark, violet eyes? Desolation, fear? Jenny was puzzled. Rob wouldn't dare threaten or hurt her again. She would pick up once the divorce was finalised. And she had Finbar now. He was crazy about her.

Shannon had nothing to fear. Not any more.

Shannon hurried along a corridor, through swing doors and down two flights of stairs to the cells. She pressed a buzzer, passed through a black metal mesh gate and nodded to the Group 4 security guard who unlocked the door.

It was cramped and stuffy down in the Bridewell. The Victorian building had originally been a workhouse; she thought the old smells and despair lingered in the thick walls. The cell doors were painted grey and had chains on the outside. Except for the strip lighting and Group 4 personnel milling around, it was like stepping back into the nineteenth century. She said hello to a duty solicitor who leaned against the counter talking on the phone. As a member of the Liverpool Duty Solicitors Scheme Shannon did stints down here herself and did not enjoy them, especially at night when the holding cell along the corridor was full of shouting, cursing drunks peeing in corners.

'Keely Breeze?' she said to a petite, bespectacled female guard with short, fair hair. 'I need a cosy chat.' The woman nodded and walked off, dangling keys on a chain. Shannon went into one of the tiny, windowless cubicles where solicitors conferred with their clients, dumped her files and bag on the table and squeezed into the chair behind it. She took a biro from her bag and started to leaf through papers in the top file. The note crackled in her pocket, as if it was not an inanimate object but had taken on an evil life of its own. *Who?* she wondered again.

Shannon stared at the papers without seeing what was written. Her left arm ached. She dropped the biro and leaned her head against the cold brick wall. I'm knackered, she thought. All these sleepless nights. Should have had that double espresso. God, I can't go on like this. A couple of well-meaning friends advised counselling, but Finbar knew better than to mention that C-word.

'Hiya, Blondie! Sleeping on the job, eh?'

She jerked upright and grabbed her biro. 'Morning, Keely.'

The tall, sharp-faced woman in her mid-thirties slumped into the chair opposite. She wore jeans, dirty trainers, a blue fleece, and had that hollow-eyed look. Her wispy, aubergine-tinted hair resembled a bird's nest.

'You gonna get me out of here this morning?' Keely demanded. She examined her long, sparkly blue nails.

'If you don't smack any more police officers.'

'Yeah, it's only them's allowed to do the smacking, isn't it! I told you, that was an accident. Self-defence. I thought that hard-arsed bitch was gonna clock *me* one. I did, Blondie, honest to God!'

Shannon's efforts to stifle a huge yawn brought tears to her eyes. She riffled through Keely's file. There was always so much bloody paperwork.

'Bastards won't give me a lighter. Or pen.'

'Standard procedure. Those things can do a lot of damage in the wrong hands.' Shannon didn't ask what Keely wanted to write. 'So, we've got these four counts of credit card deception as well as the alleged assault.'

'It wasn't me did the credit card stuff! I never had nothin' to do with it. That's why I went apeshit when they tried to arrest me.'

'Are you claiming mistaken identity? The items bought with the nicked cards – plus the cards – were found in your possession, Keely, and two receipts dropped out of your mouth and pocket while you were struggling with the police officer.' Fancy not chucking the receipts, Shannon thought, writing notes on her pad. What did Ms Breeze plan to do, take back the clothes and demand a refund if she changed her mind and decided she didn't like them?

'I never meant to hit that cop, I told you. She went for me.' Shannon cringed as Keely fiddled with her nails, hoping she wasn't going to start scratching and chipping off bits of polish. 'I panicked, that's all.'

'The officer's got a black eye and a fat lip and she'll need to see her dentist about a new crown. But okay. We'll say you didn't mean it and you're very sorry. Do you still want to plead not guilty to the credit card deception?' Shannon asked. 'Because if you do and they find you guilty, the sentence could be higher. And it's not your first offence. The magistrates might send you to be tried at the Crown Court this time.'

'You what? They won't put me away, will they?' Keely sat up and stared at Shannon, her grey-green eyes filled with alarm. 'Okay, I did do it. But I've got three little lads under ten.' Her voice was husky, choked with tears. 'I can't go inside! It was bad enough being stuck in this shithole all night. It stinks down here. God, what'll happen to me kids?'

'Keely.' Shannon reached across the table and squeezed her hand. 'I know it's difficult, but try not to worry about that right now. Okay? One thing at a time. I'll ask for bail, we'll get you out and take it from there. I'll tell them about your boys. Who's looking after them at the moment?'

'Me mum. But she can't keep them long. She gets chest pains – angina.'

'I see.' Shannon scribbled more notes. 'I'll mention that too.' It could well be a custodial sentence. And being Mum to three young boys wouldn't save Keely this time. Shannon felt sorry for the kids.

'I could murder a ciggie.' Keely rubbed her reddened eyes. 'Got one, Blondie?'

'Sorry. I don't smoke.' Shannon stood up and gathered her files. 'Right, Keely, see you later.' She smiled and patted her shoulder. 'Take care, okay? Don't worry.' Bit late for that, but never mind.

She had three more cases first, a woman who pleaded guilty to biting her ex-husband during a row, a drug addict

11

who had nicked two mobile phones, and a middle-aged drunk driver. Shannon tried not to torture herself about the anonymous letter or the possible identity of its author, and succeeded. For a while. Keely Breeze pleaded guilty, was bailed – without conditions – to appear at the Crown Court in six weeks time, and warned of the dire consequences if she failed to attend. Shannon hurried to the lawyers room to fetch her coat while Keely was led back downstairs to collect her personal effects.

The dingy, musty room was empty. Shannon put bag and files on the desk and took her coat, sending wire hangers jangling along the rail. She slipped it on, turned and caught sight of herself in the mirror.

'Don't you look lovely,' she muttered, brushing back her hair and pulling at the fringe. It was curling up again the way it did, driving her mad. She took out the letter and the pink satin ribbon fell, curling around her foot like a snake. Shannon kicked it away because she couldn't bear to touch it again. She ripped up paper and envelope and dropped the pieces in the bin. She would admonish a client never to destroy evidence. But of what was this evidence? A sad act with a sick sense of humour. Ignore. End of story. *Was* it Rob? Shannon could not help wondering again. Someone else she knew? Friendly face, malicious heart. That was a nasty thought.

'God's sake, give it up!' she whispered, biting her lip. She walked out, telling herself the hollowness in her stomach was only hunger. She would go down the road to the sandwich place, buy a bacon-and-Stilton butty and a cup of strong coffee, head back to the office and wade through paperwork. She checked her mobile; no messages. Keely Breeze sat in the lobby transferring lipstick, nail file, lighter and king-size cigarettes from a plastic bag to her purple leather rucksack.

'Thanks, Blondie,' she grinned, waving her blue bail form as Shannon approached. 'You're a doll. Cheered me right up.'

'I'm glad.' Shannon did not want to spoil her client's good mood by mentioning the Crown Court or custodial sentences. She noticed Keely wore a very expensive coat.

'Like it?' Keely stood up and did a twirl. 'It's Armani. Pure virgin wool. Tweedy coats aren't usually my thing. But that fella's magic, isn't he?'

'Yeah.' Shannon rolled her eyes. 'Giorgio's fab *collezione* is all I wake up for.' Should have been five counts of credit card deception, she thought.

'I didn't rob it, you know.' Keely giggled as they walked out and headed downstairs. 'It was a prezzie.'

'Hey, I believe you.'

'No you don't, you sarky cow.' In the street Keely paused to light a cigarette. 'Oh, holy fuck!' she breathed, closing her eyes and drawing the smoke into her lungs. 'I needed this.' Shannon smiled.

A man in jeans and a black jacket jogged towards them. Weird, Shannon thought, noting his black woolly hat and the tartan scarf wrapped around the lower half of his face. It's not *that* bloody cold. He speeded up and she stepped back, startled, afraid he would barge into them. Keely opened her eyes and gasped. She turned and fled, dropping rucksack and cigarette.

'Keely, wait!' Shannon stooped and grabbed the rucksack, trying not to drop her own bag or files. 'What's going on?' The masked jogger sprinted past, chasing Keely into a nearby alley. Shannon raced after them, her heart pounding.

'Get back!' he yelled, his voice muffled. His dark eyes were panicked, furious. 'I'll fucking kill you.'

Shannon froze at the sight of the Stanley knife in his right hand and cried out as he swiped the air with it, thinking he meant to slash her face. Terror drained the strength from her body, and she thought her legs would give way. But he lowered the knife, raced off and caught up with Keely. He grabbed a fistful of her flying aubergine hair and jerked her to a halt. Keely gave a heartrending, terrified scream that seemed to go on and on.

13

The attacker twisted her round and pulled her head back. For a split second, it looked as if he was going to kiss her passionately. He raised one arm, made a swift, brutal movement, then shoved her away. Glanced back at Shannon. The scarf fell and she saw acne-scarred, olive skin, several days stubble, pale thin lips drawn back to reveal white teeth. He seemed to take in every detail of her appearance too. He moved towards her, the blade dripping blood.

'Don't you touch me!' Shannon shook her head, her eyes locked on him. 'Don't even think about it.' Panic leapt in her as he moved closer. 'I killed somebody once,' she heard herself hiss. 'I can bloody well do it again.' He stopped. Stared at her.

'What's going on?' A policeman and security guard from the Magistrates' Court rushed into the alley. The attacker flung the scarf around his face and sprinted off, too fast for the unfit, middle-aged men to catch him. Keely Breeze was staggering, eyes dilated with shock, hands clutched to her throat. Dark, arterial blood spurted from between her fingers, staining Giorgio's beautifully tailored coat. She sank to her knees. Shannon rushed up and saw the gaping wound in her throat.

'Oh, my God!' She crouched beside her. 'Call an ambulance,' she shouted to the stunned men. 'Quick!'

Keely's terrified face was ashen. Shannon helped her to sit against the brick wall and pressed shaking fingers to the hideous wound, trying to keep it closed. People poured into the alley and stood staring. Blood bubbled out of Keely's mouth and her eyes glazed. She sagged sideways and collapsed into Shannon's arms.

'You'll be all right, sweetheart,' Shannon whispered, not believing it. 'The ambulance will be here any second. Keep your head forward, okay? I'll stay with you, I'm not going anywhere.' She was frozen, her breath coming in gasps. Keely's blood was soaking her clothes. I saw that bastard's face, Shannon thought. He saw me. Now he's escaped. Who is he? Does he know Keely? Why did he do this?

14

'Ambulance is on its way.' The policeman squatted beside them and gently took Keely's wrist, feeling for a pulse. 'Your client, is she?' he asked. Shannon nodded.

Keely's eyes were pleading. Her lips moved. 'Don't try to talk, sweetheart.' Shannon stroked her wispy hair. The alley's cracked tarmac dug into her knees. 'Just hold on, okay?' There was so much blood.

She suddenly felt sick. Her mind flashed back to the icy January afternoon when she'd regained consciousness in her wrecked car. Thick mist swirling, glass and grit in her hair, seatbelt digging into her sore ribs. The taste of blood. Thinking, this is death and so what? Two days later, the miscarriage. Finbar holding her, his eyes full of tears, telling her how much he loved her. Begging her to forgive him.

Shannon gasped as something shattered inside her. She wanted to lift her face to the blue sky, howl with rage and grief. But she couldn't lose it now, not here. She choked on the scream, forced it back down. Stared at her trembling, bloodstained fingers.

'Help me,' Keely whispered. 'Dying.'

Chapter Two

'My previous manager was forced to quit.' Finbar Linnell glanced around the dark, empty nightclub that smelled of last night's booze, cigarettes, sweet perfumes and sweaty bodies. 'After I kneecapped him.'

'Not trying to put me off, are you, mate?' Terry the job applicant, desperate to claw his way up from bar work to management, tried to laugh but managed only a strangled cough. Bastard's got a screw loose, he thought. He stared at Finbar's calm, narrow, handsome face, his sombre green eyes and the designer facial hair that should have made him look a prat but didn't. Finbar leaned on the bar jangling keys in the pocket of his leather jacket, as if he was desperate to piss off and do something much more important.

Terry had heard about Finbar Linnell from people who had tangled with the guy and lived to boast about it in pubs and clubs when they'd had a skinful. Drug trafficking, mainly, here and in the Netherlands. Didn't say no to buying and flogging military hardware going spare in the Balkans, eastern Europe or the Middle East either. Add to that contact with some Irish dissident terrorist group – maybe others too – and you had one busy bastard. All that was over now though, or so Terry had heard. The word was that Finbar Linnell had gone soft, knocked his hobbies on the head all for *lurve* of a natural blonde criminal law solicitor with violet eyes and a Page Three body. This club and his air cargo business was no longer a front for anything. Bor-*ing*.

Was that why the guy looked so pissed off, wondering if his natural blonde was worth the sacrifice? Terry did not imagine being a dodgy Irish entrepreneur in Liverpool when dissident Republicans – or so the police believed – had not long ago decorated Water Street with the body parts of the Defence Secretary helped Finbar feel happy-clappy either. That was supposed to be ancient history already, and the politicians said the war was over. Trouble was, not everyone agreed with them. Especially these breakaway paramilitary groups that kept popping up.

Do I really want this job? Terry wondered, thinking of the kneecapped ex-manager. A mate of his, Eddie, a bouncer at the Carmen Club, had helped drag Finbar's screaming, bleeding victim out of the office and down the back stairs. It was the stupid bastard's own fault, Eddie said. He'd lied to Finbar, tried to rip him off. He was lucky Finbar fired the bullets into his fat, white, hairy knees and not his thick skull. Terry frowned, clenching his hands inside his coat pockets. Finbar offered good money, a lot more than he earned now. He wouldn't get bored here either. Then again, Terry liked his adventure risk-free.

'Okay.' Finbar straightened up and pulled the keys out of his pocket. 'You've got yourself a job.'

'Eh? Oh! Cool. Thanks, mate.'

Finbar was amused by Terry's startled reaction. The guy wasn't that experienced as a manager, just full of self-promoting guff about being left in charge by an unprecedented number of absentee bosses. He was keen though, not too cocky, and not thick. Terry was frightened of him, and that was good too. Being Eddie's mate, he knew the score.

'Can you start this evening?'

'Sure. No problem.'

'Right. Come back about six. In a better suit. I'll explain everything else then. You'll have to excuse me.' Finbar nodded towards the door. 'Got to shoot off.'

'Sure,' Terry repeated. He backed away. 'See you later.'

'Don't worry,' Finbar smiled. 'You'll be fine. I've got faith in you.' I might sell this place, he thought suddenly. I don't need it any more. It's too much hassle.

Terry turned, still stunned, and left the club of which he now found himself manager. Alone, Finbar went up to his office, walked in and shut the door. He sank into the big leather desk chair, leaned his head back and sighed. He didn't feel like checking the books or making phone calls. Didn't feel like doing anything. He just went through the motions these days, kept busy so as to avoid going mental.

What was Shannon doing now? Trying to save some tosser from jail or a Community Punishment Order? Protecting the bewildered from fit-ups? Finbar hoped going back to work would make her feel better, help break her out of that silent, preoccupied world she had locked herself in, and to which he couldn't gain access. I love her more than ever, he thought. But how can I help when she won't let me? How does she feel about me now? About anything?

Shannon had to be still in shock. Her life had been complicated enough before a car crash and miscarriage blew it apart. Finbar wished again that she had confided in him about her bastard of a father-in-law sooner, instead of putting herself at deadly risk by hiring that moron who described himself as a hit man. At least he had sorted *him*. The police had only recently stopped harassing Shannon when their search for evidence turned up nothing. Who wanted to find the murderer of a paedophile anyway? Most people thought Bernard Flinder's killer was a hero, said they would have done the same themselves. If that bitch of a Detective Sergeant had not taken a ferociously jealous dislike to Shannon, the investigation would never have got off the ground.

He stood up and started to pace. The phone's red eye winked at him, but he couldn't be bothered to check his messages. He had made big changes in his life because of

18

Shannon. Given up the drugs, the arms, broken off with his contacts. Some of them were very unhappy about that. But none of it seemed important any more. Now Finbar wondered if was going to be so easy. Things were quiet – too quiet. Like a nerve-racking, eve-of-battle silence. Or was he being paranoid? He felt like somebody just back from a war zone who couldn't get used to not living with the threat of imminent death.

Irritated by the phone's winking light, he stopped and erased the four messages without listening to them. Glanced at the array of bottles on a nearby table. No. Booze would only make him feel worse. The phone rang and he turned away. It wasn't Shannon, she would be in court. Finbar did not imagine himself being arrested and put on trial – if it ever got that far he would be dead before the arresting plod reached the bit about anything he was thick enough to say being given in evidence. The phone stopped ringing and he walked to the door. It rang again.

'Fuck's sake!' He strode back and snatched up the receiver. 'Yeah, who is it?'

'Good morning!' a female voice sang. 'This is the Irish embassy in The Hague. One moment, please, I have the Consul on the line for you.'

'Hi, Finbar. Dominic. How are you?'

'Fine, thanks,' Finbar lied. What did his big brother want? They hadn't seen one another for a year, or spoken for almost three months. He stared out of the office window, down into the alley where his Maserati was parked. 'How's life in the foreign service?'

'Deeply unsatisfying, as usual. Still spending most of my working hours fending off wannabe immigrants to fair Erin. They get into the Netherlands from the Balkans, Romania, Afghanistan, you name it, and then want to move on. Anyway, I've got some news for you.'

'Yeah. I thought you might.' Dominic never called just to pass the time of day.

'Auntie Sylvia died.' Dominic cleared his throat. 'She's

19

left you all her worldly goods. Including that rambling old pile on the island.'

'She *died*?' Finbar echoed, shocked. 'When? How?'

'Ten days ago, massive heart attack. Very sudden, but things like that tend to happen when you're eighty-four. The funeral was last Friday.'

'And no one thought to invite me,' Finbar said, stung. Although he would not have wanted to leave Shannon moping silently by herself in the apartment, and he doubted if she would have gone with him to Ireland. He felt stifled by his brother's cold, indifferent tone. Sylvia had never made much fuss of Dominic, and he wasn't one to forget such slights. 'Did you go?'

'No, I was tied up here. Jill and the girls went. Ma said she didn't want you there. Too much water under the bridge. Etcetera.'

'You mean because I didn't fancy being a Cardinal at the Vatican or a Harley Street specialist, abandoned the Holy Roman religion and refused to marry the doctor's daughter of her choice?'

Dominic ignored that. 'She's furious about Sylvia leaving you everything. Especially the house. You know she always fancied living there herself.'

'Maybe she should have been nicer to her sister then, instead of laughing at Sylvia and calling her the old spinster. Takes more than biology, Dom. She and Dad never could get their heads round that.'

'Don't go all bitter on me,' Dominic said, bored.

'So the only human being in our family's gone? Well, thanks for letting me know. Eventually.'

'What will you do with the place?' Dominic sounded interested now. 'Flog it to some rich bastard – a pop star or actor, maybe – for at least ten times its market value? I would. And retire on the proceeds.'

'I'll go down and take a look at the house before I do anything. Jesus!' Tears stung Finbar's eyes. 'I can't believe Sylvia's dead. I was going to visit her soon and take Shannon, but...'

'Oh yes, your girlfriend. Sorry, fiancée. I'll have to meet her one day. Has she got over her accident yet?'

'Not exactly.' Finbar flinched. 'She's more or less physically okay now, but–' He stopped. He hadn't been able to bring himself to tell Dominic about Shannon's miscarriage, and he wouldn't now.

'But not psychologically. Hmm. Takes time, I suppose. Listen,' Dominic said briskly, 'you can get Sylvia's keys and stuff from her solicitor. Let him know what you decide about the house.'

Death came in threes, Finbar thought. He and Shannon had lost their baby, and now Sylvia was dead. Whose turn was it next? He stared at the closed office doors, one of which led into the club, the other down the back stairs to the alley.

'Sorry, Dom,' he said. 'Got to go now.'

Today was getting more depressing by the minute. Shannon shutting herself off, slipping away from him. He felt menaced by some unknown enemy. And he hated the cold March weather. March winds, the ides of March, Julius Caesar striding into the Senate saying better to die once than be always afraid of it.

'Me too,' Dominic sighed. 'A bunch of excited Nigerians just arrived. Give me a call sometime, okay? Let me know about the house.'

'Yeah. 'Bye.' Finbar hung up and stood looking out of the window, his eyes wet. A minute later the phone rang again. He picked up the receiver, wishing it would be Sylvia to tell him it was a stupid mistake and she hadn't croaked it after all.

'Good morning, am I speaking to Finbar Linnell?'

'You are.' The man's voice was cheerful and polite, upper-class git English. Finbar tensed.

'Excellent. I've got a message for you, Mr Linnell.' Silence.

'So what is it?' Finbar asked after a few seconds. Something's wrong, he thought. 'Who is this?' A click, followed by the dial tone. 'Shit,' he whispered. *'Shit.'*

21

He dialled 1471, but of course the caller had withheld the number. He put the phone down and stood still, his eyes locked on the door to the back stairs. Fear gripped him. He had no gun in the desk or safe, had got rid of them in case the police dropped by for a cosy chat. 'Cosy chat' was how Shannon described visits to clients in jails and police cells. Conferences with barristers, meetings with murderers. Finbar couldn't remember the last time she'd been in the mood for a cosy chat with him.

His mind flashed back to the freezing room of the office building, regaining consciousness to find Lenny Dowd standing over him pointing the gun. Sirens and screams outside, his sickening realisation that he was too late to stop the politician's murder. Did they think he knew too much, that he was a security risk now? Life's crap, Finbar thought, fighting fear. But I don't want to die.

He pushed the blinds aside, opened the window and scanned the narrow alley. Nobody was lurking there, as far as he could see. He climbed out, hung painfully by his arms and dropped to the concrete floor. He glanced around, rubbing his sore hands. Nobody. He got down on all fours and checked under the car. Nothing that looked like a bomb. A torch would be handy, but that was in the Maserati's glove box and he wasn't going to open the car yet, no way. The door to the back stairs showed no signs of a break-in. He strode out of the alley and peered up and down the quiet street of terraced Georgian houses. Nothing suspicious there either, or not that he could see.

Maybe someone with a twisted sense of humour was just trying to freak him. Well, they had succeeded. The mystery guy on the phone was a Brit; many members of breakaway paramilitary groups were Brits with Irish connections. Or could it be Special Branch? he wondered. Maybe other more sinister members of Her Majesty's Civil Service? Ex-contact, old enemy? Finbar could not decide which possibility was the most deeply creepy.

He walked back and checked the interior of the car, looking for stray wires, anything different. It seemed undisturbed. Even the cellophane wrapper of the Cheddar cheese sandwich he'd bought for breakfast did not look as if it had crumpled another centimetre.

'This is starting to piss me off,' he muttered, frowning. He decided to go back into the club and check there, close the office window and lock up. Stay cautious, try not to be paranoid. This might be all in his head, maybe he wasn't in any danger. Shannon wasn't the only one screwed up by post-traumatic stress.

He unlocked the door and re-locked it behind him, ran up the stairs and stood in the silent office. No sound except his own breathing. Outside in the street a lorry rumbled past. Finbar hesitated and opened the door that led into the dark club. Who might be hiding there? He stepped out, his heart thudding, wishing he had a gun. He was skirting the small dance floor when he saw the heavily taped package lying on the bar, lit by a single spotlight.

'Fuck!'

He sprinted for the front door and slammed it behind him. Raced into the street and away. Imagined his tombstone with, *'See? I was right!'* carved on it. Shannon, sexy in black, weeping over him. If she still cared enough to weep.

'Get back!' he yelled to two startled workmen in paint-splashed overalls. 'There's a bomb. Move!'

'Jesus Christ!' They dropped their cans and metal ladder and ran back across the street. Finbar raced for some area steps that led down to a basement.

The force of the blast shook the ground beneath his feet, swept him up as he ran and hurled him headlong, engulfing him in a dark, billowing cloud of dust and glass fragments.

Chapter Three

'I was soaked in her blood, Mi-Hae.'

Shannon shivered as she stood in the huge, warm living room of the Albert Dock apartment, with its expanse of shiny wooden floor and view of the River Mersey. She clutched her blue bathrobe around her and shook back her damp curls.

'My God!' Mi-Hae Kam breathed. 'It's unbelievable. You think you're in for a boring morning at the Mags Court, then you witness a horrific attack on your client. Are *you* okay, Shannon? You must be in shock.'

'I'm all right. At least, I think so. I had to come home and get a shower once I'd finished at the hospital and police station.' Shannon transferred the phone to her other ear and glanced at a yellow carrier bag on the floor by one of the sofas. 'I've still got Keely's posh coat. I had it with me at the hospital and completely forgot to hand it to a nurse or cop.'

'That can wait until tomorrow. Stay home for the rest of the day. Try to relax.'

'Keely told me it was a present, but–'

'If that's a present, I'm a jar of kimchi!' Mi-Hae interrupted. 'Who'd give *her* an Armani coat? The Keely Breezes of this cruel world don't attract Armani kind of guys, Shannon. Shell suits, trainers and lager, and you're right on the money.'

Shannon frowned. 'Another cutting edge social comment from Ms Kam.'

'If you think I'm a bitch, say so.' Mi-Hae laughed. 'I thought only submissive little Korean girls beat coyly round the bush, not in-your-face Western women.'

'Hey, stereotypes too. You'll be asking Khalida why she doesn't wear a burqa next.' Shannon sighed. 'Why would anyone want to hurt Keely ... *murder* her? It doesn't make sense. Of course we don't know the facts.'

'I can't understand it either,' Mi-Hae replied. 'Her ex-husband remarried a couple of years ago and they meet when he picks up or drops off the kids. All seems very civilised on the domestic front. Keely works in some pub in town, and she never mentioned trouble there either. Apart from the trouble anyone who works in a city-centre pub might reasonably expect to encounter.'

'Which is quite a lot. We can't be sure there's no boyfriend,' Shannon argued. 'Just because no one accompanies her to court looking all self-important and conscious of being a man taking manly responsibility.'

'You think Keely knows her assailant?' Mi-Hae asked.

'Possibly. She was terrified the second she saw him – she knew instantly that he was after her. She just took off and left me gasping. This wasn't a random attack. I got a good look at him,' Shannon said. 'Made a statement.'

'And he got a good look at you.' Mi-Hae was silent for a few seconds. 'Did Keely seem nervous or frightened before the attack?'

'She was depressed after a night in the Bridewell – as you would be – and she panicked when it sank in that she could be looking at a stretch for the credit card thing. She was freaked about what might happen to her kids. But once bail was granted she cheered right up, only seemed to need a nicotine fix to make her happiness complete. You certainly wouldn't have thought she expected to get her throat slashed any minute.'

'God! Did you get a chance to question her in hospital?'

'No way.' Shannon started to shiver again. 'It looks really bad for her. I got the impression the paramedics didn't think she'd make it to A&E.' She picked up her mug and took another gulp of hot, sweet coffee. Tea was the recommended drink for shock, but her body craved strong coffee. 'I went with her to hospital and managed to have a word with one of the doctors. He said when that bastard slashed her throat he cut right through the larynx. It might be irreparably damaged – there's a lot of swelling and tissue damage. Keely's airways closed up. Forget talking, she couldn't breathe.' Shannon paused, biting her lip. 'They had to make a hole in her neck.'

'A tracheotomy? Jesus! She can write down her attacker's name though, can't she?' Mi-Hae persisted. 'If she knows him. Or knows who's behind this.'

'Keely's terribly weak, Mi-Hae. Barely conscious. She nearly died.' Shannon flinched and blinked back tears. 'They were transfusing her when I left.' She put the coffee mug down because her hand was shaking.

'Blood loss and transfusions? This is a *déja vu* nightmare for you, Shannon! Have you got a drink there?'

'Coffee.'

'That's no damn good. Tip it down the sink and pour yourself some firewater.'

'I might do that.'

'Shall I try to distract you by talking about boring old work?'

'Please do.'

'Okay. There's two new cases just in. A guy accused of shooting a student and concealing the body in a landfill site. He claims he's –'

'Innocent. Well, he could be. How did they manage to dig out a body *there*?'

'A tip-off.' Mi-Hae laughed at Shannon's groan. 'And there's a guy charged with threatening behaviour and unlawful possession of firearms. Name of Demetrio Montana.'

'Sounds like a footballer.'

26

'Yes, I thought that. He wants our Ms Flinder to act for him. Insists on it.'

'Why me?' Shannon tensed. 'I don't know the guy, I've never heard of him.'

'Why not you? This could be good for us, Shannon. Raise our profile.'

'Depends what kind of profile you want to raise.'

'Behave. I've sent Leon our trusty accredited representative down the nick to visit him and get the details, but you'll have to take over from tomorrow. I know you hate anything to do with firearms, but I can't handle it because I'm up to my eyes in fraud documents. And Khalida's gone to Leeds for that rape case.'

'I know,' Shannon sighed. Solicitors could not make moral choices about what kind of clients they wanted to act for. It was the cab rank principle – take what comes and apply the law. It's work, she thought. That's what you want, isn't it? 'I wonder how Mr Montana came to pick on me?'

'Dunno. What does it matter? Don't sound so uneasy, Shannon. Listen, you've had a horrible shock, what with Keely and everything. Go and rest now. And it's Friday tomorrow. Not doing any Duty Solicitor stints this weekend, are you?'

'No. Thank goodness.'

'That's a relief. Sleep, eat, read a novel. Watch crap on telly.'

'I'll be spoilt for choice there. Right, Mi-Hae. See you tomorrow.'

Demetrio Montana did not sound like anyone's real name, Shannon thought. She slid her cold hands inside the robe's sleeves, moved to the windows and gazed out at the steel-grey river. The spring sunshine had faded, and there were no boats out. Everything looked dead, deserted. Firewater, she thought. But not too fiery. She went into the kitchen and poured herself a glass of Pouilly Fumé, took a packet of salt & black pepper crisps from a cupboard. Back in the living room she sat on the sofa, opened the crisps and took a gulp of white wine. Pointed the remote control at the television.

A series about a pathologist, a movie about a woman who had just suffered a miscarriage. Imbeciles arguing furiously on a talk show. Worst of all, the news headlines. She flipped on, and found a comforting cookery programme. Shannon tried to stop thinking about Keely Breeze and the horrific attack. The anonymous letter came back into her mind.

Maybe she should not have destroyed it. There was zero reason to keep it, however, when she had no intention of involving the police. If Rob was behind this, what the hell did he want? He had hated his parents, especially his father, was relieved that they were dead. And he had more than enough money now. Did he want to torture her because she refused to halt the divorce proceedings and go back to him? He hated her being with Finbar. Should she seek a confrontation? But what was the point? Rob would only deny he'd written the letter, and maybe he would be telling the truth. It didn't look like his handwriting, although he could have disguised it. But it did seem a bit previous to blame the impending ex just because she couldn't think of any other culprit right now. *Wipe it*, Shannon told herself, staring at the screen. Don't let this moron get to you. That's what they want. You've got more important stuff to worry about. Like Keely Breeze. And being witness to an attempted murder. She remembered the attacker's face, his furious eyes. The knife blade dripping blood. Could she herself be in danger from him now? Shannon doubted it, but the possibility was there. It had certainly crossed Mi-Hae's mind.

She took another gulp of white wine and almost dropped the glass in fright as the front door slammed. She gasped and her heart beat furiously. She was sick of being so jumpy. Finbar walked in and stopped when he saw her.

'Well, hello. What are you doing home in your bathrobe in the middle of the afternoon?' He frowned, noting how pale she looked. 'What's happened?'

'Bad day at work.' Shannon glanced away, drank more wine. 'I came home early.'

'Don't get me wrong, it's a delightful surprise.' He slipped off his jacket and draped it over the back of a sofa, crossed to the sideboard and poured himself a small Ardbeg. 'Are you okay? Now there's a stupid question.' He wanted to sit next to Shannon and put his arms around her, but wasn't sure she would welcome that. He sat on the opposite sofa, sighed and stretched out his long legs. Raised his glass in a salute, then took a sip. 'So what about this bad day at work?'

'I could ask you the same question.' Shannon was staring at him. 'You're as white as that wall paint and your hair's full of dust. Your forehead's bruised. How did you get those scratches on your face?'

'Never mind me.' Finbar took another sip of malt. 'I asked you first.'

'Oh, no. Never mind you.' Her voice was subdued, her deep, dark blue eyes sad. 'All right.' She put her wine glass on the coffee table and leaned back. 'Keep your damn secrets.'

'I'll tell you,' he said, his heart pierced by her vulnerability, the slumped shoulders and air of dejection. 'No more secrets. Or lies.' Finbar frowned at the television. One chef had finished with sticky toffee pudding and another was now giving a bloody demonstration of how easy it was to gut fish. 'Mind if I switch this off?' he asked. 'Unless you're watching it.'

'No.' She shrugged. 'Go ahead.' She had seen enough gore for one day.

Finbar imagined himself buried in rubble. Trapped, choking, unable to breathe or move. He licked his lips; his mouth felt dry. He switched off the television, swigged the rest of the whisky and went to pour himself another.

He was still shaking, still weak, could not believe he had survived the explosion which had destroyed the Carmen Club and hurled him across the street head first into iron railings. Incredible that neither he nor anyone else was dead or

29

maimed. The hospital had given him a scan and assured him there was no damage. His ears were ringing, he had a headache, minor scratches caused by flying glass. Sore muscles. And that was it.

Finbar would not call this a miracle because he didn't believe in them. Only in luck and coincidence. Why should one person get a miracle and some other poor sod not? Some people never asked themselves that pertinent question. Another pertinent question: Had whoever was responsible meant to just blow up the club, or were his body parts supposed to be scattered amongst the rubble now? It might be a warning. But about what? Was he expected to guess? Whatever their intention, the perpetrators were not desperately concerned for his personal safety. What now? Finbar wondered. I can't let this go. Sit around and wait for next time. He had to find out what this was about. But so far there was no clue.

Drink was bad for the headache but he needed something after the shock, and the fraught hours at the hospital and police station. The plods didn't believe him when he said he didn't understand what the fuck was going on. Finbar walked back across the room, hesitated, then sat beside Shannon, edged close to her so that their thighs touched. He could smell her perfume. He lifted her soft, cool hand and kissed it. The diamond on her finger flashed blue-white fire. How much longer would she wear his ring?

'My Auntie Sylvia died,' he said.

She gasped and twisted round to face him. 'Oh Finbar, I'm so sorry! I know you loved her very much. I'm sorry I'll never meet her now. When's the funeral?'

'Ten days ago.' He kept hold of her hand. 'I wasn't invited.'

'But that's awful! I'm so sorry,' she repeated.

'And someone blew up my club.'

'What?' She pulled her hand away, her eyes dilated with shock. 'But who? Why...?'

'I don't know who or why. I'm trying to run through the

possibilities, but that's difficult right now because I'm some-what overwrought. As I'm sure you can imagine.' Finbar looked at her and raised his eyebrows. 'Well, that's me done.' He slid one arm around her shoulders, leaned over and gently kissed her on the lips. 'How was your day, darling?'

Shannon burst into tears.

Chapter Four

'Bacon and women's underwear.'

'*What?*'

Pascale Stephens frowned as she grabbed the bottle off the coffee table and poured herself another brandy. 'That's what Demetrio used to nick and flog around the pubs and clubs when he first came over from Holland. Underwear any size. You could always find a woman who'd fit it. And not many people say no to a few cheap bacon rashers.' She shook her head, then delicately touched one finger to her swollen lower lip. 'He'd go ape if he knew I was telling you this.'

'Go ape? He *is* an ape.' Her friend Janie smoothed back her long fair hair. 'Yeah,' she said, blowing out smoke. 'Doesn't want anyone knowing about his sad little past, does he?' She glanced at the empty gun cabinets around the sitting-room walls. 'Not now that he's made it big. Or likes to think he has.'

'Those coppers took his guns away. But that's not the half of it.' Pascale's big brown eyes filled with tears. 'He's up to something else, Janie, I'm sure he is. Something worse than having a few dodgy weapons knocking around.'

'Like what?' Janie brushed a speck of ash off her denim skirt.

'I haven't a clue. I don't see a way out.' Pascale's voice trembled. 'For me, I mean.'

'Leave him,' Janie urged, butting her cigarette in a

saucer. 'That's the way out. I've only been telling you for months.'

'But Janie, where am I supposed to go? This is my house.'

'And that's a broken nose.' Janie pointed at the dressing on Pascale's face. 'What'll it be next? It's not just you – look what he's done to *your house.*' She flung out one arm. 'Iron bars on the windows. Alarms. Drop bars, dead bolts–'

'Demetrio had to have extra security when he got his gun dealer's licence.'

'Extra security?' Janie started to laugh. 'Jesus Christ, it'd be easier to break out of Death Row! You know what, Pascale? You are allowed to just shag a bloke, you know. I mean, enjoy yourself.' She swigged brandy. 'You don't have to let him move in, take over your life and turn your house into frigging Strangeways.'

She paused, studying her friend. Pascale looked slim and gorgeous in her tight blue jeans and stretchy pink top, her long, straight dark hair falling over her shoulders. She had the usual frightened look in her eyes. Her pretty face looked weird with the dressing taped to it; her nose wouldn't be so pretty any more once the dressing came off. Janie felt depressed at the sight of her. And worried. Pascale hadn't been bursting with confidence before she met this bastard. Now she was afraid of her own shadow, didn't dare go anywhere or do anything without asking the great lord and master's permission.

'You're lovely,' she went on. 'You've got your hairdressing business, your brother down south. Me and other friends – the ones you've managed to hang on to. Everything going for you. You don't need some abusive creep who just got chucked out of a gun club for threatening to blow someone's head off.'

'Demetrio said he never threatened him. He said the guy was just jealous because he lost in some competition. There weren't any witnesses, it's that guy's word against his.'

'Oh, wake up and whiff the coffee! I know who I believe, and so do you. You've lived with him for months, but what

33

do you actually know about him – I mean, about his past? He could have a criminal record as long as your arm. And if he's supposed to be Dutch, how come he's got a Brit passport?'

'Because of his English mother. He could have two passports if he wanted. His mother's dead. She died a few years ago.'

Janie sneered. 'How bloody convenient. What about his father?'

'He walked out on them when Demetrio was twelve. Janie, I do want him out of my life.' Pascale looked pale and strained. 'He was nice at first, charming. He fooled me. I realise now, we're not suited. He's not suited to any woman. But I can't just tell him to get lost. It's not that easy.'

'How easy does it have to get? You could start by having the locks changed. Now.'

'It would cost a fortune to call a locksmith out at this time of night. I can't afford it. Besides, Demetrio would go mental when he found out. He'd manage to break in, I know he would. And then . . .' Pascale put up one hand and brushed away a tear.

'All right. Look. The gun club guy Demetrio threatened shopped him and now he's in the nick. They won't let him out tonight. Get your stuff together, come and stay with us. Alan won't mind.' He would, but he'd just have to lump it. 'You can find a solicitor, get Demetrio evicted if he won't leave. Tell him you'll go to the police if he hits you again. He's in enough trouble now, he won't want more. He'll give up when he sees you mean business. Remember, Pascale, bullies like him are always cowards. Anyway,' Janie said, her pale blue eyes brightening, 'fingers crossed, he could be looking at an eight- or ten-year stretch. Possessing illegal firearms is one bloody serious offence.'

'I know it's not the sort of thing you get community service for. But I didn't realise he could get as long as *that*.' Pascale stared at her friend, trying to fight back a rush of treacherous hope. Treacherous because it might not be realised. 'Are you sure?' she asked. 'How d'you know?'

'My mate, Antonia, remember? She's a legal secretary. I phoned her this afternoon during my break and got her to ask one of the solicitors she works for. He said someone charged with that probably wouldn't even get bail. But of course you never know.'

Pascale finished her brandy and waved ineffectually at the smoky air. 'Demetrio brought some rifles and pump guns here last week. Took them away a few days later. I don't know where.'

'Well, tell the police that, for God's sake.'

'What's the point? I've got no proof, have I, if I don't know what he did with them? But Janie, I'll think about what you say.' She lowered her eyes. 'About getting him out of my life. I promise.'

Janie looked pained. 'Have you still got feelings for the bastard?'

'No! Unless you count feelings of hate and fear. He's manipulating me when he acts nice. I know that now.' Pascale got up and walked to the windows, parted the curtains. The narrow terraced street was quiet, packed with parked cars. She turned back to Janie and smiled, trying to lighten the atmosphere.

'Thanks for coming round. It's been good, despite what we've talked about for most of the evening. First time in ages I've had a friend here.'

'Having friends round is part of normal life – remember that?' Janie got up and stowed cigarettes and lighter in her bag. 'I know it's difficult, Pascale. You've had a hell of a time.' Her voice softened and her eyes behind her glasses were gentle. 'You must still miss Greg a lot. Two years isn't that long. It was awful for you to lose your husband at only thirty-three. It's hard being alone.'

'Yes.' Pascale's voice shook. 'It is.'

Alone, she thought, standing in the silent, smoke-filled living room after Janie had gone. And terrified. It was all very well for Janie to talk about solicitors and what she should say to the police. They couldn't protect her from

35

Demetrio and his temper. Nobody could. She looked at her reflection in the mirror over the fireplace.

He had been full of remorse after punching her in the face, had wept and begged her to forgive him. Said it would never happen again. And maybe it wouldn't. He had been all sweetness and light up until his arrest, feeding her painkillers and cups of tea, cooking that rice dish he said was a Dutch or Indonesian speciality: *Nasi goreng*. Pascale didn't like it, in fact the spices he put in it made her want to puke. Not a good idea. So she chewed, swallowed and said how delicious it was. He smiled, told her again that he would show her Amsterdam one day. What would he do there, chuck her in a canal if she unwittingly pissed him off?

She went upstairs and ran a bath, putting in some drops of essential oils. She closed her eyes and leaned back, enjoying the peace and silence. Although she couldn't relax completely. It was hard to believe Demetrio wouldn't stagger in drunk any minute, switch the telly on full blast and then play with his horrible guns until around four in the morning. He often woke her up for sex and made her cook him breakfast before he went to sleep. Demetrio could sleep all day of course. Mr Firearms Instructor and Ballistics Expert thought he could do better than be someone's wage slave. He had money, but Pascale didn't know where the hell he got it, and she never saw a penny. Heard the fairy tale about the bills that paid themselves?

Demetrio had to leave her, not the other way round. She couldn't leave him, because he would never allow it. Janie did not understand that. He hated Janie, called her a trouble-making bitch and worse. Something terrible in Dutch: *Kankerhoer*. The word made Pascale shiver with revulsion. It went beyond ordinary swearing and insults, sounded more like a blood-chilling curse. Was Janie right when she said he could get put away for eight or ten years? That was good, but not good enough. He still wouldn't leave her alone. He would get his mates, contacts or whatever, to harass her, make her life a misery. He would get out of jail one day. And then he would come after her. Men like that never gave up. Pascale could not imagine pursuing somebody who didn't want you, it seemed beyond pointless. But those kind of men had a different mind set. They needed power and control, wanted to feed off women's fear.

She climbed out of the bath, feeling lightheaded from brandy and the hot, steamy water. She wasn't used to drinking much any more. Janie had wanted to go to the pub, but if one of Demetrio's mates had seen her out boozing when her man was locked up ... well, it wasn't worth the hassle. Might as well be in the nick myself, Pascale thought, resentment rising in her. She dried herself, smoothed body lotion on her warm, damp skin and reached for her dressing gown.

On the landing she squeezed past the metal staircase that led to the loft and went into the front bedroom where Demetrio kept his computer, laser toner, papers and other junk. It was unlocked since the police visit and his arrest. She recalled the officers sitting in the living room cataloguing the weapons before taking them away. The desk and its contents were a mess. She opened the drawers, but did not see any papers relating to firearms licences or gun clubs. The police must have taken them. Pascale suddenly lost her nerve and banged the drawers shut. What was she doing in here, was she crazy? She looked over her shoulder, half expecting to see Demetrio standing there glaring at her. Ready to punish.

'He won't be back tonight,' she whispered, trying to calm herself. 'Go on. Do it.'

She might not get another chance to look. She felt certain the desk contained some clues about Demetrio's past life, missing gaps that she needed to fill in. But there was nothing. Only a few magazines about guns, shooting, rifle clubs. A letter – torn in half – which informed Mr Montana of the committee's decision to revoke his membership of the Osprey's Small Bore Rifle Club. He had been furious about that. In the bottom drawer was a pile of airmail letters from

37

Thailand, Australia, the Phillipines and the US. All addressed to the same Liverpool post office box number.

Pascale gasped. This was how she had corresponded with Demetrio, via a post office box in the Netherlands, before he came to the UK. He was a teacher, he wrote, working in various prisons, and had no permanent home address. She had dismissed the alarm bells that rang then. Now they were deafening. She checked the dates on the letters and chose one of the most recent, pulled out the thin folded sheet. It was from an Australian woman named Charlene who lived in the Blue Mountains outside Sydney.

Dear Demetrio,
I am so very, very sorry to hear about your girlfriend's tragic accident. I know it will take you a long time to get over her death, but when you are coping with things a little bit better I would love for you to come out here and visit me sometime.

'Oh, my God!' Pascale clapped one hand to her mouth, her body trembling. Tragic accident? Was he fantasising? That was bad enough. She suddenly wondered if Demetrio might be capable of murder. What the hell did she know about him, after all? Janie was right.

'He's written me off,' she whispered, drained with shock.

If Demetrio wanted to leave her, that was more than all right. But this sounded like he had other more sinister ideas. Surely to God he didn't seriously imagine he could just murder her and get away with it? Profit by getting his hands on her money and house, selling her business? She had made a new will after Greg's death, left everything to her brother in London. But Demetrio didn't think, period. He collected an illegal arsenal of weapons, threatened someone with a gun. Lost his temper, hit her. You didn't do stuff like that if you were worried about the consequences.

She jumped and gave a cry of terror as the desk phone rang. The airmail letter fluttered to the carpet. She didn't dare pick up the phone. Didn't dare not to. Was it him? She cringed. Surely the police wouldn't let him make phone calls at this time of night? But if it was Demetrio and she didn't answer, he would go ballistic. Go ballistic! She had to stop saying, stop thinking that phrase other people used so casually. It wasn't funny, not in her case. She reached across and lifted the receiver. It felt like lead in her hand. *Lead.*

'Hiya, love! Thought I'd just check up on you before you go to bed.'

Pascale cringed again and closed her eyes. Thank God he couldn't see her now.

'All right, mate,' he said to someone else. 'Yeah. Ta. I really appreciate this. Make sure she's okay and everything.' Footsteps sounded along a corridor. 'Good, the bastard's gone. Did you go in my room?' he hissed. 'Touch anything? Because if you did I'll fucking kill you.'

'No!' she cried, hugging herself in terror. 'Of course not. I haven't, Demetrio, I swear. I wouldn't do that.' Since when was it his room? He probably thought this house belonged to him now. With her thrown in as a job lot.

'You're lying, you devious cow. Think you can do what you like when I'm not there, don't you? You're out of control.'

'No!' Pascale gripped the phone, tears running down her injured face and soaking into the dressing. 'Demetrio, I *swear.*' How could she ever have been thick enough to get hooked up with this maniac? Was she that desperate, that frightened of being alone? It seemed she was. Being with him had taught her some unpleasant lessons about herself. She had never even imagined she would take this shit from any man. There was a brief silence.

'If you leave me I'll hunt you down and kill you,' Demetrio rasped. He had a strange accent: Dutch and American overlaid with a touch of Scouse.

'I won't leave you!' Pascale longed to stand up to him, tell him to get the hell out of her life and never come back. But she didn't have the guts. I'm weak, she thought. Pathetic. That's why he picked me.

'I'll blast Janie the *kankerhoer*,' he went on. 'Blow her ugly fat face and big backside away. I'll kill your precious brother too. You'll have nowhere to go, you'll be running scared. I'll catch you and then you'll die. It won't be a quick death because I'll have a shitload of anger to get rid of, the way you wind me up all the time. You know that, don't you, bitch?'

'Demetrio, please.'

'*Demetrio, puh-leeze!*' he mocked, laughing. 'You all right then?' His voice changed suddenly as the footsteps returned. 'Good. Okay. 'Night, darlin'. Don't worry. Oh, yeah, I'll see you soon. That's a promise.'

He hung up laughing.

Chapter Five

She shot Bernie the Bogeyman over and over, but he wouldn't die. Like Rasputin, or bogeymen in horror movies. He kept walking towards her across Salthouse Dock as she pumped bullets into his dark, menacing bulk. Moonlight glittered on the blade of the combat knife he gripped. Maybe she should have used silver bullets.

Bernard Flinder wanted to cut off one of her nipples, the way he had done with his previous victim. He liked his little souvenirs. Then slash her throat, cut through her larynx, let her bleed to death. If by some incredible chance she survived, she would never be able to speak again. She would spend the rest of her life writing messages on pink, yellow, orange and lime-green post-it notes.

She fired again. Click this time, not bang. No more bullets equals no more Shannon. Bernard grabbed her and raised his knife. She screamed for help, but no one came. A distant explosion shook the ground, sent shockwaves through her. Finbar was dead, killed. There was no hope now.

Shannon woke up gasping and sweating, her heart pounding, gripped by the nightmare's sense of evil and terror. She groaned, her eyes filling with tears. She rolled over in bed and curled up, hugging the pillow. I'll get through this, she thought. I have to. She glanced at the clock. It was three-thirty in the morning.

She was sleeping – or trying to – in the guest room as

usual, telling Finbar she did not want her restless nights to disturb him. He said he didn't mind, and she knew he meant it. But Shannon wanted to keep her suffering private, felt ashamed that even Finbar should witness her in the grip of humiliating, pathetic powerlessness. She hadn't had any bad dreams for a while. Yesterday's murderous attack on Keely Breeze and her shock at the bombing of Finbar's club was no doubt responsible for this setback.

An icy chill followed the sweat, and Shannon lay there shivering. What if the bomb really had killed Finbar? Would whoever was behind it try again? She had lost her baby, would she lose Finbar too? Serve her right for rejecting him, shutting him out, being too preoccupied with her own traumas. Guilt and panic swept over her, worse at this silent, graveyard hour.

Moonlight slanted across the floor and the river cast shimmering ripple patterns across the ceiling and far wall. No use trying to get back to sleep yet. She threw off the quilt, got up and pulled on her robe, crept out. Finbar's door was closed. She made herself a cup of tea and took it into the sitting room.

'Oh!' Finbar sat there in the moonlight, wearing pale, baggy shorts and a black T-shirt, nursing a glass of what she guessed was malt whisky. A Planet Funk CD, turned very low, whispered around the big room.

'Beat you to it,' he remarked, patting the space beside him. 'What's wrong – another bad dream?'

'No.' She sighed. 'Yes.'

'What was it this time? Let me guess. Your unfortunate client.'

'Keely Breeze. Yes, partly.'

'I won't ask about the other part.' The evil headmaster, he guessed. Shannon moved to the windows and gazed out over the river. 'Beautiful, isn't it?' he remarked, watching her. The robe belt emphasised her slender, curvy waist. 'The moon, with astronauts footprints all over the Sea of Tranquillity. Romantic Birkenhead across the water.' He picked up the bottle. 'Fancy a drop of this in your Kenya Blend?'

She turned, her face in shadow. 'No, thanks. I've hated whisky since I was five years old.'

'Five?' he echoed, amused. He put the bottle on the floor. 'Well, go on. I've got to hear this.'

'I was at a christening party in some big house. Or it seemed big from my child's perspective. Friends of my parents had christened their baby son Jason. Mum and Dad hated the name. I was bored, wandering around, wishing they'd cut the cake. Some man left his drink on a windowsill, and I picked it up and took a sip. It tasted so foul I thought I'd drunk poison and would die any second. I didn't tell anybody, certainly not Mum or Dad, because I thought they'd say it served me right for being so stupid. And I was terrified of going to hospital.'

'What, more than croaking it from poison?'

'Oh yes. I just stood watching the partying adults. Waiting to die.'

'But nothing happened, so you went home and forgot all about it.' Finbar smiled and shook his head. 'Did you get your piece of christening cake?'

'No! I was gutted.' She laughed.

He was silent for a few seconds. 'That's the first time I've heard you laugh since you got out of hospital two months ago.'

She took a sip of tea, put the cup down. 'I didn't laugh when I was in hospital.'

'You know what I mean. And yesterday afternoon you cried, actually confided in me about your client and that anonymous letter. Didn't try to hide your feelings.' He swallowed. 'Two glimpses of the real Shannon within twenty-four hours. It's almost too much for me to take.'

'Finbar.' Shannon moved away from the windows. 'Somebody tried to kill you. They might try again. You're in terrible danger, what the hell are you going to do about it? I couldn't bear...' She stopped, feeling choked.

'What couldn't you bear?' He got up. 'I'd say things don't look too great for you either. You witnessed a murder attempt and the attacker knows what you look like. Suppose he finds out who you are?'

She shook her head. 'That won't happen. There's no chance.'

'If you say so. And someone wrote you a nasty letter. They don't exactly want to be best mates, do they?'

'That's not important. I told you, it's just some deranged idiot.'

'Like Mr Ex, maybe.' Finbar's face was in shadow, his voice grim. 'I'll sort him out.'

'Forget Rob. I don't think it's him. Anyway, never mind all that. Finbar, your *life's* in danger.' Shannon stared up at him. 'I'm sorry for the way I've acted these past weeks,' she whispered, tears flooding her eyes. 'It was your baby too.'

'For Christ's sake!' He pulled her against him. 'You've got nothing to feel sorry for.'

'I shut you out. I didn't mean to, I just felt so numb. Finbar, I know we've had problems. But I don't want to lose you, I couldn't bear that!'

'Does this mean you want to stay with me?' He kissed her, stroked her hair. 'Go on wearing the engagement ring?'

'Of course I do. I love you.'

'Three glimpses of the real Shannon.' His voice was shaky as he buried his face in her hair. 'I didn't think I'd hear you say that again.' He wrapped his arms around her. 'What are you going to buy me for my birthday when I'm ninety?'

'A DVD token and some aftershave.' Shannon gasped as he kissed her neck and throat, moved up to her lips. She felt a rush of desire so strong it was painful, like blood returning to frozen limbs. 'But Finbar, what are you going to do about...?'

'If you don't mind,' he murmured, 'I'm a bit preoccupied just now.' They kissed, a long, deep kiss, and he undid her robe belt. 'Take this thing off, I want to feel your skin. God, you smell so good. I've missed you so much.' The robe slipped off Shannon's slim shoulders, leaving her naked. 'I love you. I want you back, Shannon!'

He pulled her down on the sofa. Moonlight dazzled her and she closed her eyes as his hands, lips and tongue moved over her tense, tired, aching body. Teasing, licking, kissing, stroking. Arousing.

'You're gorgeous,' he whispered. 'Beautiful. I love you, I need you.'

Shannon hadn't felt gorgeous in a long time. She clung to him and kissed him hungrily, desperately, raked her fingers through his black, silky hair. Ran her hands over his hard, muscular body.

'I want you now,' she cried. 'Please, please!'

He was moving inside her, pushing deeper, slowly and carefully. Then harder, faster. She moaned with pleasure and excitement, gave herself up to pure sensation. On the verge of orgasm she panicked for a split second and pulled back, frightened of the loss of control. But her body ignored her mind and sent her over the edge, the strength of the spasms making her gasp and cry out. Finbar groaned and shuddered as he came, strands of her blonde hair entwined around his fingers. She felt his breathing, the pulse of his heartbeat as it gradually slowed. He raised his head and looked down at her.

'Been a long time.'

'Too long.' Shannon kissed and hugged him. He grinned.

'You didn't drink your tea. Want me to make you another cup?'

'No thanks.' She closed her eyes and surrendered to drowsiness, loving the feel of his body against hers. 'I can hardly believe this, but I'm feeling rather . . .'

'Sleepy? Now there's a thing. I thought it was only the insensitive male of the species who nodded off after sex. Allow me to make a radical suggestion.'

'What's that, a new position?' She giggled. 'Don't you need a rest first?'

'Exactly. I was going to suggest we go to bed. And sleep.'

Finbar got off the sofa and lifted her in his arms. Shannon's soft blonde hair tickled his chest.

'Together,' he whispered, kissing her.

'I'm frightened,' she said at breakfast as they sat drinking coffee. The sun was shining, the wind whipping up wavelets on the Mersey. 'Whoever bombed your club could be waiting to ambush you right now. Downstairs, in the car park – anywhere!'

'It won't be in the car park, because I don't have a car any more as of yesterday. Have to buy a new one.' Finbar took a bite of buttered toast, put it down and pushed his plate away. The possibility of being stiffed any time soon tended to ruin the appetite. He picked up his coffee mug. 'Can I borrow your BMW?' he asked. 'Or do you need to drive to any outlying magistrates' courts today?'

'No, I'm staying in town. I can walk to the office, no worries. Or grab a cab.' Shannon got up, fetched her car keys and gave them to him.

'Thanks.' The metal key ring was attached to a tiny, turquoise hourglass set in a clear plastic rectangle. Finbar turned the hourglass upside down and watched the turquoise sand trickle through, his eyes brooding.

Shannon sipped more coffee, looked out at the river then back at him. 'They might try to blow up this apartment next.'

He frowned. 'I don't think so.'

'You don't *know*.' She blinked back sudden tears. 'How the hell are we going to get through today? I'll be frantic every second, wondering if you're–'

He grabbed her hand. 'Stay cool, all right? I'll be fine. I'll call you – or you call me. Don't want your mobile's little tune pissing off the judge in the middle of his *ratio decidendi*, do we?'

'I always switch it off in court. And I'm not going to the Crown Court today.' Shannon stood up, brushing toast crumbs off her close-fitting black suit. Her blonde, curly hair was loose around her shoulders. She snapped the briefcase locks shut. 'I'll see who's been arrested overnight, what's come in. After that, the Mags Court. I've got an appointment with a ballistomaniac.'

'A gun nut.' Finbar raised his eyebrows. 'Interesting.'

'I'm afraid not. They're usually obsessive, anal-retentive morons with a scarily fragile sense of identity – hence the guns. Same old, same old. Give me a shoplifter or fraudster any day of the week. Their motivations can blow your mind.' Shannon paused and looked at him again, her dark blue eyes fearful. 'Finbar, what are you going to *do*?'

'Don't worry, okay?' He stood up and took her in his arms, gently wound one of her curls around his finger and touched her pink, glossed lips. 'I'll make a few calls. Go and see that police inspector. You never know,' he said in answer to her look of scorn. 'They might have come up with something.'

'Thought you didn't believe in miracles. Be careful,' she warned. 'Neither of us is exactly best mates with them.'

'How about if we get away for the weekend?' he asked, kissing her. 'Will you come with me to Ireland? I have to go there soon anyway. We could take a late afternoon or early evening flight and hole up in Auntie Sylvia's place. Chill out.'

'Chill out? In your deceased aunt's house, surrounded by her things and memories of her and your childhood?'

'I *mean*...!' Finbar shook his head and closed his eyes for a second. 'Do some thinking. Can you get away early?'

'No worries.' Shannon nodded. 'It's Friday. And I am a partner, after all.'

'You be careful too.' He hugged her. 'Whoever did this could know about you – us.'

'What, you think they might kidnap me and post you body parts?'

Finbar's green eyes darkened. 'Don't even joke about it.'

'I'm not laughing.' Shannon slipped her arms around his neck. 'Finbar, darling, please, please be careful!'

'No need to tell me. Like I said, try not to worry.' He

stroked her hair, smelled her perfume. 'The bomb might be a frightener, not a murder attempt,' he said, trying to convince himself as much as her. 'Maybe somebody wants something from me.'

'Like who? And what? Their manner of asking leaves a lot to be desired.' Shannon looked up at him. 'Are you saying this to try to make me feel better?'

'No. It could be true.' Finbar hesitated. 'Might be, you know, certain people I don't want anything more to do with. Never did want anything to do with.'

'Terrorists?' Shannon turned pale. 'They'd better leave you alone! Don't they have enough volunteer fanatics?'

'Not as many as they used to have. And not many with funds.'

'But what about the peace process, the Good Friday agreement, decommissioning? Okay, I know that particular issue's not resolved. But surely most of it's ancient history now?'

'Ancient history one minute, car bomb outside a main railway station the next. Listen. Stay alert, but don't panic. Call me when you get back from court. Or I'll call you.' He kissed her again, felt himself harden. 'God, you look sexy.' His hands slid over her buttocks, pulled her skirt up. 'I don't know how those poor bastards in the cells stand it.'

'I have to leave in two minutes!' Shannon gasped with laughter as he manoeuvred her against the table, dragging off her tights and pants. 'You've ruined my lipstick.'

'Two minutes'll do it. Sorry about the lipstick.' He lifted her on to the table and gently moved her legs apart, stroking her inner thighs. 'I don't know if it's our weeks in the wilderness or the idea of imminent death,' Finbar murmured as he unbuttoned her jacket and blouse and unhooked her bra, 'but I've got a desperate desire to fuck you again.' He kissed her hardened nipples, unzipped his jeans.

'Don't talk about imminent death!' Shannon gasped. She did not believe it was possible to make something happen just by talking about it, but it wasn't a theory she cared to test.

Finbar laid her down and leaned over her, gazing into her eyes. 'Kiss me.'

'I love you,' she said.

'How much?'

'As much as. . .!'

Shannon cried out. She couldn't talk any more.

Fifteen minutes later she was out of the apartment and running downstairs, lipstick and knickers back in place. She could smell Finbar's subtle, aromatic cologne on her skin, and his kisses left a minty taste in her mouth. She stopped and closed her eyes. No, she thought. He'll be all right. That wasn't the last time!

She glanced at her watch; twenty-past bloody nine. She didn't feel like going to work, didn't give a damn about the tossers she was supposed to represent that morning, and she certainly wouldn't take any crap from this Demetrio Montana character. She only cared about Finbar. Getting away for the weekend was an excellent idea. As long as no one followed.

In the sunny lobby with its polished dark-red granite floor, Shannon stopped again. Better check for post. She took a tiny key from her pocket and unlocked the mail box. A couple of letters for Finbar, that month's *National Geographic*. And . . .

'Oh, no!' She was gripped by fear, suddenly felt sick. She drew out the ivory-coloured, pink-ribboned envelope and dropped it because her hand was shaking so much. She hesitated, wondering whether to tear it up and bin it without reading the contents. But no. She had to square up to this, because it obviously wasn't going to get out of her face without a fight. Like so many things.

She walked to the doors and looked out across the Albert Dock, the blue sky reflected in its waters. There were few tourists around at this early hour. A man in an overcoat

49

walked along the colonnades towards the Tate Gallery. She opened the envelope and unfolded the paper. More sprawling, looped, royal blue handwriting.

Even the police can solve a crime when someone tells them who committed it.
Have a fun weekend with your criminal lover, bitch lawyer,
Because on Monday you'll confess to the
headmaster's murder.
Or else.

Or else *what*? Shannon went cold. So they didn't want money. Not that she would have paid. This moron was insane if they believed they could force her to tell the police she'd had Bernard Flinder killed by a hit man. It isn't some stray nut job, she thought. They know me, want to destroy me. It's personal. But if not Rob, who? She shoved the letter into her briefcase and pulled open the door. Like Finbar, she needed to think. A lot. Before it was too late.

She walked out of the Albert Dock complex, through the Maritime Museum car park and past the Liver Buildings and Cunard Building, the stiff wind off the river whipping her hair. It was a beautiful morning, but cold. Shannon hurried up Water Street and turned into Exchange Street East. She pushed open the door of her building, ran up the blue-carpeted stairs and smiled at sultry, raven-haired Helena in reception, who sat typing on her word processor behind the glass screen. In the small reception area were two blue sofas and a table with a pile of magazines. The magazine with the article about multiple orgasms was falling to pieces.

Helena nodded to her, but didn't smile back. Like she was boss. Leon, their police station representative, was the only one who could get a cup of tea or coffee out of Helena; Mi-Hae, Shannon and Khalida, being of the female persuasion, had to shift for themselves. Shannon typed in the entry code, pushed the door and entered the main part of the office. A photocopier stood under the stairs, boxes of printer paper stacked around it. Her office was down the hall. The metal-meshed window faced the old brick wall of the warehouse across the alley. If Shannon looked up she could see golden Minerva on top of the Town Hall dome, goddess of all she surveyed. Minerva was supposed to help artists, poets and craftsmen. Shannon liked the idea of lots of different gods to appeal to, instead of one nasty, punishing patriarch.

'Morning, Shannon.' Leon Rossini walked in, neat and slim in his dark suit, his black hair cropped. 'You just missed Mi-Hae. She's got a conference with some barrister. She told me about Keely Breeze.' He made a face. 'Gruesome!'

'It certainly was.'

'I know she got the worst of it, and that's an understatement. Still a hell of a thing for you to witness, though. How are you feeling this morning?'

'I'm okay, thanks, Leon. But yeah, could have done without it. I'm going to call the hospital about Keely later.' Shannon took the file he handed her. 'Oh, thanks – Mr Montana's c.v.' She flipped a few pages. 'What's our new guy like?'

'Full of outraged denial. Jealous, limited minds plotting against him.'

'Hmm. Thought so. Bor-*ing*.' Shannon closed the file. 'Mr Rossini, your grave, dark, bedroom eyes look troubled this morning. What's wrong?'

He hesitated, shrugged. 'I split up with my girlfriend. But she's still pestering me.'

'That's a pain. Still, it must seem a cold, hard world to her now, deprived of your generosity, good looks and sexy Italian charm. No wonder she can't let go.'

Leon started to laugh. 'Shannon, if you want me to ask Helena for a cup of coffee and pretend it's for me, just say so.'

'No time for coffee. Which is just as well, because I ingest too much as it is.'

Leon fingered his bronze silk tie. 'This thing's knackered,' he complained. 'I only bought it last week and it wasn't cheap.'

'I'd swear Helena's got a sewing kit tucked away in that anally tidy desk of hers. And that she'd be delighted to mend it for you.'

'But what would it cost me?' He laughed again. 'See you later.'

Shannon made a few calls, grabbed her things and left for Dale Street Magistrates Court, a few minutes walk away. Down in the Bridewell she asked for Demetrio Montana. She went into one of the thick-walled alcoves and dumped her briefcase and files on the table. Was Finbar all right, she wondered? Had he left the apartment yet? Tiredness, fear and too much coffee was giving her indigestion. She wanted to phone him, but it was too soon and she couldn't make a private call down here anyway. A shadow loomed large. Startled, she glanced up.

'We'll leave the cuffs on,' the Group 4 guard said. 'And wait here while you talk to him.' He stood back, grim-faced.

Demetrio Montana had to be six-foot-five, taller than Finbar. He was powerfully built, completely bald and wore a gold earring. For Shannon, a gold earring on a man spelled the same as a medallion or signet ring: *W-a-n-k-e-r.* But she could not dismiss this man so easily. She knew he was dangerous, found him totally intimidating. Her immediate instinct was to jump up, push past him and run out. Of course she did not obey it.

'Good morning, Mr...' She half rose, sat down again. She didn't want to shake his hand. His expensive black suit was rumpled, the top few buttons of his blue shirt undone to reveal fuzzy blond chest hair. No tie, of course. If he'd had eyebrows they would have been sandy like his lashes. His skin was leathery. She could smell his sweat. His ego.

He sat down and rested his cuffed hands on the table. Shannon tried not to shrink back against the wall. She felt trapped, suffocated. She took a deep breath, picked up her pen and flipped over the top page of the file.

'So, you're charged with illegal possession of firearms.' She stopped. Demetrio Montana was staring at her as if he wanted to memorise every detail of her appearance. Steal her soul. This time Shannon did shrink. 'What is it?' she asked, dry-mouthed. She cleared her throat, coughed. She was sweating.

He smiled at her. At least Shannon assumed it was meant to be a smile. When he spoke she was surprised at how soft and light his voice was.

'People with blue eyes can get away with murder.'

Chapter Six

'Boozing at lunchtime, DC Flinder? Whatever would the Chief Con think?'

Rob Flinder, coming out of the pub after his illicit lunchtime pint, whirled round in shock and dropped his car keys. 'What the fuck do you want?' he asked, flushing. 'Did you follow me here?'

'So you do know me.' Finbar smiled as he took in Rob's terrible dark-blue suit and blue-and-gold striped tie, his angry, scared brown eyes and boring crewcut. Rob Flinder was tall and well-built though, good looking. Finbar could understand, however reluctantly, what Shannon had seen in him. Once. 'We've never been formally introduced, have we?' He stepped forward and kicked the keys out of Rob's reach. 'You saw Shannon and me that day in town a few months back when you were with your sad girlfriend. You didn't stop to say hi, but that was fine by me. I wasn't in the mood either.'

'I've heard all about you,' Rob spluttered. 'What copper on Merseyside hasn't?'

'But in the immortal words of Mae West, you can't prove anything. Still, let's forget that. My life's taken a whole new direction now.' Finbar glanced around the sunlit car park. 'Amazing what the love of a witty, intelligent, beautiful, gold-hearted woman can do for a man,' he said, his Galway accent soft. 'Isn't it? Not that you'd know how that feels any more.'

'Did you follow me here just to wind me up?' Rob's flush deepened. 'Because if–'

'Don't flatter yourself.' Finbar's smile faded. 'I've got better things to do with my time than rip the wings off insects like you. I was just down the road at your HQ,' he said. 'Went there to have a chat with one of your bosses. Find out if there were any possible early leads as to who blew up my club.'

'Oh, yeah.' Rob gave up looking for the keys, which Finbar had kicked under the car out of sight. 'I heard about that. Shame you didn't–' He stopped, clenched his fists, angry with himself because he didn't dare to finish the sentence.

'Right.' Finbar nodded. 'Always a good idea to think before one opens one's big gob. Anyway,' he resumed, 'the chat was a bit of a waste of time, unfortunately. Should have known it would be. Trouble is, the police force just doesn't seem to attract the kind of highly educated, open, analytical minds best suited to detective work, does it? Wonder why that is. But I thought, all's not lost. I can look up Rob while I'm in the area. Have a word.'

'About *what*?'

'The intelligent, gold-hearted, stunningly beautiful lady, of course. You know, the one whose love, trust and loyalty you abused, betrayed and consequently lost.'

Rob sighed, the fight gone out of him. 'How is Shannon?'

'She'll be all the better for a decree absolute.' Finbar was pleased to see Rob flinch, his eyes fill with the bitter pain of loss. 'The thing is, she's had a really tough time these past six months. As you know, given that you and your dead kiddie-fiddler father were to blame for most of it. She's been through more than enough shit.' Finbar paused, his green eyes narrowed. 'The last thing Shannon needs now is anything else to freak her.'

Rob glanced at him, startled. 'Meaning?'

'*Meaning,*' Finbar stepped right up close. 'If anyone gives her any more trouble they'll have me to deal with.'

'What trouble?' Rob backed away and stumbled against his car.

'Who's winding who up now? Don't tell me you don't know.'

'I haven't got a clue, I swear!' Rob was scared now. This bastard was a psycho, had killed people. Although like he said, no one could prove anything. 'Listen,' he begged. 'I told Shannon I wouldn't contest the divorce any more. Told her she could have a clean break. She's got what she wanted.'

'You mean you've got what *you* wanted. Made sure this clean break would cost her a fortune, didn't you? A hell of a lot more than you're worth.' Finbar controlled his rage, compressed it into a glowing space inside him. 'Come out of this laughing, won't you? I'll wipe the grin off your face, you miserable bastard!'

'Don't touch me!' Rob gasped. 'I'll have you done for assault.'

'Yeah. You'd love that, wouldn't you? I don't need to hit you. I can get the message across without that. Scared?' Finbar mocked. 'Feels different on the receiving end, doesn't it? How d'you think Shannon felt when you beat the crap out of her?'

'I didn't – I never meant to hurt her!' Rob burst out. 'I wasn't myself. I nearly had a nervous breakdown. But now I'm glad my father's dead, and I don't give a shit that my mother took an overdose on New Year's Eve. She let him abuse Melanie all those years. She was never a mother to me or Melanie.'

'Any more than you were a husband to Shannon.' Finbar's rage increased at this lame display of self-pity. Typical that Rob imagined himself badly done to, never mind what Shannon had suffered. He controlled the urge to deck him one.

'Now Melanie's dead,' Rob went on, his back to the car. 'I tried to help my sister, but I couldn't. It was too late. She was drinking, on drugs, involved with scum. My father robbed her of her childhood and youth, he destroyed her. But the worst thing of all is ...' He struggled for control, his mouth working. 'I lost my wife.'

'You didn't *lose* Shannon, you prat, so spare me the sob story. You put her through hell and drove her away. And now that she won't come back you've decided to start making her life hell again, haven't you?'

Rob jerked his head up. 'I don't know what you're...!'

'Shut up,' Finbar interrupted. 'I've had it with you. What the fuck d'you think this is, a debate? I came to warn you – leave Shannon alone!' He watched as Rob flushed dark red again. 'Just stay away from her.' He paused, lowered his voice. 'If you don't, you're dead.'

Fear shot through Rob. 'You threatened me!'

'Prove it.' Finbar glanced around the car park again. 'Where's your witnesses? Anyway, it's not a threat,' he contradicted, his voice calm once more. 'It's a fucking mission statement. You've lost Shannon. It's done, finished, ancient history, no more chances. So get the fuck over it. Because if you don't, I will personally kill you.'

He turned and walked off. Rob stared after him, breathing hard, his face shiny with sweat. Then he got down on all fours and started to scrabble around for his car keys. Finbar was shaking with rage and the adrenalin surge. He'd longed to kick the crap out of Rob, give him a taste of his own medicine. Well, he would do that and more if necessary. He'd made his point. Even if Rob wasn't the author of that anonymous letter, there was no harm in making sure he stayed lodged beneath his stone. But if it wasn't Rob, then who?

Finbar had considered visiting one or two bars to look up old contacts and ask if any rumours as to who did the Carmen Club were floating on the air, but decided against it. He doubted if anyone knew anything as yet. And he didn't want to risk crowded, enclosed places just now; might as well pin a red circle to his chest. He had been to India Buildings and the air cargo office, braved the police headquarters, and was still in one piece. That was enough for today.

He walked out of the pub car park down the street to where he'd left the BMW and checked under the car, looking for booby traps. He hoped no one was watching. He couldn't see anything, no quantity of explosive bound with adhesive tape, or little plywood box painted black. He got into the car and locked the doors, sat there for a minute waiting for his breathing to slow. Then he took out his mobile and called Shannon. Her mobile was switched off, so he tried her office.

'Kam Flinder Najeba!' Helena snapped.

'Hi there. Why not say *'fuck off and die'* and be done with it?'

'What? Who is this?'

'Finbar Linnell. I'd like to speak to Shannon, please.'

'Oh! Finbar, *hello*. Sorry! You caught me at a bad moment.'

'You seem to have rather a lot of those.'

'I'm sorry,' Helena repeated. 'How are you?'

'Terrific, and thanks so much for asking. Is Shannon about?'

'Yes, she's back from court. I'll put you through.'

Shannon sounded breathless. 'I was just going to phone you.'

'Another psychic moment in our everlasting love.'

'I was frantic all morning. Are you okay? Did you find out anything?'

'Yes to the first, no to the second. Listen, how about a change of plan?' Finbar decided there was no need to mention his visit to Rob. 'I'll pick you up at work instead of you coming home, and we'll drive straight to the airport and get the tickets there instead of calling ahead. I know it's Friday, but they'll have spare seats in Business Class.'

Shannon laughed. 'And nothing bad can happen to you when you're in Tiffany's!'

'We'll hire a car when we land in Cork. We could be at Sylvia's by ten tonight.'

'Sounds fine. But I wanted to get changed before we left. And I haven't packed.'

'You can change at the airport,' he said. 'I'll pack a bag for you.'

'Are you sure? Well, don't forget my toothbrush and moisturiser. Walking shoes, jeans. Oh, and a couple of warm sweaters.'

Finbar grinned. 'I suppose you think you'll open your bag to find nothing but black silk stockings and a suspender belt?'

'Something like that.'

'Don't worry. I'll force myself to keep a clear head while grubbing through your perfumed drawers. What time can I pick you up?'

'Let's see. I'm just going out to grab a sandwich, then I have to go and visit a client at a police station.' A rape victim. She wasn't looking forward to that. 'Four o'clock should do it.'

'Right, see you then. Be ready, okay?'

'I will. I love you,' she said. 'Take care.'

'I love you too. See you at four.'

Finbar started the car and drove through the centre of town, heading for the docks and Maritime Museum. The spring light was harsh, the sun high in the sky. It was stuffy in the car, but he didn't want to open a window. He hated being trapped in the slow afternoon traffic; if someone zoomed up on a motorbike and levelled a gun at his head he'd be literally a sitting target. He kept glancing around as he drove, trying to assess if someone was tailing him. He thought not, but it was difficult to tell. Especially if they were good. He wished to God he knew who he was dealing with.

He could hardly wait to get himself and Shannon out of Liverpool for the weekend. Of course it wouldn't be all fun and games. He had to look around Sylvia's house, go through papers, sort some of her stuff. Shannon was right, that would bring back a lot of memories. But there would be time to stand on the cliffs and watch the Atlantic waves crashing, stroll along the deserted beach. Eat wild salmon. Have wild sex. Finbar smiled at the thought of that. He wished Shannon was waiting for him at home right now.

He parked the car near the Albert Dock and walked towards the apartment building. The River Mersey sparkled in the sunshine. He shivered in the cold wind as he walked across the dock past one of the big stone museum buildings, glancing around, looking for anything or anyone who seemed suspicious. That made him angry again. He wanted to put his past behind him and live in peace with the woman he loved. How much longer did he have to go on looking over his shoulder?

He started to feel afraid again, even more afraid for Shannon. Living with him, she could be a target too. Then again, if she was in danger from this anonymous letter writer she might be in just as much if not more trouble without him. He had to protect her. But what was the best way?

He reached the apartment building, keys at the ready. Got inside and pushed the heavy door shut instead of letting it swing slowly. The lobby was silent, deserted. Finbar took the three flights of stairs at a run, getting rid of the day's pent-up tension. A pang of sadness struck him as he thought of how he and Shannon would have moved out if she hadn't had the miscarriage, because this building had no lift and she couldn't toil up flights of stairs each day as her pregnancy advanced.

Of course he had been alone when he moved in here, had wanted it that way, expected things to remain as they were. He had never imagined meeting Shannon and falling in love with her at first sight, thought she would fall in love with him too. Become pregnant with their child. Like Rob Flinder, he had almost blown it with her by keeping dangerous secrets. But he hadn't blown it, and he wouldn't now. No way.

Finbar reached the top flight of stairs. He looked up at the landing, at his apartment door. Stopped and froze.

A man stood there staring at him. He was in his early

twenties, dark-eyed, with dark brown, tangled hair. Scruffy clothes, scuffed boots. He looked familiar somehow, although Finbar was certain they had never met. But this was not the time to start reminiscing, even if his memory hadn't temporarily cut out with the shock.

All Finbar could think about, all he could focus on, was the gun pointing at his heart.

It couldn't end now. Not like this.

Chapter Seven

'Whose secretary are you, love?'

Demetrio Montana grinned at the Asian woman's glare as she hurried across the Kam Flinder Najeba reception area and typed in the code to open the door that led to the offices. Her mass of straight, shining black hair hung loose around her shoulders.

'Nobody's.' Mi-Hae opened the door and paused. 'Actually, I'm the senior partner.'

'Whoops. Pardon me.' He laughed and stood up, towering over her. 'Not much good at this political correctness stuff, am I? Still, load of old cobblers that is. Us fellas can't say anything these days without some tart getting the raving hump.'

'Political correctness can get silly, I agree.' Mi-Hae nodded. 'But it all started for a good reason.' She looked at him as if to say, *'You're it'*. 'For instance, I'm sure most people wouldn't want to go back to the days when comedians thought it was acceptable to crack jokes about pregnant women.'

Demetrio frowned at the word 'pregnant'. 'Where you from?' He picked up the bunch of cellophane-wrapped red roses and pink carnations from the magazine-strewn coffee table. 'China, Japan?'

'Korea,' Mi-Hae snapped, flushing.

'Oh, yeah?' He started laughing. 'What you having for

your tea tonight? Nice bit of rottweiler leg or alsation steak?'

'No. I do not eat dog!'

Demetrio decided he didn't like this bitch. 'They know how to treat women there.'

'Yes.' Mi-Hae cocked her head on one side and batted mascaraed eyelashes at him. 'In Korea, woman is like flower. You don't go back to work in fields until fifteen minutes after childbirth!' She turned and went upstairs, gripping her black briefcase as if she had to stop herself from bashing him over the head with it.

'Mr Montana, what can I do for you?' Shannon Flinder walked down the hall to meet him. 'We don't have an appointment, and I'm afraid I'm really busy just now.'

This one was his type big time, Demetrio thought, starting at her legs and going up. Everything in the right place, and then some. She had a good pair of tits on her, despite trying to hide them under that black jacket. He wanted to reach out and touch her hair, grab a handful of those silky, out-of-control curls. Grab a handful of something else too. He was fascinated by her long-lashed, dark-blue eyes, even bluer than his. Or were Shannon's eyes violet? They looked different, depending on the light.

'I'd like to gaze into your eyes against a background of snow,' he said, smiling.

'What?'

'Never mind. Sorry to bother you. I won't take long.' Demetrio felt depressed as he thought of Pascale, pale and cowering, that stupid dressing still taped to her nose. Stinking of the hairdressing muck she used every day on ugly bitches who needed plastic surgeons, not hairdressers. 'I just wanted to give you these,' he said, thrusting the flowers at Shannon. 'To say thanks very much for getting me off this morning.' Shannon Flinder needed a real man. And guess who was up for the job?

'There's no need to thank me, Mr Montana.' Shannon looked dismayed. 'I was only doing my job.'

'Yeah, but-'

'And I didn't get you off, I got you bail. On condition you report to the police station every Monday morning at ten, and don't contact the prosecution witness. Do you realise how lucky you were to get bail?' she asked. 'That charge carries a maximum of ten years jail time. You wouldn't have got it if the prosecuting solicitor had had more evidence to put before the court.' And if the police had done their job properly, she thought. Most people were in blissful ignorance of how the police and legal system could operate at times.

'Yeah, yeah.' Demetrio smiled at her again. '*You're* my luck. That fella's telling a pack of lies,' he said, suddenly angry. 'I never threatened to blow his head off. And I have got licences for those guns – the paperwork just needs sorting. Like I said.'

'It's really not necessary for you to bring me flowers.' Shannon laid them on top of the boxes of printer paper. 'In fact, it's not–'

'I want you to have dinner with me tonight.' He was disappointed that she seemed less than impressed with the fucking flowers. The woman in the shop had warned him that pink and red didn't really go together.

'I'm afraid that's not possible, Mr Montana.'

'Call me Demetrio. Or Demon. That's what me mates call me. DE-metrio MON-tana, get it?' He grinned.

'I get it.' Shannon's beautiful blue eyes looked nervous. 'I'm sorry, but I can't have dinner with you, Mr ... De ... Not tonight or any other.'

'Why not?' He felt angry again. 'What's wrong with me then?'

'You're a client. It wouldn't be appropriate.'

'You have business lunches and dinners, don't you?'

'Occasionally. But that's different.' She glanced at her watch. 'Sorry, but you'll have to excuse me now. I've got an appointment.'

Demetrio scowled. 'There's no one waiting back there.'

'I know. I have to go out.'

'Oh right. I'll give you a lift. I've got my car – and driver – outside.'

'No, thank you.' Shannon's voice hardened and Demetrio guessed he'd overdone things on the charm front. This wasn't some cheap pick-up who'd open her legs after a couple of Bacardi breezers. He had to start off in first gear. Nice and easy, slow and steady.

'That's cool.' He took a step back. 'Sorry I just turned up here like this.' He smoothed his black leather coat, put up one hand and played with his gold earring. 'I know I'm not the only one on your books. You must have loads of other cases – clients.' Who could all fuck off out the window as far as he was concerned. 'But like I said, I just wanted to say thanks.'

'That's all right.' Shannon backed away. 'Goodbye.'

'Yeah, see you. Got plans for the weekend?' he called as she walked back towards her office.

'Goodbye, Mr Montana.' She didn't turn round.

He strode out and ran down the stairs, seething with frustration. In the street Demetrio realised Shannon hadn't thanked him for the flowers. She was probably binning them right now, or slinging them at that narky little tart behind the glass in reception. Wouldn't be *appropriate*, he sneered to himself. He stood outside for a minute, looking up at the tall, grey Victorian office building. Shannon Flinder would have more respect if she knew what he was. What he'd done. And was about to do. Yells and shouts across the street distracted him.

Pickhead was having an argument with a traffic warden and the warden had lost, judging by the fact that he was missing his smart hat and little scribbling pad, and Pickhead was slamming his face against the brick wall of a nearby pizza restaurant.

'Let's go,' Demetrio shouted, jumping into the old white Merc. Pickhead kicked the warden down a flight of stone steps and got in, gunned the engine. 'What the fuck d'you think you're doing?' Demetrio grumbled as he drove off at speed, brakes and tyres screeching. 'Can't you go five sodding minutes without slapping somebody?'

'S'all right,' Pickhead muttered, his eyes fixed on the road, cigarette sticking out of one corner of his mouth. 'Bastard didn't get me number.'

'Well, maybe the CCTV did.' Demetrio cuffed the boy around his scabby head, his blue eyes glittering with fury. 'Just watch it, you stupid little runt!' he shouted. 'Don't want to end up back inside before the fucking day's out, do I?'.

'What you worried about? It's my motor.'

'I'm in it, you're my driver. And I've got enough to worry about. Get that cig out of your ugly face.'

'No CCTV round here, Demon.' Pickhead wound down the window and spat out his cigarette. 'Slater Street, clubland, all round there, yeah. That's all camera-ed up. But this is the posh part of the city. You're okay here.'

'Liverpool's supposed to have more cameras than any other city in Britain. And Britain's got more than any other country in Europe. This country's the dog's arse.' Demetrio slapped his chest. 'And I'm stuck in it. You can't carry your own weapons, fight back, smoke all the fucking goblins that want to grab a piece of what you've got. Wish I could go back to the States.' He didn't really, of course. That was the last place on earth he wanted to go back to. Texas, trailer parks. Death Row.

'The States?' The Merc lurched to the right as Pickhead gawped at him instead of the road, almost scraping the red paintwork from a parked Mini. 'Thought you came from Holland – clog land?'

'Yeah, I do. But I spent years in the States. I used to work for the CIA,' Demetrio lied. 'I was a special agent, hunting down terrorists.'

'Were yer?' Pickhead gasped. 'Bloody hell. Awesome.'

Demetrio cuffed him again. 'Keep your little ferret eyes on the road.' They drove past St John's Gardens, past the flight of steps that led up to St George's Hall on their left. 'How do we get to London Road from here?' he grumbled, looking around. 'This traffic system's so arsed up you don't know whether you're coming or going.'

'London Road? No problem, Boss. What we going up there for?'

'I need to visit someone at the Royal.'

'Yeah? Who?'

'Mind your own business. Just shut up and drive.'

Demetrio did not know if this was a good idea. In fact, it might be a very bad one. But he had to try. You couldn't rely on other people. They always let you down. He had to make his own luck, create his own chances. Because nobody else in this fucking world was going to do it for him.

She had a room to herself on the seventh floor. He guessed it was her room because a uniformed plod sat slumped outside reading the *Daily Mail*. He frowned and moved back out of sight. The room was also opposite the Nurses' Station. How to get past that bloody lot?

Why had he thought he could trust Phelim not to fuck up? What was wrong with him, was he going soft in his old age? Rule Number One: if you wanted something done, do it your bloody self. He had to sort her in case she wasn't frightened enough not to talk to the police. She might even talk to Shannon Flinder. Suppose she had? Then he would have to sort the lovely Shannon too. What a waste. But with luck, this nagging little problem could be contained right here and now.

'Kev! You been to see Mum?'

Shocked, Demetrio whirled round and looked down into the freckled faces of three red-haired boys, all of them under ten, the youngest clutching his brother's hand. Trust them to turn up now. Sure, he was making his own luck. Bad bloody luck.

'Oh. Hiya, lads. Ursula.' He nodded to their grandmother and she returned the compliment absently, obviously having other things on her mind. Ursula's reaction told him it was all right, and Demetrio breathed again. Her sprayed, candy floss hair was dyed black, her face heavily made up and powdered. Red lipstick bled into the lines around her mouth. Her purple trouser suit was strained across the hips. An arse as big as a porridge pot, his grandad would have said.

'You been in to see her?' Ursula asked, her voice hushed in deference to the hospital atmosphere. She probably talked this way in church too. A couple of doctors in white coats strolled past, one telling the other where he'd been skiing.

'No. Wasn't sure if they'd let me,' Demetrio whispered back. 'We're just friends, aren't we? It's not like I'm her relative or husband or anything.'

'Come on.' Ursula grabbed his arm and a strong, sweet whiff of perfume hit his nose. 'I'll get you in there.'

The plod folded his newspaper and stood up as they approached. 'Who's this, then?' he asked, frowning at Demetrio.

'Friend of the family,' Ursula replied. 'He's with us.'

'I'll need your name and address, mate.' The policeman took out his notebook.

'Kevin Hoyle.' He had got the name Hoyle from a tattered second-hand book, *Hoyle's Games Modernized (Thoroughly revised to 1909)* by a Professor Hoffman, which he'd found in the attic of Pascale's house. Inside the book was a stamp: *This book, given during the Borough's Book Appeal Fortnight, November 14th-28th, 1942, comes to you with the best wishes of the people of Weston-Super-Mare. Signed, R. Hoskens, Mayor.* The book contained chapters about old card games like Bezique, Blind Hookey and Cribbage, and there was an amusing section on the National Rules of Snooker Pool.

'Address?'

'Twenty-one Christmas Street, Kirkdale.' He'd got that out of the A to Z.

'Oh God!' Ursula gripped the youngest boy's hand and started to tremble as she looked through the door's glass panel. 'Poor little love.' Her eyes filled with tears. 'I can't believe what that swine did to her. And *why?* No reason, no reason at all.' She sniffed. 'Can hardly stop meself losing it every time I go in there.'

No reason. She definitely hadn't said anything. Demetrio peered through the panel at the motionless, bandaged object in the bed. Christ! He felt shocked, despite himself. 'Not gonna let the lads see her like that, are you?' he whispered.

'I had to bring them. Can't leave them at home on their own, can I? Although I know some who would. Their Dad doesn't want to know. He's gone off with his lady friend for the weekend.' Ursula sniffed. 'Doesn't give a toss about my little girl any more.'

'I'll watch the lads for you, love,' the policeman offered. 'They'll be okay with me.'

Ursula stared at him. 'All right. Thanks.' She pulled a tissue out of her bag and dabbed at her tears and black eyeliner.

'Why don't I have a couple of minutes with her first?' Demetrio seized his chance. 'While you get yourself together.'

'Yes, love, you go on. Good idea.'

He pushed open the door and went in. The room had a washbasin and mirror, a child-size wardrobe with one door kicked in, and walls the colour of the glutinous white medicine his father used to take for indigestion.

'Bloody hell.' He grinned at the woman lying in the bed. 'You look rough.'

Her eyes opened, widened with stark terror at the sight of him. Her pale, cracked lips moved, but no sound came out.

'Have you told anyone our little secret?' He approached the bed. 'The police? Blondie, your sexy solicitor?' She couldn't shake her head because of the tube sticking in her throat, but Demetrio thought her lips formed the word 'no'. He glanced back at the door and reached into his coat pocket.

'What's that?' he asked, looking at the black box by her side. 'Oh yeah. Morphine. You press that button when you want a fix. You must be in a lot of pain. Best if I put you out of your misery now, eh?' He unwrapped the syringe, pulled the plastic cap off the needle. 'You won't want to spend the rest of your life writing what you can't say and wearing roll-neck sweaters to hide the scars. Not to mention all that trauma – I mean, you'll never feel safe again. Even if you don't grass me to the plods or Blondie sexpot Shannon.' He held the syringe poised. 'I know you don't want to help me, that you told me you'd keep it shut and we were finished. Thought that was the end of it, didn't you?' Anger rose in him. 'Thought you could just walk away. Nobody does that to me, Keely.'

She couldn't move because of the bandages, drip and tube, all the other things going in and out of her. Her eyes were frantic. A whistling sound came from the tube in her throat. Demetrio pointed the syringe at her left arm.

'Just need to find a vein and inject this, then you'll go off to sleep and–'

He jumped in fright as the door swung open and a nurse marched in, wheeling some kind of machine with a dark-blue cuff dangling. He whipped the syringe out of sight, trying to jam it back into his pocket without stabbing himself in the process. The nurse paused and looked him up and down.

'Okay?'

'Yeah, fine.' *Shit.* Could nothing go right for him lately? Demetrio stood back, furious, his heart thudding. He had come here hoping to finish the job. The sight of the copper had put paid to those hopes. But then Ursula had come along. And this chance, now blown.

'She can't have visitors for long, you know. She needs a lot of rest. Hiya, Keely!' The nurse smiled at the helpless, terrified woman. 'Just come to check your blood pressure, darlin'.' She moved closer. 'You been cryin'? What's up, love?'

'I'll leave you to it.' Demetrio touched Keely's wispy auburn hair and shot her what he hoped was a sufficiently warning glance. 'You take care now.' He felt her shrink from him, as much as she could shrink. 'Lots of rest, like the lady said.'

70

He strode out and down the corridor, one hand over his face, pretending to be too upset to say goodbye to Ursula and the brats. He was shaking. He had so nearly done it. What next? Keely knew he wanted her dead now. Would she tell the cops everything she knew about him? Or write it down – she couldn't tell anyone anything!

Demetrio didn't think she would. Keely was in enough trouble herself, and could get into more trouble if she confessed to hiding guns and cash for him. He had given Keely a false name, of course. But the plods might put two and two together. Eventually. He just had to hope she would be too frightened to grass him up.

He swore and thumped the wall, broke into a run and shoved through doors that led to the stairs. He wasn't going to use the lift, which of course had bloody CCTV in it. That did not stop him giving the closed lift doors a good kicking to relieve his feelings, after he'd checked to make sure no one else was around.

The nurse took the piece of paper from Keely and gasped at the words slowly pencilled in shaky handwriting: *Help. He's Kev Hoyle. Tried murder me. He'll be back.*

Chapter Eight

'What's going to happen to me now?' the woman in the rape suite sobbed. 'He said he'd kill me if I told the police what he did!'

'Deborah, listen. If your ex-boyfriend threatens you or comes anywhere near you, he'll be in even bigger trouble.' Shannon laid down pen and notepad and put one arm around her. The WPC had gone out to get Deborah a cup of tea. 'He won't be that stupid.' She hoped she was right. 'They've issued a warrant for his arrest and he'll be kept in custody over the weekend.' The Magistrates' Court would very likely grant him bail on Monday morning, and the Crown Prosecution Service might decide there wasn't enough evidence. Only about 10% of rape cases resulted in a conviction. Proving a rape allegation against someone known to the victim, however briefly, was extremely difficult. And proving it against an ex-boyfriend who claimed consent as his defence would be near impossible, especially when there was little or no evidence of physical violence. But Shannon did not want to tell Deborah any of this right now.

'I know you don't feel safe any more,' she said, her voice gentle. 'Your whole world's turned upside down. You feel so powerless. But you'll get through this.' She hugged her. 'You will.'

Shannon shivered suddenly, felt herself turn pale. She was

still jittery after the menacing Demetrio Montana's un-expected visit earlier that afternoon. And the invitation to dinner, what on earth was all that about? Did he seriously think she would accept? She removed her arm from Deborah's shoulders, got up and turned away, folding her arms tightly across her chest. She felt stifled.

She hated these places, even though the pictures on the walls and leafy green plants dotted around were supposed to make them look like somebody's living room. Rape suites smelled of fear, panic, violence.

Shannon tried to push away the image of Rob pinning her to their bed, his once loving brown eyes cold and hostile as he forced himself inside her, ignoring her cries of pain and terror, her frantic pleas for him to stop doing this, stop hurting her. Whispering in her ear, *'See? I am a monster.'* Telling her they were finished and he wanted a divorce. That he was leaving and she shouldn't try to find him. She closed her eyes briefly. When she composed herself and turned round Deborah was staring up at her, her crumpled face streaked with tears. She pushed back her dark hair and rubbed her reddened eyes.

'It's happened to you,' she whispered. 'Hasn't it?'

Shannon stiffened and glanced back at the door. Was it that disconcertingly bloody obvious? She had to pull herself together, be professional. This was a bad day, but it wasn't the first and wouldn't be the last. She came forward and sat down again.

'Deborah, you asked for a solicitor to come and talk to you. That's why I'm here.' Strictly speaking Deborah didn't need a solicitor, not at this stage anyway, because in the eyes of the British legal system she was no more than a witness to her own violation. 'This is about you, your allegation. Not me.'

'Tell me something.' She jumped as Deborah touched her arm. 'Did you report it?'

Shannon ignored the question and picked up her pen and notepad. She might feel very sorry for Deborah, but no way was she going to get into any personal stuff with a client. And certainly not in a police station where the walls, ceilings and light fittings might have ears. 'Deborah, I told you, I'm here to–'

'No,' Deborah interrupted, her voice breaking. 'Of course you didn't report it.' She got up, hugging herself, and started to pace, raking her hands through her wild hair. 'Not thick like me, are you? And you're a lawyer. You knew damn well you'd end up getting fucked all over again in court. I've changed my mind,' she cried, more tears streaming down her face. 'I don't want to take this any further. I won't – I can't!' She grabbed her Victims of Crime leaflet and tore it to shreds.

It was another twenty minutes before Shannon could leave. She hailed a cab and sat glancing at her watch and cursing silently as it crawled through the afternoon traffic. Ten-past four already. She had promised Finbar she would be waiting. The cab driver, wanking on about some Big Match, was making her incandescent with irritation.

'Can you give it a rest?' she called, opening her bag and taking out her mobile. 'I hate football.'

He shot her a dark look in the mirror. 'You can still get your head chopped off for treason, you know. They haven't taken it off the statute books.'

'I wouldn't be at all amazed.' Shannon dialled Finbar's mobile; after six rings his voice came on saying to leave a number and he'd call back. She frowned. Strange. She phoned the Kam Flinder Najeba office, hoping he had arrived and was waiting for her there.

'No', Helena sighed. 'Finbar isn't here.'

Shannon stopped herself asking, *'Are you sure?'* 'Well, when he arrives could you tell him I'm on my way? Thanks. I'm stuck in traffic on Lime Street.' People with bags and suitcases crossed the road in front of them, heading to and from the station. Rubbish littered the pavements, and although it was stuffy in the cab she didn't want to open a window and get a lungful of exhaust fumes.

She tried Finbar's mobile again and got the same message. She phoned the apartment, then India Buildings. No answer there either. Finbar must have switched off his mobile and forgotten to switch it back on. He did that sometimes. And maybe he had been delayed for some reason. *What* reason? Don't start freaking, Shannon told herself. He's fine. Nothing's wrong.

Not much was right though. Maybe it was too soon to start work again. Not only had Demetrio Montana rattled her, she had nearly let her professional mask slip back there in that rape suite. And what the hell did this anonymous letter-writing idiot plan to do when she refused to obey the crazy order to go to the police and confess that she'd had Bernard Flinder killed? It all felt like too much bloody hassle.

Shannon closed her eyes and leaned back against the seat, telling herself not to panic. She was about to fly away with Finbar, spend two days in a beautiful part of Ireland. They would be alone together, surrounded by mountains and ocean. She tried to relax her mind and body, imagine the sound of Atlantic breakers crashing on a deserted, golden beach. But fear was taking hold, tightening her throat and stomach muscles, settling like a weight on her shoulders. The cab crawled forward and stopped again, the driver now grouching about overpaid footballers who didn't deliver enough goals or general entertainment. She wanted to scream. By the time she got back to the office it was four-thirty. She rushed in.

Finbar was not there.

Chapter Nine

'Don't fuck with me. You know who I am!'

The man was frightened and sweating, his dark eyes darting everywhere, the gun trembling in his hands. All of which meant it was highly probable that he would do something stupid any second. Like blowing my head off, Finbar thought. He tried to unlock his brain and think straight. The threat was no longer faceless. Nameless, yes, so far. But he didn't feel relieved to know the worst. This wasn't the worst.

He pictured Shannon getting back to her office to find he wasn't waiting. She would be terrified, wondering if some bastard with a gun or bomb had turned nightmare to reality. Rush back here and burst in on this little lot. Her life was in danger now. Because of him.

'I told you.' Finbar kept his voice calm, low. 'I don't know you from that guy in the Bible. Would you like to tell me what this is all about?'

'You *know*,' the man shouted, furious. 'You know what it's about!'

Finbar shook his head. 'I don't. I swear.' The phone on the small table by one of the sofas started to ring.

'You're lying, you bastard. Don't touch that fucking phone,' he shouted as Finbar glanced round and shifted sideways. 'Keep your hands out where I can see them.'

The phone rang a few more times then stopped. Finbar knew it was Shannon. She would have tried his mobile before calling the apartment. She must be back at her office now, frantic, wondering what had happened. Wondering what to do. And when she did it, he was powerless to stop her. She might be back within the next ten minutes, get home to find him shot dead, sprawled in a lake of his own blood. If this freaked dickbrain was still here, he would kill her too. How the hell was he supposed to stop this worst-case scenario playing itself out?

'Who was that?' The man gestured at the phone with the gun, pushed back his dark, tangled curls and wiped his forehead on his denim sleeve. Finbar shrugged.

'Most people lose what psychic skills they have around the age of seven.'

'Jesus Christ, you're full of it, aren't you? Was it your girlfriend?'

'I don't have a girlfriend,' he lied. 'I'm between relationships just now.'

'Yeah, right.'

Finbar swallowed, shook his head. 'A business contact said he'd call me around this time to discuss a deal. It was probably him.' He cleared his throat. 'How'd you get inside this building?'

'Helped some old dyed-blonde tart just back from a shopping spree.' The man grinned suddenly. 'Weighed down with labels, so she was. Like most of the tossers who live round here. *Dying* for a cappucino, dahling!' he mocked. 'Good job there was a member of the proletariat waiting to give her a hand.'

Finbar guessed he meant Angelique, the tall, fifty-something Donatella Versace lookalike who gave him the glad eye every time they met, unfazed if Shannon was with him. No use expecting Angelique to have the sense not to let a stranger gain access to the building with such an obvious ruse. She hadn't a thought in her head except where her next botox injection was coming from.

'So what do you want with me?' he challenged, desperate to do something before Shannon walked in on them.

77

'As if you didn't know. To kill you, of course. A life for a life.'

'Whose life? I really don't know, and I want some answers. I'd also be interested to know how you think you can dodge the CCTV on your way out of here after you've murdered me,' Finbar added, throwing in what he hoped would be a reality check. He was finding it hard to talk.

'This isn't murder, you bastard. It's execution.' The man's voice trembled. 'You shot my brother!' His eyes filled with tears. 'The day you and he stiffed that politician. Don't deny it, because I know everything. You shot him and walked away. I loved him. Don't act the hardarse with me!'

'Your *brother*?' Finbar sat up straight, dry-mouthed with shock as enlightenment struck. Lenny Dowd. No wonder this guy looked familiar. So this was about the revenge of the grief-stricken rellie. He hadn't even considered something that simple and obvious. But it did not necessarily explain everything. Had this nervous idiot blown up the club himself? He couldn't imagine him being that cool and competent. Was he acting alone? Or did he have help, was he maybe part of some group?

'Get it now, do you? Spot the family resemblance? Don't move!' The man levelled the revolver at Finbar's face and stepped closer. 'Didn't you know Lenny had a younger brother?'

'My association with Lenny Dowd was strictly business. We didn't swap cosy details about family on the few occasions we met.' Finbar paused. 'What's your name?'

'Declan. And don't think you'll get a dialogue going and that'll stop me blowing your fucking head off.'

'Lenny knew all about my family though.' Finbar looked him in the eye. 'He murdered my wife and baby daughter.'

'What?' It was Declan's turn to look shocked. 'You're–'

'No. I'm not lying. Neglected to mention that, did he?' Finbar slid forward a few centimetres. 'It suited Lenny to let me think some trigger-happy Brit squaddie had killed them. So that I'd want revenge, go along with his plan to stiff the politician. But when Lenny decided to kill me off because he thought I was a liability, he told me the truth.' Finbar's breath came quicker and a choking feeling rose in his throat. 'We struggled, I got the gun. It was him or me. But yeah.' He nodded. 'Once I knew, I wanted to kill him.' He paused. 'Losing a child ... that's the worst. Nothing else comes close. I hope you never find that out.'

'You're telling me Lenny shot a wee girl and her mother?' Declan gasped. 'He wouldn't ... *why*?'

'Majella, my wife, would have kept quiet about that arms dump she found him and his mates unloading. She hated Brits, wouldn't even set foot in England. Lenny knew that, but he didn't care. Roiseann would have been five now, starting school. I have to live with their murders every day, live with the fact that your precious brother took my daughter's life, stopped me being able to watch her grow up. And sometimes it feels like I can't live with it any more.' Finbar stared at the revolver. 'Lenny said he wished he could let me live, once he'd told me. He said I'd be more tortured that way. He was right.'

There was silence in the huge, sparsely furnished room. The playful spring wind blew in through the open balcony door, bringing with it a smell of engine oil, molasses and the sea. Distant children's laughter. Normal life going on all around. The late afternoon sunlight was fading, receding from walls and floor. Declan seemed to be thinking hard. He kept the gun levelled, stayed well out of reach.

'I'm still going to kill you,' he said at last. 'I have to.'

'No, you don't. You can put that thing away and walk out of here.' Finbar edged further forward. He had to try and jump him. If he was going to die anyway, he had nothing to lose. But whatever he did had to be swift and decisive. 'I'm already a dead man,' he said. 'Like I told you. Besides,' he said, probing for information, 'you blew up my club. I could have been blown to bits along with it. Don't you think you've done enough?'

Declan didn't reply. He seemed to be thinking hard again.

'D'you know who did it?' Finbar persisted. He had a feeling Declan didn't know what he was talking about.

Declan grinned again. 'I bloody do an' all.'

'So share it with me.' Finbar wondered if Declan was telling the truth. Maybe he wanted to look as if he knew more than he did. 'Go on,' he urged. 'What difference does it make now? I'm not going to grass you up for getting to me first, am I?'

'I did it. For a laugh. I thought if the blast doesn't get the shit, I'll finish him off meself with a couple of bullets. Up close and personal, like. Stop playing time-wasting games with me, you bastard!' Declan shouted, suddenly furious again.

'Do you know what it's like to shoot somebody?' Finbar asked, hoping he didn't. 'It's not as easy as you might think. It's messy, horrible, it freaks you.' He looked into Declan's angry, frightened eyes. 'It can fuck you up for the rest of your life, no matter how hard you think you are. Look at those armed response plods,' he went on. 'They think shooting someone's going to be the buzz of their life, but what happens? Months of sick leave, post-traumatic stress, whinging to therapists twice a week. They leave the force and think they're lucky to get work as a security guard. Which they are. Sad, isn't it?' he smiled. 'Not exactly Dirty Harry.'

Don't come back here, Shannon, he prayed. Stay away, stay safe. The thought of her terror, the danger she faced, tortured Finbar so much it was hard not to lose it. But he had to stay cool, keep thinking. The palms of his hands slid on the soft blue leather sofa where he had fucked her only last night, cradled her in his arms afterwards as he breathed in the scent of her hair and skin, the moonlight slanting over her beautiful naked body. He thought how much he loved her, how he was getting her back at last. Now he was within seconds of death, of saying goodbye to their love, to the joys life might hold for them if they could get past all the shit that had happened. And they were starting to get past it. Finbar wasn't ready to say goodbye.

'You think shooting you'll fuck me up?' Declan shouted, tossing the hair out of his eyes again. 'Not for five seconds, never mind the rest of me life. You murdered my brother and now it's time to pay.' He pointed the gun, his finger on the trigger. 'Want to say a quick "Hail Mary"?' His laugh was edgy, almost hysterical.

'I won't bother, if you don't mind. I'm not a fan of organised religion. Your big brother asked me if I wanted to pray.' Finbar's heart flipped as he thought he heard the front door click shut. Had he imagined it? Declan didn't seem to have heard anything. He raised his voice. 'I told him to go fuck himself!' He took his eyes from the bleak blackness of the gun barrel and looked beyond Declan. Stared in horror as Shannon appeared in the living-room doorway. Their eyes met.

'Get out!' he screamed. *'Now.'*

'Jesus Christ!' Declan spat, startled. 'That's the oldest fucking trick in the book.' He couldn't resist glancing around nonetheless. 'I knew there was no one there. You stupid bastard,' he mocked. 'It's like they all say, you've gone soft. You'd try anything, no matter how pathetic. You're just a limp dick now. I'm doing you a favour, killing you. What's up?' he asked, seeing the anguished look in Finbar's green eyes. 'Scared now, are you?'

'Not of you any more than I was of your brother, you little shit!'

The beer glass Shannon flung arced across the room and smashed against one of the stone pillars that rose up through each floor of the old warehouse, narrowly missing Declan's head. He gasped and swung round, both hands gripping the gun. Swung back towards Finbar and fired, but missed. The bullet hit a radiator pipe which gushed water. Finbar flung himself at Declan's legs and brought him thudding down in a brutal tackle.

'Get out,' he screamed at Shannon. 'Go!'

But she didn't. She ran forward, white-faced, blonde hair flying, and kicked at Declan's hand holding the gun. He cursed, gave a shout of pain and let go. The revolver spun, hit a leg of the coffee table and skidded beneath one of the sofas. Finbar lashed out and punched Declan on the jaw. Not hard enough. Declan brought up his leg and kneed him in the stomach, forcing him sideways. Finbar rolled on the floor, gasping for breath, his mouth open. Declan staggered to his feet, lunged at Shannon and grabbed her.

'Fucking bitch.' She screamed and struggled as he shoved her into a kneeling position and twisted one arm up her back. She swept her free arm over the coffee table. Papers, magazines and a Waterford crystal bowl of floating candles crashed to the floor.

'Let go of her,' Finbar gasped. 'Don't hurt her.' Declan crouched, trying to keep a grip on Shannon's twisted arm, and scrabbled under the sofa for the gun. Finbar crawled forward, and Declan kicked out at him. Shannon screamed in pain and fear. Finbar grabbed his lunging foot and brought him down again, forcing him to let go of Shannon. She struggled to her feet. Her hair was wild, her clothes soaked. Finbar climbed on top of Declan and punched him several times in the face and head, panting with the effort. His knuckles hurt like hell.

Declan groaned and stopped struggling. His head rolled sideways, blood dripping from his nose and mouth. Finbar got off him and reached beneath the sofa. His fingers touched dust and hairs, a few scattered cashew nuts. Cold metal.

'Finbar!' Shannon screamed. Declan was on his feet, staggering towards her again. She jumped back and ran for the door. Finbar gripped the revolver with both hands, index finger curling around the trigger.

'Stop!' he shouted. 'Leave her alone, or I'll kill you.'

Declan paused and glanced round, breathing hard. His lips curved in a contemptuous smile. 'Gonna shoot me, are you, big man?' he taunted. 'You wish! You've lost it. That thing won't be much use to you when I'm holding a knife to your wee girlfriend's throat, will it? You can shoot me then if you

can get up the nerve, but she'll be dead before I let her drop.'
He turned and ran after Shannon, determined to grab her
before Finbar got to them. She was gorgeous, a real looker.
Pity he couldn't have some fun with her first.

Finbar squeezed the trigger and fired once, then a second
time. The gun was fitted with a suppressor, but it still made
a loud enough noise. The shock and recoil flashed up his
arms and across his shoulders. Both bullets hit Declan in
the back and he staggered, almost theatrically, like an actor
in a movie. Then he collapsed, blood pooling out from
under his denim jacket to mingle with water from the punc-
tured radiator pipe and broken crystal bowl. Finbar dropped
the gun on the coffee table, ran to Shannon and pulled her
into his arms.

'You okay?' he gasped, hugging her tight. She was dazed,
trembling. 'You're brilliant, you saved my life. We're safe
now, it's all right. Don't worry.'

She looked up and stared at him, her face ashen. 'Don't
worry?'

'Bad choice of words. I mean, it's over now.' But was it?
He gasped again, panting like he'd run a marathon. 'What
made you think to throw the glass?'

'Every police officer and criminal lawyer knows a beer
glass is the number one choice of assault weapon in the UK.'
Shannon pulled free and raked her fingers through her hair,
brushed her hands over her wet skirt and jacket as if to rid
herself of Declan's touch. She glanced at his inert body,
looked away. 'Who is he?' she whispered, shuddering.
'What does he want?'

'To kill me,' Finbar said.

'Yeah, I guessed that. Why?'

'He's Lenny Dowd's brother. I didn't even know–'
Finbar's voice trailed off. He felt cold, shivering with shock
and the adrenalin rush. He could still feel the gun's recoil in
his arms and shoulders.

'Lenny?' Shannon stared at him. 'That Real IRA commander who tried to kill you after he'd murdered the

Defence Secretary – the one who murdered Roiseann and Majella too?'

'The very same.'

'Oh, my God! Did he – I mean, *him*–' she pointed to Declan '–blow up your club?'

'He said he did, but I don't think I believe him. I don't really know what to think right now.' Finbar's face twisted in a grimace. 'Wee Declan, out to discharge his blood and honour debt. Pathetic, isn't it?'

'We'll have the cops all over us now,' Shannon groaned, her eyes filling with tears. 'They'll think it's Christmas! We'll never get them off our backs.'

'The police?' He paled. 'You're bloody joking, aren't you?'

'For Christ's sake, Finbar, you just shot somebody!' She flung out one arm, gesturing at the, sprawled figure. 'I know it was self-defence. You did it to save me as well. But he's unconscious, he must be seriously injured. He could die. We have to call an ambulance right now. And how can we not call the police? If we don't, the paramedics will. And they'll wonder why we didn't – it'll look worse for us. Oh, *God*.' Shannon turned away, her shoulders shaking. 'This is the perfect end to a perfect day, isn't it?'

'Calm down,' he said, looking at her. 'Just stay cool.'

'Yeah, right. Whatever you say.'

Finbar walked to Declan and stood over him. He crouched and grasped a handful of dark curls, gently turned his head to one side. Declan's face was ashen, his dark eyes staring. A string of saliva, mingled with blood, drooled from one corner of his mouth. He was young, Finbar thought, could not be much more than twenty-two or three. Too young to be yet another casualty of fucked up beliefs, his own and other people's. Especially big brother Lenny's; filling him with shit about the glory of the cause. As Lenny himself had been fucked-up. Still. There came a time when people had to think for themselves, take responsibility. And if they didn't they were likely to do themselves and others a lot of damage.

Shock, horror and revulsion at this violent act against another human being, even though he had done it to defend himself and Shannon, overwhelmed Finbar. He touched Declan's clammy skin, feeling for pulse and heartbeat, then got slowly to his feet. His body was stiff and aching. He felt like an old man, like his soul had the stain of several life-times. Shannon was staring at him from the doorway, hugging herself and shivering. Finbar moved towards her then stopped.

'How is he?' she whispered. 'He's not...?' She couldn't go on. The vulnerable, frightened look in her eyes tore at his heart.

'He won't need the paramedics,' Finbar said. 'He's dead.'

PART TWO

Chapter Ten

Shannon's a criminal law solicitor, spends her days dealing with society's spume and spindrift. She probably imagines she knows the innermost workings of the scroat psyche. So she should, given that she lives with that green-eyed Mad Mick bastard. She doesn't believe there's any such thing as evil. Only drugs, alcohol, divorce, neglect, the shortcomings of the education system and the strains and stresses of deprived, inner city existence. Speaking of inner city existence, the Council stick asylum seekers in the tower blocks these days – the blocks that have so far escaped demolition. Poor sods think they're in Paradise. That's if they're genuine asylum seekers, of course, not the illegal kind who start shouting the odds the minute they untangle themselves from the high-voltage cables beneath Channel tunnel trains, and demand cash on the hip and tolerance of customs and beliefs that would make a mediaeval Cardinal appear enlightened and progressive. But I digress. Let's get back to the feisty Ms Flinder.

I wonder what Shannon thinks of my letters? Does she appreciate the pretty pink ribbon and best quality writing paper that it's difficult to find these days? I suppose she only writes e-mails, scribbles post-it notes and signs letters she's too high and mighty to type herself. She won't find any DNA on my missives, if that's what she's hoping for. Or maybe she hasn't bothered to send them to a lab for tests. I mean, what's the point? She won't want to tell the cops about her private post. And of course she may not have got the message yet.

Shannon will know that the vast majority of people who pen anonymous, threatening letters are cranks, bewildered sad acts whose threats stay well within the realms of their rich fantasy life. Or poor fantasy life, depending on how you look at it. Nasty, but not dangerous. They get bored after a while and look for other objects of obsession. Or take their medication and go quietly. You don't have to be a cop or hot bitch criminal lawyer to know that.

Where does she keep the letters she's received so far? In her bag, her desk? The bedside table? Does she take them out and read them over, wondering who the hell I am? She must be terrified, wondering what I'll do next. The Mad Mick's got his troubles too. Together in adversity, finding comfort in one another's love. Ahh. How sweet, how romantic. That's what it's all about, innit? I'm weeping into my gutsy Burgundy as I write!

I hate people who get away with things. It fills me with resentment and fury. Well, okay – jealousy, too! I glow green in the dark with envy. I never got away with anything. Couldn't even steal my favourite pink bubble gum from the corner sweet shop without getting nicked by that old bag who ran it. I can still feel the shame and humiliation. My mates laughed themselves soft, despised me for getting caught. I despised myself. Not that I'd call that a formative experience. It's just an example.

Most people have got some dream or ambition. They want to sing, act, publish a book, get their ideal job, buy a house, have kids, win the lottery, seduce their object of desire. You name it. My dream is to get away with murder. Or what the law would describe as murder. (Fine point there!)

Shannon had that car crash and the miscarriage. So what? Lots of people have bad stuff happen to them, even when they don't deserve it – especially when they don't deserve it! Shannon deserved everything. But it doesn't count, because she got away with all that – she survived.

And now she's got everything she wanted. The evil headmaster's dead, she's dumped her poor sod of a husband –
who's devastated now – and got to keep her career and good
reputation as well as her handsome, rich, criminal lover.
Sorted!

Don't get me wrong, I've got no problem with her having
the headmaster stiffed. Bernard Flinder was a murderer, a
paedophile. He deserved to die. It's just that if I'd killed him,
or had him killed, I'd have got caught. I'd be doing time
now. Besides, Shannon didn't do it for the right reasons.
Flinder got in her way, threatened to destroy her life, and
our Shannon wasn't going to let that happen, oh no. She
didn't give a toss about him raping, mutilating and murdering those young girls. She just wanted to save herself.

Hope I haven't spoiled her weekend, tee-hee! She'll
wonder what to do now, how to respond to my last letter.
Considering her response, that's how people like the hot
bitch lawyer talk. They live in a world of considered
responses and formal denials. When you stampede through
life trampling anyone who gets in your way you've usually
got plenty to deny. Formally or informally.

I WANT HER TO KNOW HOW IT FEELS TO LOSE
EVERYTHING!!!

I saw the usher give her that first letter, watched her open
it. She looked so freaked I had to turn away for laughing.
And of course I didn't want her to clock me. I stood and
looked at the notice board with the list of scroats up before
the Mags that morning, black printed names against a
yellow background. I love that building, the old workhouse,
although I'm sure Shannon thinks it's depressing with those
high walls and ceilings, and the church-like windows you
can't look out of. I suppose the Victorians who built it didn't
want the inmates to gawp out into the street and get distracted from their oakum picking, or whatever they were
forced to do in return for their daily ration of gruel, cold
lumpy porridge, stale bread and cholera or typhus-infected
drinking water. Every time I go in there I try and find a quiet

spot so that I can sit and soak up the old atmosphere and smells, hear the voices, see the ghosts.

Down in the Bridewell there's a corridor that's usually deserted, with a long old wooden bench that must have been upstairs in the days when scroats could be trusted to wait their turn in front of the Magistrates without going ape and trashing everything in sight. That's a good place. Last time I was down there sitting in the silence I saw this little girl, a toddler. She wore a coarse grey dress that was too big for her and she had long, matted, dark curly hair partially covered by a dirty cotton cap. Huge, frightened brown eyes. Her nose was running. Her tiny bare feet must have been frozen on that stone floor. She was a darling. Poor little thing was crying, I think her mother had just died. I didn't see any love or warmth around her, any protection. That made me sad. I was filled with pain because I couldn't scoop her up in my arms and make her feel safe, loved. Then she dissolved around the edges and was gone.

I never tell anyone about the ghosts, of course.

Chapter Eleven

'What the hell are you going to do now?' Shannon sobbed, trying to fight her rising hysteria. 'Hack off his hands, feet and head so that he can't be identified?' She curled up on the bed and hugged the pillow, her body shaking. Her black jacket and shoes lay on the floor. The sky beyond the windows was clear dark blue with a pale half moon reflected in the still dock waters.

'Yeah, right. Very funny.' Finbar sat on the bed and laid one hand on her hip. 'Look, this isn't exactly easy for me either, you know.' He was trembling with revulsion and felt sick. 'I've taped the radiator and cleaned up all that water,' he said, his voice low. 'The blood, too. Everything. There's no trace.'

'Oh, you reckon?' Shannon rolled over and sat up, her eyes glittering with tears. 'Have you heard of luminol tests, *darling*?' she hissed. 'They can show up bloodstains on walls, floors and anywhere else even when you think you've been a regular Lady Macbeth.'

Finbar's lips tightened. 'Well, thanks for that, my little forensic detective.' He took her cold hand, kissed and stroked it. 'Try to calm down, okay? Nobody's got any reason to come in here and carry out fucking luminol tests. Or any other kind. As long as we stay cool.'

Shannon pulled her hand away and wiped her tears. 'You can't do this, Finbar, you just can't!'

93

'Do what, precisely?' he asked, grim-faced.

'Cover up a killing!'

'All I'm doing is trying to protect us. Come on, Shannon!' he pleaded, worried about her. 'I can understand you're in shock – so am I. But why take a pop at me, for Christ's sake?'

'I'm not–'

'That little bastard would have murdered us both.'

'I know! What I'm saying is, the longer you delay reporting his death, the more suspicious it's going to look. The police might think you let him die, maybe even that you murdered him. They'll want to think the worst anyway. You shouldn't have cleaned up that blood, or touched anything. You're crazy,' she wailed. 'They'll arrest you, charge you with murder. Start investigating your past. Which means you could get put away for the rest of your future!'

'Better not give them any reason to arrest and charge me then, had I?'

'It's too late for that, you've let too much time pass. You interfered with the crime scene. And what about me? I'm an accomplice. I've aided and abetted a killing!'

'Let's get one thing clear, Shannon. This is my problem. Not yours.'

'Of course it's my bloody problem. I'm here, aren't I? I saw it happen – I helped you. I know it was self-defence, but a man's dead.' She gulped for breath, gave another sob. 'There's a dead body in the living room!' she wailed, her voice rising to a scream. 'This is bizarre, it's. . . What the hell are we going to *do*?'

'Ssh.' Finbar pulled her against him and wrapped his arms around her. 'Quiet now. Everything's going to be all right.' He rocked her gently as he held her, his lips against her soft hair. 'I promise you. You've got to trust me, Shannon.'

'It won't be all right, how can it? Oh God, I'm so frightened!'

'Don't be. There's no need. It *will* be all right.' He stroked her back and shoulders, the nape of her neck, trying to still the trembling in her body. 'This is too much for you, I realise that,' he murmured. 'Especially on top of everything else. But you musn't panic.' He reached for the glass of white wine on the bedside table. 'Here. Take a swig of this.' He'd wanted to give her something stronger, but she didn't like cognac and loathed whisky.

Shannon gulped the wine and gave a long, shuddering sigh as its warmth spread throughout her body. She pulled a couple of tissues from the box on the bedside table and wiped her eyes.

'That's better.' Finbar put the glass down and took her in his arms again. 'You're strong,' he murmured, kissing her and smoothing back her hair. 'You'll be fine, you can deal with this.'

'I'm sick of being strong and dealing with things.' Exhausted, she leaned her head on his shoulder and closed her eyes. She wanted to shut all this out, make it go away, pretend it hadn't happened. But it wasn't going to go away, so she might as well stop wasting valuable energy weeping and wailing. She sniffed and swallowed, forced back more tears. Shannon suddenly wondered if the price of loving Finbar Linnell was just too high.

'Okay. This is what's going to happen.' His voice floated, soft and gentle, somewhere around the edges of her consciousness. 'I'll get him out of here,' he said, holding her tight. 'Dump him where he'll never be found. There's nothing to link him to me. You stay here while I do it. It's too late to fly to Cork now. We'll leave first thing in the morning.'

Shannon raised her head and stared at him. Finbar's green eyes were calm, his gaze steady. 'You're serious, aren't you?'

'Of course I am,' he said, surprised.

'I need another drink.'

He gave her a look. 'Okay.' He got up, went out and came back with the bottle. The Pouilly Fumé had lost its chill, but she liked wine better that way. He poured her another glass and she drank half of it.

'I don't like to be a spoilsport and criticise your cunning plan.' Shannon put the glass down. 'But it's got more holes in it than that pair of tights I binned yesterday. Are you *crazy*?' she exploded. 'Even if you manage to drag his dead weight out of here and bump him down three flights of stairs without any of our fellow residents happening to notice, how are you going to avoid the CCTV at the entrance? You then have to get him to the car, where he's bound to leave a few hairs and fibres and the odd drop of body fluids. Someone might witness you–' she paused, biting her lip '–disposing of him. And how can you say there's nothing to link him to you? For a start, he must have been caught on the CCTV when he got into this building – where *you* live! How did he get in, by the way?'

'Angelique,' Finbar sighed. 'Helped her with her shopping bags. He was hanging around looking for some way to gain entry.'

'Oh, terrific.' Shannon wiped away a tear. 'So the airhead of the Albert Dock saw him? That's all we need.'

'Better her than somebody with a brain who might have got suspicious. Besides, Angelique wouldn't have had a clue that Declan wanted to see me.'

'I don't like to state the bleeding obvious, but you're both Irish. She might guess.'

'I doubt it. She probably didn't give it another thought. Not much thought process happening generally in that head, wouldn't you say?'

'All right, forget bleached blonde lipliner lady. Suppose this Declan told other people – family, friends – that he intended to avenge his dead brother?' Shannon argued. 'They won't need to be Einstein to work out what's happened when he disappears without carrying out his plan. What will they do then?'

Finbar frowned. 'Killing me was Declan's private initiative. Probably no one else gives a fuck. Or not enough to come after me themselves. I can't be certain, but–'

'You like that word *probably*, don't you? No, you can't be

certain. And even if he didn't tell any family members or friends, they'll *probably* report him missing sooner or later.' Shannon scrambled off the bed and stood up, panic sweeping over her. 'You said you didn't believe him when he told you he'd blown up your club. If he didn't do it, who the hell did?'

'If I knew *that* . . . !' Anger rose in him. He'd be after them right now, get to them before they jumped him again. 'I suppose Declan could have done it,' Finbar said reluctantly. 'I may have underestimated his capabilities.'

Shannon was staring at him. 'But you don't think so.'

He shrugged. 'I still think somebody wants something from me. I just don't know who or what. Declan could have a connection with whoever it might be, but I doubt it. I mean, if they want something from me they're hardly going to let him come here and blow my face off.' He paused. 'Unless Declan was a loose cannon.'

Or unless his own death was what they wanted. Unless Declan was expendable. They could be sadists, psychos, just torturing him for the fun of it until they decided to deal the final blow. Finbar thought again of the Brit on the phone just before the club blew, saying he had a message. Did that mean this was a game of cat and mouse, with him as mouse? He did not share that chilling thought with Shannon. He wondered if there were any clues on Declan. Searching a stiff was distasteful of course, not the kind of thing you queued up to get tickets for – although some might. But it was nothing compared to shooting someone dead then having to clean up the gore. Finbar swallowed hard as saliva rushed into his mouth.

'What a mess.' Shannon walked to the window, more tears flooding her eyes. She gazed out across the lights of dockland, at the illuminated mast of the clipper ship berthed outside the Maritime Museum. The moon rose higher and a few stars glittered. 'You won't get out of this one, Finbar.' Her voice shook. 'There's no way.'

97

'I admire your optimism, darling. And while you're at it, stand in front of the window looking freaked, why don't you?' He strode across and pulled the blinds closed, gripped her shoulders and turned her to face him. 'I told you what's going to happen, and I meant it,' he said, his voice low and fierce. 'This could all be down to him alone. If so, it's over. If not, I'll sort it. We'll be safe. And never mind the bloody CCTV. Tapes get lost, stolen, wiped. That's not a problem, so don't stress about it.'

Shannon was silent. She felt dizzy with wine, exhaustion and fear. 'I got another letter,' she whispered. 'This morning. It was in our mailbox.'

'Jesus Christ!' Finbar relaxed his grip. The silk of her pale pink shirt slid beneath his fingers. 'Why didn't you tell me when I called you at lunchtime?'

'I couldn't talk about it over the phone. I decided to tell you later. I thought whoever put the letter there might be caught on camera,' she said. 'But I don't know what excuse to make for asking to see it. It's not like I'm going to tell the police. Who deals with CCTV in this building anyway?' she asked. 'I never thought about that.'

'A few dozy bastards who take it in turn to sit in a little room in the basement. They keep the tapes for a month then destroy them. Or that's what they're supposed to do. I've seen the images,' Finbar said, thinking of Declan. 'They're not great. The most crap defence barrister in existence could get them ruled inadmissible. Not that it'll come to that. Most people can't reliably identify suspects' faces even from high-quality imaging. But it won't come to that either.'

'I'm suitably impressed by your knowledge.' Shannon moved away from him and sat on the bed again. 'You still don't want to be on camera dragging away a corpse.' She pushed back her hair. 'Even if you get him out of here without being spotted, where will you take him?' She couldn't bear to use the word *dump*. 'The car number might be tracked. People in the UK can't go anywhere or do anything nowadays without some miserable little power junkie spying on them.'

'The watchers have to know what they're watching for.' Finbar sat beside her and slid one arm around her shoulders, hugged her tight. 'We're wasting time,' he said, kissing her. 'I've got a job to do.'

Shannon caught her breath. 'Let me help,' she whispered.

My God, she thought, shivering. I've aided and abetted a killing, now I'm conspiring to conceal it. And before this, she had had Bernard Flinder killed. That was self-defence too, but would anyone believe her? Someone convicted of that lot would get the book thrown at them, especially if they were a respected criminal law solicitor. They would make an example of her. She would get put away for a lot longer than any of the clients she represented.

'You want to help?' Finbar said. 'Okay. I'll grab his shoulders, you lift his legs.'

'*Don't!*'

'Sorry. But you asked for it. Forget about it,' he murmured, kissing her again. 'There's no way I'm going to let you get involved in my dark, dirty deed.'

'I already am.' Shannon trembled. 'It's too late.'

'Maybe it's better if you don't stay here by yourself. Phone Nick or some other friend, get them to come round. Talk, laugh, drink some more wine – not too much. Pretend everything's normal. And before you know it, everything will be.'

'No,' she groaned. She leaned forward and rested her head on her knees. 'I can't!'

'You can. You have to. Just do it, okay?' Finbar put his arms around her and gently raised her, turned her to face him. He touched one finger to her lips, stared into her tearful, dark-blue eyes. 'You know you can. Please, Shannon.'

She pulled herself out of his arms and got up. Started to walk away. Stopped and turned, hesitating. She loved him and he loved her. No matter what happened now they were inextricably linked, bound together by secrets that each knew about the other. Secrets that Shannon hoped no one else would ever find out. Because if they did, she and Finbar were lost.

'All right,' she whispered.

Chapter Twelve

Rob Flinder slammed the porch door of his deceased parents house in Tanunda Avenue, posh Woolton, noting the cracked pane of coloured glass that he still could not be bothered to get replaced, despite the estate agent's nagging. What was the hurry, anyway? People were not exactly queueing up to buy the house of a murdered paedophile whose wife had committed suicide and whose daughter had been murdered by person or persons unknown. It just didn't have that *je ne sais quoi*. Couples with young children wouldn't touch it. And there was still the possibility, almost four months after his father's death, of some outraged vigilante crashing another brick through the front windows.

The few people who did come to look over the house were usually the wrong kind; time-wasting, obscenely curious sensation seekers. Rob sometimes thought he should organise an Evil Headmaster Tour, along the lines of the Jack the Ripper Trail in London. With the added titillation for the punters of being shown the house, school and bloody murder scenes by the son of the murderer. Who, incidentally, was himself a CID detective. Rob could see them now, oohing and aahing, searching his face for the family resemblance, wondering if sonny boy had inherited Daddy's perverted sexual tastes and murderous propensities? Oh yes. There were big bucks waiting to be made. Shame he couldn't be arsed.

He had dropped the price by several thousand, but there were still no takers. The only person who liked this mausoleum was Katy. They had moved out of her poky flat because of the damp and knackered central heating, and there had been nowhere to go but here. Rob knew he should look for another place. He had more than enough money, even though this house hadn't yet sold. But it was too much hassle. Everything was too much bloody hassle.

Depression hit him as he stuck his key in the front door and walked into the hall, smelled the familiar mustiness. He felt the ghosts of his mother, father and sister crowd around him. Blaming, demanding, threatening. But this evening there was another smell – authentic home cooking. Katy came out of the kitchen and walked smiling down the hall to greet him. She was putting on weight, Rob thought, noting how tight her jeans looked. And he could swear her tits had got bigger. Unless it was because she had on that clingy, purple Mexx sweater she liked so much. Katy's dull, fair hair hung around her long oval face, and her pale-blue eyes looked more animated than usual. She was flushed, like she'd had a couple of drinks.

'Hiya, darlin'!' Katy flung her arms around his neck, kissed and hugged him. Rob stiffened and drew back. Coming home from work was one of the times he missed Shannon most. He wished it was her kissing him now, back in their old house in Eaton Road. The pain was worse because he had lost her through his own fucking stupidity. Let her down when she needed him most. Rob knew he had to get over his broken marriage and move on. But intellect was one thing, his emotions another.

'I've done us cottage pie,' Katy grinned. 'With chopped spring onions and grated mature Cheddar in the mash. Ready in about five minutes. And there's apple crumble with your favourite Lemon Chiffon ice cream for pudding. Come on, I'll get you a glass of wine.'

Rob slipped off his mac and jacket, hung them up and followed her into the dining room. Katy had spread one of his mother's stiff white linen cloths and set the table with the best silver cutlery. Four red candles glowed in crystal holders, and the big lamp by the mantelpiece was switched on. A fire burned in the grate. Rob frowned as he loosened his tie. She was making herself a bit too bloody much at home.

'It's more like December than March,' he commented, gazing around.

'Cold this evening though, isn't it?' Katy rubbed her hands. 'I thought a fire would be nice. More cosy. There's plenty of coal and wood chips out the back. I lit it without using firelighters,' she said proudly.

Rob sat at the table, in his father's old place, and took the glass of red wine she poured him. 'Aren't you supposed to be on nights this week? Scouring for scum in clubland?'

'You don't listen to a word I say.' Katy laughed, but her eyes were anxious. 'I told you I'd swopped with Sharif. Besides, I've had to take a couple of days off. Haven't been feeling too good lately.'

'Oh, yeah. Your stomach bug.' Rob sipped the wine and leaned his elbows on the table. It was true, he hardly listened to her. There were too many other voices in his head. Katy lived with him – her idea, not his – and cooked comforting cottage pies, stews, stuffed baked potatoes and rich pasta dishes. She talked, poured him glasses of wine, cups of tea or coffee, and kept telling him she loved him. Coaxed him into screwing her two or three times a week. He gave nothing back. Katy knew he wasn't really interested, that she had caught him at a vulnerable time and that normally he wouldn't have given her a second glance. He had never given any woman a second glance when he'd had Shannon as his wife. Rob sighed and sipped more wine. Bonfire Night, he thought, gazing at the burning candles and the glowing coals of the fire. That's when it all started.

Katy hesitated. 'Bad day? How's that murder inquiry going?'

'About as well as *that* Jack the Ripper inquiry went.' Rob gulped the rest of his wine and poured himself a second glass. 'Finbar fucking Linnell had the nerve to waylay me today,' he said, his voice thick with rage. He dragged off his tie and threw it on the table. 'I went for a quick pint at lunchtime after a morning from hell. The bastard was waiting outside.'

'Finbar? Oh, you mean Shannon's...?' Katy took the tie and began to roll it up. Don't say 'boyfriend', she thought. Certainly not 'lover'. But 'partner' wouldn't be appropriate either. Jesus! Her hard-won mood of cheerful optimism faded as cold disappointment and apprehension struck. She didn't need to hear about Rob's nearly ex-wife at the best of times, and she didn't want the shadow of the golden goddess whose beauty, charm and sex appeal she could never even come close to ruining her carefully planned evening. Wouldn't Rob ever get over Shannon? They were finished, the divorce would come through soon. He had to accept that and move on, he just bloody had to! Katy started. Her body was tense, rigid, and she was gripping the tie as if it was a ligature.

'What did he want?' she asked, keeping her voice light and unconcerned. 'His club got blown up, didn't it? Nobody knows who did it. Or why.'

'Yeah. And it's a pity that bastard didn't get blown up along with it.' Rob's face flooded with colour. 'He threatened to kill me.'

'What?' Katy gasped.

'Said he'd kill me if I didn't leave Shannon alone. Stop making her life hell. He wouldn't believe me when I told him I didn't know what the fuck he was on about.' Rob did not want to tell Katy how much Finbar's threats and intimidating presence had frightened him, made him feel a hopeless prat. He blushed with humiliation at the memory of it. His fingers tightened around the glass.

'You can't let him get away with that,' Katy said, shocked.

'What am I supposed to do?' Rob jumped up. 'He made sure there were no witnesses and he didn't assault me – he was too bloody clever for that! You don't know what he's like.' He jabbed an accusing finger at her. 'That tosser is the biggest bloody villain–'

'I do know what he's like,' Katy interrupted. She dropped the rolled-up tie on the mantelpiece. 'You've told me often enough.'

'Oh well, I'm sorry to bore you.' Rob turned to leave.

'Rob, no! Wait.' She ran after him in panic. 'Please! Look, I'm sorry, okay?' She tried to put her arms around him again, but he shook her off. 'I hate to see you upset, that's all. I just want us to have a quiet, relaxing evening.'

'I'm not upset.' Rob wouldn't meet her gaze. 'Not by *him*. I just wonder what he meant, that's all. Shannon must be in some kind of trouble.'

'That's not your problem any more.' Katy's voice was gentle. She put an arm around him, guided him back to the table. 'I know you still care about Shannon.' Didn't she bloody just. 'I understand that. Let's have dinner,' she pleaded. 'Try to relax. You've had a long day.'

He sat down again and stared into the fire. She went back to the kitchen, took the cottage pie out of the oven and stuck the apple crumble in to cook. In the dining room she served the golden, bubbling pie with a flourish. It really was good, she thought, the cheese and spring onions in the mash especially delicious. She was relieved that the smell and taste of food didn't make her want to chuck up again. She poured Rob more wine. He didn't notice she was only drinking Seven Up.

Rob calmed down and ate his way through two large portions. Then he sat back and picked up his glass of wine.

'Was it all right?'

He nodded. 'Excellent. Terrific. You're a great cook,' he said. 'My mother never had a clue about cooking.'

His mother hadn't had a clue about most things, as far as Katy could gather. Gratified and encouraged, she stood up and began to clear the plates. She was even more encouraged when Rob smiled at her.

'Give me a break!' He patted his stomach. 'I'll need a

good ten or fifteen minutes before I can tackle that apple crumble and ice cream.'

'Yeah, sure. Me too.' She sat down again and took another sip of Seven Up, tried not to burp. She studied him for a few seconds. Decided that this was The Moment.

'Rob,' she began, suddenly rigid with nerves again. Her heart pounded and her stomach rumbled embarrassingly. 'I've got something to tell you.'

'Yeah, what's that?'

'I...' What was the best way to say this? There was no best way. Might as well come straight out with it. 'I'm going to have a baby.'

There was a silence. A *pregnant* silence, Katy thought, suppressing an unfortunate and untimely desire to burst into hysterical giggles. Rob pulled himself up and dumped his glass on the table, slopping red wine on the immaculate cloth.

'You...?' He looked at her, really looked at her for the first time. 'You're *what*?'

'It's why I haven't been feeling well. I've missed two periods. I bought a home pregnancy test kit and it showed positive. So I went to my GP. She confirmed it. It was a shock, of course, but once I got used to the idea I felt really happy. I hope you will be too.' Katy wanted to reach across and grab his hand, but didn't dare. 'I'm supposed to have a scan in three weeks time – I'd love it if you'd come with me. Rob, I've been thinking.' She knew she was babbling, but couldn't stop herself. 'Can't we go on living here, at least until our baby's born? I love this house, and it's so much bigger and better than my flat. I can understand you don't want to live here permanently though, it's got bad memories for you. So why don't I sell my flat? With that money and yours we could get a really nice house when the baby is, say, a few months old. I know you hate the hassle of moving, but don't worry. I'll organise everything. You won't have to lift a finger.'

Rob stood up and shoved back his chair. 'How could you do this to me?'

She paled. 'Rob, please don't be horrible! Like I said, it was a shock to me as well. I didn't plan this.'

'Didn't you? You told me you were taking the Pill.' He clenched his fists. 'Taking the piss, more like. You conniving bitch.'

'No! I came off the Pill because of irregular bleeding,' Katy cried, panicked at the fury in his brown eyes. 'You know I did. It was only temporary, just until my periods got back to normal. Look, it's just as much your responsibility as mine,' she argued. 'I don't see why I should get the blame, this isn't an immaculate conception! It's what can happen when two people make love.'

'Fuck, you mean.' His eyes were like stones or bullets. 'That's all I've ever done with you, you stupid cow. You threw yourself at me, you were there. A convenience. I don't love you. I don't even fancy you that much.'

Katy gasped with hurt. 'Because I'm not Shannon.'

'Yeah, because you're not Shannon. I miss her, I want her. I always will. You don't even come a poor second – you're nothing compared to her.'

'Oh, Rob! Please, please don't be like this.' Katy burst into tears, pouring out the emotion that had been building in her for the past days. She had expected him to be shocked, angry even. But not as awful as this. She was gutted. Crushed.

'What's Shannon going to think?' he yelled, thumping his fist on the table.

'Shannon?' Katy raised her tear-streaked face. 'What the hell's she got to do with this?' Her voice was a squeak of outraged astonishment.

'She lost her baby, remember? *Our* baby.' Candle and firelight flickered over his contorted face, giving it sinister shadows. 'She said I wasn't the father, but she lied because she was with *him*. I was the father! If Shannon hadn't had the miscarriage she would have come back to me. Everything would have been all right between us.'

'Rob, for God's sake! You don't really believe that,' Katy

sobbed in despair. This was a disaster. He was crazy, even more obsessed than she'd realised.

'I do fucking believe it! How's Shannon going to feel now? She'll be so hurt – devastated. Of course I know you hate her, you always did. You'd like to kick her in the guts. Now you've done it, you rotten, scheming slag. You planned all this. Should have seen you coming, shouldn't I? Well, let me tell you something.' He jabbed his finger at her again. 'Your plan won't work. I don't want you, and I don't want your fucking foetus. If you try to screw me for maintenance I'll contest that it's mine. You'd better go back to your bloody GP and tell her you want a termination.'

'*No!* Rob, this is our baby. I don't want to kill it, I won't!'

'It's not *my* baby. It's your problem, so you sort it. It's got nothing to do with me.' He paused, breathing heavily as he glared at her. She was frightened by the hate in his eyes. 'I'm going out now and I don't want to find you here when I get back. Take your stuff and fuck off out of this house – out of my life. I'm finished with you.'

'Please, Rob,' Katy wailed, 'don't treat me like this! I love you, I want our baby.'

But he was out of the room. The front door and porch door slammed and his car started, crunched over gravel in the drive and accelerated up the road. Silence took over. She stood there staring at the rolled tie, his half full glass of wine, the red stain on the cloth. The smell of apple crumble floated in from the kitchen. She felt sick again.

Katy drew a big breath and screamed, long and very loud. She picked up the wine bottle and hurled it against the wall. It smashed, and red wine dribbled down like blood. She threw Rob's tie in the fire and watched it burn. That wasn't enough, so she smashed the glasses and crystal fucking candleholders too. Dizziness and nausea overwhelmed her. She couldn't make it to the loo in time, so she vomited on the carpet.

Let Rob clean up the mess. He never lifted a finger. She was supposed to be so bloody grateful to him for having had anything to do with her. Keep her mouth shut, wait on him hand and foot, not have any needs, wishes, desires or opinions of her own. Because she wasn't even second best.

Shannon.

It was always Shannon.

Chapter Thirteen

'Bloody hell, she's got some tits on her!'

Harry Devlin the security guard chuckled as he turned a page of the magazine and saw the naked girl lying there feigning ecstasy, legs and pink gloss-slicked lips parted. Good job she was lying down, because she wouldn't be able to walk in those heels. Her eyes were half closed and her head on one side, strands of dark hair arranged across her face. The phone rang and he swallowed the chewed remnants of another Everton mint before picking up.

'Hello, yes?'

'It's me,' his wife Corinne said. 'Did you manage to get Emma's birthday present?'

'I certainly did, my love.' Harry closed the magazine out of respect at the mention of his adored granddaughter. He frowned. 'Cost me a fortune though. Those Barbie outfits and the fixtures and fittings are a right bloody rip-off.'

'I know, but think of her little face when she sees what Granny and Grandad have got her. She'll be made up.'

'Yeah.' Harry smiled. 'The shop assistants were giving me some funny looks.'

'Well, who did they think you were buying doll clothes for, yourself? None of their business anyway.'

'Maybe they thought I was a pervert.'

'Well, you are.' Corinne laughed. 'Listen, love. I've put your tea in the oven.'

'What am I having?'

'Salad. Only joking. It's lamb chops, broccoli and potato croquettes. I've had mine,' Corinne said. 'I was starving when I got in from work.'

'I've got to go,' Harry said, his voice hushed. 'Someone's coming.'

'Right, love. See you soon.'

Harry hung up, whipped the magazine out of sight and stared at the black-and-white screen that covered the building's entrance, trying to look alert and on the case. All he could see were several rows of mailbox flaps, the big glass front doors and beyond those cobblestones and dark, shiny dock waters. He swivelled round in his chair as the office door opened.

'Oh. Hiya, Finbar.' He raised his eyebrows. 'Don't often find you slumming it down here in the dark depths.' He yawned and stretched. 'Saw you go out earlier.'

'Did you? Well, now I'm back. No privacy around here, is there? I suppose it's the price we pay to keep out the criminal hordes.'

'Go anywhere exciting, did you?'

'Only to get a van and crate. We're having a clear out.' Finbar lounged in the doorway, hands in the pockets of his leather jacket. 'Books, mostly. Got a load to get rid of, promised we'd give them to a hospital. I'm supposed to deliver them tonight.'

Harry sniffed. 'I haven't got time to read. Not books, anyway. My missis is a great reader though. Why don't you sell them?' he asked. 'Still, I don't suppose a load of old books is worth much. And you rich gits with guilty consciences like to do your bit for charity now and then, don't you?' He wouldn't dare talk like this to any of the other snob residents, as they definitely would not see the funny side. But Finbar Linnell was different. He was all right. You could have a laugh with him.

'Yeah,' Finbar replied, smiling. 'Especially when, as in this case, the charity work won't cost anything but time and van hire. And no, a second-hand book dealer wouldn't give me more than a few quid.'

'That's how you stay rich though, isn't it, Finbar? Watching the pennies. Very important, that. Tell your girl-friend to ask for discounts at Cartier and Tiffany.'

'Thanks for the advice, but she's never been to those places. Neither have I.'

'That's right, lad,' Harry laughed. 'Keep your hand in your pocket.'

'Problem is, the books weigh a ton and I can't lift the crate by myself. Should have thought of that before, of course, but I had other things on my mind.' Finbar glanced around the small office, his eyes lingering on the screens. 'That other guy not on duty this evening?'

'Stevie? Lazy little sod called in sick. Sick, my arse.' Harry sat up and squared his shoulders at the mention of his young colleague. 'Want me to give you a hand getting these books downstairs?' he asked, knowing he wouldn't be expected to do it out of the kindness of his heart.

'That'd be good. Sure you can manage a bit of lifting? What about your hernia?'

'I haven't got a...!' Harry realised Finbar was on a wind-up. He heaved himself out of his chair and struck a body-builder pose, trying to pull in his sagging stomach. 'I'm all muscle, me,' he grinned. 'Then again...' He glanced back at the screens. 'I'm not supposed to leave me post except in an emergency. Could get in big trouble if I do. Lose me job.'

'Only if you're rumbled. Which won't happen.' Finbar pulled out his wallet and held up a twenty-pound note. 'And of course there's a small financial incentive for you.'

'Wouldn't say no.' Harry smoothed his shirt and the creases in his dark-blue trousers. 'Funny you have to deliver them tonight. What's the big hurry?'

'I haven't got time in the morning. My fiancée and I are going to Ireland for the weekend. Early flight out.'

'Oh, I see.' Harry rubbed his hands. 'Right, let's get

moving.' He took the note Finbar handed him and stuck it in his shirt pocket. 'Ta, lad.'

Bloody hell, he thought as he walked into the top-floor apartment. I'm in the wrong job. He had never been in any of the apartments. The space, the acres of white wall and shiny parquet floor, stunned him. Although it was a bit bare for his taste. Corinne wouldn't like it either. She would want lots of pictures, rugs, vases, photographs and trinkets to make it look cosy. The kitchen door was open and Harry could see the fiancée standing there with her back to him. Gorgeous arse, he thought, looking at her tight skirt. And legs. She was pouring herself a cup of coffee. It smelled good, the proper stuff.

'Evening!' he called. She turned, startled, and almost dropped the cup. She looks rough, Harry thought, staring at her beautiful flushed face and untidy hair. Wonder what's up with her? Finbar walked into the kitchen, slid one arm around her shoulders and hugged her.

'Won't take long,' he murmured. 'I'll be back soon, all right?'

She nodded and pulled away. Weird, Harry thought, sensing an atmosphere. Had they had a row? Maybe she'd wanted him to move the books sooner. Women got upset about crap like that. He remembered the time Corinne had blown her stack about the dusty *Amateur Photographer* magazines he'd kept in neat piles around his armchair, shouting at him to get rid of the bloody things before she tripped over them again and broke her neck. He followed Finbar into the living room and paused to stare out at the river. He whistled.

'Nice view.'

'Yeah.' Finbar pointed. 'Over here.'

The crate stood in the middle of the floor. It was bigger than Harry had anticipated, and full to the brim with sodding books. Bloody hell, he thought, grimacing. If I don't have a hernia now, I will after shifting this lot. He wasn't going to say anything though, because he didn't want to look like a

113

wimp. Or worse, have to give Finbar the twenty back. They would manage somehow. He strolled over and picked up a novel on the top layer.

'Okay if I take this for the wife?' he asked. 'Seeing as you're giving them away.'

Finbar seemed to hesitate. Then he shrugged. 'Help yourself.'

'Ta. She's mad on crime and thrillers,' Harry laughed. 'Probably looking for ideas on the perfect way to bump me off.'

'Come on, Harry, let's get going.' Finbar stepped forward and grabbed his arm as he started to rummage further. 'I haven't got all night, and you'll want to get back to your video cubbyhole, won't you?'

And you'll want to get back here and relieve your blonde bombshell of her knickers, Harry felt like saying but didn't. He knew Finbar's sense of humour wouldn't stretch that far. He put the book back, stooped and they lifted the crate. 'Jesus!' he gasped. 'I think me blood vessels are going to rupture. What you got in here, a whole bloody library of encyclopaedias?'

'No, a dead body.' Finbar's face was grim, flushed with effort. 'Can you manage?'

'Just about.' They staggered out of the living room and down the hall. The fiancée hurried out of the kitchen and thoughtfully opened the front door for them. Somehow they got the crate down the stairs. When they reached the lobby Harry was panting, sweating and groaning, and his heart felt as if it was about to burst from his chest like in some horror movie. He couldn't see his face, but was sure it must have turned blue or purple. They gave themselves a minute's rest, then dragged the crate towards the doors.

'You couldn't do me another favour and bring the van round?' Finbar straightened up, rubbing his back. 'Don't fancy dragging this thing all the way to the car park. And I've got to go back upstairs. Forgot something.'

'I deserve another twenty for this,' Harry wheezed. 'Bet my poor old blood pressure's shot off the scale.'

Finbar gave it to him. He handed him the van keys and told him the licence number. 'See you in about five minutes,' he called.

Harry staggered towards the car park, the wind from the river cooling him down. Forty quid was a nice little earner, but he was worried about the sharp pain around his midriff which stopped him taking a full breath. Had he done himself a mischief? He paused, loosened his belt and leaned against a wall. The pain eased after a few seconds and he was able to breathe properly again. He went into the car park, located the white van Finbar had hired, and drove it round to the building's front entrance. Better wipe this off the tape once I'm back in the office, he thought. Just in case the big boss man watches it and finds out I deserted my post.

Finbar was waiting. One last heave, and the crate was in the van. Finbar slammed the doors, turned and handed him the book.

'Your wife's crime novel, with my compliments. Hope she enjoys it, I did. Thanks a lot, Harry. You've been a big help.'

'Oh, good. If you don't see me again, lad, you'll know I'm in intensive care. Or that I've croaked it. No flowers, please, just donations to the charity of your choice.'

'I'll remember,' Finbar grinned. 'What'll you spend the forty on if you don't croak?'

'A truss and a bottle of brandy, mate. See ya.'

Harry strolled back down to his office and collapsed in the chair. He leaned forward and pressed the button to rewind the tape. Stopped it and rewound again.

'That's weird,' he muttered. 'What's up? Bloody machine hasn't recorded a thing!'

He remembered the two laughing girls who had hurried past earlier, just before Finbar came in, but he couldn't find any footage of them. The entire tape was wiped. Must be a dud. Or was there a problem with the video itself? Whatever the reason, there was no Harry and no Finbar. No van, no crate of books. Only blank, grey nothing.

As if it had never happened.

Finbar was driving, he wasn't sure where at first, because he was too busy checking to make sure he wasn't being followed. Past St Nick's church, along the Dock Road, past the horrible pub where he and Lenny Dowd had met one icy afternoon last December to talk about murder. He had been in a hurry to get home to Shannon, Lenny to pick up a prostitute. Now he had Lenny's dead brother Declan in the back, his body wrapped in binliners and curled beneath the books in the crate. He had searched the body for clues, but hadn't found anything except Declan's passport and wallet stuffed into the back pocket of his jeans. The cheap wallet contained a credit card, a tenner and some Euro coins. The passport looked brand new and had no immigration stamps.

Finbar could not believe he had got this far. And it wasn't over yet. He slowed, gripping the steering wheel as horror and revulsion overwhelmed him again. How could he have thought it would be easy to shake off his old life and start anew? He was worried about Shannon; how would she cope with this on top of her other problems? Would it change the way she felt about him now, wipe out the magic of last night? Finbar thought he already sensed some withdrawal in her.

He imagined Shannon back at the apartment, anxiously scrutinising the tapes with that day's date which he'd nicked from the tiny storeroom next to Harry's office. Desperate for some clue as to the identity of the anonymous letter-writing bastard. She would watch until Nick or some other friend turned up. Finbar hated to leave her, but he had to dump Declan's body quickly. Driving around Liverpool with a stiff in the back of the van was tempting fate big time. It would be just his luck to get pulled over by a couple of polizia short of something to do.

'Fuck!' he gasped, cutting speed as the idea struck. Why

hadn't he thought of it sooner? He didn't know whether to laugh or be angry. How could he have forgotten until this moment the all-time, perfect body dump? Of course he had not visited his secret hiding place in months, and had almost forgotten its existence. Being here, driving along this road, reminded him. But the keys? He thought. They were in the safe at his India Buildings office. He pulled up, did a U-turn and drove back towards the city centre. He hated to leave the van with the body in it, even for a few minutes while he fetched the keys. But he had no choice.

Twenty minutes later Finbar was bumping the van over grassy cobblestones between two big, round stone gateposts into dark, deserted Clarence Dock. He parked outside the old clock tower, took a torch from the glovebox and got out. It was pitch dark here and very quiet, the river sloshing close by. He checked the studded iron tower door; the padlock he had put there months ago was secure. Everything looked undisturbed.

He unlocked the door and went in, flashed the torch around the small space. The walls were damp and crumbling, covered with mould spores, and the cold air was musty. Finbar was surprised that this part of dockland had so far escaped renovation. He could hear the water slapping and gurgling; the dungeon beneath his feet was below the water line. The sound was creepy in the blackness.

He crouched and undid the trapdoor bolt, shoved the torch into his pocket and jumped down into the dungeon. Switched it on again and shone it over the ancient, circular, thick stone walls from which rusted chains dangled. Rumour was that French prisoners from the Napoleonic Wars had been kept here, the clock tower built in 1840 on the foundations of a previously demolished building. The torchlight picked out the white skull and ribcage of what Finbar presumed had been one of the unfortunate prisoners, chained up to die in the dark.

The rough stone floor was bare now. No more drugs, weapons or explosives. This had made the perfect hiding place, but he didn't need it any more. It could go back to being a tomb. Finbar heaved himself up again through the trapdoor and went back out to the van. He stopped and listened. Only the river, the city sounds remote.

He lifted the books out of the crate, upended it and tumbled out Declan's dead weight, revolted by the feel of the wrapped body and hating the fact that he had shot Declan. But what was he supposed to do? Let himself and Shannon be murdered on the whim of this idiot with his warped perceptions and inability to face the ugly truth about his precious big brother?

Anger flared in Finbar, giving him renewed strength and resolve. He hadn't asked for all this shit and he was damned if he was going to let any of it stick to him. He dragged the body inside the tower, heaved it towards the trapdoor and rolled it, letting it drop into the pitch black space below. He did not wince at the horrible thud as the body hit the stone floor. Declan Dowd couldn't feel anything any more.

'Gone soft, have I?' Finbar whispered, staring down into the black dungeon. 'Looks like you're the limp dick from where I'm standing.' He kicked the trapdoor shut, locked and bolted it, and padlocked the tower door. He had to lean against the wall for a minute because he was trembling and out of breath. He coughed the damp, musty air out of his lungs. Jesus Christ! he thought. There's better ways than this to spend an evening.

But he couldn't rest yet. He checked the interior of the crate to make sure it was clean, then piled the books back in and shut the van doors. He switched on the torch again and walked through a pair of old dock gates towards the end of the quay. Torchlight flashed on the murky waters of the Mersey, and on a huge, rusted iron ring set in a stone slab. Finbar switched off the torch, raised his arm and hurled the clock tower keys into the river. Heard them splash. Declan could rot until, like the French prisoner, there was nothing left of him but bones. Someday someone would build a leisure complex, shopping mall or multi-storey car park on top of him.

He got back in the van and drove off again, constantly checking to make sure he was not being tailed. It was nerve-racking. He wanted a drink, but that would have to wait. He delivered the crate of books to the Royal Liverpool Hospital, where they were received by a couple of porters and left in a small room near Accident & Emergency. The porters didn't seem surprised; maybe people often delivered donations of books or other stuff at this time of night. He had to do it, in the unlucky event that he ever had to tell a story which needed to be checked out. Then he drove to the airport and parked the hired van in one of the car parks, ready to return it early the next morning before flying to Cork. It was cold and windy, the smell of aviation fuel in the air, and the scream of jet engines. Finbar walked into the terminal and called Shannon on his mobile.

'Hi,' he said when she answered. 'It's me. How's things?'

'Okay.' She sounded subdued, as he had expected. 'Nick's here,' she said. 'We're having a glass of wine.'

'Good.' Shannon's old friend and his accountant, Nick Forth, currently caught up in marital strife. Finbar hesitated. 'How are you feeling now?' It was a stupid question, but he badly needed some reassurance from her.

'I'm okay.' Well, what else could she say at this moment? There was a pause and he heard Nick's laugh in the back-ground. 'Nick says hello.'

'Tell him hello back. Everything's fine here,' Finbar said. He didn't ask if Shannon had spotted anything on the stolen tapes; it would take a while to zap through them. And maybe Nick had turned up before she'd had much of a chance to look.

'We've decided to go out for some dinner,' she said. 'Should we wait for you?'

'No. Tell Nick I'm at the airport. Just sorting some last-minute details about a cargo. Although last minute doesn't mean it might not take a while. I'm sorry to miss him.'

'Okay,' Shannon said again. 'Did you deliver those books to the hospital?' she asked, her voice carefully neutral.

Good girl, Finbar thought, cheered. She had calmed down, she would be fine. 'Yes,' he said. 'No problem.'

'I'll see you later then.'

'Yeah. Shouldn't be too long.' Finbar gripped the phone as he looked around the busy terminal. 'You take care, okay?' he whispered. He wished he could hold her right now. 'I love you.'

She hung up without replying. He frowned, stuck the phone back in his jacket pocket and walked out. He hailed a black cab and settled down for the ride back to the city centre. The driver left him alone after guessing correctly that he wasn't in the mood to chat.

Finbar was still trembling, and he felt exhausted. He stared out of the window and thought of his club, blown to bits. Being hurled across the street, escaping death by some incredible chance. And Declan Dowd, now dead and left to rot in a secret place. He hated to have another man's blood on his hands. Even if he had killed him in self-defence. But what choice did he have?

He wished he could believe Declan Dowd really had blown up his club for a laugh, then come after him to finish the job properly. That he was alone, hadn't told anyone of his murderous intent. That there was no one else who wanted him dead. It would be so convenient to be able to think that, to believe the danger was over.

Finbar believed it was just beginning.

Chapter Fourteen

'I don't know where Demetrio is, Janie!'

Pascale Stephens glanced down the narrow hall at the locked, bolted and chained front door as she nervously gripped the phone. 'He walked out of court this morning, got bail. I know that much because some mate of his phoned. Said he'd had a pint with Demetrio at lunchtime, and assumed he'd come back here. But he hasn't. I haven't seen him all day.'

'Well, that's good, isn't it? Jesus, I can't believe they gave him bail. Those magistrates must be out of their minds. Is his stuff still outside where you left it?'

'Hang on a sec.' Pascale laid down the receiver, hurried into the sitting room and moved the curtain aside. The three bin bags full of Demetrio's clothing and papers still sat in the tiny, walled front garden. She walked back into the hall and picked up the phone. 'Yep. Still there. If he doesn't pick it up soon, the binmen will. Janie, I'm terrified!' she confessed. 'I can't believe I'm doing this.'

'You should have done it months ago, Pascale. You'll be okay. But it'd be better if you could get him locked up again, just to be on the safe side. Did you tell the police about those other guns you think he might have stashed somewhere? Or that you think he's into other bad stuff, even though you don't know what it is? I'm sure he wouldn't have got bail if the police had had more evidence against him.'

'But I can't give it to them, can I?' Pascale argued. 'I told you, I don't have a clue what he did with those guns. He'd just deny it. I only suspect he could be into other stuff – I don't know for sure.' She paused. 'Look, Janie. I've dumped his stuff outside, had the locks changed, and that's it. I don't want to try and make any more trouble for him. I just want him to go away, get out of my life.'

'And you think he'll do what you want? Just like that?'

'He won't bully me any more once he realises I mean business. You said so yourself, remember? Well, now I do.'

'Yeah. Right. Good for you.' But Janie didn't sound so sure of herself now.

Demetrio's threats and recent violence terrified Pascale, but it was his letter from the Australian woman, Charlene, more than Janie's persuasion, that had finally pushed her into taking this leap for freedom. *'Dear Demetrio, so sorry to hear about your girlfriend's tragic accident.'* What kind of moron must this Charlene be? The same kind of moron as herself, of course. Not picking up on warning signals, not hearing the alarm bells. Not wanting to hear. Well, Demetrio Montana would just have to be someone else's problem from now on.

Pascale shivered and glanced at herself in the ornate gilt mirror over the hall table. She had taken off the dressing, but her nose was still swollen and bruised. Make-up didn't help much, but it was better than nothing. She glanced at the front door again, thinking she'd heard a tiny sound. Where the hell was Demetrio, what was he doing? She had expected him to come straight back here after the police station and court. She dreaded his return but also longed for it, wanting to get the terrifying confrontation over. The endless, tension-racked hours of waiting tortured her already overstretched nerves to the limit, picking and chipping away at the courage and resolve she had tried so hard to build. Pascale was tempted to unlock the door, drag the bin bags back inside and unpack all his stuff, hoping she would have time to put everything back in place before he reappeared. Demetrio was probably in some pub getting hammered. That would make things even worse.

'And don't be soft with him.' Janie's voice was belligerent again. 'Don't take any shit. Call the police if the bastard tries anything.'

'Just give it a rest, will you?' Pascale suddenly felt filled with resentment at her friend's badgering. Sometimes she thought Janie got a kick out of her situation, a few vicarious thrills to brighten her sad, boring life. 'It's okay for you, isn't it?' she snapped. 'No one's ever raised their fist to you – you don't have a clue what it's like to be hit, or how it makes you feel.'

'Pascale, don't bite the head off me! I'm just trying to help.'

'Are you? Sometimes I think you enjoy this.'

Janie gasped. 'That's a terrible thing to say!'

'You think it's all so bloody easy, don't you?' Hot tears stung Pascale's eyes. 'Show him the door, Pascale, show him you mean business! Do this, do that. I shouldn't have listened to you,' she cried. 'I should do this my way.'

'Oh, yeah?' Hurt, Janie lashed back. 'We know what your way is, don't we, Pascale? *"Hey, I'm the doormat, walk on me!"*'

'Go to hell.' Pascale slammed the receiver down and started to sob with fear. What was she doing, was she crazy? Demetrio would give her the beating of her life for this. She had to get his stuff back inside right now. She grabbed the shiny bunch of keys from the hall table, ran to the door and fumbled with the new and unfamiliar locks, undid the chain. Flung open the door and gave a cry of terror.

Demetrio stood there. Smiling.

'Ughh. What the *fuck*. .?'

Rob Flinder was pissed, although not pissed enough to ignore the horrible stink of vomit that hit his nostrils when he dropped his keys on the hall floor and stumbled into the dining room. The lamp was still on, the fire burned low. He stared open-mouthed at the table with its depressing clutter of dirty plates, dishes and glasses, the huge wine stain on the wall, and the bits of red candlewax and chunks of broken, sparkling crystal everywhere. He stepped back just in time to avoid putting his foot into the mess on the carpet.

'Jesus *Christ*!' He wheeled round and stumbled out, put up one hand and clicked off the light. She'd gone to bed and left all the bloody lights on. Thought he was made of money though, didn't she? That she'd struck gold. Well, Katy was just about as wrong as she could get. He'd drag the bitch down here and make her clean up all this shit while he watched. Pregnant or not. Then he'd kick her out. He had told her to go, but of course she wouldn't have obeyed him. There was only one woman Rob wanted in his life, and that woman was Shannon.

He staggered into the sitting room and grabbed the bottle of Chivas Regal he had left on the floor by the sofa, took several big gulps. Then he went back into the hall and made his way upstairs, crawling on hands and knees. His head swam.

'Katy!' He raised his voice. '*Katy!* Wake up, you bitch. Get out here and–'

He kicked the bedroom door open and stood there staring, swaying slightly. The double bed was empty, the flowered pillows and quilt smooth. She wasn't there. The wardrobe door was open, the old-fashioned, three-mirrored dressing table cleared of brush, comb, make-up, Nivea cream and the perfume bottle shaped like a woman's body. So she really had gone. Amazing. Rob shivered as the oppressive silence of the big Edwardian house crowded in on him.

'Good riddance,' he muttered. Anger drained away, leaving him desolate and full of self-pity. He didn't care about Katy and the baby she said was his. He loved and missed Shannon, wanted her so much. If only they were still together, happy the way they used to be. Rob imagined his joy if he had come home to Shannon and she had told him she was going to have his baby. He would have been – *could* have been – the happiest man in the world. But that chance was gone. All gone. He'd messed up. It hurt too much.

He collapsed on to the bed, fully dressed, and stared at the white period ceiling with its meandering cracks. He had to get up in another few hours – hungover – and go to work. Push himself through another day of boredom and hassle, thinking of what he could have had, what he'd lost. There was nothing to look forward to, nothing good would ever happen again in his life. He'd have to carry on though, because he was too bloody gutless to top himself. Maybe that would change.

'Shannon,' Rob groaned, closing his eyes. He started to cry.

Chapter Fifteen

'Shut up!' Demetrio shouted. 'Or I'll really give you something to whinge about. I haven't started yet!'

Pascale was curled sobbing in an armchair, trembling hands hiding her bruised face. Her whole body was shaking like a terrified animal. He strode to the television and turned the sound up. There was some old, dyed-blonde celebrity yakking away on a chat show. She had a loud, posh, bossy voice, the voice of someone who believed in her own importance.

'Women really should think about what they're doing to men.'

'Woof!' Demetrio laughed. 'You never said a truer word, you old doggie.'

He didn't know why he was laughing when he felt bursting, boiling with rage. He was jittery too, frightened after spending last night in the nick; he didn't want any more of *that*. He knew how lucky he was to be back on the street and that his freedom might be very temporary. He'd been drinking all afternoon, but it didn't make him feel any better. Old Demon was in deep shit all round.

Keely was still alive, for a start. He'd screwed up there. He didn't know when – if – he'd get another pop at her. He couldn't go back to that hospital. Worst-case scenario was that Keely would grass him up about the guy he'd killed. Okay. Even if she could prove it, she didn't have a clue why he'd killed him. He should never have taken her out that night, never have thought he could trust her or even that she might help him. That brought Demetrio's confused thoughts back to Haytham, his contact from the organisation or group, whatever they were. He couldn't let *them* find out he was charged with illegal possession of firearms and free only because he'd got bail. He hoped they wouldn't find out. He was supposed to meet with Haytham Monday lunchtime, and he had to have something to give him by then. Demetrio still wasn't sure what kind of group Haytham belonged to, not that he really gave a fuck. He suspected they were a variety of terrorist. Nut jobs, of course, like all fanatics. But if they wanted him to stiff people for them and steal their identities they had to give him a break now and then, realise it wasn't all easy-peasy. The money was nice, but the stress he could live without.

Another nasty surprise he did not need was this snivelling bitch in the armchair. Pascale might look like a frightened, mad cow, but she'd still had the nerve to dump his stuff outside in binbags and seriously think he would turn up, grab them and just piss off out of her life. She had to be bloody joking. He couldn't handle trouble with Pascale on top of everything else. Demetrio needed her quiet, frightened of him, doing what she was told.

'I know Janie – that *kankerhoer* – put you up to this. I'll kill that interfering bitch.' He stood over her, had to raise his voice above the sound of the television. 'You shouldn't have listened to her. Why'd you try to get rid of me, eh? That's the most stupid thing you could do.' Demetrio was about to grab her again and haul her out of the armchair when he noticed his right fist was still clenched. He opened it, stretching his fingers; a handful of Pascale's dark hair floated on to the carpet. He picked it up, took out a lighter and set fire to it, let the hank of burning hair fall back on her head where it belonged.

'No! Don't!' Pascale leapt up, screaming in pain and fright, brushing frantically at the little fireball. The smell of the singed hair and black acrylic sweater she wore filled the

127

room. 'Don't hurt me any more,' she whimpered. 'Please don't.' Tears poured down her bruised, reddened face and her eyes were wide with shock.

'Not so pretty now, eh?' He laughed. 'Better keep away from the salon tomorrow, you'll frighten the clients. Why'd you try to throw me out?' he repeated.

'Because I can't take any more! We're finished. And leave Janie alone,' Pascale gasped, rubbing at her burned scalp. 'It wasn't her made me do it. It was that letter.'

'What fucking letter?' He seized her arm, dragged her towards him and knocked her to the floor, forcing her head down.

'The airmail letter,' she sobbed. 'From that Australian woman – Charlene. You told her I'd had an accident. I thought you didn't want me any more. I thought you'd want to leave.'

'You...!' Fresh outrage gripped him. 'What did you do with that?' he yelled, shaking her by the hair so that she howled in pain. 'Where is it, in one of those bags?'

'It's upstairs. I forgot to–'

'What, pack it? You bloody bitch.' He kicked her, dragged her to her feet and smashed her across the face. More tears poured from her eyes and her nose starting bleeding. He dragged her out into the hall and up the steep stairs.

'I told you never, *ever*, to touch my things,' he panted. 'Never to go in that room. Didn't I?' He shook her again. *'Didn't I?'*

'Yes. I'm sorry,' Pascale mumbled. 'I was frightened. Didn't know what to do.'

'Oh, you knew, all right. You whore.'

'I'm not a–'

'What?'

She gasped for breath. 'I'm not a whore!'

'Yes, you are,' he said, kicking her again. 'And I'll prove it to you.' They reached the top of the stairs and he pulled her across the landing into the room where he kept his computer. Pascale was crying, snivelling, trying to wipe her bloody nose on her sleeve. Demetrio shoved her against the wall and kicked her legs from under her, watched her crumple to the floor.

'What does it take to make you listen?' he shouted. He hated the sight and snivelling sound of her, felt as though he could never hurt her enough to make her understand. He banged her head against the wall with its stupid flowered paper. 'Are you listening to me now, bitch?'

'Yes,' Pascale whispered, dazed. She shut her eyes and slowly curled up her body, gasping and groaning. Demetrio turned to his desk and riffled through the drawers, in between flashing her looks of hate. She had been in here, searching. While he was locked in that stinking cell, expected to eat pigswill.

The letters were in the bottom drawer where he'd left them. They were his insurance. He had to know there was somewhere he could move on to if necessary. Now this bitch knew about the other bitches. Had she read them all?

'What were you gonna do with these?' He shook them in her face.

Pascale opened her eyes. 'Nothing. I swear.'

Demetrio looked over a few of the letters, then gathered them into a neat pile and put them back. He slammed the drawer, turned and stared in outraged disbelief. Pascale was at the door, scrambling out on all fours, her round bottom outlined by the tight blue jeans. The soles of her bare feet were black with dust. That was another thing – she never even kept this bloody dump of a house clean.

'Get back here!' By the time he reached her she was on her feet, gripping the newel post at the top of the stairs, her bruised face a mask of panic. Demetrio lunged and grabbed her. She screamed again and struggled fiercely. The neckline of her sweater ripped in his hand and unravelled. Pascale jerked away from him and teetered backwards.

For a split second she was poised, balanced like a ballet dancer on the top stair, arms flung up, her dark eyes dilated with terror. Then she wasn't graceful like a dancer any more.

She fell, arms and legs flailing, tumbled down the stairs and landed in a clumsy heap at the bottom. Lay still.

'Come on.' Demetrio's voice was harsh in the silence. He couldn't see her face. 'Get up, you stupid cow!'

She didn't move. Anger and tension drained, leaving him weak and shaky. This was all her fault. Look what she did to him, how she wound him up. It was always the same. He sat on the top stair and waited for his breathing to slow.

'Ninnie! Ninnie!' A child's voice broke the silence, followed by a giggle. *'Ninnie!'*

He gasped and jerked his head up, staring around the dimly lit landing and stairs. He was imagining it, of course. He was in shock, exhausted. But why that name, why now? Then he remembered. Pascale had once told him her great-grandmother had lived in this house. Everyone called her Ninnie. She had been killed one night during the Second World War while Luftwaffe planes overhead dropped sticks of bombs all over Liverpool. But Ninnie hadn't been blown up by any bomb. She had tripped and fallen downstairs in the blackout, on her way to fetch a drink of water for a sleepless child. Cracked her head open and died instantly. The stairs were steep and sharp-edged, uncarpeted.

Demetrio sighed and rubbed his eyes. Pascale wasn't dead, of course, just unconscious. Or pretending to be unconscious, acting more injured than she was. This was her own fault, she couldn't deny she'd asked for it ten times over! He hoped she hadn't concussed herself or broken any bones; he didn't want her going down the hospital. But she wouldn't grass him to the doctors or nurses. He'd frightened her enough for tonight. She had surely learned her lesson now.

'I *said*, get up!' he called. 'I've had enough of your carry on.' He was sweating, his heart beating uncomfortably. He wanted a mug of coffee, more Scotch, something to eat, wanted to stretch out and relax in front of the telly while she went and had one of her perfumed baths. There was a faint smell of essential oil of lavender on the landing. He got to his feet, went slowly downstairs and stood over Pascale. Crouched and shook her by the shoulder.

No response. She just lay there. Angry again, he seized her and rolled her on to her back, sweeping the long strands of dark hair off her face. He swallowed hard, gasped and broke out in an icy sweat.

'Christ!' Pascale's mouth was open, trickling blood. Blood also came out of her nose and ears. Her dark eyes stared past him. Demetrio thought he could still see the fear in them.

He pressed one hand to her chest, feeling for a heartbeat. Lifted her wrist and checked for a throb of pulse. Nothing. His lips moved as he gazed down at her. He wanted to tell her she was a stupid cow, that she'd brought this on herself, that she must know he hadn't meant to kill her. It was an accident, pure accident. But Pascale couldn't hear anything he had to say to her now. Demetrio dropped her slim wrist as freezing panic gripped him.

'Shit,' he whispered. 'Oh, bloody *shit!*'

Even a slight, slender woman like Pascale weighed a ton as a stiff. Demetrio sweated and cursed as he carried her limp corpse out into the back yard and dumped it in the boot of her blue Volvo. He had switched off all the house lights. Part of the yard was roofed over to make a car port, which meant that no gawping insomniacs could see him from their back bedroom windows. One of Pascale's suitcases was also in the boot. He went back into the house for the rest of his stuff. He had to find another place now, of course. There was no way he could stay here.

Demetrio made sure the front door was locked but not bolted or chained, and slipped the new keys in his pocket. He would get rid of them later. He crept through the downstairs rooms, looking at everything by the light of the street lamps. He had cleaned up the blood and burned hair, made sure there was no trace of a struggle. It looked as though Pascale had left in a hurry, pausing just to grab a few clothes. He straightened up and gasped with shock as the phone rang, loud in the silent house. Demetrio counted fifteen rings before it stopped. He had to get out now.

He strode through the kitchen, locked the back door behind him and reversed her car out of the yard, trying to be as quiet as possible. Closed the yard doors. He drove down the alley and out into the road, parked the car a couple of streets away and walked back. The three bin bags Pascale had stuffed his clothes in were still outside the front door. Amazing that no one had nicked them. Then again, the tiny garden was surrounded by a wall and a hedge. And it was pretty dark.

'Pascale!' he yelled, banging on the door. 'Pascale, please, love! Come out, I want to talk to you.'

Silence. Demetrio glanced up and down the street before pounding on the door again. One or two lights came on in the bedrooms of neighbouring houses. He saw the old woman from next door peer through her bedroom curtains then move hastily back when she caught him looking up at her. The old bat liked Pascale, said she was a 'lovely girl'.

'Pascale!' he yelled, banging again. 'Open the door, will you?' He went on shouting and banging, wanting to wake up the whole street if he could. A couple of minutes later a car turned the corner into the road and pulled up outside the house.

Janie got out. She left the door open and only came as far as the gate.

'What are you doing here?' he snarled. The nosey bitch next door might have phoned her, he thought, not wanting to challenge him herself. Or maybe it was Janie who'd called before. That was fine. He looked at Janie's long, limp fair hair, the steel-framed specs that he would have liked to swipe off her ugly gob and stamp on, and the black jacket that failed to make her look slimmer. He noticed she had her mobile clutched in one pale, chubby hand.

'You can't get in,' Janie called, her voice high with nerves. 'Pascale's had the locks changed. She doesn't want you back. Get lost and leave her alone, or she'll call the police. And if she doesn't, I will.'

'You mind your own business, you fat whore,' he shouted. 'Or I'll–'

'What? Land me one? Blow my face off?'

'That's not a face you've got, it's the back end of a cow.'

'You touch me, you'll end up in more trouble,' Janie shouted back. 'This is the twenty-first century, you know. You can't go round harassing and beating women and acting like they're your personal property. Not in this country, any-way.'

'Fuck off.' Demetrio picked up the bin bags and marched down the garden path. Janie retreated, jumped back in the car and locked herself in, mobile at the ready. He paused and threw her a contemptuous glare, then hitched up the bags and walked down the street. What would she do next? Probably ring the bell and shout for Pascale herself. He didn't think Janie would have the nerve to tail him in her car.

Demetrio glanced back before rounding the corner. Sure enough, Ms Four-Eyes Blobby was out of the car and open-ing the gate. She would ring the bell and get no answer. Maybe she would piss off then. Or maybe she would call the police. No worries. She had seen him outside, believed he couldn't get in. Watched him walk away. Janie didn't know it but she had fallen in with his plan, done him one great big bloody favour. He smiled as he turned the corner and quick-ened his pace, heading back to the car.

Pascale wasn't dead. She wasn't even missing.

She had gone away.

Chapter Sixteen

'I shouldn't have come here.' Shannon checked her last message and switched off her mobile. 'There's too much going on back in Liverpool.'

'Tell me about it. I know you only came with me because you were in a state of shock and didn't know what else to do.' Finbar pushed away his unfinished plate of scrambled eggs and smoked wild salmon. 'Can't you try and forget work for a while?' he asked, studying her pale, anxious face. She needed to rest.

'It's Sunday, I haven't checked my messages since yesterday morning. And I don't want to forget work,' Shannon said, her blue eyes cold. 'It helps keep my mind off ...' She glanced away. 'Other things.'

She pushed the mobile into the pocket of her hooded grey sweatshirt and rubbed at the coffee stain on her jeans. There was another message she had not mentioned to Finbar: Rob wanted her to call him, said it was urgent. He begged her not to tell Finbar. Shannon didn't feel like talking to her almost ex. What did Rob want? The divorce details were sorted. All they had to do now was wait.

Finbar got up, taking his coffee, and walked across the kitchen to the open door. He looked out over the long back lawn with the moss-covered stone balustrade that ran along the gravel walkway to the right. The sea whispered in the bay below and the spring wind smelled of earth and salt. The sun warmed his face. He loved the peace and beauty, the isolation. All of which he especially needed now. Shannon needed it too, but not surprisingly she was finding it impossible to relax after Friday's trauma. That was his fault, of course. He felt guilty and worried about her.

The big old house was warm and welcoming. He could not believe Sylvia was dead, that she was not going to hurry in any second and complain about how the gardens were running wild and what in the name of God would this summer's visitors – probably all botany experts, damn them! – think? The dog baskets were empty; Sylvia's two golden retrievers had been found a new home at a farm several kilometres up the road.

'Someone made another attempt on Keely Breeze's life,' Shannon said.

He turned. 'When?'

'Friday, of course, our favourite day of the week!' She moved restlessly. 'Turns out Keely knows the would-be murderer. He gained access to her hospital room and tried to inject the contents of a syringe into her drip. With a police officer outside!'

'Was it the same guy who attacked her outside court?' Finbar asked. 'The one you got a look at – and who got a look at you?'

'No. She didn't recognise the guy who slashed her throat. But this one she's known for some time, apparently. I don't understand,' Shannon sighed. 'But then there's a lot I don't understand! He ran off after a nurse disturbed him. Nobody knew he'd tried to murder Keely until she scribbled a note. She must be terrified.'

'This doesn't help you then, if the police are none the wiser about who attacked her outside the Mags court?' That was all Finbar cared about.

Shannon shrugged. 'It must be someone connected to the guy who got into her hospital room. I still don't know why anyone would want to murder her.'

'Look, I know it's important.' Finbar drank his coffee,

walked back and put the cup on the table. 'But just try to put it out of your head, at least until we get back. We came here to–'

'Relax?' she flashed. '*Chill*? Would you mind telling me how I'm supposed to do that when I've aided and abetted a homicide, then conspired to conceal it? You do realise what will happen to us if anyone finds out?'

'I think I could paint a picture if I wanted.' Finbar watched her hand tremble as she lifted her coffee cup and set it down again. 'I just don't see the point in freaking about something that won't happen.'

'You can't be sure it won't.'

He dragged a chair forward and sat close beside her. 'How many more times do I have to tell you?' He kept his voice calm. 'Nobody's going to find out about Declan bloody Dowd. Ever. I sorted it, we're safe.' He tried to take her hand, but she snatched it away. 'What happened was horrible. We're both in shock now. We'll feel bad for a while, but then we'll get over it.'

'What, just like that?' Shannon's voice trembled.

'Yeah.' He nodded, wishing she would let him hold her, comfort her. 'Just like that.'

'Well, I suppose I should trust to your greater experience in these matters!'

'Have a go at me, Shannon, if that makes you feel better.' Finbar felt hurt nonetheless. 'But is any of this my fault?'

'Not directly,' she admitted. 'But it's your past, isn't it? The drugs and arms deals, your involvement with para-militaries, however unwilling. You can't get tied up with all that and expect to break free when it suits you. The past keeps catching up with you – with *us*.' She brushed away a tear. 'I don't think I can take much more.'

'You won't have to. Declan Dowd's dead. He's no longer a threat.' But who else is? Finbar wondered yet again. 'In the meantime, we've got other stuff to worry about.'

'You mean the anonymous letter writer? I'm not worried about *that*.' But Shannon's eyes were frightened. 'Okay, I'm disappointed that the tape didn't show up anything. But people who do that sort of thing – well, they're not dangerous,' she argued. 'If someone wanted to hurt me they'd go ahead and do it, not make things difficult for themselves by advertising their intentions. Anyway, what intentions? The threats aren't exactly clear and concrete. And that moron can't seriously believe I'm going to go to the police tomorrow morning and confess to–' She broke off, twisting her hands, afraid to speak the words: *'I hired a hit man who killed the headmaster.'*

'You don't still feel bad about *him*?' Finbar asked, knowing she did. 'Jesus, Shannon, you had no choice! The fucking pervert would have murdered you.'

'I know. I know all that. But it still feels horrible. It's like a stain on my soul. And now look what's happened!' She sniffed, sat up straight. 'There won't be any more letters,' she said, trying to steady her voice. 'Once this person realises I won't do what they want. They'll get bored, give up. No fun picking on someone you can't bully, is it?'

Finbar looked grim. 'Well, let's hope you're right.' If the anonymous author was Rob the letters would stop now, after their little chat. But if it wasn't Rob...?

'I still can't believe Friday happened!' Shannon blinked back more tears. 'That he's dead. You never told me,' she said. 'What did you do with his ... ?' She gasped, jumped up and ran out of the kitchen, along the corridor to the hall. Finbar followed her into the drawing room.

'D'you really want me to tell you what I did with his body?'

'No.' Shannon walked to the windows and stood gazing out over the gardens and the sea, her arms tightly folded. Her body was rigid with tension. 'What I don't know they can't torture out of me!'

'For Christ's sake!' He crossed to her and tried to take her in his arms, but she pushed him away. 'Shannon, please try to calm down and relax a bit. It's over now.'

'It's not over.' She turned to him, the tears flooding her eyes. 'It never will be.'

'What the hell d'you mean?' he asked, stung.

'There's always going to be something with you,' she cried. 'I can't take any more. Coming home to find you held at gunpoint. Seeing you shoot a man, even though it was self-defence. Having to chat to Nick over a glass of wine then talk to you on the phone about whether or not you'll join us for dinner, act like we're a normal couple when all the time I know you're out disposing of a corpse! I can't live like that, I can't function. I'll end up crazy – if I'm not already!'

Finbar turned pale. 'I thought I was getting you back at last – after the other night. That you were starting to get over everything.'

'I was.' Shannon wiped her eyes on her sleeve. 'But Friday's events have caused something of a setback. Made me realise it's impossible with you.'

'No!' he said, panicked. 'Shannon, I don't want to lose you again. Certainly not because of some stupid little bastard with an imaginary blood feud! Come *on*. We were starting to get back on track before this happened, it was like it used to be. I love you, you love me. Don't let that go, Shannon, please! Just give yourself time. You'll feel better.'

'You mean until next time?'

He gripped her shoulders. 'There won't be a next time!'

'There will, Finbar. It's not a question of giving myself time to feel better. I wish it was that simple.' She tried to free herself from his grasp. 'I want to go for a walk now,' she said. 'Alone.'

He let go of her and stood back, his green eyes filled with anxiety. Shannon went into the hall, took her jacket and walked out. She was conscious of Finbar's gaze on her, watching from the drawing-room windows as she passed along the gravel walkway. She felt consumed with sadness. She longed to get back to Liverpool and busy herself with work, even the traumatic case of Keely Breeze. Being here in this beautiful place with nothing to do but think only tortured her more. Finbar was still entwined in the threads and strands of his past life. And she did not want to be trapped with him.

Shannon walked down a narrow path with huge ferns on either side and came to a white-painted gate and stile. On the gate was a notice: *Private Property. Fierce Dogs.* She had to smile at that, despite her mood, thinking of the two gentle, lazy golden retrievers Finbar had mentioned. She climbed over the stile and carried on down a grassy slope, trying to avoid sheep droppings, until she came to the rough stone steps which led down to the beach.

The sand was smooth and golden, engraved with wave patterns from the last tide. Breakers crashed further out. The cold, salt wind whipped her hair, and she could taste salt on her lips. Seagulls swooped and cried overhead. The sky was blue, fluffy white clouds massing on the horizon. There was nobody about. Shannon paused to gaze out at the ocean. Next stop, America.

Wasn't she being an idiot? Overreacting to all this? Finbar was doing his best, trying to put the past behind him and move on. What had happened on Friday wasn't his fault. She loved him and he loved her. Why couldn't she just run to him now, fling her arms around him, make love where they fell? Put this latest nightmare behind her? Because too many nightmares had happened. Shannon had given up thinking she and Finbar could ever lead a normal life – whatever *that* was. Friday's horror was the last straw. Living with Finbar was like being with someone who had a high-risk occupation. Every time he walked out the door Shannon wondered if she would see him alive again. And she couldn't stand it any longer. Love was not enough.

She walked along the beach, found a sun trap amongst some rock pools and sat down. Pulled out her mobile and dialled Rob's number. He answered after a couple of rings, sounding breathless and eager.

'It's Shannon.' She raised her voice above the wind and the crash of breakers. 'What did you want to talk to me about?'

'Shannon! Where are you now?'

'What does that matter?' she asked, irritated. She realised she had had some vague hope that Rob might have something useful to tell her, some information he had come across during the course of his CID work. That even though he wasn't working on the Keely Breeze case, he might have picked up some gossip.

'I think it's better if we talk face to face.' Rob paused. 'Is *he* around?'

'If you mean Finbar, no. And we can't talk face to face, at least not today. Rob, what's this about?'

'Shannon, you've got to promise me you won't tell him we've talked. He'll kill me!'

'Don't be ridiculous.' The wind suddenly felt colder, sharper. She shivered and closed her eyes for a second. 'For God's sake, just get on with it.'

'He – your boyfriend – cornered me outside the pub Friday lunchtime. Threatened to kill me if I didn't leave you alone.'

'What?' she gasped.

'He accused me of making your life hell, said you didn't need anything else freaking you. I told him I didn't know what he was on about, but he wouldn't listen. He was ballistic, Shannon. I thought he was going to kill me there and then.'

She stared at the blue ocean with its white-crested waves. 'You're telling me Finbar just waylaid you outside a pub and threatened to kill you? Without anyone else noticing? Where were your mates, back at the custody suite kicking the crap out of some mobile phone thief?'

'You don't believe me? Jesus Christ! Look, I was alone. It happened in the car park. There was no one else around, or not near enough to notice us and realise what was going on. Shannon, please listen,' Rob begged, distraught. 'I know I can't change the past, how I put you through hell and let you down and everything. I can never make up for what I did – or what my father did. But I want to help you now. That's

140

why I called, despite what that ... what *he* said. You're in some kind of trouble, aren't you?'

Shannon was silent, listening to the crash of the waves and the cry of a curlew overhead. She believed Rob suspected her of having had his father killed, although he had never asked and she would never confess. He had refused to cooperate with the detectives who accused her of her father-in-law's murder and tried to get him on their side, telling them they were crazy and that his wife wasn't capable of murder. When they persisted he had warned them to leave him – and her – alone. Rob could have made big trouble for her then, but he hadn't. He had stopped pestering her to go back to him as well, kept his promise not to bother her. He was behaving impeccably. Too impeccably?

'Are you still there?' he shouted. 'This is a crap line. Shannon?'

'I'm here. I've had a couple of anonymous letters,' she admitted, wishing she could read his mind. She wanted to say they're not serious, the saddo who wrote them will give up and go away, but she restrained herself. If Rob was the author she didn't want to make him more angry by pretending she did not take them seriously.

'Anonymous letters?' He paused. 'So that was the reason for your boyfriend's visit.' He sounded hurt, bewildered. Not angry. 'You think it's me, don't you?'

'Rob, I was trying – *am* trying – to think who could be responsible. I won't deny that you crossed my mind.'

'I didn't write them, no way! Shannon, please. You've got to believe me.'

'Finbar's visit wasn't my idea. It was his private initiative.' Which he had neglected to inform her about! 'He shouldn't have threatened you,' she said. 'That was wrong.' What else had Finbar done that she didn't know about?

'Got any other suspects lined up?' Rob asked.

'Not really. I went through the list of clients I'm acting for, plus people I've acted for in the past. Couldn't come up with anything there. Or nothing obvious. Friends,

141

acquaintances, ditto. I'm also checking out closed cases that I prosecuted, where people did time. All that will take a while, of course. I thought it might be some crank who'd read about the Bernard Flinder case in the papers and seen stuff on tv. But now I'm not sure.'

'It could be a crank,' Rob said. 'It probably is. And you know those morons set out to cause fear and distress. That's not nothing, of course. It can freak you big time. But you know what I mean. They're highly unlikely to turn up on your doorstep wielding a–'

'Chinese cook's knife. Machete, meat cleaver, mezza-luna.'

'I can see it's got to you. What do the letters say?' Rob asked. 'What does this bastard want?'

'He – or she – would very much like me to go down my nearest nick first thing tomorrow morning and confess that I had your father murdered.'

Another silence. 'What exactly is your doing that supposed to achieve?'

'Well, nothing, seeing as I'm innocent!' Shannon gave a short laugh. Never, ever would she confess to Rob, no matter how friendly and supportive he might seem. 'But I presume the author has fantasies of me being arrested, charged, struck off the Roll of Solicitors and getting lots of nightmare publicity before I'm dragged away to spend the next God knows how many years inside. Basically, they want to destroy my life.'

'Nothing else?'

She felt a jolt of anger. 'Isn't that enough?'

'I mean – don't they want money?'

'No,' she sighed. 'Just blood.'

'Do they say what'll happen if you don't comply with their crazy demand?'

'Only *"or else"*. And they call me a hot bitch criminal lawyer, so they obviously think I need kicking down several steps.'

'Shannon – I promise you, I *swear*, I'm not behind this!'

Rob's voice was high, desperate. 'I'd never even think of trying to freak you like that, especially not after all you've been through. I really care about you. I still. . .' He stopped. 'Oh, Christ. Sorry. Listen. Do you believe me?'

She hesitated. Hard to imagine that this was the man who had fallen apart when he'd found out his father was a murdering paedophile. Who had rejected her, raped her in a fit of drunken rage. Now it seemed Rob was piecing himself back together, becoming more like the man she had married. Shame it was just too bloody late. Shannon felt a pang of sadness and regret. It could have all been so different.

'If this nut job has read the papers and watched tv, they'll know the police dropped the investigation against you for lack of evidence,' Rob said. 'It's finished, it won't be resurrected. You're not going to confess to a murder you didn't commit.'

Nice one, Shannon thought. 'I don't suppose reason and logic dominates their thought processes.' She turned her head and looked along the golden expanse of beach to her right. A tall, broad-shouldered man in jeans and a dark-blue sweater was coming down the steps: Finbar, the man for whom she had abandoned reason and logic!

'Can we meet sometime this week?' Rob asked. 'Talk further about this and see what I can do to help? Bring the letters, let me take a look.'

'I can't. I burned them,' Shannon confessed. 'Well, tore up the first.'

'You *what*?'

'I know, it was stupid. I just hoped there wouldn't be any more. Couldn't face it.'

'I suppose I can understand that. And let's hope there aren't any more. But if you do receive another, don't burn it.' Rob's tone was brisk now, the CID detective talking. 'Have you got time? We could have lunch, or a drink after work.'

'I'll call you,' she promised, her eyes on Finbar's approaching figure.

'Right. See you soon, Shannon. Take care of yourself.'

'Yeah. 'Bye, Rob.' Shannon stuck the mobile in her jacket pocket. She picked up a pretty pink shell nestling at her feet. She was dabbling it in a rock pool to rinse the sand off when Finbar reached her.

'You threatened Rob,' she said, not looking up as his shadow fell across her. 'You had no right to do that. Or lie to me.'

'What's this? I didn't lie to you, darling.'

'You went behind my back.'

'Oh, a lie of omission. Sorry. For a minute there, I forgot my Holy Roman indoctrination. So it was Mr Ex you were talking to just now. Been whingeing, has he? There's a lot of things *he* had no right to do, if you remember. Fucking sad act.'

'He asked me if I was in trouble. Said he wants to help.'

'Yeah, I'll bet!' Finbar laughed angrily and stuck his hands in his pockets. 'Get you wound up and terrified–'

'You haven't done a bad job of that yourself!'

'So that he can step in and be Sir Knight. Rescue poor Shannon from the big, bad, ravening wolf she's gone and got her fluffy little self entangled with.' Finbar sat beside her on the rock. 'Trouble is,' he said, smoothing back her wind-blown curls and kissing a cold earlobe, 'Rob's not the type to wear the old shining armour, is he? Finds it a bit too bloody heavy. I thought you'd have got your head around that by now.'

'Don't patronise me!' Shannon jerked away. His handsome, angry face was reflected in the clear water of the rock pool. She stood up and glared at him, clutching the wet pink shell. 'The point is, I am not some cliché, frightened, passive female who needs the pop-up macho hero to run her powerless little life for her!'

'So I'm a macho hero? Well, thanks for that. I'm not trying to run your life,' Finbar said quietly. 'I just want to help. Protect you.'

'I've had enough of your so-called help,' she cried. 'I've had enough of everything!'

'Yeah.' He stood up. 'I know you have. Look, I'm sorry, okay?' His brilliant green eyes were anxious, pleading. 'I shouldn't have done it. I just wanted to protect you. I love you, I've got your interests at heart, remember?'

'Have you really?'

'You're shivering,' he said, taking a step towards her. 'It's cold out here. Let's go back to the house. Have more coffee or a drink. Sit down and talk about everything.'

'You mean like why I get the raving hump whenever you have to dispose of a stiff?' Shannon started to cry. 'I can't live with you any more, I just can't! We're finished.'

'No! Shannon, please!' Finbar grabbed her arm, the wind ruffling his black hair. 'You left me once before, remember? I told you I'd be a dead man if you did it again. I wasn't joking.'

'You won't be a dead man.' Choked and half-blinded by hot, stinging tears, Shannon wrenched her arm away, stumbled back and flung the shell at him. It hit him on the cheek, and he flinched. 'It's the people around you who end up dead!'

She saw the shock in his eyes, the hurt. She instantly and bitterly regretted her words. Too late. They could not be taken back. The barb had found its mark and inflicted the wound.

She turned and ran away from him down the beach.

Chapter Seventeen

'Don't cry, Mum.' Nine-year-old Craig, Keely Breeze's eldest son, stroked his mother's hand and smoothed her rough auburn hair. 'I know it's horrible to have an operation, but you'll be all right afterwards. Your voice'll get better. I'll look after them two,' he said, meaning Paul and Robbie, his brothers who were waiting outside. 'I'll look after you an' all. Gran says we can have a party when you come home.'

There won't be any more parties for me, Keely thought, as the tears slid over her cheekbones and dripped on to the white pillow. She stared at Craig's earnest, freckled little face, felt the pressure of his hand on hers. There was an anxious look in his grey-green eyes. He hated to see her upset, always had done, but this time Keely couldn't control herself. She wanted to sit up and fling off all this paraphernalia attached to her, pull Craig into her arms and tell him how much she loved him and her other two sons.

That was impossible, of course. She couldn't speak or feed herself, couldn't do bloody anything except lie here helpless, terrified and in constant pain. Her life had become a nightmare that she wasn't going to wake up from. Keely looked past Craig to the young, dark-haired policewoman standing by the window, her arms folded as she gazed out at the hospital buildings and car park. The officer had told her – great timing, just before she was due to be wheeled to theatre! – that there was still no sign of Kev Hoyle, the man who had tried to murder her.

Keely was terrified of having another anaesthetic – the last time she'd got a horrible choking, burning sensation in her throat just before she went under. Even if she woke up from this one, she might not survive much longer. Kev would be back. Or he would send someone else, like he'd done the first time. The police had to find him before he got to her again.

She had to stop thinking of him as Kev. That wasn't his real name. He didn't live in Christmas Street, Kirkdale, either; an old couple lived there, had done for donkey's years, and they had never heard of him. Keely had scribbled answers to the police questions, and written a statement. Post-it notes weren't enough, of course, she'd had to have a writing pad. Getting it all down on paper had exhausted her nearly as much as trying to remember everything. She had scribbled about his weapons and the drug deals he had boasted of, but which she'd never actually witnessed. How Kev had spent time in America, talked about how he loved going to city dumps to practice marksmanship by shooting *rattus rattus*. Worst of all, that night she had been drunk in the car with him when he had stalked and shot that guy walking from a bar near Slater Street. She had been terrified, dumb – oh, God! – with shock and sat frozen while he heaved the body into the boot, drove miles out to Otterspool Prom and dumped it, then returned to town to break into the poor guy's flat. Keely remembered his cruel eyes gleaming, the street light shining on his bald head.

'This is what I'm after,' he'd said, shaking a passport and bunch of papers at her. 'I want his identity – his *life*.'

She hadn't understood, but maybe it would make sense to the police. Did Shannon Flinder know about the murder attempt on her yet, Keely wondered? Shannon would be in court now, or have gone back to her office and grabbed some lunch on the way. Lunch. Keely imagined eating a sandwich, a good sandwich made with ham cut from the bone. Butter,

147

soft brown bread. Tasting, chewing, swallowing. Smoking a ciggie afterwards. So many things she had taken for granted. All she had now was this filthy stuff that flowed through the feeding tube. Greyish muck that looked as though someone had already eaten it and chucked it back up.

Keely didn't worry that one day she might have to give evidence against 'Kev' and bring more danger on herself. How could she be in any more danger than she was now? Anyway, she couldn't think that far ahead. Why the hell didn't you grass him sooner, you stupid cow? she fretted again. You should have gone to the cops after he shot that poor guy.

She had been too frightened, of course. And she had never dreamed he would try to murder her. 'Kev' seemed to accept it when she told him their friendship was over, that she didn't like the kind of stuff he was into and wanted nothing to do with murder. She would keep her mouth shut, and no hard feelings. Thanks for the prezzies, especially the gorgeous coat. He had nodded, smiled, got up and walked out of the pub. Keely had thought that was the end of it. She was surprised, if relieved, because she hadn't expected this big, arrogant bastard to let her go without a fight. Of course he hadn't been letting her go, only pretending to. He had planned to kill her the minute she finished with him. Keely had felt depressed at having got herself mixed up with another bloke who turned out to be rubbish, and gone on a spending spree with a few nicked credit cards to cheer herself up. 'Kev' or someone else must have been tailing her, must have freaked when she got arrested. If she hadn't been locked in the Bridewell all weekend he would have done her sooner. The second she'd seen that guy running towards her everything had become terrifyingly clear.

Keely's mind was all over the place. She was going mental lying on this bloody awful bed in this hideous room. Craig was talking again, but she didn't hear. She flinched as the door swung open and a nurse and that doctor they called the houseman came in. She hated the houseman, who was a bloody idiot. He had tried to find a new vein for her drip that

148

morning and had a hell of a job doing it, impatiently order-
ing her to relax – relax! – while he squeezed the green cord
around her arm so tight she thought he'd cut off her circu-
lation as well as bruise her yellow and ink-blue. All the while
stabbing her with the needle. She would have screamed if
she'd had her precious voice, told him where he could stick
his fucking needle. Keely had the terrifying feeling that
because she couldn't talk any more some people thought she
was retarded. And she was unable to put them right on that,
because the only voice she had now was the one inside her
head.

'Going to pop you down to theatre in a minute, love,' the
nurse said, smiling as if that was great news. Her mother
came in and smiled too, her lips trembling. Keely didn't
wonder how Ursula could manage to look after the lads by
herself, especially with the angina bothering her, because
she couldn't think about things like that now. Or what use
she herself would ever be to her family again. She wondered
if the attack on her had made the telly. She knew a reporter
had tried to get in to see her, because she'd heard the nurses
talking about it. The thought of that would have made Keely
laugh, if she'd been capable of laughter. What did they
expect her to do? Sit up in bed and tell them how she felt,
what her reactions were? Maybe they would like a gruesome, full-colour photo to thrill the readers.

'Come on, Craig, love.' Ursula leaned over the bed and
kissed her daughter's wet cheek, gently wiped away the
tears. 'Don't be scared, darlin',' she whispered, trying
desperately to smile. 'Everything's going to be all right. I'll
see you later when you get back here, okay?' She patted her
hand.

If I get back here, Keely thought. The houseman wrapped
a blood pressure cuff around her arm, then hurried out when
someone called him. Two porters came in and wheeled her
bed and all the attached paraphernalia down the corridor to
the lift. They looked scruffy, bored, couldn't be bothered to
give her a smile or a comforting word. There was a smell of

food; the nurses were serving lunch to the people who could eat. Down in the lift then along another corridor, this one cold and silent, into a room with four empty, unmade beds. The porters left and the Theatre Sister came in, wearing green overalls and a shower cap.

'Won't keep you long, love,' she promised. 'You know what they're going to do, don't you?'

Something to her silent, slashed voice box. Keely lay shivering with cold and fear, trying not to think about what they would do with their scalpels, needles and God knew what else. She felt cramps in her lower belly; her period was starting, but she couldn't ask for a tampon. By the time she was in the little room next to the operating theatre she was crying again with sheer panic. The anaesthetist was there, a different one from last time.

'Don't be scared.' He smiled and patted her shoulder, looked into her eyes. 'We'll take good care of you, Keely. I'm just going to give you something to relax you.'

It really did relax her. And there was no horrible, choking sensation. This guy knew what he was doing. Keely closed her eyes, opened them, closed them again. She felt her mind and body melt. Suddenly she was flying. Christ, she thought drowsily. This is bloody fantastic. I could get used to this stuff, whatever it is.

'That's better, isn't it, darling?' The Theatre Sister stroked her hand. 'Now think of something nice. Something you really like.'

Mine's a double vodka-and-tonic! the voice in Keely's head shouted as she went under. And I could murder a ciggie.

Chapter Eighteen

'My dear Shannon, why on earth are you staring at me in terror?' boomed Roy Gardner, friend and cliché, larger than life, claret-swigging barrister, an image which most barristers were desperate to dispel. 'You look like you've seen the Grey Lady of the Bridewell. I'm just guessing,' he said. 'There's usually a grey lady, isn't there?'

Her startled eyes dropped to the pink-beribboned letter he held, and she took a step back. Shannon herself looked somewhat grey-faced, Roy thought worriedly. Although polished and beautiful as always, that mass of soft blonde hair curling over her shoulders. Roy envied the Irishman, Finbar Linnell, who he had met a couple of times and liked, although initially he had been horrified when Shannon took up with him.

'Is it from one of your lovers?' he joked, holding out the letter. 'Or some disturbed client?' Shannon had been through the mill these past few months, of course.

'You make my life sound much more exciting than it is, Roy.' Shannon forced herself to take the letter. 'This isn't from you, by any chance?' Surely not, she thought, barely able to conceal her shock and dismay. She would never have dreamed that dear old Roy Gardner who she had known and loved for years might write her threatening letters.

'Good God, of course it isn't from me!' Roy looked indignant. 'Pink ribbon's hardly my style, is it? Why would I be writing you letters anyway? It was in the Lawyers' Room,' he said. 'On the desk. I was in there earlier, hanging up my old Burberry and trying to dry off. Thought I'd deliver your missive, because I knew we'd meet up at some point.' He rubbed his balding head. 'Rotten bloody weather this morning, isn't it?' he grumbled. 'I got soaked just walking from my car into the building.'

Shannon breathed again, let go of some tension. She had just dealt with another drunk driver who had hit and seriously injured an old man crossing the road, a GBH and two assaults, plus a mobile phone thief. Somewhere, in the midst of today's chaos, she had to try and find time to start looking for another place to live. And now, already, another anonymous letter. She didn't want to read it, hated to touch it. Of course she hadn't complied with the demand of the last letter, that she go to the police and confess to having had Bernard Flinder killed. So now it was *'Or else'* time. She just had to hope that was an empty threat.

Shannon felt as if her heart was breaking. She wanted to go home, lock herself in and crawl back into bed. But where was home? She swallowed as a choking feeling rose in her throat. Blinked hard and straightened her shoulders. Don't lose it, she warned herself, and certainly not here in the Mags Court. All this crap has happened and you've just got to deal with it.

'Was anyone else in the room?' She slipped the letter into her briefcase. No time to open it now, even if she wanted to. Besides, she had to be alone when she read it.

Roy shook his head. 'Just me, an old desk and some wire coathangers.' He took her arm and guided her into a quiet corridor away from the throng of solicitors, their clients, policemen and court officials. 'Look, what on earth's the matter?' he asked, lowering his voice. 'Do you know who that thing's from? I thought you were going to faint when you saw it. My God!' he exclaimed as an alarming thought occurred. 'Have you got a stalker?'

'Hasn't every self-respecting criminal lawyer?' Shannon

152

smiled. 'No, seriously, Roy, it's nothing like that. Just some idiot propositioning me,' she lied. 'I suppose he thinks a fluffy female should be bowled over by the romance of pink ribbon and posh writing paper. When all it does is make me sick.' That wasn't a lie. 'Minor hassle,' she shrugged. 'Doesn't bother me.'

'Are you certain about that?' Roy frowned. 'Where is the tosser? I'll kill him for you.'

'Not necessary,' she laughed.

'Have you told the Irishman?'

'No. Look, forget it. Really, it's not a problem.'

'But you looked so shocked, so on edge. Still . . .' Roy was silent for a few seconds. He laid one hand on her shoulder. 'It's an understatement to say life hasn't been kind to you these past months. And it's not long since you came back to work. Things must be tough. Minor hassles get to you more than they normally would.'

Shannon nodded. 'That's it, exactly.'

She tried to suppress another rush of longing for Finbar. He had been up before her this morning, out of the warm, silent apartment by the time she left her bedroom and trailed into the kitchen to get herself a cup of coffee. He was giving her space, of course. Shannon felt sorry for the things she had said to him the other day on the beach in Ireland, knew how much she had hurt him. But it was all too late. The best thing now was damage limitation; move out as soon as possible and try to pick up her life again. She would miss Finbar terribly. But when were things ever easy?

Her existence seemed pointless, just one great stretch of endless punishment. And she was tired. Incredibly tired. Sometimes Shannon could not believe that her evil, murdering father-in-law really was dead. It felt as if Bernard Flinder still threatened her, that he could still leap out from some dark corner and destroy her. And now she had aided and abetted in another killing. She went cold again as she thought of Declan Dowd's body sprawled on the living-room floor.

Roy straightened up. 'I'm going to take you in hand, young lady,' he said, concerned at how frightened and desolate she looked. 'We'll have dinner one evening this week or next – you, me and Rosemary. She was only complaining the other day how it's ages since she's seen you. You can tell us all your worries. And a couple of glasses of Chateau Pétrus will soon put the roses back in those wan cheeks.'

'I'll look forward to it.' Shannon turned and they began to walk back along the corridor. 'So, Roy. What are you doing slumming it in the Mags Court?'

'A despicable tosser wanted to bring in a big gun for the opening round. GP accused of professional misconduct.'

'God. Another one?'

'Fraid so. Still, at least he hasn't murdered any of his patients – as far as we know. I suppose we should be grateful for that. You got anything else this morning?'

'No. I'm finished here.'

Shannon said goodbye to Roy and watched him disappear into Court Seven. Then she sat down on a metal bench and checked her mobile for messages. There was one from Nick Forth asking her out for dinner, another from Rob to say that Wednesday or Thursday would be good days to meet, either at lunchtime or in the evening. A couple of other friends wanted her to call them. God, she thought, grimacing. A lot of social attention for a soon-to-be-divorced female. Maybe I won't be the spectre at anyone's dinner party after all. Silence from Finbar. Would he try to talk to her again when she got back to the apartment this evening? Shannon stood up, left the lobby and hurried along the corridor to collect her coat from the Lawyers' room.

She hesitated outside the closed door, suddenly afraid. Don't be thick, she told herself. Okay, somebody went in and left that letter. But they won't do anything, they won't attack you! She wasn't sure though. If they knew about the Lawyers' Room, this person must be familiar with the layout of the building. They could watch her, follow her, and how would she know? It was almost lunchtime and the long,

154

narrow corridor was deserted. It didn't sound as if anyone was inside the room. This was the perfect time and place for someone with evil intent to do ... what?

'Behave,' Shannon whispered, biting her lip. She took a breath, opened the door and pushed it wide before walking into the room. The cold draught made the wire coathangers jangle. Her coat, Roy's Burberry and a couple of damp jackets hung on the rail. Shannon grabbed the coat and thrust her arms into the sleeves. Or tried to. The garment slithered off her arms and shoulders, the black virgin wool folds and silk lining falling in a soft heap around her ankles.

'What...!' She stooped. 'Oh, my God!' The coat's back, shoulders and sleeves had been cut from top to bottom, sliced with sharp scissors. It was ruined. Finbar had bought it for her one Saturday afternoon last December when they were shopping in town. They had gone home, dropped the bags and collapsed on a sofa, kissing and laughing as they pulled each other's clothes off. Shannon had tried the coat on again after they had made love, enjoying the feel of its soft, light, warmth around her naked body.

She reached for her briefcase, took out the letter and tore at the stupid pink ribbon, wishing she were tearing off this bastard's head. She unfolded the single sheet of thick, ivory paper and saw the familiar handwriting in royal blue ink. Gasped in fear as she read the words:

You won't do what I said, will you, bitch lawyer?
Why doesn't that surprise me!
You've just signed someone's death warrant.
But you're used to playing God.
Isn't it a shame how it's always the innocent who
suffer in this lowest of all worlds?

'I'm sorry, Mr Linnell, but we can't pay any money on the policy until the police have ruled out foul play.' The insurance man snapped his briefcase shut and got to his feet. 'And as yet they haven't been able to do that.'

155

They wouldn't either, Finbar thought, because they didn't seem to give a fuck. He stood up, waited as the man struggled into his expensive camel coat, then held out his hand.

'I'll be in touch, Mr Linnell.'

'Yeah.' Finbar shook his hand. 'Thanks for your time.'

The man left, and he heard the outer door slam. Paula his office manager came in.

'Did he hand over a nice, big, fat cheque then?'

'No. That's going to be a long time coming, I'm afraid.'

'I didn't like him.' Paula scowled. 'He reminded me of my last boyfriend.'

'Really? You surprise me. Didn't think you'd go for the young fogey type.'

'I don't,' she said darkly. 'Not any more. I'm shagging an unemployed poet now.'

'Good for you. Any phone calls while the nice gentleman was in here telling me exactly how he couldn't help?' Finbar strolled back to his desk and sat down.

'The warehouseman at Speke – I mean, John Lennon airport – wants to know if you're going out there later this afternoon.' Paula shook back her long, dark hair and examined her French-polished nails. Finbar knew her outfit was Prada because of the little red leather or plastic logo near the skirt hem. Sometimes he wondered if he was paying her too much.

'What's wrong with that guy?' he asked, irritated. 'I already told him I'd see him this afternoon. Anyone else call?'

'No. That was it.' Paula saw the hope in his gorgeous green eyes and felt sorry to disappoint him because she guessed he wanted Shannon to phone. 'Okay if I take my lunch break now?' She flashed him a bright smile.

'Sure. Go ahead.' Finbar hadn't expected Shannon to phone. Not really. Misery and apprehension welled up in him. Was she serious about leaving him? Restless, he got up again and stared out of the windows at the office block opposite India Buildings. The narrow, wet street several floors below was choked with cars as usual. Dark grey clouds over the river threatened more heavy rain. 'Hope you brought an umbrella,' he said.

'My boyfriend's meeting me downstairs in the arcade. He's taking me to lunch.'

'Sounds like fun.' Finbar turned. 'But how's an un-employed poet going to take you to lunch? Treat you to a piece of mouldy bread in his freezing garret?'

'Well,' Paula said, 'I guess I'll take him to lunch.'

'Have a good time. You can be late back, if you like.'

'Oh, thanks, Finbar!' Paula flashed the smile again. 'You're great, you are. I'll see you later.' She walked out gracefully and closed the door behind her.

Paula had only been working for him for a couple of months, but she could run the place practically single-handed. Plus the friendly Scouse girl was as legit as his import-export and air cargo businesses now were. Paula did not wear fur coats or carry combat knives, like his ex-secretary and courier, the Dutch girl Mariska. She didn't try to flirt with him either; at just twenty-two she looked on a man in his mid-thirties as already having one foot stuck in the grave. Maybe he wasn't paying her too much after all, Finbar thought.

He was thousands of pounds out of pocket because of his bombed club, and losing more now that he could no longer make money out of it every night. Luckily money wasn't a problem; he had plenty stashed away in offshore accounts, and did not need to join in battle with insurance companies. Nick Forth looked after his finances very diligently. He had met Shannon through Nick.

Finbar leaned on the stone windowsill, reliving the sunny September day when his life had changed for ever. Standing outside the Crown Court gazing into Shannon's blue eyes, not wanting to let go of her hand, sledgehammered by the instant knowledge that this was a once in a lifetime thing. Several lifetimes! Shannon had blushed, pulled away, looked annoyed. He thought she didn't like him. So much

157

had happened since that day. He loved her even more now, if that was possible. And Finbar could not bear the thought of losing her.

He sat down again and drummed his fingers on the desk, glanced at his watch. It was hard not to phone Shannon, even go round to her office and try to talk to her, but that would only piss her off. He had wanted to go into her bedroom this morning, take her in his arms and start pleading with her, but he hadn't done that either. He felt terrible, had a headache and stomach pain. A feeling of hollowness, a hunger that only Shannon could satisfy. He cursed Declan Dowd. Just when he thought he'd got Shannon back, that little bastard had to come along and ruin everything! The sky darkened further and he clicked on the desk lamp. The phone started ringing.

'Fuck!' He didn't feel like answering. It could be the dimwitted warehouseman at the airport, one of Paula's mates, or a client. It wouldn't be Shannon. Finbar could not resist picking it up though, just in case it was her.

'Mr Linnell himself, how nice. Aren't you going to thank me for saving your life?'

Finbar froze, silent with shock at the sound of the upper-class git male voice, the Brit who had phoned him minutes before the club blast. He gripped the receiver, started as a shower of rain hit the windows. His heart raced.

'Obviously you're not going to thank me,' the man went on, calm and friendly. 'Well, that's all right. I'm used to base ingratitude. Never mind. I just want you to agree to meet me so that we can talk.'

Finbar got his voice back. 'You must be bloody joking!' His head throbbed and he felt sick with dismay. He heard Shannon's voice again, saw her beautiful face, her eyes full of tears. *'It's not over! It never will be.'* 'Forget about it,' he snapped.

The Brit sounded amused. 'You don't even know what I want to talk about.'

'Tell you what – I don't *even* care.'

158

'You don't care about your life?'

'What bloody life?'

'Oh dear. Like that, is it?'

Finbar's anger increased. 'Just fuck off.'

'Not possible, I'm afraid.' The voice was sharp now. 'If you don't care about your own blighted existence, perhaps you give a damn about that of the delectable Ms Shannon Flinder?'

'Shannon?' Somehow Finbar managed to laugh. 'You're on a hiding to nothing there,' he said roughly. 'We've broken up. She's history.'

'Well, even if that were true – and I don't believe it is – I'm sure you wouldn't want your intransigence to result in her untimely and agonising death.'

'What?'

'Mr Linnell, I don't wish to resurrect what must be traumatic memories for you, but several years ago you lost your wife and baby daughter. Now Ms Flinder's the closest person to you. I'm sure you wouldn't want to lose her as well, in equally tragic circumstances.'

Finbar closed his eyes as he thought again of the words Shannon had hurled at him on the beach, the words that had really hit where it hurt, had been burning him ever since: *'It's the people around you who end up dead!'* She was right. So right.

It wasn't going to work, this attempt to throw off his old life and start anew. Or to be happy with the woman he loved. Other men could do that, but not him apparently. Despite all his efforts, his determination, the new start wasn't going to happen. Everything was against him.

'And apart from the mortal danger to yourself and the lovely Ms Flinder,' the man went on, 'I happen to know you've got some very dark secrets that you'd strongly prefer never saw the light of day.'

Which particular dark secrets, Finbar wondered? The politician? Declan Dowd? Did this bastard know he'd killed Declan, maybe even know where he'd dumped the body?

But he could swear no one had followed him that night! He broke out in a sweat, staring at the rain-lashed windows and lowering sky beyond. Knew despair and hopelessness again. He was trapped. He didn't give a fuck about himself, he would take on anyone and if he didn't come out the winner, so be it. But he couldn't put Shannon in danger – more danger.

'Mr Linnell? I'm waiting very patiently.'

Finbar heaved a long, silent sigh. If there was any way out of this one, he couldn't see it at the moment. Rain drummed against the windows, car horns blared in the street below. He thought of Shannon, of how much he loved her. She had whirled into his life, loved him, given him hope and made him feel alive again. That was over now. Only loss was forever. Not love.

'What do you want?' he asked.

Chapter Nineteen

What was I thinking of?!

Why did I tell Shannon Flinder the bitch lawyer that she'd signed someone's death warrant? Now I'll have to follow through. Can I do it?

That's what I hate most about this world, how it's always the innocent who suffer. The guilty get away with murder and all kinds of outrages. It makes me sick, I can't stand it. If there's something on the news about a man or woman who was wrongly convicted of a crime and spent years inside, I can hardly bear to watch. It upsets me too much to think what they must have suffered, their families as well as them. And if I feel like that, how must they feel? It also makes me think of others who are locked up for crimes they didn't commit, people who won't be lucky enough to attract the attention of some prominent lawyer or journalist who'll turn things around for them. The prominent people don't help out of the goodness of their hearts – what hearts? – of course, or because their sense of justice is outraged. They do it because it suits them, brings them publicity, advances their careers. They've always got their own agendas. Self-promotion is their thing. That's why you can never trust them. Shannon's one of those people.

Problem is, I'm not sure I can do it. Kill a fellow human being, I mean. I can't bring myself to just go out one night, pick on some innocent, unsuspecting person and murder them so that I can give Shannon bloody Flinder her wake-up call. It would be totally unjust. I'd be no better than all those lawyers, judges and journalists then.

It would also mean Shannon's crimes were still having repercussions, still leading to other people getting hurt and killed. I don't want that to happen. But if I do nothing, she'll only laugh at me. Think she's got away with it again. She'll believe the nut job got bored or scared, picked the wrong person to intimidate. She's so strong, doesn't get freaked by a few silly anonymous letters! She'll think she's won. Ms Flinder won't be playing God then. The bitch will think she IS God.

I can't imagine killing somebody, don't even have a clue how I'd do it. Except that I wouldn't want to spill their blood. Not just because I don't want it all over my clothes. I've just got this thing about not spilling blood, I'm not sure why. In the Middle Ages they burned witches at the stake or hanged them because they believed you must never spill a witch's blood. They weren't just being sadistic. Dear God! How the hell am I going to work this one out?

When I had to deliver the bitch's letter this morning I entered the Magistrates' Court building from downstairs, around the back, and walked along that corridor where I sometimes sit on the old wooden bench. I wanted to sit down for a few minutes then actually, but there wasn't time. I had a job to do. Besides, my mood was agitated. That meant I wouldn't see any ghosts. It's best to be in a calm, meditative state. That's when you can bridge the gap between worlds.

I don't mind if I'm seen by someone who knows me. I am entitled to be there, walk around the building. It's not as if anyone would be suspicious. Not many people notice me anyway, really notice me. Sometimes I feel as if I'm invisible, in the sense that those snob lawyers, court officials and the more macho guards and coppers think I'm insignificant, not worthy or interesting enough to warrant their attention. Just another loser with a small life. But this morning I didn't want to be seen by anyone. And that wasn't easy.

Several times I had to dodge into various rooms, and just when I'd pushed through the swing doors to that long, narrow corridor which leads to the Lawyers' Room I had to dash up the flight of white-painted, winding, wooden stairs to my right. Good job they are winding, because otherwise I couldn't have hidden. As it was, they're not carpeted, so I had to be careful not to make any noise. I crouched there until whoever it was had walked past. I got a fright when I heard something drop, or at least thought I did. Just a small sound. Maybe a bit of plaster flaked off the wall.

I finally got to the room, crept in and placed our Shannon's letter on the desk, knowing she'd either find it herself or that one of her lawyer pals would hand it to her. Then it was party time. I didn't realise how much I'd enjoy cutting up her coat, how hearing, feeling and watching the sharp scissors slice through that soft, fine wool and silk lining would be such a pleasurable, even sensual, experience. I got quite carried away, was shocked to hear myself gasping and laughing. I was proud of my work – I even managed to hang the coat up again in such a way that it looked undamaged. I felt really pissed off that I wouldn't be able to witness Shannon's shock when she came in, slipped her coat on and then watched it fall apart around her. That would have been bloody fantastic.

It was a beautiful, classic coat, of course, some incandescently expensive Italian label. I bet her rich bastard Irish lover bought it for her. Bitches like Shannon Flinder never buy those things for themselves, even though they've got plenty of money of their own. Oh no. That's what Shannon thinks men are for – to support her financially and emotionally, buy her endless presents and give her endless shuddering orgasms. And if they don't come up with the goods she kicks them out of bed and out of her life. I suppose that's her idea of feminism.

I took a big risk staying to cut up her oh-so-beautiful designer coat. If someone had walked in and caught me...! The scissors are here on the table beside me, a few black wool threads and a strand of sexy silk clinging to them. It's just occurred to me how much I'd love to cut Shannon's soft, curly blonde hair too. By the time I'd done her coat and got out again I was dizzy, sweating and scared stiff. Drained, that's the word. I reached the main hall where the hordes were starting to arrive, and soon blended into the throng of assorted scroats. A sit down and a cup of good, strong tea restored me. The tea's much better than the coffee. That's when I discovered my fountain pen was missing.

I knew I'd had it before I left home. It's a Mont Blanc Le Grand. Very expensive, black with a thin gold rim around the cap, the signature tiny white star on top. An eighteen-carat gold nib. You can either fill it with ink or buy cartridges. I buy bottles of the best quality ink. If you go on a long journey, especially one that involves flying, it's recommended that you use cartridges. I'm forced to write this journal with a biro now, and it feels like punishment.

What did I DO with the Mont Blanc? Where did I lose it? I went back and searched, but couldn't find it anywhere. Not on that cold stone floor downstairs, or in the rooms and corridors above. I thought I might have dropped it on the stairs and that the little noise I'd heard was the pen falling, but no joy there either. Did I leave it in the Lawyers' Room? I just don't know! I've racked my brains, looked everywhere and it's no use. I can feel the panic again, making my mouth dry and my heart pound, giving me that uncomfortable sensation of pressure around my diaphragm. I love that pen, and I'm very upset to lose it. I've drunk a couple of glasses of white wine, but that hasn't helped me calm down.

It might be lying somewhere unnoticed. Or some thieving sod could have found it and decided to keep it for themselves. They might try to sell it if they guess it's valuable. Or just toss it in the nearest bin. I'm not worried. Just upset. I mean, nothing can happen. It's a bloody nuisance, that's all. I hope I find it soon.

But back to this huge challenge I was stupid enough to set myself. The signed death warrant. Am I really up for it? I'll have to be, won't I? If I don't want to lose all credibility in Shannon's eyes. Just the thought of killing somebody makes me break out in a cold sweat of horror. But I'll have to do it.

When I last saw her in the Mags Court she was talking to a barrister friend, that big, old fat bloke with the out-of-control eyebrows. The one who kindly delivered my letter. Shannon looked so shocked at first, I think she wondered if he'd written it. Must be tough – poor cow can't trust anyone right now, can she? When they'd finished their little chat and she walked off, I heard him shout something about a dinner. Maybe he'd like to be more than friends, despite the fact that he must be at least thirty years her senior. Fat old bastards like him aren't our Shannon's type though, are they? Oh no. She only does long, lean, sharp and sexy.

I started keeping this journal once I'd made up my mind to destroy Shannon Flinder. Most people use diaries and journals to indulge in limitless introspection, interesting only to themselves. But I haven't got much inclination to write about myself, my job, or my life in general. Only insofar as it relates to Shannon, my beautiful hate object.

How dare she defy me like this! Who does the bitch think she is? She looked so cool, talking to her father figure with the eyebrows. Cool clothes, hair, make-up, attitude. That self-confidence I loathe and long to crush. It's about time I got some confidence. I want to be powerful, able to make changes. In her life and my own.

I can't hurt or kill the innocent of this world. I don't feel ashamed of that. It's a strength, not a weakness. So I'll have to pick on somebody who's guilty. It won't be so difficult then. I can imagine doing it if I feel angry enough, if I feel it's justified. Yes.

The phone's ringing. I can guess who it is.

Got to go.

Chapter Twenty

'Are you crazy?' The dark-haired man shook Pascale's passport in Demetrio's face, his brown eyes and low, angry voice brimming with contempt. 'This is a woman. We've got no bloody use for bloody women!'

'What, not even to make butties? Or are you telling me you bat for the other side?'

'Just watch it, you ... !'

'All right, mate, all right. Take it easy.' Demetrio held up one hand placatingly, remembering how this little arsehole was permanently incapable of seeing the humourous side of life. 'Look,' he said, 'you told me you wanted another one by today, and I've done it. Are you sure you don't want this?' he persisted. 'She was young – young enough.' He decided to risk the lie. 'And she can't be traced. No family to kick up a fuss. That's what you wanted, isn't it?' He looked irritably around the busy café in the middle of Lime Street Station. 'Christ, I can't hear meself think in this bloody place.'

He would have preferred to meet in a pub. They could be noisy too, but not as bad as this. And at least you could have a proper drink. But this prat in the dark blue ski jacket – Haytham, he called himself, although Demetrio no way believed that was his real name – didn't like pubs and wouldn't touch alcohol. Miserable, self-righteous git. No wonder he couldn't see the funny side.

'Yes. I notice you've got a problem with thinking, big old

bald man!' Haytham smacked the passport on the wet table then shoved it back at him. 'No fucking use,' he hissed. 'Just like you, you ugly bastard.'

Demetrio's anger ratcheted up a notch. 'You never said no women!'

'I was thick enough to think that'd be bleedingly obvious.' Haytham pushed aside his cooled coffee and lit another cigarette. 'I'm losing faith in you, not to mention patience,' he grumbled. 'So are the others. Even if we wanted to use this one, how can I believe you when you say she can't be traced? That the police will think she's only missing, not dead? Maybe you fucked that up.'

'Now, just hang on a minute, mate.' Demetrio was losing his temper as fast as the other was losing faith. He was in a panic too. He'd hoped he could shove Pascale off on them because he didn't want to – couldn't – do another one already. He had enough problems as it was.

'No. *You* hang on.' Haytham leaned over and gripped his wrist, making him wince with pain. 'How can you be sure she won't be traced?' he repeated. 'What did you do with the body?'

'I sorted it, all right?' Demetrio, flushed. 'Not a problem.'

He wasn't going to give this bastard the details of how he'd got a mate of his who owned a garage and picked up abandoned cars for the council to hoist one more car on to his wagon. Of course he wasn't stupid enough to leave Pascale's body in the boot. The people at the scrap yards always checked car boots for gas cylinders or old tyres before the cars went in the crusher. Demetrio had taken up the carpet, underlay and squabs – the part of the seat your arse went on – and shoved her in there before putting it all back again and throwing some junk on top. They never checked the insides of cars. He had hung around, watched Pascale and her car go in the crusher. She was all chewed up now.

'She's history, mate,' he said. 'Another unsolved case in Detective Dickhead's file.'

'I hope you're right.' Haytham glared at the passport. 'For your sake, that is, not ours. Because you're on your own, big man.'

Demetrio opened his mouth to tell him to piss off, then shut it again. He liked the money and wanted to go on doing business with these mystery people, however unreasonable they were at times. He wasn't scared of them, of course, no way. But it was best to try to stay friendly.

Haytham shot him a contemptuous look. 'You want to ask a question? I can save you the trouble.' He stubbed out his cigarette and patted his chest through the padded jacket. 'You don't get paid.'

'What?' Demetrio flushed again. 'Come on! I did what you asked,' he protested.

'No, you fucking didn't.' Haytham stood up. 'I'm giving you one last chance, ugly man. You bring me something good next time,' he warned, pointing his rolled-up computer magazine as if it were a semi-automatic. 'Really good. Then maybe you'll get paid.' He smiled, revealing yellow teeth. There was a brown mark on the front left eye tooth where the enamel was chipped. 'Or maybe I'll kill you. Remember,' he said, 'I've got the group to protect me. Some of them are watching us right now. Don't bother,' he laughed as Demetrio glanced around, startled. 'You won't spot them. We don't normally work with scum like you. You only want money, that's all you give a fuck about. So maybe you'll get some if you don't fuck up again. Right.' He gave a mocking salute. 'See you next time.'

Demetrio watched him stroll out of the café, a shortarse trying to look tall, smacking the palm of one hand with the rolled up magazine. Bloody little weasel, he thought, I could kill him with one punch. Unfortunately it was true what the bastard said. Demetrio sighed. He'd been counting on that money. He hadn't dared tell Haytham he couldn't do another one for a while.

He felt in his pocket and touched the plastic sandwich bag of crack cocaine rocks. At least he could flog this stuff for now, as long as he didn't tread on anyone else's turf. And he had sold the guns. But it was all small stuff. Nothing was working out, his plans to be the big man coming to nought. He had to report to the bloody police because he didn't dare break his bail conditions – for now – and worry about whether or not Keely would grass him up. Even if she didn't know his real name, she could give a description and they would issue – what was it called? – an e-fit? Murdering people, stealing their identities, even though he didn't know what for, had given Demetrio a fantastic buzz. Now pleasure had turned to aggravation.

He missed the comfort of Pascale's house, but of course there was no way he could go back there. He had rented a flat near Princes Park, in the same road as Pickhead, and that would have to do until he found something better. He winced as he imagined her crushed body again; the skin and blood, the hair, the broken teeth and bones. He didn't want to think about it, but the image kept flashing into his mind.

Demetrio still hadn't got over the shock her death had caused him, especially as he hadn't even meant to kill the stupid bitch. It was all Pascale's fault for winding him up, so why did he feel so bad? Look what she did to him, giving him the shivers even after she'd croaked it! Demetrio swore at the memory of last night, how he'd woken in a drenching sweat after dreaming he was back in the silent house with Pascale collapsed in a heap at the bottom of the stairs. He'd turned her over and screamed when he saw that her face had decomposed, fat worms slithering in and out of her eye sockets and lipless mouth. And all the time that bloody unseen kid was giggling and calling *'Ninny!'* He had to pull himself together. There were no ghosts. It was all in his fucked-up head. He sighed, got up and strode out of the café.

The station hall was noisy and crowded, some disembodied voice booming announcements that no one could understand. The place stank of old diesel trains. Demetrio didn't so much as glance at two patrolling coppers. He walked past W.H. Smith and felt aggrieved as a really fit, twenty-something blonde refused to catch his eye and smile back at him. He must be losing his touch. The fact that she was blonde reminded him of Shannon Flinder. Shannon didn't bloody want to know him either, except at arm's length as client and solicitor. And as his solicitor, was she doing enough for him? He might give her another call later or go round there. Sod whatever bloody appointments she had! Shannon was Keely's solicitor as well as his. Shame he couldn't get friendly enough with her to squeeze some info about Keely out of her. He would keep trying.

Demetrio stopped and froze as he clocked another woman gazing into the shop window at a display of some new novel and a glam photo of its sexy, smiling author. He gasped and broke out in an icy sweat. The woman looking in the window was slim, dark-haired, wearing jeans and a denim jacket. Just like . . .

'Christ!' he breathed, going weak at the knees. The woman turned her head, revealing the curve of her profile. She had calm grey eyes and a preoccupied expression, unaware that she had almost been mistaken for a murder victim. By the murderer himself. She moved away. Demetrio jumped and cursed again as someone tapped him on the shoulder. He whirled round, his fists clenched.

'Take it easy, Demon!' The young man with the black baseball cap pulled down over his face took a startled step back.

'What the fuck are you doing here?' Demetrio felt furious at the sight of Phelim. If he'd done his job and killed Keely outside the Mags Court, that would have been one less problem. 'Have you been following me?'

'I saw you cross Lime Street and come in here. I hung around 'til you'd finished talking to that bloke.' Phelim had to hurry to keep up with him. 'Who is he?'

'None of your business. Get lost.'

'I had to see you, you won't talk to me on the phone. I'm scared, Demon! It's been in the *Echo*. On telly.'

'You mean the job you fucked up?' Demetrio glanced around, breathing heavily.

'They've got an e-fit.'

'So what? Since when did anyone look like their e-fit? I dunno what you're worried about anyway – she never saw you before and she won't recognise you 'cause you had the hat on as well as that scarf over your stupid gob.'

'I'm not talkin' about *her*.' Phelim grabbed his arm, his dark eyes angry and frightened. 'I mean that one who was with her, the one who chased me. The blonde. She must have helped them with the e-fit. She saw me when the scarf fell – she can ID me!'

'The blonde?' Demetrio stopped suddenly. He laughed.

Phelim's voice rose. 'You know who she is, don't you? Who?'

'Get off me.' Demetrio shook his arm free.

'She said she'd killed someone,' Phelim went on.

'What?' Demetrio stared at him.

'Told me she'd killed someone before and could do it again. I think she was just fronting it out, scared like, 'cause she thought I was gonna do her.' Phelim paused, his lips tightening. 'I wanted to, but she looked like she'd be trouble. And I had to get away.'

Demetrio thought for a few seconds, frowning, then shook his head. Who the hell would Shannon Flinder kill? That was crazy. 'She was just saying that,' he said. 'She was scared. Got some guts though, hasn't she?' He smiled, admiring. He needed a woman like Shannon, someone with spirit. Not whimpering, frightened bitches who started whingeing even before he'd taught them who was boss.

Phelim grabbed his arm again. 'Who is she?' he hissed. 'What's her name? Fuck's sake, Demon! She can ID me. I can't get to the other one, not now she's in the hossie with the bizzies all over her. But I've got to do that blonde.'

'You're not doing her!' Demetrio wrenched his arm away and shoved him. 'You're not doing anyone. She's not a problem,' he said. 'Leave her to me.'

171

'But—'

'I *said*, she's not a problem. Nothing's a problem. Now fuck off and leave me alone,' he ordered. 'If you follow me again I'll do *you*. Get lost!'

Demetrio turned and strode on out of the station, leaving Phelim staring after him. He felt angry and isolated, frightened. The pressure was piling on. Everything and everyone was getting to him. What was he going to do next?

First he needed a drink.

Chapter Twenty-One

'My name's Iain Blick. Good of you to meet me, Mr Linnell.'

Finbar did not shake his proffered hand or make the obvious reply about having had total bloody lack of choice in the matter. The body attached to the voice on the phone was about thirty, dark-haired and well built, a few inches shorter than him. Iain Blick was casually dressed in jeans and black sweater and looked fit, as if he did a lot of training.

'Sure you wouldn't like me to order coffee? Or something stronger?' Blick lifted the hotel suite curtain and peered down into the rainy street. 'You can understand I didn't want to linger in the lobby,' he said. He glanced around the room. 'You'd think there'd be a mini bar, given that this place is supposed to be four-star. But that's English hotels for you, isn't it? Sit down,' he smiled, gesturing at the hideous red-and-green striped sofa. 'Relax.'

'I'm afraid I don't feel very relaxed.' Finbar pulled Declan Dowd's gun out of his coat pocket and levelled it at the man's face. 'Why don't I just kill you right now?'

Blick stared at the gun without flinching. 'Because that would be stupid.' The bedroom door opened and three men in ski masks appeared, stood there silently.

'What's this, the punishment team?' Finbar looked at them, at their guns. He wasn't Clint Eastwood and this wasn't a movie where one man could vanquish three others and survive without so much as a flesh wound for the distraught heroine to bandage. He slowly lowered his gun.

'That's better. Much more sensible.' Blick nodded to the men. 'Okay. I'll call you when I need you. Shut the door.' They disappeared.

'Tell me what you want.' Finbar stuck the gun back in his pocket. 'And just because I've come here doesn't mean you're going to get it.'

Blick sat in an armchair. 'I would have approached you sooner,' he said. 'But I wanted to unsettle you first. Show you what I could do, make you more amenable to suggestions. Perfectly timed, wasn't it?' he smiled. 'The club bomb. I've got a good man who arranged it just the way I wanted. You ran out, got blown across the street and suffered no more than the shock and minor injuries I intended.'

'How do I know it was you who blew up my club and not someone else?' Finbar asked. He hadn't believed Declan Dowd was responsible and now it looked like he was right.

'Well, there was my phone call just before the explosion,' Blick said, the smile more fixed now. He didn't like being challenged. 'And as you ran out the front door, you must have seen that neatly taped package left on the bar. In the spotlight, where you couldn't miss it. There were those two men in overalls you shouted at to get out of the way – before you flew head first into the railings. We watched it all from a safe distance. Anything else you'd like to ask?'

'Who's *we*? Apart from you and the masked clowns in there?' Finbar nodded at the bedroom door.

'I represent a–' Blick paused, frowning slightly '–how can I put this? A group of what you might call disaffected people. With Republican sympathies.'

'There's a hell of a lot of them about. Let me take a wild guess,' Finbar said, his heart sinking. This was exactly what he'd feared. 'Paramilitary, breakaway, splinter group, dissident, loose cannon? Ongoing danger to the Peace Process? That's what the politicians and journalists say, isn't it?'

Blick's eyes gleamed. 'We know you don't like politicians.'

'Tell me someone who does.' Finbar moved away and sat on the bed.

'Not liking is one thing. Murder's another.'

'I don't know what you're talking about.'

'Yes you do, but I'll indulge you anyway. I'm talking about the late Defence Secretary. You're the mystery man who got away after the killing, left poor old Lenny Dowd with a bullet in his head to take the rap posthumously.'

'What bullshit—'

'It's not bullshit. You were there. And now something funny's happened.'

'I can't wait to hear what that is.' Finbar's heart sank further. He had a nasty feeling he knew what was coming. 'Funny strange, or funny ha-ha?'

'Depends on your viewpoint. I got a disturbing report that Lenny Dowd's younger brother had set out to avenge the hero commander's death. Disturbing, because it conflicted with my interests. You see, I've got plans for you. I made some discreet inquiries. Turned out Declan Dowd was something of a hothead – basically, a security risk – who'd been quite vocal about his intentions to kill you, and even disobeyed the orders of the group he was with to go off and pursue his private vendetta. He set out on his mission, but didn't return. Still hasn't, days later. And here you are, alive and in the pink.' Blick smiled. 'He came after you, didn't he? And you killed him.'

Shit. 'I don't know what you're—'

'I'm glad you did it. If he'd killed you he would have ruined everything. Problem is, Declan's superiors are wondering what action to take. They're relieved he's gone, and they've got nothing personal against you. On the other hand, for credibility's sake, they're not sure if they can let you get away with stiffing one of their men. Even if he was a bloody liability.'

'I didn't—'

'Please.' Blick raised one hand. 'Let me finish. We talked, and I managed to persuade them it was best to let it go,' he said. 'See the bigger picture.'

Finbar went cold. 'What bigger picture?'

'That's for me to know and you to find out. Eventually.'

'I don't know anything about this Declan Dowd,' Finbar protested again. 'No one tried to kill me. Anyway, why would they automatically assume he's dead? It's a hell of a conclusion to leap to just because he hasn't come back from wherever he said he was going. And mouthing off about how you want to kill somebody is one thing – doing it's another. He could have changed his mind, bottled out. Doesn't want to go back home and be laughed at as the limp dick.' Finbar paused. 'For all his bloody superiors know, *you* could have killed him! If he was a threat to your bigger picture, you obviously had a motive.'

'Shame you don't work for the police or intelligence services,' Blick said coldly. 'They're crying out for people with analytical minds like yours. People with analytical minds have usually got better things to do though, haven't they? Deny it if you like,' he went on. 'I would in your situation. Fact is, Declan Dowd went to kill you and didn't come back. We know you, your history. Enough said. Anyway, let's forget that for now.' Blick paused. 'I want your help, Mr Linnell. Can I call you Finbar?'

How much does Blick really know, Finbar wondered, and how much is speculation? Albeit bloody accurate! He can't be sure I was the so-called mystery man who got away. And if he knows I shot Declan and dumped his body in the Clock Tower dungeon, surely he wouldn't be able to resist freaking me with his knowledge? I made damn sure I wasn't followed that night.

'Who exactly are you lot?' he asked. 'The Real IRA, or some other variety? I know there's quite a few Brit members. Got Anglo-Irish parents, have you? Meet up with some local psychos during holidays in Fair Erin?'

'We're not the Real IRA. Another variety, as you say. You don't need to know. The less you know, the better. And let's not discuss my personal motivations just now.' Blick shifted in his armchair. 'I'd prefer to focus on the cooperation I

176

require from you. When I say I need your help I'm talking about you renting premises for us, obtaining cars, false driving licences, arranging banking facilities. We need more explosives, bomb-making equipment–'

'I wouldn't have thought you were short of that!'

'Oh, always, I'm afraid. We can never get enough. But you can. It's the sort of thing you're very good at.'

'The sort of thing I don't do any more!'

'Well, it's time you came out of retirement. Especially if you want the lovely Ms Flinder to celebrate her next birthday.' Iain Blick glanced around again. 'Horrible room this, isn't it? No wonder you can't relax.' He leaned forward, clasped his hands. 'Let me outline a little scenario for you. You do what we want, everything goes smoothly, end of story. We leave you alone – Declan Dowd's superiors leave you alone – and Ms Flinder gets to go on plying her trade in the law courts.' He smiled. 'That's when she's not getting fucked by you, of course. I bet you don't give the poor girl much rest.'

Finbar felt furious, frightened. 'I told you,' he said. 'She and I are finished. She's moving out.'

'I'm starting to find all these denials rather irritating. So spare me, all right?' Blick held up one hand, his dark eyes cold. 'Just spare me. So, as I said. You cooperate, everything stays cool. No more worries. Now let's imagine you don't cooperate. We kill Ms Flinder.' He smiled as Finbar turned pale. 'I'm afraid it won't be a quick bullet. She's very beautiful, isn't she? We'll want some fun first. Unfortunately it won't be much fun for her. One of the guys in the other room is something of a sadist. Slow strangulation is his thing, plus various other unorthodox and highly uncomfortable sexual predilections – uncomfortable for his victims, that is. It's always been his ambition to direct as well as star in his own snuff movie. You'll get to watch it being made.'

Finbar felt sick. His mind raced. He had to protect Shannon. What could he do? Warn her, tell her to get out of Liverpool? Where could she go, where could she stay safe?

177

She was in terrible danger because of him. She would hate him now. But the only thing that mattered was her safety.

'Of course you might warn Ms Flinder,' Blick said, his cold eyes studying him. 'But what's the point? You'll only terrify her, and if you're sensible there'll be no need for her to be terrified. She can't escape. And of course you might go to the police. But one can of worms will certainly lead to others being opened. You really don't need that, do you?'

Finbar was dry-mouthed, sweating. He stayed silent. Trying to think, hold on.

'Once the lovely Shannon's dead, we won't kill you. We won't be that kind.' Blick stared at him, his eyes shining. 'We'll make it look like you murdered her. She was a slut, went with other men. You caught her *in flagrante delicto*. A lot of men kill their wives and girlfriends, don't they? Nothing unusual there. And with your past, who'll believe you're innocent? To complicate things further, a witness will come forward to state they saw you run out of that Water Street office building a few minutes after a rocket launcher hit the Defence Secretary's car and blew his body parts all over the place. Don't tell me you weren't there!' he shouted, seeing Finbar's expression. 'It'll be just the break the police have been looking for. Fit you up good and proper. I'll also let you take the credit for my scheme. The one I need your help with.'

Finbar cleared his throat. 'This would be the bigger picture you mentioned earlier?'

'Right. And there's the mysterious disappearance of Declan Dowd.' Blick laughed, shaking his head. 'Any one of those things would be enough. The police, QCs and judges won't know where to start. You'll spend the rest of your life as an A category inmate in a top-security prison. With vivid flashbacks of the beautiful Shannon's degrading, agonising last moments to fill those endless days, months and years.' He took a breath and sat back. 'Dear God. That's a hell of a lot to cope with. On the whole, I think I'd prefer death.'

It didn't matter what Blick knew or didn't know. The fact

was, if he didn't do what the bastard wanted Shannon would die. They both would. Finbar's sweating hand inside his pocket slid on the gun metal. He didn't want to speak in case his voice came out as a croak.

'Maybe you don't believe I can do what I say.' Iain Blick's smile was pleasant and friendly again. He stood up, stretched his arms above his head and sat down again. 'Ms Flinder's spending this rainy afternoon at the Queen Elizabeth II Law Courts, isn't she? Court 35, to be precise. In her role as instructing solicitor, sitting behind some chinless boy barrister who's trying to elicit – in a really unclever way – the facts from a thug who head-butted an innocent clubber. Ms Flinder's wearing a sexy, elegant, dark-brown trouser suit, one of her favourites. We know that because we've observed her for some time. Despite her sexy beauty, however, our man in the public gallery seeing justice seen to be done is a bit bored. He says the trial's all very polite and quiet, really just a fact-finding exercise. No barristers screaming at witnesses, like you see on television, or the judge browbeating the jury.'

Shannon often made remarks to that effect. And Finbar knew she was at the Crown Court this afternoon. She had mentioned the head-butting case, remarked how it was dragging on longer because the prosecuting barrister was an idiot. Finbar cleared his throat again. Was it him, or was it freezing in here? Rain beat on the windows.

'I wonder,' Iain Blick went on, 'will Shannon get safely home to you this evening? Her mobile's switched off because she's in court, so you can't warn her she's under surveillance. Even if you could, you can't give a description of our man. Or men. The police won't be any help – all that explaining! If you go to them you'll only make things even more horrendously complicated for yourself. And waste time – precious time that you and Ms Flinder can't afford.'

'Why bother with all this?' Finbar got his voice back. 'You lot are as dead as the extreme right! Haven't you heard of the Peace Process, decommissioning, all that? No one supports you any more, the public aren't bloody interested.'

'Ah, well.' Blick's smile faded. 'That's their tragic mistake, isn't it?'

'Go and be a computer programmer or work for MI6 or something.'

'Actually, I wouldn't fancy either of those careers.' Blick's voice was icy.

'Why me in particular?' Finbar remembered his conversation with Shannon that morning he'd pulled off her knickers and made her late for work. 'Anyone can organise transport, bombs and banking facilities. Don't you have enough fanatic volunteers to do all that stuff?'

'Not enough with your money, skills, contacts and resources. Plus the stunning possibilities for blackmail.' Blick glanced at his watch. 'Right. I suggest we get down to business. That's if you want Ms Flinder to come home tonight? I'll take that as a yes,' he said when Finbar stared silently at him. 'Let's do the banking first. I want you to get me fifty grand by tomorrow. And don't try to tell me you can't do that.'

'I know this is a stupid question, but where's the money supposed to come from?'

'You're right, that is stupid. From your account, of course. Or one of them. Don't tell me you haven't got it. I could ask for a lot more. Bring it here by noon tomorrow. Or Ms Flinder co-stars in a snuff movie. And you start your life stretch.'

Finbar stood up. 'Tell me what you're planning. What's all this for?'

'I'll tell when I get evidence of your good faith and common sense. When you're implicated. One of us. Oh, and I'll relieve you of that gun, if you don't mind.' Finbar hesitated then gave it to him, thinking how two of its bullets were lodged in Declan Dowd's decaying flesh.

'Thanks. Hey!' Blick called. The bedroom door opened and the three masked men reappeared.

'Do they wear those things all the time?' Finbar asked. 'Bit sad, isn't it?' They came forward and crowded silently around him. He looked at each man in turn, the eyes behind the masks, felt the waves of hostility emanating from them. They were dying to hammer his head in, no question about that. He pushed away a sudden, horrible image of Shannon in their sadistic, murderous hands.

'I wouldn't be in a mood for sarcasm if I were you.' Blick searched Finbar's pockets and pulled out his mobile. 'Call your bank and get things started,' he ordered. *Now.*'

Ten minutes later Finbar walked out into the cold, rainy street. He was shaking. He experienced a strange sense of detachment, as if he couldn't feel the ground beneath his feet. For a few seconds he could not remember where he had parked his new Maserati. He looked up and down the street, searching faces. Was he being watched now? Followed? A red-haired girl in a black mac moved her umbrella aside as she passed, gave him a shy smile. Finbar did not smile back. He strode on along the street of Victorian buildings, cold rain running down his face and the back of his neck. He could smell fast food, traffic fumes, the river. Somewhere in the midst of all that, a scent of spring.

He could phone the bank back right now and tell them to cancel the transaction. Rush down to Derby Square and drag Shannon out of her courtroom non-drama. Tell her the whole horror story, try and persuade her to flee with him. But would she? She wanted to leave him. There were lots of places they could run to, but how long would they stay safe? They might be followed and murdered. What was this nut job Blick planning? Even if he did what the bastard wanted, there was no guarantee he and Shannon wouldn't be murdered anyway. Fear and despair swept over him. Finbar walked down Mount Pleasant and went in to the multi-storey car park.

No more lies, he thought. I have to tell Shannon. She's got a right to know the danger she's in, even if it does make her hate me. At the same time, he wondered what good being honest would do. Knowing the threat she faced wouldn't help Shannon protect herself. It wouldn't help him protect her either, at least not until he found out more about them. To think she was being watched right now! He reached the top of the stairs, pushed through swing doors and paused in the dank, petrol-smelling gloom to wipe the rain off his face.

'Jesus Christ!' he muttered. 'What the fuck do I do?'

He had no time to think about that any more, because headlights blinded him as a car shot forward and screeched to a stop alongside, trapping him against a stone pillar. Doors were flung open. Dark figures jumped out and grabbed him. Finbar was manhandled into the back of the car and pushed down, boots all along his vertebrae.

'What's going on?' he shouted. 'Who are you?' He didn't know why he asked, because he didn't expect an answer. Face down, in pain, barely able to breathe, he struggled furiously. 'What the fuck are you ... ?'

'Shut up,' someone said. 'Keep still. You're all right, we won't hurt you.'

Of course Finbar didn't believe them. In their place, he would have said the same.

'No!' he shouted as they pulled his arms behind his back and slipped something around his wrists. 'Get off me, you bastards!' The car screeched forward and swerved. He kicked out furiously, heard one of them gasp and swear. His face was squashed against the dirty, blue-grey carpet.

'Listen,' the voice said. 'I don't want to have to bash you over the head and risk giving you a subdural haematoma. So just relax, okay? We'll be there soon.'

Where? The car was speeding down and around corners, bouncing over a ramp. The boots pressed harder into his neck and vertebrae. Finbar's wrists were tied tight and a thick, suffocating hood pulled over his face. Everything went black. He felt sick and dizzy, disorientated.

Who were they? Declan Dowd's associates, concerned

about their credibility? Maybe Blick had underestimated his powers of persuasion. Someone else he hadn't seen coming? Well, he would find out now. Too late.

They're going to kill me, Finbar thought.

Chapter Twenty-Two

'So you won't come out for a drink with me tonight?'

'Mr Montana, I already told you I don't socialise with clients.' Shannon gripped the receiver, stared out of her office window at the brick wall across the alley, then raised her eyes to golden Minerva on top of the Town Hall dome. She didn't need this creep pestering her, especially now. She had just got back from the Crown Court and hadn't had time to dry off after walking through the pouring rain without coat or umbrella. She had missed lunch, and another client was due in five minutes. Worst of all, she was deeply miserable at the thought of splitting with Finbar.

'It's not socialising exactly,' Demetrio Montana argued. 'We can talk about my case. I mean, it's your job to keep the bizzies off my back, isn't it?'

'I'm a criminal law solicitor who does mainly defence work,' she snapped, nervous and irritated. 'You make me sound like personal attorney to some Mafia boss.'

'Hey, I like that.' He laughed his creepy laugh. 'I just think we've got stuff in common. Maybe I could help you. Maybe I already am helping you,' he said slyly.

'What on earth do you mean?' Shannon asked, mystified. This was one big time bullshit artist. And worse.

'Come out with me tonight and I'll tell you.'

'Mr Montana, if you persist I'm going to have to inform

my associates about your behaviour, and I – this firm – will refuse to act for you any longer.'

'All right,' he said sullenly. 'Forget it for now. Let's talk about my case. I phoned you before, but you were out. Where were you?'

'That's my business, Mr Montana,' she said stiffly.

'Got a mobile, haven't you? What's the number?'

'If I'm not available you can leave a message with our receptionist. Or if it's outside office hours, there's a pager number.' Shannon had no intention of giving him or any other client her mobile number. 'Right, your case.' She reached for his file and flipped it open. 'The best way you can help is to get me that paperwork you promised. For the weapons. Remember?'

'Yeah. But Pascale – me ex-girlfriend – kicked me out a few nights ago, chucked all me stuff in binliners. I've only just found a new place. Haven't sorted everything yet.'

'Well, I need to see the licences as soon as possible. It's vital for your defence.' Shannon had a feeling that neither she nor the police were going to see any paperwork that proved Demetrio Montana's confiscated weapons were legit. And she couldn't imagine the ex-girlfriend daring to kick him out. But good on her if she had. She glanced at her watch. 'I've got to go now. I'm very busy.' Where did he get off, thinking he could phone her any time he liked?

'Don't tell me,' he sneered. 'An *appointment*.'

'That's right. Goodbye, Mr Montana.'

She hung up and leaned back in her chair, closing her eyes and massaging her temples. Her hair was damp, smelling of rain and peach conditioner. She had to look at another property after work, then she was meeting Rob for dinner. Shannon wasn't looking forward to that. But he had offered to help her, and she might need his help. It would also give her a chance to assess his mood. She didn't think Rob was the author of the anonymous letters, but she still couldn't be sure. If he was serious about helping he could make discreet inquiries, maybe get hold of a list of Mags Court personnel, as it appeared the author was in some way connected with that place.

Shannon also wanted to stay out of Finbar's way as much as possible until she could move out of the Albert Dock apartment. She hoped he wouldn't be there when she went back to shower and change. One look from him, one word – if he tried to touch her – and she was afraid she might not be able to resist. She opened her eyes and glanced at her brief-case lying against the desk leg.

This latest letter was more of a shock than the previous two. And her coat getting cut up and slashed, that really gave her the shakes. The angry words whirled around her brain, pausing to form again and again that chilling message: *'You've just signed someone's death warrant.'*

Who's bloody death warrant? Had this bastard killed, or were they about to? If so, how could she – or the police – stop them when she didn't know the identity of either mur-derer or intended victim? She had to hold on to the fact that it was rare for writers of threatening letters to carry out their threats. The alternative was too terrible to con-template. This person was a nasty piece of work, but a coward. If they'd wanted to hurt her they would have slashed her, not her coat. She would find out who it was and confront them, make them realise they had no power to frighten her.

Shannon tried to force the matter out of her mind, but it was like a nagging headache that wouldn't shift. In the mess of papers and files on her desk she caught the gleam of the tiny pearl in its sparkling crystal oyster, a gift from Finbar. She picked it up and gazed at it, felt the treacherous force of her useless longing for him sweep over her, pull at her body and soul.

'No,' she whispered, biting her lip. Splitting up was hor-rible; she would feel horrible for a long time afterwards. But it was the right thing to do. And she would get over Finbar Linnell, because she just bloody had to. Shannon sniffed and blinked hard, wrapped the crystal oyster in tissues and put it in a desk drawer. She shivered and sneezed. There was a knock at the door and Leon Rossini walked in.

'Thought this might warm you up.'

'Oh, thanks Leon!' Shannon took the mug of hot tea and the chocolate digestive he handed her. 'You saved my life.' She took a sip of tea. 'That's great.'

'Demetrio Montana phoned earlier. While you were in court.' Leon fiddled with his tie. 'He's a pain.'

'Tell me about it.' She took another sip of tea and a bite of biscuit. 'He just called again now. Asked me out for a drink, if you please. I've never been pestered by a client before. Well, not like this. Let's hope he gets banged up soon. This is one time when I won't mind losing. Speaking of pestering,' Shannon said, 'has your ex-girlfriend stopped bothering you?'

'She seems to have. Changing my home and mobile phone numbers helped,' he grinned. 'And she hasn't turned up at the flat again.'

'Good.'

Shannon's next client, Keith Gould, wore his usual baggy jeans, check shirt – blue today – and blue baseball cap over his lank blond hair. He reeked of stale cigarettes, and his nervous expression and fidgeting hands meant he was dying for a fag now. Shannon got down to business.

'Would you like to tell me your version of what happened, Keith?'

He flushed. 'I did smack that fella.'

'You're talking about the assistant supermarket manager?' She looked at his hands, the bitten nails. 'I don't mind if you want to smoke.'

'No,' he said. 'S'all right. I'm tryin' to knock it on the head. Yeah, I'm talkin' about the assistant manager.' Keith played with his green plastic lighter, turning it over and over. 'Didn't hit him hard. It was just a bit of a slap, like. I was pissed off. I lost it. He came and started narkin' at me when I wasn't doin' nothin'.'

'You mean, not–'

187

'Not stealin', no.' He shook his head. 'I don't do that no more, Shannon. Honest to God. You know me and me girl-friend have got little Danielle now?' Shannon smiled and nodded. 'Well, I don't do nothin' like that any more, not since she was born. Don't wanna miss her growin' up 'cause I'm stuck inside half the time, do I?'

'Of course not. Go on, Keith.'

'Well, this – this *bastard* – comes up to me and tells me to get out. I said, what's the problem, mate? I'm just buyin' milk, teabags and nappies. I mean, just mindin' me own business. And then–' Keith dropped the lighter and picked it up '–he said. . .he said. . .' He flushed crimson again, and his lips trembled.

Shannon's voice was gentle. 'What did he say, Keith?'

Keith's eyes were full of tears as he looked at her. 'He told me to leave the premises because he said I was a – a known shoplifter.'

Shannon put down her pen and sighed. She could under-stand the assistant manager didn't want him in the shop, but she felt sorry for Keith. He was trying hard to be a good father to his baby daughter, put his past behind him and start afresh. No one would give him a chance. Like you're not giving Finbar a chance, she thought suddenly. But that was different. Wasn't it?

She rushed out of the office at six and managed to be only several minutes late for her appointment to view the next property, a large, unfurnished apartment in a renovated Georgian house near the city centre. It had a view of the river, although nothing like the panorama visible from Finbar's apartment. Shannon liked the space, high ceilings and big windows, as well as the beautiful red marble fire-place in the sitting room. The apartment was only about ten minutes walk from her office. The estate agent had launched into his old chat about location, view and modcons com-bined with delightful period features when she cut him short.

'I'll take it. When can I move in?'

He gaped at her. 'Couple of days suit you?'

It would do for the next year or so, Shannon thought as she hailed a cab to drive her back through the wet, grey city streets to the Albert Dock. Maybe longer. All she needed now was something to sit on, lie on, eat off and drink out of. She glanced nervously around as she got out of the cab, keys at the ready, shivering in the cold wind that blew off the river. The idea of moving was a massive bore, apart from the pain of leaving Finbar. She would have to let people know her new address, and hated the thought that she might inadvertantly give it to whoever was writing her the anonymous letters. Shannon climbed the stairs, exhausted and dispirited.

The silence in the huge, empty apartment spooked her. Finbar was out, and there was no sign he had been back since this morning. Shannon wondered where he was, then reminded herself that it was nothing to do with her any more. The red button on the phone was flashing, but she didn't bother to check the messages. She went to shower, feeling lonely and desolate. Early evenings had usually been taken up with talk, cooking, laughter and lovemaking. Or going out for dinner. Shannon imagined herself in her new apartment, eating dinner off a tray while she watched television, doing paperwork before going to bed early. Alone. Well, there were worse things than being alone. After what she'd been through, she could certainly stand some of that. She dried herself, put on her robe and went into the kitchen to get a glass of white wine. She felt she needed a drink before she could face Rob.

She stood at the window gazing out at the river and darkening sky, sipping the cold wine and eating a few crisps because she was starving after having had nothing since breakfast except the chocolate digestive biscuit. I'm so tired, she thought. Tired, empty-hearted, scared and lonely. I don't want to go out and meet Rob, I just want to curl up here, stay safe, warm and cosy. I want Finbar. She turned and dumped the glass on the table, went to get dressed.

When the bedside phone rang Shannon wondered if it might be Rob calling to cancel their enchanted evening. No such bloody luck, she decided. He wouldn't dare phone the apartment number, only her office or mobile. Was it Finbar? Suddenly she was desperate to hear his voice, speak to him. She dropped her lipstick and ran to grab the receiver.

'Hi, Shannon. It's Paula from the India Buildings office. Is Finbar there?'

'No,' Shannon replied, disappointed. She sat on the bed.

'D'you happen to know where he is?'

'Sorry, I don't.' Shannon stopped herself asking why, what's up? She had to be strong.

'Shannon, I'm really worried,' Paula confessed, despite not being asked. 'He wasn't here when I got back from lunch and he didn't keep any of his appointments this afternoon. He was supposed to go to the airport, but he didn't do that either. The warehouseman kept phoning to ask where he was. I stayed late at the office, but Finbar still didn't turn up. I can't reach him on his mobile. I don't get it,' Paula said, her normally cheerful voice subdued. 'This is totally unlike him.'

Shannon felt a pang of fear. Then she wondered if Finbar was doing this deliberately to worry her. She dismissed the thought as quickly as it occurred; such cruel, petty behaviour definitely wasn't his style. Maybe he thought she didn't give a toss where he was. She was going to leave him, wasn't she? Why should she care?

'Shannon? Are you still–'

'Yeah, I'm here. Just thinking.'

Declan Dowd was no longer a threat. Horrible as it was, Finbar had sorted him. But he didn't believe Declan had blown up his club. That meant there might be someone else after him. But who? A friend or relative of Declan? Or was Finbar in some other kind of trouble, someone or something he'd kept locked away in a secret compartment of his existence? Whatever, there was nothing she could do to help him. She might even be in danger herself. That was one of the reasons she was leaving him.

'Did Finbar get any unusual phone calls or visitors recently?' Shannon asked.

'How d'you mean?'

'Well, I don't know – just anything out of the ordinary. Weird, even.'

'No. At least I can't think of anything.' Paula gasped. 'Shannon, d'you think he's okay? Maybe something's happened to him. An accident.'

'I'm sure Finbar hasn't had an accident.' Or not the kind Paula was thinking of. 'We would have heard. He might have just met some friend and gone for a drink or dinner.' Shannon thought how lame that sounded.

'Really? So you're not worried then?'

'Well, like you, I'm concerned.' That was the understatement of the month. Shannon caught sight of her pale face and frightened blue eyes in the dressing table mirror. 'But Paula, I'm sure Finbar's all right. He'll probably be back later this evening. I'll get him to give you a call, shall I?'

'Yeah, just to reassure me. Okay, Shannon. Thanks.'

Shannon hung up and stood trembling with fear. What the hell was going on? Maybe nothing. Finbar might just be staying out of her way, giving her space. She went into the sitting room and checked the messages on the answering machine; they were all from Paula. Then, because Shannon did not know what else to do she finished her make-up, spritzed herself with perfume, blew her hair dry and slipped on a simple black dress. The silence in the apartment was like a weight pressing on her shoulders. She couldn't stay here, waiting. Waiting for what? That was the trouble with Finbar Linnell. You never bloody knew.

She scribbled a note telling him to phone Paula, stuck it on the kitchen table and prayed he would come back to read it. Then she pulled on a black leather jacket and took her bag, looked at her reflection in the hall mirror. Her blonde hair curled around her face and shoulders, her lips were glossed red, cheekbones dusted with blusher. She looked like someone heading out to enjoy herself. How inaccurate was *that*. Shannon could not imagine enjoying herself again for as long as she lived. Endurance was her lot.

191

What if Finbar was in danger? Suppose he was even dead – murdered? Tears filled her eyes. He's not dead, Shannon told herself, hoping desperately that she was right. She sniffed, swallowed, squared her shoulders. If he was in danger, how could she help him? The simple and terrible answer was that she couldn't. She wouldn't know what to do, where to start looking. Neither would the police. And if Finbar was all right – please God! – he wouldn't thank her for getting them involved. No. There was nothing she could do. And anyway . . .

'Not my business,' she whispered, clenching her hands.

More tears welled up, and she blinked them away. She went back to the kitchen and gulped the rest of her wine. Took a last glance at the note. A tear fell on it, smudging the ink. She thought of the anonymous letters.

Shannon walked out of the apartment and slammed the door.

Chapter Twenty-Three

'So I'm between the devil and the deep blue sea.'

Finbar wasn't sure he should feel grateful not to have been dumped on some stretch of wasteground with several bullets in his brain. He leaned back and folded his arms, looked at the four men lounging around the small, dingy sitting room of the flat where they had brought him after abducting him in the car park. The place smelled of cigarettes, instant coffee and damp. Finbar had no idea where it was, but guessed that the drive from the city centre had taken about fifteen minutes.

'Iain Blick and his paramilitary mates will probably kill me even if I do help them with whatever they're up to,' he said. 'And if I don't go along with it and at the same time try to find out what atrocity they could be planning, in order to assist you gentlemen from Special Branch with your sting operation, you'll get me and Shannon Flinder killed anyway.' He paused, shaking his head. 'Someone should make a movie of this.'

'Maybe they will.' Carl Mactire, the tall, dark, heavily-built man in his forties who was in charge and whose high rank Finbar was so impressed by that he'd forgotten it, got up and came forward. He had brown, bloodshot eyes and his crinkly black hair was grey at the temples. 'With you as Executive Producer in charge of Creative Development. If you live to tell the tale. We think you were involved in the Defence Secretary's murder three months ago,' he said.

'That you knew Lenny Dowd, one of the murderers. Dowd and another unknown man carried out the killing then this man, for reasons best known to himself, shot Dowd.' Mactire felt in the pockets of his crumpled suit and pulled out a pack of cigarettes. 'That was you, wasn't it?'

Not again. Forget the movie, Finbar thought. Better make it a pantomime. 'Well, it's all very interesting,' he said. 'Certainly creative. But I'm afraid I'm going to have to blow your half-arsed theory out of the water. I missed the horrific spectacle of the assassination and its aftermath because I was in Dublin at the time. On business.'

'Yes,' Mactire nodded, lighting his cigarette. 'Staying at the Shelbourne. Nothing but the best for you, eh? You paid for the room in advance and didn't check out in person, just phoned and told them to bill your credit card for the extras. Unusual, that. Plus a few other things we found unusual.' He paused and waited for Finbar to ask what. Looked annoyed when he didn't. 'It might have seemed quiet to you these past months–'

'Not really,' Finbar interrupted, thinking of his blown-up club and all the other shit.

'We've been doing a lot of investigating into you.'

'Yeah? So why can't you tell me who nearly killed me when they blew up my club? And if you think I'm involved in the politician's murder, why don't you charge me?'

'We may well do that.' Mactire paused. 'Lenny Dowd's younger brother's gone missing,' he said. 'Rumour was he was with some breakaway paramilitary group somewhere in the UK.'

'Gone missing?' Finbar nearly groaned aloud. 'Well, there you go,' he said. 'The dangers of falling in with the wrong people.'

'Declan Dowd told some of his mates that he'd heard you were the one murdered Lenny, and he wanted revenge. Said he was going to blow your face off. Now suddenly he's disappeared.' Mactire paused. 'I don't suppose you'd know anything about that?'

'Why would I? Never heard of the guy.' Finbar shifted on the hard wooden chair and stretched his arms above his head. His back and neck ached and he felt sick, exhausted. In shock after the terrifying car journey, blindfolded on the floor, thinking he was going to be tortured and then shot. 'If you've got any more incomprehensible questions,' he said, 'I'm afraid I'm going to have to insist on speaking to my solicitor.'

'You mean your girlfriend?' one of the men asked. The others sniggered.

'We could search your apartment,' Mactire said, pointing the glowing cigarette at him. 'Investigate your finances. Basically, put your whole bloody existence under the microscope. Your girlfriend's, too. Could prove very damaging for her.' He smirked. 'Criminal law solicitors have to be careful about the company they keep.'

Finbar remembered Shannon talking about luminol tests that could show up bloodstains even after walls, floors or anything else spattered with them had been scrubbed clean. 'Well, even in these civil liberties-challenged times you still need reasonable suspicion to be able to do all that to an individual,' he said, trying to project a calmness he was far from feeling. If they started digging, he was fucked.

Mactire laughed suddenly, blowing out smoke. 'Oh, we've got it. Don't you worry. However, the Defence Secretary's murder and Declan Dowd's disappearance – as well as whatever else you may have been involved with – aren't our primary concerns. They will be, though, if you refuse to cooperate with us.'

'What about Shannon Flinder?' Finbar asked. 'She's *my* primary concern.'

Mactire shook his head. 'I don't want to talk about her.'

'Well, I bloody do! You just threatened to fuck her over big time. Not to mention me. You accuse me of all this shit and try to force me to agree to risk my life for you bastards – as if I wasn't in enough danger already!' Finbar shook his head. 'Forget about it.'

195

'You've got no option.' Mactire glared at him. 'You said it yourself, they'll kill you anyway. And Shannon Flinder. Help us, and you've got a chance. Once it's over – and you survive – you're in the clear. No more worries about your past bouncing back up to smash you in the gob. But if you don't cooperate, you're in the shit with us as well as them.' Mactire's voice lowered, became more menacing. 'It won't even matter what you did or didn't do. We'll put it out that you were an informer, that you worked undercover for us for years.'

'Oh, really?' Finbar went cold. That was a surefire death sentence. 'And just who or what am I supposed to have informed on?'

'Want a list?' Mactire smiled. 'I'll make one, no problem. I enjoy a bit of creative writing.' More sniggers.

Finbar felt furious as well as frightened. He was trapped. He knew it and so did they. He sat up straight and folded his arms, looked the grinning Mactire in the eye.

'If I'm not convinced that Shannon Flinder will stay safe, you can forget about my help,' he said slowly. 'I mean that. I don't care what you or those other bastards do to me.' He wasn't in any position to make demands, but there was no harm in trying.

'Must be *lurve*,' one of them laughed. Finbar looked at him and he went quiet.

'Listen.' Mactire stubbed out his cigarette. 'The best thing to do re. Ms Flinder's safety is to just get her out of your life. Tonight, if possible. Don't speak to her, meet her, have any contact whatsoever. Blick and his gang will see that and start to believe you're finished with her.'

Finbar got a choking feeling. 'Even if they do, they might still think I care about her. Or that I'm trying to fool them.'

'Well, if you stay together they'll definitely think you care about her! We'll put someone on to her, keep an eye out. Make sure she's safe.'

'I've only got your word for that. And it's not good enough.'

'It's in our interests as well as yours that we keep tabs on her,' Mactire argued. 'But get real. We can't whisk her to some safe house, can we? Even if she agreed. Blick would know something was up if she disappeared, the whole operation would be blown. You'd be dead then, and so would she sooner or later. These people don't give up on their grudges. You know that.' He turned away and signalled to one of the other men, who got up and headed towards the kitchen. 'Sure you don't want some coffee?'

'I'm sure.' Finbar was silent for a few seconds. 'Tell me more about *these people*,' he said eventually. 'I know you said something earlier, but you'll appreciate that I'm in a state of shock at the moment and find it difficult to absorb information.'

Mactire sat at the table and leafed through some papers. 'Iain Blick – that's his real name, by the way – used to work as an Intelligence Officer for MI5.'

'*What?* Oh, Christ!' Finbar started to laugh. 'This is a wind-up, right?'

Mactire glared at him again. 'No wind-up!'

'It's almost worth being kidnapped, hooded and dragged to this dump for. Thanks, Carl. You've really made my evening.'

'Now, look–'

'Hey, lighten up. It's a blast. Better forget the movie though,' Finbar grinned. 'The critics would slam it for being too far-fetched. How d'you know Iain & Co. didn't follow you here?' he asked. 'If he's been one of *that* kind of Her Majesty's civil servants, he'll know a trick or two. Your sting could be neutralised as we speak.'

'There's no way we were followed here.' Mactire's puffy face was flushed.

'Okay, let's say you're right about that. Let's *hope* you're right. Won't they have got a teeny bit suspicious when I walked into that multi-storey car park and didn't drive out? I mean, what the hell would I be doing?'

'We know you weren't followed from the hotel.' Mactire

calmed down and lit another cigarette. 'No need, was there? They know you're going to do exactly what you're told. For now, anyway.'

'Incidentally – how did you know I was meeting Blick?' Finbar asked. 'Surveillance, phone taps? More sophisticated techie things that average citizens like myself don't know about? It's been bugging me, if you'll pardon the expression.'

'I'd hardly call you an average citizen. Like I said.' Mactire frowned. 'We've been doing a lot of investigating.'

'But not enough to find out what Iain and his mates are up to?'

'If we knew that, we wouldn't need you.'

'What happened to cause Iain's apparently radical switch of loyalties?'

'Who knows, really?' Mactire shrugged. 'He has an Anglo-Irish background, parents moved from Dublin to London when he was nine. Went back to Ireland for holidays, to visit relatives. He went to Oxford and got an indifferent political science degree. He was too busy doing all the student things except studying. Worked for some government department after he left university, then joined MI5. He was posted to Belfast for a few years. Basically, he wasn't much good at his job. Immature, naive, having rows with everybody about operations. Major pain in the arse. He got a bit partisan, went around saying to anyone who'd listen about how he hated loyalists. Any op he was involved in went tits-up.' Mactire paused and nodded his thanks as someone handed him a mug of coffee. 'He was a total bloody liability. He's dangerous. Unstable.'

'Funny. I had that impression too.' Finbar was sick of liabilities fucking up his life. 'So why the hell did they hire him in the first place? And then not fire him?'

'These things aren't always immediately apparent. Besides, the security services don't like to fire disaffected people who might go whingeing to the media. But when this moron actually tried to form links with republican paramilitary groups and sell them information, his employers had no choice. A psychiatrist's report described him as unstable and suffering burnout. God knows how he got burnout. He was lucky he didn't get a long stretch at HM's pleasure.'

'Or a bullet,' Finbar said. 'That's a lethal game.'

'So he left Belfast and went back to London. Then he disappeared. He attracted our attention again recently when we heard he'd got hooked up with the Real IRA, but had rowed with them and gone off to form his own brand-new splinter group.'

'And now you think this little wanker wants to make a big splash?'

Mactire nodded. 'He's not interested in changing the political process. Only in killing. You could prevent an atrocity.'

'Is that meant to motivate me?' Finbar smiled. 'If I've done everything you accuse me of, why's the possibility of a bunch of stiffed Brits supposed to get me all upset?'

'It isn't. If everything works out we forget about the Defence Secretary and Declan Dowd. Plus other stuff. You and Ms Flinder get to stay alive. And of course you'll be immune from prosecution in this particular case.'

'I should bloody well think so.' Finbar didn't need to ask what would happen if things didn't work out.

Mactire raised his straggly eyebrows. 'Sure you can get that fifty grand by lunchtime tomorrow?'

Finbar sighed. 'Getting hold of cash is the least of my worries right now.'

Half an hour later he was climbing the stairs to his apartment, too tired and drained to feel angry or frightened any more. He just felt numb and hopeless. If there was something he could do to get himself and Shannon out of this mess, he couldn't see it. He wouldn't give up, of course, wasn't going to let these bastards fuck him over. But defiance would have to wait until tomorrow. He needed to rest. Think, plan.

Shannon wasn't home. He was glad because he dreaded

facing her, didn't have a clue what to say. He wondered where she was. Out with a friend, probably. To think Blick's bastards knew where she was and he didn't. He shrugged off his jacket in the hall and let it drop, went into the kitchen and saw the note on the table next to an empty wine glass and half-eaten packet of crisps. So Paula was worried about him. Well, that was heartwarming. A glimmer of light in a cold, dark world. Finbar picked up the phone and called her, reassured his sleepy office manager that he was fine and would be in tomorrow as usual.

'Don't do that to me again,' Paula muttered as he rang off.

Finbar poured himself an Ardbeg, went into the dark sitting room and stood looking out at the river lights. The sky above the city was clearing, clouds parting to reveal a sliver of pale moon, several glittering stars. Might be a beautiful day tomorrow. For someone.

He couldn't believe his life, the things that happened and just kept on fucking happening. It felt unreal. He didn't want his life to end though. Even more, he didn't want Shannon's to end because of some stupid bloody mess he'd got himself into. No matter what her other problems, she was better off without a fuck-up like him. That was the bitter truth.

He finished his drink, went into his bedroom and switched on the television. He stripped, walked into the adjoining bathroom and got under a hot shower. The stream of water, combined with the whisky he'd drunk, eased his aches and pains and made him more sleepy. But there was no way he could sleep until Shannon got back.

Finbar wrapped himself in his robe and looked at the silent phone. Glanced at his watch. Then he stretched out on the bed to rest and think.

To wait.

'Hope you don't mind me saying, but you look absolutely gorgeous tonight,' Rob smiled, his eyes shining in the candlelight as the waiter served Shannon the Café Americano and petit fours she didn't really want. 'I remember that dress.'

Shit, she thought. Trust me to pick it out. He'll think I did it for sentimental reasons. Although what he thinks I've got to be sentimental about...! 'I hope you're not driving,' she remarked, watching as he drained his glass of Burgundy and picked up the large cognac he'd ordered. Rob hadn't always drunk like this. But when you discovered your father was a murderous paedophile, your mother had looked the other way while he got on with it, your abused sister had been murdered by person or persons unknown and you were about to get divorced, you needed something to soften the hard edges.

'Of course I'm not driving. I took a cab here.' Rob's smile broadened. 'Nice of you to worry about me though.'

'I wasn't.' She added sugar to her coffee. 'I was worried about who you might kill.'

He laughed as if she'd made a joke. 'It's so great to see you again, Shannon, just sit here talking and having dinner. Reminds me of old times. Did you enjoy your monkfish?' he asked. 'You didn't eat much of it.'

'It was fine.' If you liked your fish overcooked. She was glad she'd had the crisps before she came out. 'So, can you get a list of Mags Court personnel?' she asked for the second time, trying to get back to the important subject in hand. This evening had been a bloody waste of time.

Shannon's anxiety about Finbar was mounting. Her head could keep telling her that what he did or what happened to him was no longer any of her business, but her heart wouldn't buy it. She longed to get back to the apartment and find him there, just know he was all right.

Rob swilled cognac around the balloon glass, sniffed and took a gulp. 'I'd have to give a good reason for wanting to get hold of that list,' he said. 'Of course the fact that someone who appears to be connected with the Mags Court is writing you threatening letters is a bloody good reason.' He lowered his glass. 'But you don't want me to tell anyone about that, do you?'

Shannon sighed. 'There's no point.'

'There's every point. Shannon, this is serious. This bastard's done more than just write letters now. It could have been you who got slashed, not your coat!'

'Reassure me, why don't you?'

'I'd love to reassure you, but I can't. Would you rather have a false sense of security? Now they're threatening to murder someone. They might be bluffing, but we can't be sure. You – and someone else – could be in big danger. We can help, you know,' he said. 'We're not total idiots.'

'I never thought you were,' Shannon lied. 'But you said you could help without involving your colleagues. Make a few discreet inquiries.'

'That's what I thought. But now I've had a look at the latest letter and heard the full story, I really think you should report this.'

'I suppose I'll have to,' she said reluctantly. She took a sip of coffee. 'But the police won't have any more clue than I do.' My God, Shannon wondered suddenly. Might this person try to kill Finbar to get at her? No, she thought. She had a feeling they wouldn't want to take him on. They would pick someone they perceived as easy, weak. If they picked on anyone at all! 'That sergeant,' she said, frowning. 'Cindy Nightingale, the one who tried to put me in the frame for your father's killing.' Shannon couldn't bring herself to say *'murder'*. 'Is she still in the division?'

'Oh yeah.' It was Rob's turn to frown. 'Bitch got promoted to inspector.'

'I'm so happy for her. If she gets wind of this she might see it as the perfect excuse to start harassing me again. She hated me, Rob. I'm sure she's still got it in for me.'

'Hey, come on.' He reached across the table and squeezed her hand. Shannon flinched at his touch. His hand felt unpleasantly warm and moist. 'Don't worry about that cow, okay? There's no need. She got a stinger of a reprimand over the way she conducted the investigation into my father's murder, and she was warned to pull in her horns. Because I complained about her. I sorted it, Shannon.' He let go of her hand and picked up his cognac again.

Shannon was silent, sipping more coffee. Rob hadn't sorted anything. It was Finbar who had saved her, called in a favour owed to him by some high-ranking police officer. Rob had no reason to feel pleased with himself. She put the coffee cup down, wishing she could get hammered and blot everything out for a while. But how would that help? She didn't even have a couple of paracetamol for tomorrow morning's hangover. She glanced out of the restaurant window at the river, the lighted buildings across the water. She hadn't told Rob she was splitting with Finbar, moving out. His delight at that news, however much he might try to hide it, would be unbearable.

'Are you still living with . . . sorry, what's her name?' She looked at him again.

'Katy.' Rob's handsome face darkened. 'No.'

'Didn't work out then?' Pity, Shannon thought. If he could find someone he liked it might get him off my back.

'She went all moony and broody and domestic,' he said, tracing the curve of the cognac glass with one finger. 'I'm not ready for all that. Don't know if I ever will be.'

'I thought you liked domesticity. Roast dinners, apple pies, evenings in front of the telly.'

'Yeah.' His brown eyes were suddenly sharp again, focused. 'I did. With *you*.'

Oh, God. Shannon looked at her watch, started to frame excuses about how it was late and she was tired, had a heavy day tomorrow. Rob grasped her hand again, making her jump with fright.

'Sorry,' he said. 'Didn't mean to startle you. Listen – Shannon, please don't get mad at me for saying this. But I still love you. I think you know that. I don't want this bloody divorce! Given time – and a hell of a lot of talking, of course – is there absolutely no chance we could get back together some day?'

Shannon's heart sank, and she felt crushed with

disappointment and misery. Rob wasn't interested in helping her. He was only interested in himself, in trying to win her back. He just wanted to sit here, get pissed and talk mawkishly sentimental bullshit.

'No,' she said. 'There's no chance. I thought you knew that by now. I don't know how you can ask, how you can even think–' She broke off and stared over his right shoulder. There was some sort of commotion going on at the restaurant entrance. A scuffle, raised voices, people arguing.

'What is it?' Rob looked round. 'Oh, Christ!' he groaned. 'She must have followed me. Bloody bitch. I'll kill her for this.'

'Is that ... Katy?' Shannon stared at the distraught, dishevelled, fair-haired woman in the blue jeans and bright red jacket as she shoved her way past concerned waiters and headed for their table, attracting nervous looks from other diners.

'Wouldn't think of taking *me* to dinner in some posh restaurant, would you?' Katy glared at Rob as she banged her clenched fist on the white cloth, making glasses and cutlery jingle. 'Oh no. I'm not good enough, am I? That's only for the likes of Lady Shannon. You fucking bastard,' she spat.

Rob stood up, dropping his napkin. 'I don't know what you hope to achieve by this,' he said, his voice low and furious. 'But all you're doing is making me hate you more. I told you we were finished and I meant it. Now get out of here and leave me alone.'

'I'll go when I'm good and ready. I've been watching you eat your posh meal.' Katy's eyes were full of tears. 'Drinking wine. Talking, laughing. I saw you hold her hand. You're bloody pathetic, you know that, Rob? You're so sad. I feel sorry for you.'

'Stuff your sympathy. No one could be as sad as you.' Rob's eyes glittered with fury, but he kept control of himself. 'I *said*, get out of here.'

'Katy, why don't you sit down and have some coffee with

us?' Shannon interrupted, wondering what the hell all this was about. 'Or a drink. Rob and I just had some things to discuss. That's all, honestly. We're not–'

'*You* shut the fuck up!' Katy turned on her, her face contorted with rage. 'Don't come that we're-all-girls-together shit with me, you patronising cow. I wouldn't drink with you. Anyway, I'm pregnant,' she shouted. 'It's Rob's baby. Foetus, he called it.' She gave a twisted grin as Shannon gasped with shock. 'Didn't tell you that, did he? He's afraid it'll upset you.' She wiped her eyes on her sleeve and glared at Rob again. 'Doesn't give a bloody toss about upsetting *me*. Throwing me out, making me move back to a damp flat without heating. In my condition. I bet you don't live in a dump, do you, you scumsucking bitch lawyer?'

Shannon turned pale. 'What did you call me?' Police officer, she thought. Familiarity with Magistrates Court. Means, opportunity. And by the look of things, certainly a motive!

'Bitch lawyer!' Katy taunted. 'Bitch lawyer. Bit young to be going deaf, aren't you? Or are you just thick?' People were silent, staring, forks and spoons poised half way to open mouths. Getting their money's worth. The manager walked up to the table.

'Madam, would you please leave,' He said to Katy. 'If you don't I'll be forced to call the police.'

'Shut it, pretty boy.' Katy pulled out her warrant card and stuck it in his face. 'I *am* the police.' She turned back to Shannon. 'D'you know what that moron thinks?' she flashed, pointing at Rob. 'He thinks the baby you lost after your car crash was his. Not your Mick criminal boyfriend's.'

'What?' Shannon gasped.

Rob stepped forward and gave Katy a vicious shove. 'Shut it, you!'

'He thinks you and he would have got back together if it hadn't been for your miscarriage and the Mick criminal.' Katy laughed hysterically. 'He really believes it!'

Shannon got to her feet and grabbed her bag. Her legs felt weak and she was trembling all over. 'Finbar Linnell is my fiancé, actually,' she managed to say. 'And he's not a criminal.'

'Jesus! You must be the only person in Liverpool who believes that.'

'Don't you dare talk about Finbar! Or the baby we lost. It's none of your business.'

'Rob still loves you.' Katy was crying now, blubbering loudly. 'That's why he doesn't want me – doesn't want our baby. He told me to have a termination.'

Shannon looked at Rob. He wouldn't meet her gaze. 'You really believe the baby Finbar and I lost was yours?' she asked, her voice shaking. 'You're crazy!'

'He hates me,' Katy wailed, tears streaming down her face. 'He doesn't care. He hates our baby!' The waiters were standing around looking stunned, the manager talking urgently on the phone.

Finbar's words flashed into Shannon's mind: *'Rob's not the type to wear the old shining armour. Finds it a bit too bloody heavy.'* He's right, she thought. So right. She was filled with contempt as she looked at Rob.

'Now that you're going to be a father – for real, this time! – don't you think you'd better give some serious thought to growing up at last?' She turned to Katy. 'I'm sorry about the way he treated you, but I'm afraid letting people down is Rob's thing. It's why I'm divorcing him. If you love him, that's your problem. It doesn't give you the right to attack me. If those stupid letters don't stop, I'll give you more trouble to be going on with – pregnant or not!'

'What letters?' Katy gaped through her tears. Her face was red and wet, her eyelids swollen. 'What the hell are you on about?'

'You know what I'm on about. Right. I've warned you.' Shannon glanced at Rob again. 'Deal with it,' she snapped. 'For once in your life.' He stared at her, shocked. Stared at Katy.

'What letters?' Katy repeated, wiping more tears and snot on her sleeve. But Shannon couldn't talk any more. She had to get out of here, get away from these morons. Had Katy sent those letters? She seemed genuinely astonished; maybe it was just coincidence that she'd called her a bitch lawyer. Or the astonishment could be a front. Katy hated her. Why didn't she stick the blame where it lay, with her less than red-hot lover? All this was Rob's fault. Shannon couldn't wait for the divorce to come through so that she could be legally rid of him. How could he think the baby she and Finbar had lost was his? That they could get back together? His grasp of reality wasn't just tenuous. It was non-existent.

'Shannon, don't go!' he shouted. 'Please!'

She shook her head and held up one hand, signalling him not to follow. Walked out, hoping her legs wouldn't give way. She longed for Finbar. He loved her, he was strong, he would never let her down. How could she leave him? She loved him, she couldn't let go. They belonged together, despite everything. And how could Rob and that mad, screaming bitch in there have a baby – even if he didn't want it – when she and Finbar had lost theirs?

'It's not fair,' she muttered, her eyes filling with tears. 'It's not bloody fair!' Shannon got outside the restaurant, stopped in the cool darkness and burst into tears. She was so upset that she didn't notice the man approaching her.

'You all right, love?'

'What's it to you?' she sobbed, not caring if he was a mugger or rapist. If he touched her she would kill him. She was in the mood for violence. She noted his Irish accent; there was only one Irishman she wanted to talk to. 'Leave me alone.'

'Okay, love. Only trying to help.'

'I don't need your help.'

'Fair enough. You take care now.'

His mate joined him and they grinned at one another. They stood by a stone pillar and watched as Shannon stumbled away into the darkness.

Chapter Twenty-Four

'My brother committed suicide,' Lucas shouted in the girl's ear over the talk, laughter and stomp of feet on the club's upper floor. The thump of the dance music was like a heart beating too fast. 'Last November. He was fifteen.'

He hadn't meant to come out with it just like that, but it tended to happen after too many shots and shooters – Finnish vodka tonight, on special offer. Sooner or later, to somebody or other. Usually the wrong person, like now. He watched shock, embarrassment and that *oh-God-I-don't-want-to-get-into-this* look flit across the girl's face. She was pretty, cool, with long red hair and a skimpy, glittery blue top that showed her flat, smooth belly and pierced navel. She'd told him she was a second-year medical student. If so, this was just what she didn't need to hear after a hard day slicing up body parts. Or whatever medical students did. But Lucas couldn't help himself.

'I was angry at first,' he shouted. It was hot and crowded in here, and he was pouring sweat. 'Furious with him. I thought, how could he keep all that pain locked inside and not tell anyone? Not even me, his big brother? We did everything together. Dion always acted happy. Must have been a front.'

'That's terrible,' she shouted back. 'Tragic. A lot of young guys commit suicide.' She turned slightly, away from him, and Lucas caught sight of himself in a mirror behind the bar.

Bleached blond dreadlocks, mahogany skin. Black T-shirt. She said something else, pointed to a group of girls at the other end of the bar.

'What?' he shouted.

'I said, I have to get back to my friends now. We're going on to Cream.' She had a posh accent, came from Cheshire or somewhere out in woolly-back country. Lucas somehow didn't feel like telling her he came from Liverpool 8 and shared a flat off Upper Parliament Street with two mates. Plus a gang of ravenous rodents. He looked at his watch, trying to focus on the different dials.

'D'you think you'll get in there now? It's after two.'

'No problem,' she shouted back. 'Stays open 'til four.'

'Costs a fortune to get in, doesn't it? A tenner or more. Drinks aren't cheap either.' Lucas didn't know, it was only what he'd heard. He'd never been to Cream. It was one of the things he kept meaning to do. The usual story, having famous places on your doorstep that you never went to.

The girl shrugged, smiled and moved off, giving him a little wave. He watched her join her friends, glance back, shake her bright hair and laugh at their questions.

'Another one bites the dust,' he murmured, glaring at himself in the mirror. 'Nice one, Lucas, you fuck-up.' What was the matter with him, why did he have this irresistable desire to tell everyone he met about Dion? He downed another shot of Finnish vodka. Tasted foul, what you did taste of it, but you got a result. The result being that Lucas's head was swimming and he was afraid to move in case he fell over or crashed into someone. Or both. He couldn't see his mates anywhere. Sometimes they all got split up after they'd pulled and didn't meet again until the following morning over coffee, Danish pastries or doughnuts and newspapers.

He might not want to move, but he needed some air. And his stomach was starting to play up now. Lucas peered through the crowd, planning his way out, which tables and groups of laughing drinkers to avoid. A space suddenly cleared and he took his chance. He lifted his steadying hand off the wet, sticky bar and lunged forward. Lucas made it outside after charging into only one guy and causing him to spill half his pint. But the guy just laughed and accepted his apology, no worries. That was good. If someone got nasty he wasn't in a fit state to take them on.

He stood in Slater Street, breathing the cool night air. Thursday night – Friday morning, now – and it wasn't busy. It was better on Friday and Saturday nights. He glanced up at the CCTV camera on the corner with Bold Street, angled towards him, and gave it the middle finger. Lucas didn't like cameras. Not that he had anything to hide. He just resented the fact that he couldn't walk down a street without being spied on. He turned and headed down Slater Street, crossed Concert Square with its bars and clubs. There were young trees in the middle of the square, not yet in leaf, and the ground was littered with plastic beer glasses. He jumped on one and cracked it, laughing at the noise. Other people laughed with him. There was a good buzz, not nasty. On nasty nights Lucas always went home early because he got a bad feeling.

He reached the far end of the square, passed the Arena Bar and the Rat & Parrot, and hesitated outside the Aussie bar, wondering whether or not to have one last drink. He decided not. Which way to go now, where was the best place to grab a cab? Or should he walk home?

'Don't think so,' Lucas muttered. He swayed, stumbled slightly, shivered. Turned right and headed down a dark, narrow street of old warehouses, away from the crowds and cameras. This street was a bit creepy, but it was a shortcut. And he was too pissed to feel scared.

He missed Dion right now. It was as if Lucas could sense his young brother's presence, hear soft footfalls behind him in the darkness. Dion was here in spirit, watching him, following him on his night out. Dion would have liked that girl. Lucas's eyes filled with tears and he choked up. He stopped, fumbled in his jeans pocket for his wallet, opened it and pulled out the tiny photo of Dion that he always carried. He had moved out of his parents' house as soon as he got the job with the computer firm, because his Mum and Dad insisted on keeping Dion's room exactly the way it had been before his death. Lucas couldn't stand seeing it like that day after day, everything looking normal as though Dion had just gone out for a while, maybe down to the kitchen to get himself a snack. It ripped his heart out. He took the photo carefully between thumb and forefinger and held it up. But it was too dark to see his brother's face.

'Why'd you do it, man?' he whispered. It was a question he'd asked loads of times and would keep on asking, even though he would never get an answer now. 'Why didn't you come to me? I would have helped you. You know it.'

Lucas didn't hear the footstep and intake of breath, didn't see who or what smashed him over the back of the head then across his right temple. He collapsed, crumpled, cracked his head on the edge of the pavement as he went down. Dion's photo fluttered and whirled in the air for a second then descended, landing softly beside his brother's outstretched hand.

'Who are you?' Lucas whispered to the dark shape above him, seconds before he died. 'Why?'

'What can I do for you?' Finbar sat up in bed and pointed the remote to switch off the television as Shannon knocked and walked into the dimly lit bedroom. 'Did you have a good night?'

He thought not, judging by the state of her. Shannon looked upset, like she had been crying. Her eyes glittered. Her curly blonde hair was wild and her mascara slightly smudged, red lipstick licked off except for the outline. Her dishevelled look made him want her more. She held a glass of white wine.

'No, I had a terrible night. I...' Shannon hesitated. 'Are you okay?' she asked, an anxious look in her eyes. 'Where did you get to all afternoon – and evening?'

'Had a few people to see.' He shrugged. 'Business, that's all.'

211

'Oh. But–'

'But what?'

'You never do that. Just go off, I mean. I was worried,' she confessed, brushing away a tear. 'Paula said–'

'I know. I phoned her. It's sorted.' Finbar paused. 'So tell me about your night. Apart from the fact that it was terrible.'

'I agreed to meet Rob.' Shannon took a gulp of wine. 'For dinner. I thought he might be able to help me find out who's writing those letters, but all he wants to do is bullshit me. It was a complete waste of time. His girlfriend – ex, now – burst into the restaurant and made a scene. She's pregnant, apparently. Rob doesn't want to know – he told her to have a termination.' Shannon bit her lip and raked one hand through her curls. 'He thinks the baby we lost was *his*,' she said, her voice rising. 'I mean, can you believe that!'

Finbar willed himself to stay calm, controlled. 'I can believe anything about that fucked-up bastard.' He noticed Shannon was wearing his engagement ring again. She took a step forward.

'She – Katy, his ex, I mean – called me a bitch lawyer. Just like in those letters. I got a hell of a shock.'

He flinched, sat up straighter. 'You think she wrote them?'

'I'm not sure. She hates me enough. She's crazy with jealousy, even though she's got zero reason to be jealous. That's Rob's fault. It could have been coincidence, what she called me – when I challenged her she looked like she really didn't know what I was talking about. She could be lying, of course, trying to front it out. I told her if she wanted trouble she could have it.'

Maybe he'd had a chat with the wrong person. Finbar lay back in bed and took a deep breath. Forced himself to ask the question. 'So, have you found anywhere?'

'What?'

'Another place to live.'

'Well, I–' Shannon looked surprised, hurt '–I did look at a place after work,' she admitted. 'An apartment. Not far from here, actually.' She took a sip of wine. 'I can move in within

212

the next couple of days. Thing is ... I don't want to now.'
Her voice trembled. 'Finbar, I don't want to leave you. I
thought it was the right thing to do.' She smiled, her eyes
wet. 'It probably is! But it's no use. I just can't do it. I love
you too much.'

So she still wanted him, despite bloody Declan Dowd.
Despite everything. Finbar was silent, gazing into her
beautiful eyes that shone with wine and tears. He didn't feel
any joy. He just felt sick, despairing. Why did everything
come too bloody late?

If he didn't kill her love for him, Shannon might die. How
could he kill her love? He had to open a wound, make it deep
and bloody. In time it would close, heal over and form scar
tissue. The pain would go, making it numb, impenetrable.
He hated himself, but he'd just have to live with that. He
stretched out one hand.

'The glass.'

Shannon stepped forward and gave it to him, stood there
uncertainly. Finbar put the glass on the beside table and
leaned back against the pillows. Looked into her eyes again.

'Take your clothes off,' he said. 'Slowly.'

'I love you,' she whispered, blushing.

'Don't talk,' he said, fighting the anguish that gripped
him. 'Don't say anything. Just do it.' He watched as she
unzipped the black dress, pulled it down and stepped out of
it. She took off her bra, revealing her gorgeous breasts, and
dropped it on the floor. He stared at her hardened nipples.
She slipped off her pants. Her stockings and high-heeled
pumps came last. She stood naked in front of him. Finbar
gazed at her beautiful face and body, drinking her in, devour-
ing her. There was a tiny throb of pulse in her neck. Their
eyes locked.

'Come here.' He could hardly get the words out. Shannon
came forward and knelt on the bed, put her arms around him
and hugged him tight. He kissed her, hungrily and desperately, his hands stroking her breasts, sliding over her smooth,
curvy body, pushing her thighs apart. 'D'you want me?' he

whispered, easing her down. He kissed her breasts, flicked his tongue over her nipples.

'Yes,' she moaned, clinging to him. 'I always want you.'

'D'you love me?' He spread her legs wider, slid one and then two fingers inside her, stroking gently.

'Yes, I love you. You know I do! I want you,' she gasped.

He slid between her legs, one hand on her flat stomach. She was warm and wet, wild for him. He felt as if he would go crazy. Shannon gasped and cried out, brought up her legs, shuddered and arched her back as the orgasm coursed through her. He loved the way she came.

Finbar couldn't wait any longer. She cried out again as he entered her, her hands stroking his shoulders, back and buttocks. He kissed her as he moved inside her, pushing deep, her hair entwined around his fingers. He breathed in her perfume, the warm scent of her body. He wanted to taste the essence of her soul and being, store it all up. Shannon slipped her arms around his neck, her violet eyes half closed, her hips moving to meet his thrusts. He felt her shudder again, writhe beneath him. She screamed as she started to come again. Finbar's heart was hammering, his body slippery with sweat. He let go, gave a choked cry as incredible sensation overwhelmed him.

They lay still, wrapped in each other's arms, breath and heartbeat slowing. The scent of Shannon's body, her perfume, seemed stronger. It filled his head. Finbar leaned on one elbow and caressed her, stroking her breasts, kissing her belly, feeling the curve of her waist. Her honey skin glowed in the lamplight. Shannon smiled up at him, started to say something.

He cut her off with another kiss, long and deep and searching. Then he stroked her hair, her face, touched one finger to her lips. Gazed into her eyes and spoke the words. Gently, softly. But distinctly, so that Shannon would hear. So that she would not misunderstand.

'Now get out.'

PART THREE

Chapter Twenty-Five

I did it. I killed someone.

Christ, I was so angry! I couldn't have done it otherwise. But I don't want to write about the anger, about what caused it. Don't even want to think about that. My mind's full of little compartments that need to be kept shut. That's the only way I can deal with the life I'm condemned to lead.

So now I know what it's like. How it feels. And it's all bad news. Worse than I expected. It makes me feel evil, sick to my heart and stomach. Anguished, rotten with guilt that I don't believe will ever disappear. I wish to God now I hadn't done it, that I could go back in time and make it not happen, take a different path. But it's too late. I'm crying as I write this.

The terrible thing is, it was so easy. That's what gets to me more than anything. I didn't realise you could snuff out a human life like that. I thought it would take more effort, more strength. Unbelievable the way he went down, just crumpled. He looked so helpless lying there in the gutter. I'd followed him from that club. Just as I was about to hit him, he suddenly stopped. I heard him ask, 'Why'd you do it?' Like he'd sensed my presence, guessed what was going to happen. I panicked then. Bashed him over the head. I could just as easily have run away. Why didn't I?

I was sick with horror the second I'd done it. I wanted to stay with him, comfort him, call an ambulance, tell him I was sorry and hadn't meant to hurt him. That I was just a stupid, crazy, fuck-up. I was desperate to save him. But it was too late. He died in my arms.

Now I understand why three-quarters of murderers and violent criminals suffer from depression. Why suicide so often follows homicide. Murder is like a stain on your soul, sticky and oily, pollution that can't be washed away. I know this is forever. When I was a kid in school and the teachers talked about religion – only the Christian religion in those days, of course – I used to imagine the soul as a tiny ball of brilliant white light inside your head, your sins sticky black dots on it. You'd go to confession and your soul would be clean and new again. Until you committed another sin. I'll never be clean and new again. This is mortal sin, the kind that can never be cleansed. Some things can't be forgiven.

I feel like the Devil's got my soul now. I know old Lucifer ('lucifers' means matches in Dutch, by the way) is supposed to be a Judeo-Christian concept, a vast oversimplification dreamed up by some smart arse in the early, fundamentalist church of fire and sword to terrify and oppress the credulous masses. Projection – it wasn't me, it was the Devil dunnit! But he feels real enough to me.

I wonder if Shannon felt the way I do now? I don't think so. We're different people. I've got morals, a conscience. Besides, she distanced herself from the headmaster's murder, got someone else to do her dirty work. She didn't experience it first hand, suffer the pain and trauma that I'm going through. And the headmaster was a total bastard, no redeeming qualities. So why feel guilty anyway? Shannon probably regards herself as a Jeanne d'Arc figure who, unlike poor Jeanne, managed to escape her masculist punishers and mediaeval barbecue. Wrong, Shannon. There's still time for you to be tied to the stake and smell your own burning flesh, feel the agony and terror as you pray to He Who Never Fucking Listens.

Why didn't I pick someone guilty, like I meant to? I thought the lad was guilty at first, when I saw him lurching out of that club. I thought, yeah, here we go, another pisshead scroat out looking for trouble. An anti-social little bastard who should have been strangled at birth, not even quietly useless, but a nuisance to everyone who comes in contact with him. I'm saving valuable space in the Bridewell, doing the system and society a favour. But once I'd hit him, when I saw him lying there ... oh, Christ! He's somebody's son, somebody's brother. Father, for all I know. I can't bear this agony.

This is Shannon's fault. I'd never even have contemplated this if it hadn't been for her arrogance and stubbornness. It makes me hate her more. Why should I suffer like this? It's not fair.

When she finds out about the – I have to call it murder – she'll know this boy died purely because of her, because she won't do what I want. She has to start suffering at last, feel what I'm going through. Maybe that will make her confess to her crimes. She has to understand what I'm trying to tell her, accept the fate she's so far managed to push away. Then and only then, will there be some point to this.

I've got to know that boy didn't die in vain. In a way, I suppose I've saved him a lot of suffering, the kind all human beings go through sooner or later. He's in a better place.

No use. I can rationalise as much as I like. It doesn't help. Doesn't alter the fact that I've murdered an innocent kid on his way home from a night out. He wasn't doing anybody any harm. I get up and pace around in between writing sentences. Good job I'm alone. I look ill, crazy. Like I've lost my mind. It feels as if I have. I need another drink. Then a good sleep, deep and peaceful. No nightmares. Just crashed-out oblivion.

When will they find his body?

What will happen next?

Chapter Twenty-Six

'Pascale had changed the locks when I got back, dumped my stuff outside in bloody binliners. Like it was a load of old crap.' Demetrio folded his arms and looked indignantly at the two detectives seated across the interview room table. 'Threw me out, she did. Wasn't bothered about where I was supposed to go at that time of night.' He shrugged. 'Haven't seen her since. Wouldn't bloody want to after that.'

If it hadn't been for the sodding bail conditions – and that bossy, interfering bitch Janie throwing her accusations around – these dickheads would never have pulled him in for questioning. They had no evidence, nothing but the word of that fat, four-eyed *kankerhoer*. He felt furious. Lucky they hadn't searched his flat and found the little stash of cocaine and party pills. Thick of him to keep it there. He'd have to find another hiding place – Pickhead's flat, maybe. Let that scabby little lame brain take the rap if it was discovered. At first Demetrio had been terrified that they were going to ask him about Keely, but they hadn't mentioned her. They only seemed interested in Pascale. And that was more than enough.

'You turned Ms Stevens' house into a fortress, so that you could keep your illegal arms cache safe,' the younger, smart-arse detective said.

'It wasn't illegal.' Demetrio thumped his fist on the table. 'I've got the paperwork.'

'Yeah, right. 'Course you have. Ms Stevens' close friend, Mrs Janie Ball, says you knocked Pascale about. Broke her nose on the last occasion.'

'She'd say any shit about me. She hates my guts. Me and Pascale had our ups and downs, but–'

'You mean like when you broke her nose?' the older, grey-haired man with the nicotine moustache butted in.

'I never broke her sodding nose!' Demetrio flinched. 'I never touched her. That was an accident, it was her own fault. She'd been on the sauce one night, had a few too many. Came downstairs to get a drink of water and–'

'Let me take a wild guess. She walked into a door?'

'That's right!'

'Must have been some door. And she must have run into it, not walked.'

'Whatever.' They might wind him up, but they couldn't prove anything. He had to stay cool. Pascale couldn't tell anyone what had happened because she was dead. Not just dead either – shredded, crushed, fragmented! Demetrio sat up straight and shoved his sweaty hands into the pockets of his leather coat. 'Look mate – if the soft cow suddenly decides to frig off in the middle of the bloody night, what's that got to do with me?'

'You tell us,' the older one said, glaring at him.

'Mrs Ball and Ms Stevens' brother are very concerned,' the younger one resumed. 'They said there's no way she'd pack a suitcase, leave home late at night and go off without telling anybody. Not let them know her whereabouts even after a week. Mrs Ball says she spoke to Ms Stevens shortly before she disappeared.' He paused, his eyes on Demetrio. 'She says Ms Stevens was terrified of you, that that's why she didn't break up with you sooner. She was terrified you'd kill her.'

'Crap!' Demetrio snorted, getting more twitchy. 'I already told you, I never hit Pascale. I don't hit birds. She had no reason to be scared of me.' The fact that he hadn't meant to kill Pascale increased his rage. 'We had a few rows, but that's normal, isn't it?' They didn't answer. 'She was pissed off about me being in the shit with you lot. Typical bloody stupid woman, stressing about sod all.'

The two men exchanged glances. 'I wouldn't call a charge of possessing illegal firearms *sod all*,' the younger one remarked.

Demetrio ignored that. 'I thought me and Pascale could work things out, but no. And I told you, she changed the locks. I couldn't get back in the house. That bitch–'

'Who exactly would you be referring to here?'

'Mrs bloody Ball! She came round just as I was leaving, watched me walk down the road. She knew I couldn't get in, she even shouted that at me. It's thanks to her that Pascale threw me out. She poisoned Pascale's mind against me, she was always stirring it. Made up, she was, when she got what she wanted. Told me to fuck off.'

'You could have gone back to the house later.'

'Well, I didn't. Even if I had, how was I supposed to get in?'

'Mrs Ball thinks you hurt Ms Stevens. That you could have murdered her.'

'*Eh?* I haven't murdered anyone, mate! No way.' Demetrio shook his head and tried to smile. He'd love to murder Janie bloody Ball right now. 'Pascale didn't want me any more, did she?' He threw up his hands. 'Fine. Finito. I'm not some sad bastard who chases women who don't want me. I don't need to beg. I've got better things to do with my time.'

'Yeah.' The older detective nodded and exchanged another glance with his colleague. 'I'm sure you have.'

Demetrio looked around the small room with its blue walls. Blue was supposed to be a calming colour. They had even put a plant on the windowsill. Britain was getting like the Netherlands, plants everywhere. 'Don't I get a cup of coffee?' he asked, drumming his fingers on the table. 'I fancy a couple of chocolate biscuits too. Missed breakfast this morning. The Human Rights Act says you're supposed to keep the accused fed and watered. Especially when you've got sod all against them.'

The older guy looked pissed off. 'Know all about *your* human rights, don't you?'

Shannon Flinder certainly did. Demetrio frowned. He had to get hold of her. She hadn't been available when he'd phoned earlier, only that little wanker, whatsisname? Leon. And some other woman named Khalida. He didn't want either of them. What was Shannon doing that was so bloody important?

'Try my solicitor again,' he ordered. 'I'm not answering any more questions until I get her down here.'

'Never mind solicitors and chocolate biscuits,' the younger one said. 'You're not in any position to chuck your weight around. You're in enough trouble as it is. You're lucky to be still on the street.'

Demetrio appreciated that, although he didn't appreciate this patronising bastard telling him how lucky he was. This was all a bloody great bore, another pain he didn't need. And suppose Haytham or one of his mates was keeping an eye on him? If they saw him going in and out of a police station accompanied by detectives they might get some very worrying ideas. They already had doubts about his reliability. He was also worried about Phelim. Phelim was scared, getting stupid. Suppose he lost it and dropped himself in it somehow, ended up spilling all about Keely Breeze? Maybe he should let him do Shannon Flinder, like he wanted. But that would be a terrible waste. Besides, who was to say he wouldn't fuck that up too?

'We could charge you with murder.'

Jesus! 'Scuse me, mate.' Demetrio tried to smile again but it was more a stretching of lips and baring of teeth, like an aggressive chimp. 'I'm not a lawyer, so I don't know about these things. But if you want to charge someone with murder, don't you need ... like, er ... a dead body first?'

Finbar walked into the sunlit sitting room of his apartment and dumped the briefcase containing the fifty grand on the coffee table. He did not take off his coat because he had to go out again soon. He checked his watch, sank on to one of the sofas, leaned back and closed his eyes. Allowed the full force of his sorrow and anguish to sweep over him. His exhaled breath came out as a groan.

It was hard to believe he'd done the right thing. It didn't feel right. It just felt callous, sadistic, heartbreaking. He would remember each day until he died – and there might not be many days left – the sight of Shannon lying naked with her arms and legs wrapped around him, the feel of her warm body against his. Her perfume, his fingers entangled in her hair. The love and desire in her eyes turning to shock, dismay and finally incredible hurt when he spoke those cruel words: *'Now get out.'*

She had stared up at him, stunned. Gave a little gasp. He'd had to repeat the words. She broke down then. Pleaded with him, sobbed that she couldn't let him go, couldn't live without him. Told him she loved him, thought he loved her, that she couldn't believe this, didn't understand. Asked how he could cause her such pain, dump her in such a cruel, humiliating way? *Why?*

'You were going to dump me,' he replied. 'You've fucked me around long enough. I've had it with you, I want to make a fresh start. It's over, Shannon. Sorry to do it like this. I'm not proud of myself.' That part was true. 'But I had to show you I mean what I say.'

'Well, congratulations! You've done it.' She scrambled off the bed and stood there naked and crying, hugging herself. Stared at him, still disbelieving despite her words. He couldn't stand the terrible, wounded look in her eyes. He watched the tears roll. She swiped them away.

'You bastard,' she whispered. 'You fucking, *fucking* bastard!' She turned and walked out then, shut the door very quietly. He looked at the teardrop stain on his pillow, touched it with one finger. Knew that he couldn't feel any worse than he did at this moment.

He switched off the lamp and lay in the dark, watching

wave patterns from the river ripple across the pale ceiling. Knew how shocked and devastated Shannon must feel now. He longed to get up and run to her, pull her into his arms and tell her he didn't mean it, of course he bloody loved her, he couldn't let her go either. Finbar forced himself not to do that. He didn't know how.

Some time later he thought he heard the slight drag of a suitcase or heavy bag on the hall floor, then the click of the front door as it closed. He got up and rushed to her room, found it empty. Started to panic. He hadn't expected Shannon to leave now, for Christ's sake, not in the middle of the bloody night. It wasn't safe. And where the hell would she go? But by the time he'd pulled on a robe, located his keys, grabbed them and run out it was too late. He got down to the lobby in time to see the glowing red tail lights of a cab disappearing into the darkness. He dashed back up to the apartment and dialled her mobile. The phone was switched off.

Shannon hadn't taken all her stuff, there was too much. She'd left some clothes in the wardrobe, and her laptop in the small room she used as an office. Books, files, papers. She had to come back for those. It was stupid, pointless, dangerous even, but he needed to see her one more time. To make sure of . . . what? That his cruel act had succeeded, that she really did hate him now?

Finbar swallowed hard, opened his eyes and looked around the big, silent room. The pain of missing her, of knowing he'd never get her back, was even worse than he had imagined. He got up and paced around, walked into Shannon's room, stopped and sniffed the air. Her perfume, the scent of her body, lingered. The pain was too bad, he couldn't stand it. But he had to. Finbar suddenly noticed that the wardrobe doors were open and the rest of her clothes gone. He turned and strode into the little office room. The laptop, books and papers were gone too. She must have come back here to collect the rest of her stuff while he was at the bank getting all that shit about the fifty grand sorted. Maybe someone had helped her.

The bathroom looked bare without her shower gel, perfume, shampoo, bath oil and little pots of skin cream. The dress, panties and stockings she had stripped off last night had been swept from his bedroom floor. Finbar spotted something just under the bed, and bent to pick it up. It was one of her shoes, a black leather pump with a high heel. Cinderella must have been in a hurry. He sat on the bed and held the shoe in his hands, sniffing it like a fetishist. He relived Shannon's striptease act of last night, the look of her naked body and feel of her skin. Her hands sliding over his back and buttocks, clinging to him, her gasps and cries of passion. The look on her face when she came.

Holding the shoe, he got up and went into the kitchen. He knew what he would find here. Yes. The bunch of spare keys lay on the table, her discarded diamond engagement ring next to it. The diamond glittered in the sunshine, throwing out little rays of coloured light. There was a note, scribbled in pencil. He picked it up.

I'll let people know my new address a.s.a.p, but if any post does still come for me, could you send it on to the KFN office, c/o me? Thank you. Shannon.

Care of me. Finbar folded the note very gently and slipped it into his wallet. His mobile rang, breaking the silence.

'Got the money?' Iain Blick asked.

Murderous rage gripped him. He took a couple of seconds to answer. 'Yes.'

'Excellent.' Blick sounded very happy. 'Okay, we'll meet now. Then I'll tell you how you can help us further.'

'Look forward to it,' Finbar said. 'In fact, I can hardly fucking wait.'

'And don't worry too much about Ms Flinder.' The smile disappeared from Blick's voice. 'She'll be fine. So will you. As long as you don't do anything unclever.'

'I'm more worried about myself,' Finbar replied. 'Ms Flinder doesn't live here any more.'

'So you're having a living-apart-together thing? Good idea. Keep it spicy.'

'More like a living-apart-apart thing. I told you, we're finished. I dumped her.'

'Hmm. Did you really? Methinks you protest too much. Remember – don't do anything unclever. That is, apart from trying to get me to believe that you and the lovely Shannon are no longer an item.'

Finbar hung up swearing and dialled the number Carl Mactire had given him. He was about to do something highly unclever.

'But what *happened*?' Nick Forth repeated, his brown eyes mystified. 'Finbar must have said or done something to make you flee in the middle of the night!'

'Please, Nick. I can't talk about it,' Shannon whispered, white-faced. She collapsed into her chair and leaned back, her eyes closed. 'Not even if you've got ten boxes of extra-strength, man-size tissues handy.' Her head throbbed so much she could barely speak without feeling she had to throw up.

'Shannon, for goodness sake, you're ill!' Mi-Hae, Khalida and Nick exchanged more worried glances. 'Nick just helped you move the rest of your stuff and put it in your new apartment. I don't know why you came to the office afterwards. Nick will drive you back to my house, and I want you to go straight to bed,' Mi-Hae said firmly. 'Don't get up until that headache's gone. And I want you to stay with me for at least the rest of this week. Go to your new place and unpack a few things when you feel better. But don't move in yet.'

'Shannon could also stay with me,' Nick offered. He grimaced at her. 'I promise not to quiz you about Finbar.' What the hell had happened, he wondered again? What had that bastard done? And why hadn't Shannon come to him instead of Mi-Hae Kam?

'Nick, I don't want to intrude on you and Caroline and the baby,' Shannon whispered, giving him his answer.

227

'Don't be ridiculous. You won't be.' Nick wouldn't tell her in front of the others that Caroline had taken their daughter and moved in with her parents while she looked for somewhere else to live. 'We're old friends. You shouldn't be alone now.'

'Well, don't let's argue about it while she's feeling like death warmed up. Yes?' Mi-Hae snapped as Helena barged in without knocking. 'Can we help you?'

Helena looked offended. She held up two pink post-it notes. 'Couple of urgent messages for Shannon,' she said. 'Demetrio Montana wants her to call him, he wants her to go to—'

'Shannon is ill. She's not going anywhere except bed.'

'Yes, but he—'

'You can go,' Mi-Hae said. 'Thank you. We'll sort something for Mr Montana.'

Helena flounced out, banging the door shut. Shannon gasped and winced. Dark-haired, dark-eyed Khalida laid one hand on her shoulder. 'I'll do your Duty Solicitor stint this weekend,' she said. 'No arguments, okay?'

Shannon felt too sick to argue. 'I'm being a bloody nuisance to everyone.' She fought back the tears. If she started crying again she might never stop. And her head hurt too much.

'Nick, could you drive Shannon back to my house now?' Mi-Hae asked. 'She needs rest. She can decide what she wants to do when she's feeling better.'

'Yep.' Nick nodded and cleared his throat. 'Sure.' He loosened his tie and pulled the car keys out of his coat pocket. He just didn't get it. Finbar had been crazy about Shannon since the day they had met. She loved him too. Nick had envied the magic, the chemistry between them, something that was long gone between him and Caroline, had never really been there in the first place if he was honest. Let it go for now, Nick told himself, looking at Shannon's pale, strained face. She'll tell you when she's ready. Shannon got slowly to her feet. He picked up her briefcase and Khalida draped her leather jacket around her shoulders.

'Did you take anything for the headache?' Mi-Hae asked. 'I've got some–'

Shannon gagged and clapped one hand to her mouth as she felt a rush of saliva. They looked startled, parted quickly to let her through. She dashed out of her office and up the stairs, her head pounding harder with the sudden movement. In the cold, blue-tiled toilet she vomited up grief, shock and hurt, holding her hair out of the way. Afterwards she rinsed her mouth, washed her hands and looked at her ashen face and reddened, streaming eyes in the mirror.

'Death warmed up,' she whispered. 'That's you all right, girlfriend!'

The big question surfaced again: *Why?* Finbar had seemed desperate for her not to leave him. Now he had dumped her. Not only that, but done it in just about the most cruel way imaginable. She couldn't believe he meant what he'd said, that they really were finished. Shannon had had her doubts about their relationship – big time! – but she had never stopped loving him. Trouble was, now she didn't think she ever would. She was alone, devastated. Finbar didn't love her – couldn't, after what he'd done last night. He didn't want her any more. She still felt completely bewildered.

Her mobile rang and she groaned, dragged it out of her pocket without bothering to check who was calling. She had a wild hope that it just might be Finbar. Maybe he could give her an explanation, if nothing else.

'Shannon, it's Rob. Listen, I'm really sorry about last night!'

For a second she wondered what he was on about. Rob couldn't know Finbar had dumped her! Then she remembered Katy and the ugly scene in the restaurant. It seemed like nothing now. She had run away to a much more ugly one.

'I don't want to talk to you, you stupid... Leave me alone.'

'Shannon, wait! Please listen. I've got something important to tell you.'

'Oh, yeah, and what might that be? Did you suddenly grow up or something?' She shivered, felt freezing cold. She needed a bed and a hot water bottle, felt desperate to lie down and rest her throbbing head. 'You do realise,' she said, wanting to make him feel as bad as she did, 'that if the baby *had* been yours I would have had a termination?'

Rob gasped with hurt. 'You don't mean that.'

'I bloody do mean it. Even a moron like you can't possibly imagine I'd want to bear the child of a man who raped me. And don't tell me you were drunk and didn't mean it! I don't know why I still speak to you. I only had dinner with you last night because I thought you might help me, but all you did was talk bullshit. That baby was Finbar's and mine,' Shannon said, starting to cry. 'I love Finbar!'

'Yeah, well.' Rob's voice hardened. 'Great. I hope you'll be very happy together. And I know you don't want to hear this, but actually I *didn't* bloody mean it. I was drunk, out of my head, freaked about my father. I lost it for a while. You know that.'

'Stop making excuses!'

'I'm not. Look,' he said. 'I just phoned to warn you about something. Although I don't know why I should bother now. It's bad news for you. I wanted you to hear it from me first.'

'How thoughtful.' Shannon wiped her eyes. 'Warn me about *what*?' Nothing could be bad news, compared with what Finbar had done to her.

'There's been a murder. Last night in clubland. Near Slater Street. A young lad got his skull cracked. His name's Lucas Grant. D'you know him?'

'No, of course I don't. Why should I? He isn't a client. I've never heard of him.'

Khalida knocked at the door. 'Shannon, are you okay?'

'There was a note on the body,' Rob said. 'In his jeans pocket.'

'A note?' Shannon was puzzled, irritated, the pain in her

230

head making her feel sick again. She had to lie down. 'So why's that bad news for me?' Khalida rapped on the door again but she took no notice. 'What does it say?'

'Just one line.' Rob paused. 'It says, *"Ask Shannon Flinder"*.'

Chapter Twenty-Seven

'It's ordinary people I hate and despise.'

Iain Blick sipped his coffee, the open briefcase with its stacks of notes beside him on the sofa. Finbar hated the proprietary way he ran his hand over the money from time to time. Blick wore a pinstripe suit today, looking like the young fogey Intelligence Officer he had once been.

'Your so-called Joe Average, innocent citizen,' he went on. 'They're thick, their heads are full of shit. They don't give a toss about anything unless it affects them.' His voice hardened. 'They won't walk or drive five minutes to the nearest polling station to vote in an election, but they'll turn out in their thousands to gawp at some horse-faced minor royal or a sad little runt who's supposed to be the next big thing in pop.' He put down his coffee cup. 'Politicians, big business, the multi-nationals, you name it, couldn't go on destroying the planet if it wasn't for Mr and Ms Average letting them get away with their criminal behaviour because they don't give a fuck.' He paused. 'They need a wake-up call.'

'And of course you're the one to give it to them.' Finbar stared at his money.

The highly unclever thing he had done was to take the briefcase to Carl Mactire and his men and let them bug it. The bug was tiny, looked like a screw inserted into the briefcase handle. It had a range of several miles and its battery would last about three weeks. Finbar wondered if he would still be alive in three weeks time. He wouldn't make it to this evening if Blick discovered the bug.

'Don't get sarcastic with me, Finbar.' Blick stood up, clenching his hands. 'You're always doing that. I don't like your tone.'

He seemed different today, Finbar thought, not so calm and controlled. Well, the guy was unstable, it came with the territory. He glanced around in surprise as a woman's cry came from behind the closed bedroom door.

'The troops are getting some R & R,' Blick explained. He relaxed and sat down again, smiled at Finbar's expression. 'It's all right, don't worry. She does it for a living. Not like Ms Flinder, who wouldn't cope quite so well with the experience.'

'Can we get back to the main subject?' Finbar asked, trying not to imagine Shannon in their hands.

'Ah, yes. Your next task.' Blick leaned forward, clasping his hands. 'Explosives. As I told you, we lost that contact we had. So we'll need you to find us a large quantity of semtex.'

Christ! 'How large? Enough to blow up what?'

'There you go again, asking questions.'

'It's a reasonable one under the circumstances, wouldn't you say?'

'Not necessarily. If we hadn't already searched you, just as a precaution, I might think you were all wired up and trying to get me to say something highly incriminating.'

All wired up. How quaint. Finbar felt slightly relieved. Mactire had said Blick wasn't a techie and it looked like he was telling the truth.

'If you want me to get enough semtex for you to blow up something, how the hell am I supposed to know what quantity to get if I don't know the intended target?'

'Why don't I give you an indication of the quantity of casualties instead?' Iain Blick smiled, his eyes shining. 'Terrorists – or at least that's how your average brain-dead citizen would describe us – like to think big these days, don't they? So.' He lowered his voice. 'We're talking lots of souls. In the thousands.'

Finbar went cold. 'What is it, a building?'

Blick's smile broadened. 'Most people spend most of their time in buildings, don't they? So, yes. Of course it's a bloody building. Several under one roof, to be precise.'

Some kind of complex? Finbar tried to think. He ran his tongue over his dry lips. 'Where?'

'Not in Liverpool. We came here to stay out of the way. It's a good base. You like this city too, don't you?'

If not Liverpool, where? Somewhere else in the north-west? London? Or was Blick lying about the target not being in Liverpool? The woman's cries were louder now. 'What *are* they doing to the poor girl?' Blick glanced at the closed door and raised his eyebrows. 'She's certainly earning her money today.' He looked back at Finbar. 'D'you think the lovely Ms Flinder would have rampant sex with several different men at once for money? I mean, she is a lawyer after all. They're just another variety of prostitute, aren't they?'

I'll have you, Finbar vowed. If it's the last thing I do. Maybe it would be.

'Another sub-species I hate,' Blick went on, 'is shop-keepers. My grandfather said Napoleon was right when he called the British a nation of shopkeepers. They rip you off all the time and put their prices up the minute a war or some other crisis starts.' He frowned. 'Scumsucking bastards, they are. Same as lawyers'.

Was there anything or anyone this guy actually liked? Apart from himself and the sound of his own voice. And other people's money, of course. Finbar glanced round again as an agonised scream came from the adjoining room, followed by male laughter. Blick got up and rapped on the door.

'Keep the noise down! That's enough for now.' He came back and sat on the sofa. 'We can't stay here any longer,' he said. 'Not even now that we've received your kind donation. It's too expensive and there's not enough privacy.' He

234

laughed. 'If Ms Flinder really has moved out – for now – you must be lonely. Fancy some company?'

Finbar shook his head. 'Forget about it.'

'Yes, well, it was just an idea. We'll find somewhere today or tomorrow. A flat in a suburb. Somewhere quiet and–'

He broke off as the bedroom door opened and a dishevelled, auburn-haired, twenty-something girl staggered out, trying to pull on a sheepskin coat and fasten the zip of her mini skirt. Her legs above knee-length black boots were bare.

'Fucking perverts!' she shouted. 'I told you I don't do *that*. You bloody hurt me.' Her face was wet with tears, the makeup destroyed. 'You're worse than fucking animals.'

'You'd know all about animals, wouldn't you?' Blick looked at her with contempt. 'You've been paid,' he said. 'More than enough. Now get out.'

Finbar flinched at those words. 'So, are you going to tell me?' he asked as the prostitute ran sobbing out of the suite. 'Where and when?'

'Have you seen those old war films about Bomber Command? *The Dambusters*, for instance. They never told crews their targets until the night of the raid.'

'No, but they were told the appropriate flying techniques to practice.'

Finbar prayed that Blick wouldn't find the briefcase bug. It made him frantic to think his life and Shannon's depended on those pricks from Special Branch not screwing up. He – or they – had to find out the target as soon as possible.

'Fair enough.' Blick smiled his sunny smile again. 'All right, I'll give you a clue. More of a teaser, really. What do all these stupid, boring, ordinary people who don't give a fuck about anything or anyone but themselves enjoy doing most?' He paused. 'And I'm not talking about sex. They don't do nearly as much of *that* as they like to pretend.'

Drinking? Finbar thought. A bomb in a pub, in a street full of bars and pubs? No, that wouldn't kill thousands of people. Hundreds, possibly. Sex and drinking, sex and … He thought of the fiction genre of the 1980s and early 1990s, the kind of novels Shannon said should have been banned, along with anything written by Barbara Cartland, and all those children's fairy tales about powerless, passive virgins who had to be rescued by handsome princes. But what had people called those novels? Sex and ... what? Blick hated shop-keepers.

'Shopping,' he murmured. He sat up. *'Shopping.* A town – city centre?'

Blick was enjoying himself. 'People seem to prefer to go out of town these days, don't they? Despite efforts to keep them spending their money in high streets.'

Thousands of people – parents, children, teenagers, the middle-aged, senior citizens – concentrated in one place. Wandering around, unaware of anything except the con-sumer goods they wanted to spend their money on. Thinking – if they thought about it at all – that they were safe because they weren't at an airport, on an aircraft, or in a town or city centre.

'A shopping mall!' Finbar breathed. 'One of those out-of-town complexes.' Jesus Christ! But where? Which one?

'By George!' Blick laughed at his horrified expression. 'I think you've got it.'

'Bloody hell, Rob, you look rough.'

Rob glanced up from perusing his final divorce papers and frowned at the sight of Cindy Nightingale lounging in the doorway holding a cup of coffee. He hadn't seen the bitch all morning and had hoped she was out for the day. Cindy's brown eyes were cool and watchful, summing him up. She had certainly come out of her shell since her promotion to inspector, goose-stepping around as if she expected to be Chief Con any day soon.

'I need a quiet word.' Cindy smoothed back her straight, brown, shoulder-length hair, took a sip of coffee and looked at Rob's colleagues, Steve and Lesley, who sat staring at their computer screens, apparently unaware of her presence.

236

They both knew Rob hated Cindy Nightingale because she had launched her own personal crusade to put his wife in the frame for his paedo father's murder. Cindy wasn't crazy about Rob either.

'This isn't a good time,' Rob muttered, staring at the papers again. 'I'm busy.'

He and Shannon were officially divorced now. He'd known it was coming, of course, that it was just – *just* – one last legal formality. But he hadn't expected it to hurt this much. He had felt like staying home and getting hammered instead of coming to work. But what was the use? He'd been there, done that. Loads of times. If you put the pain on hold it only came back worse afterwards.

He had caught Shannon at a bad moment the other day. She didn't mean what she'd said about how she would have murdered their baby. It wasn't in her to do such a terrible thing, she wasn't that hard. She was upset, that was all. Frightened. The anonymous letters were getting to her. And this clubland murder, which apparently had some connection to her, must be the last straw. Rob wondered if anyone had talked to her about it yet. At least he had warned her, surely she would be grateful for that? Shannon knew he was her friend, even if he couldn't be her husband any more. She knew he would stick by her, no matter what.

'Excuse me.' Cindy's tone was sharp. 'This is important.' A DC didn't brush off a DI with the excuse that he was busy. 'What's wrong with you?' she asked, her voice rising irritably. 'You look like you're away with the fairies.'

Rob glared at her. Then he sighed deeply, got up and followed her out and along the corridor to her office. He would have loved to snatch the mug of steaming, milky coffee from Cindy and chuck it in her face, watch it spray over her pale blue sweater and denim skirt. But that would be his job gone straight to hell in a handbag. And if he didn't have his job, what else was left?

He thought of Katy again. He hadn't set eyes on her since the horrible scene in the restaurant when she had so upset and insulted Shannon. Not to mention the humiliation she'd caused him! He wouldn't show his face there again for a while. If the stupid bitch didn't realise by now that he didn't love her, she never would. Shannon was right, it was Katy's problem. In one sense though, it was a shame the way things had turned out.

Katy wasn't Shannon, of course. No way, didn't come close. And she had infuriated him at times. Once his initial anger at her pregnancy and subsequent pestering of him had worn off, however, Rob started to miss having another human being around the house. He missed Katy fussing over him, cooking him great meals, listening to him whinge about work, her compliant body available whenever he got the urge. She was undemanding, vaguely comforting. And it was nice to feel loved, even if you couldn't return the compliment. What did the silly cow have to go and get herself up the duff for?

With his baby. *His* baby. Rob couldn't stop thinking about that the last couple of days. He had come close to regretting his outburst when Katy had told him the news. Of course it was a hell of a shock, the last thing he needed. He had only ever wanted to have kids with Shannon. But still, this baby was his. Maybe he shouldn't have dumped Katy like that, been so rough on her. He of all people knew how it felt to be dumped by the person you loved.

He would be a father in a few months time. It was a strange and frightening, but intriguing thought. Flesh of his flesh. He didn't want Katy, but he did want to see, want to know, this child. He was the father, he had rights. He could get access, maybe share custody, whatever parents who weren't together did these days. He was prepared to support his child, be much kinder towards his little son or daughter than his fucking cold bastard parents had ever been to him and poor Melanie. The more Rob thought about it, the more he liked the idea.

He would go and seek out Katy once Inspector Cindy had finished hassling him, talk to her or make a date to talk. They could work something out. Katy would be delighted and relieved that he meant to take an interest and wasn't going to leave her to struggle alone. Who knew, it might even make Shannon more sympathetic towards him. She would see that he had grown up, taken responsibility, admire and approve of him the way she used to. Fantasy might even turn to reality; he and Shannon could have kids of their own one day. Happiness was still within his grasp, providing he acted wisely. He would give Shannon time, space. She still had a lot to get over.

'What the hell is up with you?' Cindy demanded, angered by Rob's dreamlike state, the lack of attention and respect from someone who ought to know a lot better. She stalked into her office, dumped the mug of coffee on the desk and turned to him.

'Nothing's up.' Rob frowned at her hectoring tone and shook himself out of his daydream. He blinked, squared his shoulders, looked at her. 'What d'you want to talk about?'

'The Lucas Grant murder. I've been put in charge of the investigation.'

Oh great, Rob thought, cold reality striking again. Terrific. 'Let me take a wild guess,' he said slowly. 'You want to pin it on my wife.'

'Ex-wife, isn't it? Or almost ex.' Cindy smiled. 'Now why would I want to do that?'

'Because you hate her. You didn't get her for my father's murder. And because of the note on Lucas Grant's body: *"Ask Shannon Flinder".'*

Cindy's smile faded. 'How'd you know about that note?'

Rob flushed. 'It was all over the division.'

'Was it?'

'Yeah. The morning after the murder. That's when I heard. You know how these things do the rounds.'

'Do I? This is – *was* – confidential! Who told you?'

He shrugged. 'Can't remember.'

'No. Of course you can't.'

'I don't think anyone actually told me,' Rob said. 'Like I said, I just heard.'

Cindy sat on the desk and folded her arms. 'A lowly copper such as myself wouldn't dare go after your ex-missis. I mean, she's a lawyer, isn't she? Got good friends shitting on the likes of us from some very high places.'

Rob started. 'What's that supposed to mean?'

'It *means* that the investigation into your late Dad's murder went nowhere, did it?'

'Not this again.' Rob felt furious. 'It went nowhere because the people conducting it had tunnel vision. And they kept going down the wrong bloody tunnel. You don't care who blasted his arse to kingdom come any more than I do,' he said. 'Whoever killed him did society a favour. Saved innocent lives.'

'As opposed to guilty ones.'

'And if you're thinking of going after Shannon again, it might be a good idea to remember that she's a criminal law solicitor. You won't want to chuck the rule book out of the window a second time.'

'Never stop protecting her, do you? I suppose that's because you still love her. How sweet.' Cindy gazed at him, her eyes narrowed. 'Or sick.'

Rob tried to control his anger. 'What do you want?'

'Well, even you must realise we've got to have a chat with your ex-missis about that note. Don't get me wrong. I'm not saying she murdered Lucas Grant, that she's stalking club-land looking to crack the skulls of any young lads she comes across.'

'No. Even you couldn't be that obsessed.'

'Watch it!' Cindy snapped. 'I'm just saying there must be a link somewhere. I wondered if you could give us any pointers before we speak to Shannon? Seeing as you're supposed to have stayed mates with her.'

'Shannon's never heard of him,' Rob said. 'He's not one of her clients – past or present.'

'I see. So you've warned her,' Cindy said softly. 'Thought you might. That was a bit naughty, wasn't it, Robert dear? Very naughty, in fact.'

Rob flushed again, kicked himself. He had so much on his mind lately that he couldn't think straight. Now he'd dropped himself in it and the bitch had him by the unmentionables.

'We wanted to talk to the glamourous Shannon sooner, but we couldn't get hold of her all weekend.'

'Did she go away then?' Shannon hadn't told him she was going anywhere.

'No. She's left home, apparently.'

'What?' Rob looked at Cindy in astonishment. 'She lives with Finbar Linnell. In that Albert Dock apartment.'

'Not any more she doesn't.'

'I don't understand.'

'She moved out.' Cindy's grin was pure malice. 'You mean you didn't know? Dear me. You're obviously not as pally with her as you think. We dropped by the apartment and Mr Linnell showed us a note she'd left, asking him to send any post on to her office. She didn't leave him a forwarding address. Poor guy,' she sighed, batting her mascaraed lashes. 'Him getting his club blown up and all. Now he's lost his girlfriend. Life can be so cruel.'

Rob was staring at her, shocked. 'When did Shannon move out?'

'Friday, Mr Linnell said. She'd been shopping around estate agents.'

'I don't get it,' Rob stammered. 'I just don't–'

'Never mind what you don't get. Which seems to be quite a lot of things.' Cindy glared at him. 'If you can think of any reason for the note on that stiff, you'd better tell me right now. Otherwise,' she snarled, 'I'll be chucking the rule book at your dozy head, not out the bloody window!'

Rob's shoulders slumped. Shannon wouldn't thank him for this. It was what she'd dreaded. Why hadn't she told him about leaving her Irish criminal lover?

'Do sit down, Robert dear,' Cindy invited, back to her nice cop routine.

'Well.' Rob pulled up a chair. 'Shannon's been getting these anonymous letters,' he began. 'I told her she should report them.'

Chapter Twenty-Eight

'Another magic day on Metal Mountain!'

Marty, owner of a scrapyard along the Dock Road, gazed up at the huge pile of flattened scrap metal glinting in the sunshine as he inhaled cigarette smoke and the molasses-scented breeze off the Mersey. 'Makes you glad to be alive, dunnit? Oh, Ma!' he laughed, adopting a drawling US accent, 'the Chinook is blowing.'

'The *wha*'?' Lee, the new lad, whose dark-blue overalls hung on his skinny frame, squinted up at him.

'Haven't you ever seen *Little House on the Prairie?* No, don't suppose that'd float your boat, would it? Even as a kid.' Marty looked disgustedly at Lee's vacant expression, his half-open mouth. 'Well, it was winter on the prairie–'

'What's a prairie?'

'Bloody hell.' Marty rolled his eyes. 'It's a big flat stretch of land in America. Anyway, it was winter and when the temperature went up to twenty below zero the family thought the cold snap was over. Their house was all snowed in and they were freezing their arses off. And then one night the thaw came. The spring wind. They called it the Chinook.'

'Fascinatin',' Lee sniggered. He yawned to show how impressed he was. Fucking dickbrain, he thought. Triple sad. All these years in the scrapyard had done something to Marty. The metal must have got into his system, poisoning

243

him. Pulled his face out of shape and made him bark instead of talk.

'Where's that tea you were supposed to be makin'?' Marty shouted. 'Go'n stick the kettle on, you useless little sod.'

'That's charmin'.' Lee slouched off, blackened hands stuck in his overall pockets. He slouched back a minute later. 'It's on.'

'Good.' Marty pointed his cigarette at the huge piles of scrap. 'D'you know where that lot's going?'

Lee shrugged. 'Haven't a clue, have I?' He didn't give a fuck either.

'Eastern Europe. Romania, to be exact. Also goes to the Third World. Very good with scrap metal they are there.'

Lee sniggered again. 'Not much good with anythin' else.'

'Like you'd know. You think Manchester's a foreign country.'

'It is.'

'Shut it, I haven't finished. The scrap'll be melted down for recycling.' Marty sighed, dropped his ciggie and trod on it. He'd taken Lee on as a favour to Lee's uncle Danny, who was one of his mates, and he was already regretting it. His wife Angie said he was too bloody soft, and she was right.

Was he just pissed off with Lee's general uselessness and total bloody lack of enthusiasm for the job? Or was there something else bugging him? Marty wasn't in the habit of analysing his feelings. He normally left that to Angie. But there was definitely something bothering him lately. Things had been hectic here though, and they had just been away for the weekend, visiting Angie's sister in North Wales. He hadn't had a spare minute to think about it until now.

It was that fella, Marty realised. The big, bald, forty-something bastard in the black leather coat. With the earring, piercing blue eyes and evil expression. He had a funny accent too, which Marty couldn't place. The guy had come along with Colin in his wagon and hung around to watch the cars go in the fragmentor. People called it the crusher or shredder, but what the machine actually did was fragment the car parts, chew them up and spit them out, steam-cleaning them in the process. Marty was sure one of those cars on Colin's wagon that day belonged to the big fella, and that he'd wanted shut of it for some reason. A dodgy reason. You got a sixth sense about these things. Of course Marty didn't ask questions. He never did that, because he preferred to mind his own business and lead a nice, quiet life. He didn't care if some people called him a boring bastard.

Of course people often came to watch the cars going in the fragmentor. Nothing unusual there. Some brought their kids; he got the feeling one or two parents would have liked the kids to go in the fragmentor along with the cars. One woman wanted to see the red Ford Sierra she'd shagged her cheating ex-fiancé in get flattened and chewed, because she said if she flattened the tosser herself she'd get twenty years. They thought it was a laugh.

This fella hadn't been having a laugh. He was nervous, jittery. Something about him gave Marty a bad feeling, a nasty taste in his mouth. The feel of those cold blue eyes on him gave him the creeps. The fella had shoved Colin a few quid and Colin had slipped the cash to the crane driver so he'd do that lot of cars right away. They didn't think Marty would notice, but he had.

'Behave!' he whispered, shaking his head. What was up with him? Stressed, that's all. Who wasn't these days? Too much telly as well, mesmerised by all that crap every night. What was it doing to his brain? When Marty watched the news or read the tabloids he wondered if most of the population was chronically depressed and fuckwitted. He turned and looked at his reflection in the dirty hut window. Late thirties, overweight, sparse red hair. Football fan, couch potato when he got the chance. He looked like a character in a soap. Lee came out of the hut with two mugs of strong tea.

'Yours is Earl Grey with a lemon slice, innit?' he sneered. Marty looked at him, stunned.

'Don't go and fall into one of your daft bloody daydreams,' he ordered as Lee took his tea, went to sit on the oil-stained ground against the wall and lifted his face to the sun. He pointed to the guy in the orange fluorescent jacket with *Environment Agency* across the back, who sat some distance away on a low stool by the giant scrap heaps, three trays on the ground in front of him. 'Aren't you going to ask him if he wants a brew?'

'If he does, he can friggin' well make it himself,' Lee muttered, scowling. 'Not a sodding waiter, am I?' He took out his cigarettes and lit one. 'What's he doing there anyway?'

'He's picking out samples to take to the lab for analysis. To make sure we're complying with all the bloody EC directives against pollution.'

Lee blew out smoke. *'Eh?'*

Marty sighed. 'When the machine chews up engine blocks and all the other car parts, it separates the steel from the aluminium,' he explained. 'Aluminium's worth a lot more than steel. It also separates out what we call the fluff pile – carpets, underlay, seat leather, plastics. Gives everything a good clean at the same time. Like a giant washing machine. So when the metal gets melted down in Eastern Europe or the Third World it won't give off toxic fumes from grease, oil, paint, you name it. That's why you've got three piles.' Marty paused and took a gulp of tea. 'You'd know all that by now,' he said, 'if you'd taken any bloody notice of what goes on around here, instead of sitting on your arse dreaming about being a record company executive shagging your way through girl bands.'

No response. Marty stared out at the Mersey, on which the wind was whipping up little waves, then at the cranes which lined the docksides. Across the water he could see a Korean ship, the hull so rusted he wondered how it could put to sea. He turned back to the glinting metal mountains. The Environment Agency guy's slow, lazy movements had turned urgent all of a sudden. He was scrabbling in the fluff pile like someone demented.

'What's up with him?' Marty murmured. 'Dropped his wallet or something?' But the sky was blue, the sun was warm and he was enjoying his tea. He couldn't be bothered to go over and find out. Lee butted his cigarette and tossed it away.

'Can I climb up them heaps?' he asked, pointing.

Marty frowned. 'Not unless you want to bring the whole bloody lot crashing down on you, slice yourself to ribbons on rusted metal, and get blood poisoning. Then again, you'd probably bleed to death before you had time to get blood poisoning. Only a dickhead would even think of it. Still, you go ahead if that's what you fancy. Call the paramedics now, shall I? D'you know what blood group you are?'

'All right! Only asked.'

The loading shovel was about to scoop up another bucketful of fluff, but the Environment Agency guy waved his arms at the driver to stop, nearly getting himself scooped up in the process. He grabbed something and held it up, stared at it. Then he turned and came running towards them.

'What's up, mate?' Marty asked as the guy stopped, panting for breath. The bad feeling was back suddenly. Big time. It was going to be one of those days – with knobs on.

'Look at this!' The guy was shocked, white-faced, could barely get the words out. He held up the object. Marty looked at the jagged piece of jaw bone with the few teeth sticking out of it. The skin and gum would have been ripped off by the fragmentor, any blood removed by the cleaning process.

'It's human,' the man gasped. 'You'd better call the police.'

'I knew it,' Marty said hoarsely. 'I bloody knew it.'

'My God!' Mi-Hae exclaimed, exchanging a horrified glance with Khalida. 'So this anonymous letter-writer could have murdered somebody now?'

'Looks like it.' Shannon stared out of the window. They were in Mi-Hae's office upstairs, which overlooked the busy, narrow street.

'And you no longer think Rob's ex-girlfriend wrote them?'

'Well, she's certainly full of jealous, irrational rage towards me. But murder's something else. Besides, Rob tells me she's got an alibi for the night Lucas Grant was murdered. Some friend stayed with her at her flat, phoned Rob to tell him Katy was in a terrible state and wouldn't he talk to her or come over? He refused. Of course that will have to be verified. But no. I don't think it's her. I was never sure anyway. Besides', Shannon said, thinking of Katy's pregnancy, 'she's got other things on her mind.'

'And you've no idea who else it could be?'

'No. All I know is, I'm to blame. A young man, murdered because some big-time whacko's got it in for me! It's terrible, it's been doing my head in all weekend. More than—' She stopped.

'Oh, come *on*.' Khalida got up and hugged her. 'For God's sake, Shannon, you can't blame yourself for any of this! As you say, this person's a whacko. How could you have prevented them from murdering that poor boy, any more than the police could? You can imagine their reaction if you'd told them about the letters before – go away, love, don't bother us, people who write nasty letters never carry out their threats.'

Shannon nodded. 'That's the reaction I anticipated. It was my reaction when I got the first letter. I was shocked, upset. But I didn't think it was serious.'

Mi-Hae glanced at Khalida again. 'Shannon, I'm disappointed in you. You've been going through all this trouble, and now it looks as if you could be in danger. But you didn't say a word to either of us about it until now. We're friends, you know, not just colleagues.'

'Yes.' Shannon sniffed. 'But we're always so damn busy here and – oh, I don't know!' She pushed back her hair. 'It was just personal stuff. I thought I could sort it.'

'It can never be one thing at a time, can it?' Khalida commented. 'Your life must have been hell these past six months, what with all the stuff that's happened to you. And now you and Finbar have split.'

Shannon turned. 'I'm not going to fall apart over *that*,' she said, her voice hardening. 'Life goes on, etcetera.'

That's a relief, Mi-Hae thought. She smiled. 'You're very cool about it. And you look much better than you did a couple of days ago.'

Shannon did not feel better. She was very frightened now. She also felt lonely and isolated, crushed by misery, as if her heart was literally breaking. But maybe it wouldn't if she acted as though it wasn't, refused to give this break-up the attention it didn't deserve. She had more important stuff to think about than being rejected by a man. Useless to torture herself, re-live that bedroom scene over and over. Wonder what, why? *Why?*

Finbar had broken through her defences, fucked her, listened to her tell him how she couldn't leave because she loved him too much. Then he had told her to get out. And she had. End of story. It was what some men did. It was her own stupid fault for falling in love with him. Shannon was determined not to make the even more stupid mistake of letting herself sink into a deep, dark well of self-pity from which she might not emerge for a long time.

'Shannon, you will be careful?' Mi-Hae looked worried. 'Maybe you shouldn't live alone right now.'

'I'll be fine. I've got to get on with my life.' Shannon hoped she would have a life to get on with. 'That's enough about me, okay? Let's talk about other things.'

'What are we going to do about Demetrio Montana?' Khalida asked. 'He was very aggressive and uncooperative when I went to see him at the police station on Friday. Insisted he wouldn't see anybody but Shannon. I told him she wasn't available, and he flew into a rage.'

'Yes. Well.' Mi-Hae looked grim. 'One more strike and he's out, as they say.'

'Suits me.' Shannon glanced at her watch. 'Right. Think I'd better head off to the Mags Court.'

'What about the police?' Mi-Hae asked. 'Don't they want to pay you a visit?'

'I'll pay them a visit,' Shannon said. 'When I'm ready.'

'I don't remember wha' 'appened in that fight,' the spotty, tired-looking youth assured her as she had her pre-court chat with him. 'Don't remember being in no fight. I was rotten drunk, like. But it's all camera-ed up around Slater Street and the coppers kept telling me it was on video.'

'Yeah. A video which they've had two months to produce.' Shannon did not wonder why the police had failed to produce it, despite repeated requests by herself and the CPS solicitor, because she had given up trying to get her head around things like that. 'Okay, Darren,' she said, gathering her files. 'See you in there.'

'Don't suppose you've lost a posh fountain pen?' an usher asked later after she had come out of Court Seven, said goodbye to a grateful Darren and gone to re-check the list of cases before she left. Shannon carried her leather jacket; she didn't want to go anywhere near the Lawyers' Room, and hated going down the empty stairs and deserted corridor that led to the Bridewell. The usher pointed to the notice written in black marker. 'A Mont Blanc, no less.'

'Hmm. Seriously posh,' Shannon commented, scanning names on the list. 'Unfortunately, however, the Mahblah is not mine.'

He laughed. 'The *what*?'

'Mahblah. It's a derisory term employed by jealous, sniping individuals who despise Mont Blanc pens as outrageously expensive and elitist, and think their owners are snotty snobs of the worst variety.'

He laughed again. 'How d'you know that? Have you got one?'

'No. Somebody I once knew owned a Mont Blanc.' Shannon would not tell him that somebody was her late father-in-law. She remembered an incandescently dull, inedible dinner at Rob's parents house one evening, when Bernard had treated them all to a long lecture about Mont Blanc pens, their history and culture. He had a Le Grand, which he used only for signing letters. And showing off. He needed things like that to prop up his fragile sense of identity. She felt depressed again as she thought of the anonymous letters, and the author's possible connection with the Magistrates' Court. Who the hell was doing this? Who hated her this much?

The police could compare the letter Shannon had kept with the note found on Lucas Grant's body. Have the writing analysed to see if the same person had written both, perhaps even used the same pen. Forensic handwriting analysis was not to be confused with pseudo-scientific graphology. Forensic handwriting and document analysis dealt with class characteristics formed from learned writing systems, the individual characteristics of the writer, and any features not common to a particular group. Also form, line quality, arrangement and content. Problems with identification could of course occur if the handwriting was disguised, as was usually the case with threatening letters. Shannon sighed. She dreaded seeing the police. But it was out of her hands now.

'Shannon!' She jumped as someone tapped her on the shoulder. Turned and gasped with annoyance at the sight of Rob.

'What are you doing here? What do you want?'

'I need a word. In private. Please – it's urgent.' Rob wore a charcoal suit and expensive-looking tie beneath his grey jacket, but his dark hair was a mess and his eyes reddened and bloodshot. He looked pale, distraught. The usher glanced curiously at him then drifted away.

'What do you want?' Shannon repeated. 'I hope you haven't come to wank on about how you don't want the divorce,' she said, irritation rising in her, 'because I am definitely not in the mood.' She dumped her files and briefcase on a nearby bench while she dragged on her jacket. 'It's done,' she hissed. 'Finished. Get over it.'

'Can we talk outside?' Rob asked hoarsely. 'Shannon, please! I need–'

'Shut up!' She glared at him. 'All I ever hear from you is what *you* need. I'm sick and tired of it. What about *my* needs for once in a bloody millenium?' She marched off. He ran after her and grabbed her arm.

'You've left Finbar Linnell. Why?'

'Get your hands off me!' Shannon pulled free. 'That's none of your business,' she snapped. 'How the bloody hell do you know anyway? Stalking me now, are you?'

'Of course not. The people conducting the Lucas Grant murder inquiry were looking for you. They went to Linnell's apartment and he told them you'd moved out. Where are you living now?'

'Again – none of your business. I'm warning you.' Shannon turned, agonising pain flooding her at the mention of Finbar. 'Leave me alone! I'll get an injunction if that's what it takes.' She ran down the stairs past the guard and out into the street. Glanced around the way she'd done ever since the attack on Keely Breeze. She was seeing Keely later today. Or maybe tomorrow. There was so much to do.

'I told them about the letters,' Rob burst out. 'I had to. Cindy Nightingale cornered me. She's in charge of the Lucas Grant case.'

'You're joking.' But she knew he wasn't. Shannon stopped, despair sweeping over her. 'Well, today just gets better and better, doesn't it?'

'Don't worry. I've warned her not to hassle you,' Rob said. 'I sorted it.'

'Give me a break, will you? You never sorted anything in your life. All you do is fuck things up. Have you warned Katy to lay off me too?'

'We've been through that. She swears she didn't write those letters. And she's got an alibi for the night of the murder.'

'Still hates my guts though, doesn't she? And we know who's to blame!'

'That's not important.' He started to cry. 'Shannon, please!' he choked, his shoulders shaking. 'I'm in a terrible state. You've got to help me.'

252

'What?' She stared at him, enraged. 'Forget about it, you stupid, selfish bastard. Don't you think I've got enough trouble of my own?'

'You're right,' he sobbed, oblivious to curious glances from passers-by. 'I am selfish. I do fuck things up. I just went round to Katy's. She was off work, she called in sick. I wanted to talk to her about the baby. I thought we could work things out so that I could get access. Share responsibility.'

'What a typically male turnaround,' Shannon sneered, infuriated even more by the fact that Rob was going to be a father when she and Finbar had lost their baby. 'Suddenly decided you want the flesh of your flesh to bear your name, did you? *Access*. Why don't you say what you mean? You want control. Not responsibility.'

'No! You don't understand.' Rob covered his face with his hands as a huge sob burst from him. He leaned against the building's dirty wall and slid down until he was crouched on the pavement, huddled like some homeless drunk. 'I wanted to be a proper dad,' he wailed as Shannon stared at him, her body suddenly rigid with alarm. 'I wanted to know my little girl or boy, be around to watch him or her grow up. Wanted to give love – all the love Melanie and me never got. But Katy just laughed at me, told me to fuck off. Asked why was I making such a fuss when I'd got what I wanted?'

'Got what you wanted?' Shannon gasped. 'You mean–'

'I can't believe what she's done – she hates me!' Rob looked up at her, his reddened, contorted face drenched with tears. 'She got rid of it!' he screamed. 'That bloody bitch murdered my baby!'

253

Chapter Twenty-Nine

'Finbar, my old friend! It's great to see you. Welcome back to Amsterdam.'

A smiling Jan-Willem Hendriks got up, grabbed his hand and shook it as Finbar walked into his panelled office in the gabled, seventeenth-century *herenhuis* – 'gentleman's house' – on Keizersgracht, one of the city's famous canal streets. 'Man,' he laughed, 'I never thought to see you again.'

'It's great to see you as well.' Finbar smiled, trying to appear enthusiastic, although he felt depressed at the sight of his old contact. It brought everything back, the bad old days. Still, he was lucky that Jan-Willem was so happy to see him after he'd sent his courier, Mariska, back months ago with the curt message that their mutually beneficial association was at an end. Through the window Finbar could see boat-loads of tourists passing slowly to and fro along the canal, their camera lenses glinting in the sunlight, guides pointing up at the gables of the old houses.

'You don't look so good,' Jan-Willem said, frowning. His blue eyes looked pale in his deeply tanned face, and his hair was the usual mop of tousled steel grey. He looked like any other middle-aged Dutch businessman. Except that he wasn't just any businessman. 'I don't mean sick,' he added hastily. 'Just not so good. A little bit depressed, maybe?'

'No,' Finbar lied. 'I'm fine. Bit tired, that's all.'

'Hm. All right. If you say so.' Jan-Willem gave a sly smile. 'Is it a woman?'

'Perish the thought. How's the arms trade these days?'

'Difficult. Still good though. One market closes, another opens. I went to a fair in Dubai recently, made some new contacts there.' Jan-Willem grabbed his mac from the hook. 'Let's go out and have a drink,' he suggested. 'We can talk properly then. Shall we go to my current favourite bar in the Jordaan? Or head for Rembrandtsplein? You are the guest, you can choose.'

'The Jordaan's nearer. We could walk.' Finbar liked the Jordaan, one of Amsterdam's oldest neighbourhoods. The streets were named after plants and flowers: Lily, Violet. There was even a Lindenstraat, Lime Street.

'How long are you staying in Amsterdam?' Jan-Willem asked as they went out of his office and down the building's scarily steep, narrow stairs, a typical feature of Dutch houses old and new. The scarcity of land meant people always built upwards rather than outwards.

'I'm just here for the day. Have to be back at Schiphol by eight-thirty. My flight's an hour later.' All Finbar had to do was meet with Jan-Willem and get the deal fixed. Nothing else. No need to go anywhere near Leidseplein with its bars and cafés or head for Leidsestraat, on one corner of which was Shannon's favourite shop in Amsterdam, Australian Homemade Chocolates. He would normally have bought a big box to take home to her. Not any more.

'Such a quick visit,' Jan-Willem commented, shaking his head regretfully. 'Then maybe we can have a *very* early dinner.' They walked along Keizersgracht, skirting the lines of parked cars and avoiding speeding cyclists, crossed the bridge by the Westerkerk, the church mentioned in Anne Frank's diary, and turned down Prinsengracht. Finbar looked at the barges and houseboats, the young trees dotted at intervals along the canal sides, and at the tourists milling outside the old house where Anne and her family had hidden until someone betrayed them to the Gestapo in 1944. Behind him on the bridge was the roar of traffic and the clanging of tram bells. The Westerkerk bells joined in, chiming the hour. Prinsengracht could still be reached by trams 13 and 17, as Anne had written in her diary.

Shannon loved this city. She had come with him on his previous visit months ago. The pain of missing her, feeling frantic at the thought of his cruelty and wondering how she was doing, seemed to intensify until it became a sharp pain that made him catch his breath. Finbar hadn't wanted to come back here and be forced to remember the streets, shops and museums that he and Shannon had explored, their elaborate dinners and even more elaborate sex sessions in the suite at the Krasnopolsky Hotel. But as with everything in his life at the moment, he had no choice. Shannon would be safe, as long as he did what Blick – and Special Branch – wanted. Trouble was, Finbar hated doing what other people wanted.

'That's a lot of semtex,' Jan-Willem remarked when they were settled in a corner of the quiet, dark bar down a tiny street in the Jordaan, glasses of Amstel beer on the table in front of them. He chuckled. 'What are you planning to do, blow up the world's major airlines?'

Finbar smiled. 'Nothing like that.'

'So what is it then?'

Finbar took a gulp of beer. 'You know better than to ask. I'm sure it'll be all over the world's media when it happens though.'

'I can't wait.'

'When do you think you can deliver the consignment?'

'Couple of days. The old route?'

Via Linnell Air Cargo. Finbar nodded. 'That's fine.'

It was all so easy. Horribly bloody easy. As if he'd never been away, never tried to start afresh. Maybe he was meant for this kind of life and should just stop fighting. He had lost Shannon, and he would probably end up stiffed soon anyway. What was the point? That's right, Finbar thought. Nothing like a positive attitude.

Jan-Willem lit a cigarette and signalled for two more beers. 'So now we have to discuss price.'

Finbar's right foot nudged the briefcase on the floor. 'I'm sure you'll find more than enough in there to cover it.'

Jan-Willem smiled with satisfaction. 'That's what I like about you, Finbar. You're a pro. Always have been. We trust each other, eh? There's so few people you can trust these days, don't you find?'

'Tell me about it.' Finbar folded his arms and stretched out his long legs.

'Anything else I can supply you with?'

He thought for a few seconds. 'No. That's it.' He had no intention of making any further purchases that could be of use to Blick and his gang.

'Why don't you marry my daughter?' Jan-Willem laughed. 'I'd love to have you for a son-in-law. You could come into the business with me, I'd make you a partner. Oh, but I forgot. You don't like Dutch women, do you?'

'What makes you say that?'

'Mariska once told me you said something uncomplimentary to her.'

'She deserved it.' Pain knifed Finbar as he thought again of what Shannon had not deserved. What was she doing now? Did she miss him anything like as much as he missed her? Or was the wound already healing over, forming its scab of hate? He hoped so, because hating him was the best thing that could happen to her. He didn't want to think about what the worst would be.

'How's life in Liverpool?' Jan-Willem asked, picking up his beer. 'A guy I know moved there a few months ago,' he said, before Finbar could answer. 'A real bastard. He fucked up a job he was supposed to do for me – I won't go into details. Said he was a ballistics expert, but he knew nothing about guns.' He snorted. 'He's half Dutch, half Brit. Spent a lot of time in the US. He told me he'd been on Death Row in Texas for murdering two social workers who tried to take his girlfriend's baby away. He lived with her in some trailer trash park. His lawyers got him off, can you believe it? I don't know – maybe it was all bullshit what he said. Anyway, he left the US and came back to the Netherlands.'

'So what's he doing in Liverpool?' Finbar asked, to be polite.

'Living with a woman, I think. He boasted he had a world-wide stable of women who wrote him penfriend letters. Stupid bitches.' Jan-Willem frowned. 'He had to leave Amsterdam in a big hurry. Beat his girlfriend so badly that she died – the police were looking for him. He came to me before he left, gave me a post office box number to contact in case I had another job for him.' Jan-Willem drained his glass. 'I told him he had to be joking. His name's Demetrio Montana,' he went on. 'He might use a false name now, I don't know. But you can't mistake him. He's a big guy, mid-forties, piercing blue eyes. He always says people with blue eyes can get away with murder! If you come across him, keep away. He's real bad news.'

'I'll remember.' Finbar nodded, barely listening, his head full of Shannon. 'Thanks for the tip.'

Jan-Willem nudged him. 'Can you tell me when this great big bang's supposed to happen?'

'Soon.' Or so Finbar assumed. Where and when was still the big question. He wondered if the briefcase bug had revealed any secrets to its eavesdroppers. Of course, planting bugs in rooms was very much yesterday's technology. And Finbar had noticed Blick and his men did not use mobiles, which could be tracked by specially adapted laptops. Each mobile phone, when activated, was a mini tracking device because of the digital technology required to pinpoint users for incoming calls. Blick and his mates had left the hotel and rented a flat in Newsham Park. He was supposed to go there and meet with Blick when he got back late tonight. Contact Carl Mactire afterwards if he had anything to tell. Finbar knew that whatever Mactire might say, Special Branch did not give a fuck about him or Shannon. They were just pawns in the usual game. And Finbar wasn't sure he could win this one.

The thoughts went round in his head as he drank Amstel beer and carried on the conversation with Jan-Willem, picked at the very early dinner in an Indonesian restaurant on another tree-lined canal street. He had no appetite for the array of spicy little seafood, meat and vegetable dishes that constituted the *rijsttafel.* Jan-Willem drove him to Schiphol. His flight to Liverpool took off on time.

For once, Finbar would have welcomed a delay. Anything to put off the moment when he had to walk back into the apartment and not find Shannon there. Reading a novel or listening to music, cooking a meal, whizzing through paper-work she'd brought home, lying in bed watching tv. Making him laugh with stories about some of her crazy clients. It's finished, he told himself, looking out of the cabin window as the aircraft climbed into the clear, dark-blue sky. Get over it. The smell of her perfume still lingered around the apartment, or so he thought. He could be imagining that. But it was doing his head in.

He took a cab from the airport, got out at the Albert Dock and was paying the driver when a horn beeped and head-lights flashed from a nearby car. Finbar glanced across and recognised Blick at the wheel of an Audi TT, two of his men in the back. He noted the number plate, walked over and got in.

'Thought I was supposed to come to your place?' He slammed the door.

'I decided to surprise you.'

Finbar looked round at the two in the back. 'Scared to meet me alone?' When he might have had a chance to do something with the bastard.

Blick ignored the question. 'So how did it go in Amsterdam?'

'The consignment is being delivered day after tomorrow. Via Linnell Air Cargo. The manifest will describe it as spare parts for engines, from a client I've dealt with often in the past. There won't be any problem.'

'I hope not, for your sake. And the blonde lawyerine.'

Blick looked at the lighted apartment building in front of him, the dark stretch of river to his left. 'It appears Ms Flinder really has moved out,' he said. 'D'you know her new address?'

Finbar swallowed. 'I don't give a fuck.'

'No. Of course you don't. I've been to Amsterdam a few times,' Blick said. 'It's a really happening place.'

'*Happening*?' Finbar mocked. 'So there are people who still talk like that.'

'Famous for stretching to the limits tolerance and political correctness,' Blick went on as if he hadn't spoken. 'Problem is, most people think the rest of the Netherlands is like that. They don't know the Dutch have their own Bible belt, like in the US. I wonder what they'd think of Ms Flinder in the more rabidly conservative parts of that little country? Unmarried, childless. Lovers. A *career.* I don't think someone like her would be very popular, do you?'

'Are you finished?' Finbar hated it every time the bastard mentioned Shannon. He tried to control his anger. 'All right with you if I go home to bed now?' He opened the car door. 'It's been a long day.'

'And there'll be more. Aren't you going to ask me about the target again?'

Finbar paused. 'Is there any point?'

'No. Even after your kind cash contribution and good work today, you'll understand that I can't reveal the target to you. Not until it's time for the actual strike, in fact.'

Not until it's too bloody late, you mean, Finbar thought. For the victims. And me. Maybe Shannon too.

'Well,' he said. 'I'll say goodnight.'

'Sweet dreams!' Blick called. Finbar got out of the car and walked away.

Like Lily Bart, Edith Wharton's heroine in *The House of Mirth*, all she had now was her dignity. And a bit more money than poor Lily. Oh God, Shannon thought, rolling over in bed, don't tell me I'm going to start cuddling up to literature for consolation. Thinking of cuddling – had Finbar got himself another girlfriend yet? They might be having sex right now while she sobbed into her pillow, acting out the tragedy of the abandoned lover. Time for a change of role.

She sat up, rubbed her eyes and looked at the bedside clock. Ten-past two in the bloody morning. Still, no use trying to sleep. She would be exhausted tomorrow, but so what? Being in a semi-somnolent state might just help her make it through another shit day. Shannon got out of bed, pulled on her robe and walked to the windows, looked down into the rainy street. The apartment was warm and peaceful, a refuge, but she did not feel at home. She went out of the bedroom, stopped and looked down the hall at the solid front door, chained and bolted. She'd thought she heard a noise, but no doubt that was overworked imagination. No one could get in downstairs unless they lived here or were visiting one of the other tenants. She walked to the door and peered through the spyhole. Nobody.

In the kitchen she pressed the switch on the shiny, new, fast-boiling kettle. Another vital piece of equipment, the coffee machine, stood next to it. Shannon really wanted wine, but drink would only make her feel worse. Having a whinge in the small hours was okay – hitting the booze wasn't. She took her tea into the sitting room, which was empty except for some boxes and a folded quilt on the floor by the fireplace. The gas fire looked like natural flames. She had furniture in storage from the house she and Rob had lived in, but the last thing Shannon wanted to be reminded of was scenes from her disintegrated marriage. There was more than enough to depress and frighten her.

Shannon did not want to act for Demetrio Montana any longer. Especially not since the police had questioned him about the disappearance of his girlfriend – who he had assaulted several times in the past. She had the feeling there was a lot she didn't know about him. And it was difficult not to fear the worst about the missing girlfriend. There was still no clue as to who wanted Keely Breeze dead, or why. And now Rob had screwed things up for her by telling his cop colleagues – Cindy Nightingale, of all people! – about the anonymous letters before Shannon could do that herself. He had screwed things up for Katy too; she must have been desperate, to go ahead with the termination. Rob had rejected her, let her down, and she must have felt she had no choice. It was a bit bloody late for him to get all upset now. Shannon did not want any more contact with him. She wanted to forget he existed.

She sipped her tea, then dragged one of the boxes towards her. Maybe sorting through some of this junk would make her feel bored and sleepy enough to go back to bed. Tights, tops, knickers, bras, books, all thrown in together. One shoe, a black leather pump with a high heel – where the hell was the other? She wasn't an accomplished packer at the best of times. She pulled out another book and gasped with dismay; it was a book of baby names and their meanings. Finbar had bought it when they had found out she was pregnant. They had been looking at it together when the pains that signalled the miscarriage started. Shannon frowned and bit her lip, her vision blurring with tears. She got up, took the book into the kitchen and binned it. The phone rang.

She stood still, gripped by fear. Who would call her at this hour? No clients knew her private number. Was it Nick, perhaps, guessing she was unable to sleep? Mi-Hae? It couldn't be Finbar. Could it? He wouldn't know her new number. Unless Nick had given it to him. And why the hell would Finbar want her number anyway? Shannon let it ring a few more times before she answered.

'Hello?' No reply. 'Who's there?' Her voice was sharp, nervous. Silence. If it was a wrong number why didn't the caller say so and apologise, or just hang up? Maybe they liked the idea of scaring a woman in the middle of the night. Shannon waited another few seconds then hung up. She wasn't going to stand there like some hysterical idiot, asking over and over who was calling. The phone rang again. She swore and picked it up. Her heart was racing. She wished she wasn't alone here.

'Who is this?' Silence, a slight background crackle. Someone was there, listening. Wanting to enjoy, feed off her fear. 'So you haven't got the guts to tell me who you are.' Shannon kept her voice calm, although she was trembling. 'I'm not surprised. Sad bastards like you are all cowards. You don't scare me,' she lied. 'So just bugger off and get a life, because I'm going back to sleep.'

Back to sleep? Nice one, Shannon. She was about to hang up for the second time when the breath came, gathering force until it turned into a whisper.

'Bitch lawyer.'

Chapter Thirty

'You've let me down big time, Blondie!'

Demetrio Montana glowered at Shannon as he charged into her office and slammed the door, breathing hard. 'Those bastard coppers keep harrassing me, trying to make out I've murdered my ex-girlfriend when I don't have a frigging clue what's happened to the stupid bitch. She's doing this on purpose – trying to get me into trouble.'

'Why would she want to do that?'

'She's a bloody woman, isn't she?' He thumped his fist on the desk, causing a heap of files to slide off and crash to the floor, spilling papers. 'And what are you doing to get those coppers off my back? Fuck all, that's what!'

His anger increased as Shannon Flinder just sat in her swively chair, tapping her pen on the desk and giving him a dirty look, like she didn't need to be frightened of him. He wanted to grab her by her corkscrew curls and pull her face close to his, rip her posh suit and tell her exactly what he'd do to her if she didn't show some respect for a change. The door opened and the soppy, Italian-looking lad in the pin-stripe came in.

'What's this?' he sneered. 'The muscle?'

'You okay, Shannon?' Leon asked.

'Yep, fine.' She nodded. He picked up some files and put them back on the desk.

'Thanks, Leon. You can leave the door open.'

'Don't think so.' Demetrio grabbed Leon and shoved him out. 'I'm having a private consultation with my solicitor.' He kicked the door shut.

'I'm not your solicitor any more.' Shannon threw down her pen. 'This firm no longer represents you. As of this minute.'

He gaped at her. 'You *what*?'

He noticed Shannon had a copy of yesterday's *Echo* on her desk, could see part of the headline that had scared the shit out of him: *Mystery Female in Crusher Horror.* They were carrying out DNA tests on the piece of jawbone, getting dental records checked. It was Pascale, he knew it. Unless someone else had also had the bright idea of concealing a dead woman in a car and taking it to the same yard. But that was too much coincidence. Demetrio was sure the crusher horror was Pascale, and that it was just a matter of time before the police drew the same conclusion. They still couldn't prove he'd murdered her though – could they? Anyway, he hadn't bloody murdered her. Some interfering bastard from the Environmental Agency had discovered the piece of jawbone. Didn't they have anything better to do than scavenge around in rubbish heaps like the rats he used to shoot?

'I *said*,' Shannon repeated, 'this practice no longer represents you.'

'Come off it.' He glared at her. 'Don't give me an attitude, Blondie. I need you on my side. I liked you,' he said. 'Thought I could trust you.'

Shannon wouldn't give him the time of day, personally or professionally. Thought she was a cut above. Phelim was going out of his head, having nightmares about being picked out of ID parades by her, however much he got told that there was no chance of that happening. And Demetrio didn't dare go back to the hospital for another go at Keely. He had to wait until she got out, whenever the hell that might be. But he couldn't wait. He was on borrowed time.

'Mr Montana.' Shannon stood up. 'I've done my best for

you, but you wouldn't cooperate with me right from day one. You make it impossible for me to get your defence together–'

'You haven't even tried to get my bloody defence together,' he shouted, enraged. 'Where were you all the time those bizzies were harassing me? Threatening to charge me with murder? I couldn't get hold of you.'

'You were offered representation by my colleague, Ms Najeba, on that day I wasn't available,' Shannon replied. 'But you refused it. You've made highly inappropriate comments to me – and Ms Kam – on several occasions. And now you burst in here and try to intimidate me and other staff members. I'm afraid you'll have to seek representation elsewhere. I'd like you to leave now.'

'I'm not going anywhere, darling!' Who did this bitch think she was? Demetrio stepped forward and lunged across the desk, grabbed Shannon by the arm and pulled her towards him. 'You better cooperate with *me* from now on,' he snarled, ignoring her struggles and cries of protest. 'You better be *very* available.'

'Let go of me,' Shannon cried, struggling fiercely as he tried to drag her over the desk. More files and a thick hardback book thudded to the floor. 'Help!' she yelled. The pinstripe boy and Khalida Najeba burst in.

'I'm calling the police,' Khalida said, her dark eyes frightened.

'Don't bother, love. I'm out of this dump.' Demetrio let go of Shannon. She regained her balance and straightened her clothes, stood there massaging her arm and looking shocked.

'Get out,' she gasped. 'And don't come back here. You won't be allowed in any more.'

'You don't seem to realise, darling.' Demetrio jabbed a finger at her. 'You owe me. I've been protecting you.'

'Protecting me? What are you talking about?'

He'd got to her now, Demetrio thought, seeing her frightened, mystified expression. She pushed back her hair. Her hands were shaking. Shaky voice too.

'You're still my solicitor,' he barked. 'That's all you need to know. I'll be back. And you'll let me in. Because if you don't show some respect from now on ...' Demetrio paused, smiling at Shannon's look of horror as he drew one finger slowly across his throat. 'Things could get very nasty for you.'

She looked like she was going to faint. 'What do you mean?'

'I'm your guardian angel, babe.' Demetrio gathered a mouthful of spit and gobbed on her desk; it hit a letter on which Shannon had been scrawling her signature when he walked in. Khalida cried out in shock. Shannon was always busy. Too bloody busy. Acting as if he didn't matter. She had a big lesson to learn.

'See ya,' Demetrio sneered. *'Blondie.'*

'They won't tell me the target.' Finbar walked to the window of the horrible flat in a block which looked on to a patch of rubble-strewn wasteland. Anyone who had to live here would need regular, large doses of mind-altering substances.

'Stay away from the window,' Mactire said sharply. 'So, no date or location then?' he asked, irritated and disappointed. 'Nothing at all?'

'Nothing,' Finbar confirmed. 'Why don't you put a tracking device on that Audi Blick's got now?' he asked. 'There's forty-seven different locations where you could place the thing, he can't check them all every time.'

'They keep using different cars,' Mactire said. 'Even public transport sometimes. And the surveillance unit has turned up nothing so far.'

'How about the briefcase device that I delivered at great personal risk?'

'Sounds are muffled.' Mactire stood there morose and smoking, one hand in the pocket of his leather jacket. 'Like it's in the bottom of a wardrobe or something. They've probably taken out the money and stowed it elsewhere. We daren't put anything in their flat either, even if we got the chance. It's too risky, too obvious. If they find it, the operation's blown.'

'And I'm dead. You forgot to mention that bit. I suppose they're still tailing Shannon?' Finbar asked. 'Blick won't believe me when I tell him we've finished.'

'They might come to believe it.'

Mactire's hesitation and lame answer told Finbar what he suspected. 'You don't know, do you?' he said. 'You're not bloody keeping an eye on her.'

'We are,' Mactire protested. 'Just not all the time. We haven't got the resources. It's all about priorities. Budgets.'

Crass bastard. 'Look.' Finbar shoved his hands into his pockets because he wanted to punch Mactire. 'Why don't you just go in and arrest them? They're fucked then, they can't do anything, and it's all over the news about how you lot prevented an atrocity and might actually be worth taxpayers' money. Could even mean a bigger budget next year. I mean, what more d'you want?'

'It's not enough. We need to catch them in the act. As you know, that's where you come in. And so far you haven't given us much to keep yourself alive or out of that cell on A wing.'

'Well, excuse me for lack of enthusiasm. I've only provided them with fifty grand and enough semtex to blow up the world's major airlines. Which I also paid for, incidentally. And told you they're planning to blast an out-of-town shopping mall.'

'You can't be certain of that.'

'Seems a good bet, given what I've managed to find out. Blick's not joking when he says how he hates so-called ordinary people. And letting me guess his plan, but keeping me in the dark about the details – that's typical of him, it gives him a buzz. A hit like that could kill thousands.' Finbar frowned. 'They'll probably pick a Saturday. That's when you'd get the highest number of–'

'Stiffs. Okay, even if you're right – which bloody mall? And where?'

'Could be somewhere local,' Finbar said. 'He might be lying about using Liverpool just as a base.'

'*Could* be. *Might* be!'

'I'm doing my best, okay?' Finbar took a deep breath. 'Now, why don't you drop me back in town at the multi-storey car park so I can continue my day? I've had enough of this place. Not to mention you.'

'Continue your day?' Mactire's dark eyes were cold. 'I like your humour. You talk as though you had an infinite number of days left.'

'Well, no one's got an infinite number left, have they? Not even you.' Finbar smiled at him. 'Been a pleasure as always, Carl.' Even if the sting succeeded, Mactire wouldn't be gutted at seeing him murdered by paramilitaries, or locked up and the key permanently misplaced.

There was the usual uncomfortable ride back to town, huddled on the floor of their car. Then they changed to another car. They went to a lot of trouble – as long as it suited them. But they didn't think Shannon was worth protecting. Finbar wondered where her new place was. Some post for her had arrived that morning and he couldn't bring himself to send it on to her office like any other letter, because this wasn't just any letter. But he couldn't deliver it personally.

'All right?' Paula looked up from her newspaper as he walked into the India Buildings office. 'Had a nice lunch?'

'Not really.' Finbar hung up his jacket. 'I didn't eat anything.'

'You're mad, you are.' She shook her head, amused. 'I'm going out in a minute. Want me to bring you back a sandwich? With plenty of napkins so you won't get crumbs on that posh suit.'

'Go on then.' Finbar supposed he had to force food down now and again. 'I'll have ham. Just ham, no mayonnaise or soggy salad with it. And a coffee.' He felt in his pocket and gave her some pound coins.

'You'd better not want me to come in a week on

Saturday.' Paula stood up and reached for her coat. 'Even if it's an emergency. I'm giving you advance warning.'

He looked at her, surprised. 'Since when have I ever wanted you to come into the office on a Saturday? Why, what's up?'

'There's no way I'm going to miss *this*.' Paula pointed to the page she'd been reading. 'It's opening at last,' she said, 'more than six months late. And look who's snipping the ribbon.'

Finbar stared at the big colour splash ad and the fuzzy photo of a simpering, chinless boy pop star. 'The Village?'

'It's called The Village, but it's bigger than that. Oh, Finbar! You must have heard of it.' She laughed at his blank expression. 'They've been building it for ages, on that old stretch of dockland. Up the road from here, just out of town. It's supposed to be one of the biggest malls in the country – bigger than the Trafford Centre.'

Finbar had a friend in Dublin who was a writer. He always said that when a novel was going well, all kinds of information that he needed but could not see how he was going to obtain suddenly seemed to fall into his lap out of nowhere, like gifts from the gods. He felt as if he was having a similar experience now. I bet that's the place! he thought. I bet it bloody is. Of course he couldn't be sure. But maybe he could find out. He was sick of feeling powerless, being at other people's mercy, having his life fucked up by imbeciles. He had to act fast. It was risky, but doing nothing was more risky. It was time to take back control.

'You can get every label in existence there,' Paula chattered on, her eyes shining. 'They've got gourmet restaurants too – well, they *say* gourmet. On opening day there'll be free offers, free food. All kinds of goodies up for grabs.'

'Sounds irresistible,' Finbar commented, still staring at the ad.

She nudged him. 'Why don't you take Shannon? I know she always swears she hates shopping, but I bet this place'll change her mind. She'll go mad – you won't believe it's the same woman!'

270

'You might as well know,' Finbar said, frowning. 'Shannon and I have split.'

'*What?*' Paula's eyes widened. 'You're joking.'

He swallowed, glanced away. 'I wish.'

'Oh, my God! I can't believe it. So that's why you seemed depressed lately. I'm sorry,' Paula said, dismayed. 'I really thought you two were for keeps. You've destroyed one of my romantic illusions.'

'Sorry about that. But illusions are meant to be shattered, aren't they? Especially the romantic variety.'

'Why did you split? Oh, sorry.' Paula grimaced, patted his arm. 'That's none of my business. But it'd be a shame to give up, wouldn't it? Can't you work things out?'

'No,' he said shortly.

'I'll shut up,' she said. 'I can see it's the last thing you want to talk about.'

'Thanks.' Finbar was relieved. So many people never knew when to shut up.

'There's just one thing.' Paula smiled suddenly, and batted her long, black eyelashes at him. 'As the sole, glamorous, sexual female around here, I don't have to worry when the big boss man gets desperate, do I?' she teased.

'No!' That made Finbar smile despite his mood. 'Your knicker elastic is safe from me. See you later,' he called as she grabbed her bag and ran out laughing. He walked into his office, sat down and unlocked the top drawer of his desk, took out the transparent plastic bag that contained Shannon's letter.

He recognised the looped, slanted handwriting on the envelope, this time in biro not fountain pen. The envelope was elegantly addressed to '*Bitch Lawyer Shannon Flinder*'. It was postmarked Liverpool, had a first-class stamp. No hand delivery this time. The bastard obviously didn't know Shannon had moved. Finbar longed to open it, but was afraid to contaminate whatever DNA might be inside. Shannon had to give the letter to the police for forensic analysis. Whoever was doing this wasn't going to stop, and she couldn't deal

271

with it on her own. He felt a rush of love and longing for her. Wanted desperately to see her, speak to her. But what the hell could he say? He picked up the phone and called Nick Forth's accountants firm.

'It's Finbar,' he said when Nick himself answered. There was a silence. 'Sorry to bother you, Nick, but I need to meet you. Right now, it's urgent. Have you seen Shannon recently?' he asked when the silence continued.

Still no answer. He thought Nick was going to hang up on him, or that they'd been cut off. But finally he did answer.

'Yes, I've seen her.' Nick's normally friendly, slightly diffident tone was cold, filled with anger.

'How is she?'

'What? You mean, like you give a fuck?'

'Oh, yes,' Finbar said. 'Believe me, I do.'

Blondie. It was just a word used by lots of people, usually of the politically incorrect variety. Demetrio Montana employed it to belittle and intimidate. With Keely Breeze, it was friendly and joshing. Shannon walked into the hospital lobby, bought a bunch of mixed flowers trimmed with green fern and took the lift to Keely's floor.

What the hell did that nut job mean when he said he was protecting her? Nothing, probably. Demetrio Montana lived a broken, destructive life, was a control freak, had a limited mind filled with rage. Other people were just objects to be used to satisfy his desires. Especially women, whose submission he regarded as crucial in defining his scarily fragile and distorted sense of identity. Poor Pascale Stevens, Shannon thought. I bet he did something terrible to her. He must have done it while he was out on bail. Bail I got him. Last night's phone call came back into her mind. She had tried to find out the number, but it had been withheld. How did the caller know her new home number? She had only given it to a few people: Mi-Hae, Khalida, Nick, several other friends. She couldn't imagine any of them being the anonymous letter writer or caller. Could someone else have got hold of her number without her knowledge? It was terrifying to think that this person had murdered Lucas Grant. Who was next on their list? Herself?

Shannon's unease heightened as she neared Keely's room. She hated hospitals, their smell and atmosphere. She steeled herself for the sight of Keely surrounded by all the tubes and other paraphernalia. The latest operation on her larynx had repaired more damage, but there was a lot of swelling and Keely still couldn't talk. Or breathe without a tube. The police guard on her room had been stepped up since the second murder attempt. Although not much, Shannon thought as she approached the two bored officers who looked her over like she was a prime joint of meat for sale in Tesco. Resources, resources.

Hiya Blondie. Keely held up the yellow post-it note as she walked in. Shannon smiled, trying to hide how shaky she still felt after the encounter with Demetrio Montana. He was no longer a client, but she had a nasty feeling she hadn't seen the last of him. Keely was propped up in bed, her dry, tangled hair showing a few centimetres of grey at the roots. She wore a silky blue lace-trimmed nightgown.

'Very sexy,' Shannon commented, 'but aren't you freezing?'

Keely scribbled another note. *Pretty flowers. Ta. You look shot at. More slap.*

'Thanks for the brutal honesty. I'll just nip out and get a vase. The days are gone when you could chuck flowers at some nurse and say, "Deal with these, darling".' Shannon was back a minute later. 'Apart from wanting to know how you're doing,' she said, placing the cut-glass vase of flowers next to another one full of white tulips, 'I also came to tell you your Crown Court appearance is postponed indefinitely. I know that seems trivial now, but at least it's one thing less to bother about.'

Keely scribbled again. *Police tell sod all. No sign Kev Hoyle?*

'I'm afraid not.' Shannon shook her head. 'They're doing all they can.'

And how much was that? If only the police could nail this Kev Hoyle, whoever he was, they might also get the man who had slashed Keely's throat. Shannon could still see his face when the scarf dropped, recall her terror, the knife dripping blood, his murderous eyes on her. Keely desperately needed to know her life wasn't in danger any more. And she wasn't the only one. Shannon watched as she wrote something else. How terrible not to be able to speak the damn words, especially when all your life you'd taken the power of speech for granted.

See his eyes. SO BLUE! Nightmares. Scared.

'I know.' Shannon pressed her hand. The bit about blue, blue eyes was a disquieting reminder of Demetrio Montana. As was the tall, shaven-headed, earringed man described in Keely's statement. Of course there had to be quite a few men who looked like that walking around. It bothered her nonetheless. Keely's statement also described the man as dealing in firearms. And drugs. Although Montana wasn't charged with dealing. 'Can you remember anything else about him?' she asked. 'Something you forgot to include in your statement, maybe. Or let me or the police know about?' She was trying not to let slip words like "tell", "said", "told".

Keely sank back against her pillows. She stared at Shannon, her eyes suddenly filled with alarm. Her dry lips moved.

'What is it? What's wrong?'

Keely gripped her pencil. *Sorry. Blanked. Forgot. He knows you!*

'What?' Shannon went weak with fright. 'Kev Hoyle? I don't understand! How can he possibly know me?'

Called you sexpot Shannon. Before he ...

The door opened and one of the police officers came into the room. ''Scuse me,' he said. 'But have you seen this yet?' He pushed a sheet of paper into Shannon's hand. 'We've been showing it around to the nurses and doctors and other

hospital staff. It's an e-fit of the guy who got in here and–'
He broke off, looked at Keely and smiled. 'All right, love?'

Shannon took the paper and gasped. It was a good like-
ness. Horrifyingly good. And it opened up too many fearful
implications for her to grasp at this moment. She glanced at
Keely, at the police officer. She was trembling.

'I know him,' she whispered.

Chapter Thirty-One

So I'm a coward, am I? Need to bugger off and get a life? Her arrogance just makes me more angry, more determined. Might even make me laugh if I didn't feel so bad, so depressed all the time. I can't deal with anything, can barely get through each day. I'm off my head, don't know what to do. No one can help me.

I bet the bitch lawyer wonders how I found out her new home phone number. It wasn't difficult, not for someone in my position. Just a few keyboard strokes, accessing the necessary info, scrolling down a list of names. Double-click. It was unauthorised what I did, of course, and I could have got into trouble if someone had discovered what I was up to. But I had a good excuse ready, and I'm sure it wouldn't have meant anything more serious than a reprimand.

Why did Shannon move out of Linnell's apartment? Did he dump her, or did the heroine herself do the dumping? I only found out the other day, which means I posted my latest letter to the wrong address. Still, I'm sure Mr Linnell will see that she gets it. Then again, it depends on how bitter their break-up was. He might bin it. Or open it himself. I hope he won't do that. I'll wait a while before I write again.

I got my pen back. I was in the Mags Court Information Office this morning, making a call on my mobile. There were a few other people in there – some middle-aged clerk in a tragic suit, a uniformed copper and a couple of girl solici-

tors, one trying to contact some scroat client who hadn't been able to crawl out of bed and turn up for his court appearance. An arrest warrant would have to be issued, more valuable time and resources wasted. None of them took any notice of me. People are in and out of that office all the time. Obsessed with their own business, thinking their little lives matter. I saw the Mont Blanc lying in the open top drawer of the old desk. I perched on one corner, having my very important conversation, shifted my arse and sent a stack of leaflets fluttering to the floor. The rest was easy. I'm glad I've got it back. Especially as it was engraved. Only a first name, nothing traceable. But still. I'd seen the notice, felt amazed that someone had handed it in. There are a few honest souls left.

Lucas Grant is cold and stiff now, lying in the morgue. The pathologist has finished cutting up and mutilating his poor, vulnerable body, and it's his funeral tomorrow. I'd love to go and pay my last respects. Pray for his soul. For mine. Tell him again how sorry I am. Problem is, a lot of murderers like to turn up at their victims' funerals. It's a well-known phenomenon. So a couple of police officers will attend and hover discreetly – or not – in the background to check out the mourners for anyone who isn't a family member, friend, or third-string journalist from some local rag. I feel guilty, gutted, stained, you name it. I drink and cry myself to sleep. But I'm not gutted enough to be susceptible to that other well-known murderer's phenomenon – taking stupid risks in the hope that I'll get caught.

The blonde bitch lawyer's got a frightened look in her blue eyes these days. Definitely fraying around the edges. How does it make her feel to know Lucas Grant died because of her selfish intransigence?

Hey, big word there. I'll start sounding like a lawyer myself soon, if I'm not careful. So, what next for Shannon? She'll have to tell the police about her nasty letters now. That's the last thing she wants, of course. Especially as one thing might lead to another, with the result that they decide to re-open the Strange Case of the Splattered Headmaster. And she doesn't know what I'll do next, does she? Except that it won't be anything that'll make her day. Oh yes. She's starting to slide down the slippery slope at last.

I sat on my bench in that silent stone corridor down in the Bridewell this morning. Not for long, because I got disturbed by a couple of Group 4 guards, a man and a woman with loud voices, braying laughs and jangling keys. I whipped out my mobile and pretended to be having a very important conversation. They looked at me and I could tell they wondered what I was doing sitting there, although I've got every right. I didn't smile or nod, just ignored them completely. The woman was boasting about getting hammered the previous night, giving a detailed account of how much booze she and her sad mates had got down their necks. And who'd chucked it back up. Socially acceptable behaviour for our times. I can understand it though, I suppose. Things are tougher than ever, so much shit to worry about, in the world as well as in your own life. Most people, me included, need something to help them forget their problems for a while.

I thought I'd be happy now that Shannon's frightened and in trouble. But I'm not. It's just not enough. It takes my breath away to realise how much and how fast my hatred for her is growing. I really want to hurt her, see the pain in her eyes. Relish her fear. Phoning her like that was stupid, it just gave her the chance to show defiance and congratulate herself afterwards on how brave she'd been. Everything – everything! – that's happened is her fault. I can never forgive her for the damage she's done. She could never atone even if she wanted to. It won't be enough even if I do manage to destroy her life.

Poor Lucas. I'm crying again. I can't stand this, I'll never get over it. And I feel this way purely because of that evil, selfish, arrogant bitch. Shannon will be terrified that I'll kill again. She won't give a toss about someone else dying, of *course, only worried how much trouble their death might cause her. Most of all, she's afraid for herself. And she should be.*

I'll get a life, all right, Bitch! Don't you worry about that.

Chapter Thirty-Two

'So you think it's the same guy?' the police inspector in charge of Keely Breeze's case asked after Shannon had explained.

'I don't think, I know!' She gripped the phone as she stared out of the window. The seventh-floor hospital waiting room was littered with empty coffee cups and torn magazines.

'Okay. But we'll need Keely – and you – to ID him. An arrest warrant for a Demetrio Montana was issued this morning,' he went on. 'We got the test results on that piece of female jawbone found in the crusher. Turned out it was part of the body of Pascale Stevens, his girlfriend. Or ex-girlfriend. Problem now is, we can't find the bastard.'

'I can help you there.' Shannon was sweating. 'I've got his mobile number. You can trace it and locate him that way.'

'Well, yeah. In theory. But it's not that easy. It'd take time – and loads of red tape.'

'But this is an emergency, for ... ! Okay, there might be another way,' Shannon said. 'But I can't guarantee it'll work. And I'll need back-up from you. I won't do anything without that, because I'll be putting myself at risk.'

'You've got it, Shannon.'

Half an hour later she jumped up as Demetrio Montana barged into her office again and slammed the door, his blue eyes gleaming.

'What d'you want to talk to me about then, Blondie? Seen the light, have you? Remembered your manners? Thought you would.' He came around the desk, grabbed her and pushed her against the bookcase, his breath on her face. 'I've fancied you rotten ever since that day I saw you down in that bloody hole of a Bridewell.' He gripped her shoulders. 'Doesn't have to be just a working relationship between us, you know. I've got plans for you, Blondie.'

'Did you murder Pascale Stevens?' Shannon asked.

His smile faded. 'What?'

'I don't want any relationship with you.' She pulled away. 'Take your hands off me.'

She watched his expression change to enraged disbelief. The door burst open and the room was suddenly full of police officers. They grabbed Demetrio, dragged him back and handcuffed him, checking his pockets. The inspector in charge stepped forward.

'Demetrio Montana, I am arresting you on suspicion of the murder of Pascale Stevens and the attempted murder of Keely Breeze. You do not have to say anything, but it may harm your defence if–'

'Bitch!' Demetrio shouted at Shannon, his eyes blazing. 'You set me up. You're one fucking dead bitch now!'

She looked coolly at the inspector. 'You can add threatening behaviour to the rap sheet. Although I realise it's a drop in the ocean of everything he's wanted for.'

'You've got that right.' He glared at the struggling Demetrio. 'Shut it, you. Get him out of here,' he snapped. He turned to Shannon. 'Thanks a lot for your help on this.'

'No worries. Any time.' Shannon kept her arms tightly folded so that he wouldn't see her clenched fists.

'I owe you one.'

'Don't say that.' She tried to smile. 'I might take you up on it.'

He laughed. 'See you.'

'I didn't murder that stupid cow,' Demetrio was yelling as

281

they dragged him away. 'I didn't do it, I never touched her. I swear!'

Mi-Hae and Khalida walked in, grim faced. 'Just another boring day at the office,' Mi-Hae commented. 'You all right, Shannon?'

'Yes.' She sank into her chair. Shock and an empty stomach made her feel weak and sick.

'We're taking you out for a late lunch,' Khalida said. 'You're going to eat a sandwich and drink at least one big glass of wine.'

'I can't, Khal. I'm already late for my appointment with Inspector Cindy.'

'No, you're not. I called and told her you couldn't make it. Oh, and Nick phoned just before this little drama occurred. He wants you to call him back. Says it's urgent.'

'You're joking.' Shannon rubbed her cold hands together. 'I can't do *urgent* now. Had more than enough of that for one day. I don't bloody want to know.'

'I agree,' Khalida smiled. 'Come on. Let's get out of here.'

'This is crazy!' Cindy Nightingale's girly ponytail bobbed up and down as she marched along the corridor gripping a handful of papers, followed by an indifferent Rob. 'We've hardly had a chance to get this Lucas Grant murder inquiry up and running, when some anorak local history man discovers a stabbed stiff in St James's Cemetery. What the fuck's going on in this city?' she snapped. 'There's only supposed to be one homicide every fortnight.'

'At least some other stuff's sorted.' Rob loosened his tie. 'Pascale Stevens's murder, not to mention the two murder attempts on Keely Breeze.'

'One attempt, you mean. Demetrio Montana won't say who slashed her throat outside Dale Street Mags Court. It's going to take a lot of persuasion to make *him* realise where his interests lie.'

'Well, you've got Shannon to thank for his arrest.'

'Oh yes, the ex-wifie.' Cindy walked into her office, threw the papers on the desk and turned, giving him one of her evil looks. 'What came over her then, doing the despised bizzies a favour? Because if she thinks it'll make me forget the little chat she's supposed to come and have with me, she's dead wrong. Some bimbo from her office called earlier, and had the nerve to tell me our Shannon couldn't make it. Of course she thinks she's above the law.'

'That's crap! Shannon's going through a really tough time just now,' Rob said quietly, hating Cindy. 'In her personal life as well as at work. And she was ill last weekend.'

'Oh dear, was she? Remind me to pop a get well card in the post. Stop it, will you?' Cindy pulled a face. 'Some of us are off to the pub in about ten minutes, and you'll have me blubbering into my Becks.'

'Shannon wants to help with the Lucas Grant inquiry as much as we want to solve it,' Rob argued. 'She's devastated to think that whoever wrote those anonymous letters could have murdered some innocent person just to get to her.'

'Devastated to think it might cause trouble for her, you mean,' Cindy snarled.

'That's not true! And for all we know, she could be next on this bastard's list.'

'Hmm. Better take her into protective custody then, hadn't we? Otherwise I'll be tossing and turning all night with the worry.'

The bitch was really picking on him lately, snorting at him non-stop and singling him out for all the shit jobs. Just because she hated Shannon, and because he had a connection with Shannon. Rob had had enough of Cindy, more than enough. He was dead tired. He thought of Katy, who was still off work. Recovering from murdering his baby! He had phoned and gone round to her flat again, but she refused to see him or speak to him except to shout through the door that they were finished, he had destroyed her and she never wanted to set eyes on him again. Rob needed her to know that she had destroyed him by what she'd done. How much he hurt, how gutted he was. He still couldn't believe it had happened, that she'd really got rid of his baby. But Katy wouldn't listen, and it was doing his head in. Rob had not told anyone at work; he didn't want something like *that* doing the rounds. It was nobody's business but his.

And Shannon's, of course. She had been sympathetic to him when he broke down outside the Mags Court the other day. She knew what it meant to lose a baby. He had the feeling she was almost as shocked about Katy's termination as he was. But Shannon had her own problems, and only limited time and attention to spare him. If he wanted to win her back one day he had to be patient and tread carefully, even though he could barely control his grief and rage at times, wanted to spill it all out to her. And if he wasn't so devastated about his cruelly dashed hopes of fatherhood, he would have been ecstatic to know that Finbar fucking Linnell was out of Shannon's life now. What had happened, he wondered? Hardly any time ago Shannon had been desperate to tell him how much she loved the bastard. But she was angry then, might have said it just to try and hurt him. Well, whatever. She was on her own now, miserable and fed up. This could be his big chance. Their mutual misery might bring them together again.

'If you don't stop mooning over this bloody divorce and your ex-missis and do some serious work for a change, I'm going to put your name forward for an official arse-kicking,' he heard Cindy snap. 'I've had just about enough of your bullshit. You sit around all day staring into space and–'

'I want some leave,' Rob interrupted. 'I'm owed it.'

She gaped at him. 'You what? Need a holiday, do you, after all your hard work? Be careful, Rob,' she sneered. 'You're a valuable team member – don't want you getting burnout, do we?'

'I want some leave,' he repeated. 'Shouldn't be a problem. I've got plenty of days saved up.'

'You know what? I don't think I'm getting through to you.'

'I'll put in my request in the morning.' Rob turned to go.

'And I'll tear it up. Just a bloody minute.' Cindy put on her red leather coat and picked up her bag. 'What are you on?' She stared at him. 'I'd like to know, just to be sure I never try it. Did the gorgeous Shannon give it to you?' she mocked. 'You'd take anything she gives you!'

Rob stuck his hands in his trouser pockets and walked out, determined to get away from Cindy's hectoring voice. Because if he didn't he might kill her. He wouldn't regret that, although he would regret doing the time. She wasn't worth it.

'Where the hell d'you think you're going?' Cindy shouted after him. 'I haven't finished with you. Get back here!'

Rob felt so alone, so crushed and desperate. He could phone Shannon on her mobile – she would probably have left the office by now – and ask her to meet him for a drink or dinner. But he was afraid she would refuse, because she had other plans. Or because she didn't want to see him. He wasn't strong enough to take any more rejection just now. Not from Shannon or anybody else. Would his and Shannon's baby have been a boy or a girl? he wondered again. And what about his baby that Katy had just murdered? He would never see that child now, never hold it in his arms. Watch it grow up. Give love, receive it.

Rob's eyes flooded with hot, stinging tears. Cindy's voice got smaller and faded away. He was alone, he had nothing and nobody. Just a job he loathed now, but was too bloody scared to pack in because he didn't know what the hell he'd do with himself if he had no reason to crawl out of bed each morning.

He kept on walking, down and down the long corridor to the doors at the end.

'So Finbar thought it would be best if I gave you the letter,' Nick finished awkwardly. He took a gulp of Scotch and glanced around the big, unfurnished sitting room lit by two lamps and the bluish gas flames. They sat on folded quilts,

Shannon huddled in her robe. Her hair was damp, her feet bare. 'Why didn't you call me back?' he asked. 'I said it was urgent.'

'Sorry.' Shannon shrugged. 'Everything's urgent lately.' She didn't want to tell Nick about her day, didn't even want to think about it. 'You know how it is.'

'Yeah. Bloody jobs swallow up all our time. Turned cold tonight,' he remarked, pulling his overcoat around him and shifting closer to the fire. 'Typical, just when you think spring's arrived.'

So Finbar didn't want to give her the letter himself. Did not want to see her. That wasn't a surprise, and she was stupid to feel so hurt. She should be grateful he had enough sensitivity not to just stick it in the post and let it land unannounced on her desk one fine morning.

'It's not that Finbar doesn't care.' Nick felt desperately sorry for her, hated to see Shannon look so defeated. 'He just didn't think it would be a good idea to–'

She looked away. 'I think I get the picture.'

Nick wondered again what kind of danger Finbar was in, why he said it was necessary for him and Shannon to split, even though he still loved her. But Nick had to stay ignorant, at least for now – and not breathe a word to Shannon. All he could do was be a friend, keep an eye on her like Finbar wanted. Finbar had made a new will and left her everything. Just in case, he said. Nick's anger at him was gone, replaced by sadness and anxiety. Finbar and Shannon had loved one another so much. What had happened to destroy that?

'Where's this letter then?' Shannon put down her wine glass. 'Might as well have a look at the damn thing.'

'Sure you want to?' Nick pulled his briefcase towards him and clicked it open. 'Might be better to wait until tomorrow when you're in the presence of the police.'

'I'd rather do it now. I don't want to give Cindy Nightingale the satisfaction of seeing me–' she paused '–react badly.'

'Okay. Up to you.' Nick took out the plastic-covered letter and passed it to her. Her hand trembled as she took it. She stared at it, bit her lip. 'You *sure* about this?' he repeated. 'I can understand you don't want to lose it in front of that police inspector, but still.'

Shannon opened the letter, flinched and gasped as something landed in her lap.

'Bloody hell!' Nick stared at the large spider, the long-legged, thick-bodied variety that crawled into houses when autumn cold began to bite and stayed until early spring, scuttling along skirting boards and getting trapped in slippery bathtubs. The thing was dead, dried out. Several more dropped from between the folds of paper. Shannon swiped them away and jumped screaming to her feet.

'It's all right,' Nick said, knowing it wasn't. 'They're dead, they can't... Shannon, wait!' He got up and followed as she ran screaming into the bedroom. 'Come here.' He grabbed her and pulled her to him. She was shaking, sobbing uncontrollably. 'It's all right,' he repeated, hugging her and stroking her damp hair, cursing whoever was doing this to her. Shannon had had just about all the shit anyone could reasonably be expected to take.

'Get rid of them,' she sobbed, her face pressed into his shoulder. 'Now. Please!'

'Of course I will. Calm down, okay? Get into bed,' he said. 'Keep warm.'

She took no notice. 'I want Finbar!' Her voice rose to a wail. 'I love him, I miss him so much! Why did he hurt me? I love him!'

Nick held her tight. 'I know you do, sweetheart.' He wished he could tell her the truth – the bit of it he knew. 'Come on, you're shivering. Get warm now, okay?'

She collapsed on the bed and curled up, crying loudly. Nick pulled the quilt over her, went back into the sitting room and looked disgustedly at the leggy, dried-out specimens scattered over the parquet. There were seven altogether. Sick bastard, he thought. He got a couple of tissues, swept them up and flushed them down the toilet. Then he unfolded the sheet of paper.

Hello, bitch. These things used to trap helpless specimens in their silken webs and suck them dry until they were all used up. Just like you do. Look at them now. Their turn to be all used up. Not pretty, eh?

Lucas Grant died because of you. A young guy, decent and intelligent, his life ahead of him. I found out he'd already had one tragedy in his family: his brother committed suicide. Can you imagine how killing Lucas made me feel? No, how could you? You've got no guilt, morals, conscience. So I'll put it this way: killing him made me feel a hell of a lot worse than I would if I killed you.

Thought for today, bitch lawyer – Mortality.

Namely, your own.

'Christ!' Nick whispered. He dropped the letter, went into the kitchen and made Shannon a cup of tea. Her keys and mobile, some paperwork, lay on the table. She was quiet when he returned to the bedroom, lying there hugging the pillow. He put the cup on the bedside table.

'I got rid of those beasties,' he said. 'They're on their way out to the Mersey.'

Shannon turned over and sat up. 'Did you read the letter? What does it say?'

'Never mind that now. Drink the tea.'

'I want to know.' She started to get out of bed.

'Stay there, okay? I'll get it.' Nick retrieved the letter and handed it to her. Shannon read it silently, folded the paper and put it back in the envelope.

'On the whole, I think I prefer dead spiders.'

He sat on one corner of the bed. 'I want you to come home with me tonight. You've had a big shock – another one – and I hate the thought of you alone in this barn of an apartment. You're unhappy, you're frightened, and there's a

288

murderer on the loose! You have to face the fact that you're in danger.'

'I am facing it,' Shannon said. 'That's why I won't run and hide and cower.'

'Very commendable. But don't you think that might be the best thing you could do until the police catch Lucas Grant's killer?'

'How long will that take? And what am I supposed to do in the meantime? I need to work, Nick, earn a living.'

'But–'

'I'll be careful, don't worry. Thanks for the offer, it's very sweet of you.'

He sighed. 'You're a stubborn lady.'

'Have to be, don't I?' Shannon smiled for the first time. 'People bossing me about.'

'Only because they care.' Nick took her hand. 'I love you, Shannon. I want us to be friends for the rest of our lives. I can't stand the thought of some fucked-up bastard hurting you, even–' He stopped, frowning. 'Drink that tea before it gets cold. Will you at least let me doss down here?' he asked. 'I don't want to leave you alone tonight.'

'You're very kind, but I'll be okay.' Shannon sipped her tea. 'I'm on my own now, and I'm determined to get used to it.'

'Determined to punish yourself, more like!' He dropped her hand. 'What are you trying to do, be the loneliest, saddest single in existence?'

'That reminds me – must stock the freezer with pizzas.' Shannon smiled again at his expression. 'There's nothing sad about being single. It certainly beats being in a crap relationship with a partner who doesn't love you. You'll be welcome to stay over once I get a guest room sorted,' she said. 'And Nick, think of your dodgy back. If you spend a night on these floors you'll need an emergency osteopath.'

She wouldn't admit to anyone, not even Nick, how frightened she was. He stayed another half hour. After he'd gone Shannon put the letter in her briefcase and went to bed, fully expecting to be plagued by horrific nightmares about spiders and murderers. Hours later when she finally managed to fall asleep, she dreamed that Finbar was touching her, his hands, lips and tongue roving over her naked body, teasing her in all kinds of almost unbearably erotic ways. Each time she was on the verge of orgasm, he stopped. She was in tears with the frustration of it. His green eyes stared down at her and he smiled, a cruel smile. He kissed her and she was desperate for it not to end because then he would tell her he didn't love her any more. Shannon was jerked out of her restless sleep by the persistent sound of the hall buzzer. She gasped and sat up in bed, her heart pounding. It was windy outside, rain-drops pattering the double glazing. The buzzer sounded again, long and hard. It was three-twenty in the morning.

'Bloody hell,' she groaned. 'Talk about endless night.' A faint thump of bass came from somewhere. One of the tenants having a mid-week party? Nice when you didn't have to get up for work. She lay down again. If she ignored the buzzer, whatever idiot was pressing it would give up and go away. But it was no use, they didn't go away. She got up, swearing, pulled on her robe and padded into the dark hall. Snatched up the intercom phone.

'Who is this?' A car swished past on the wet road.

'Your cab's here,' a male voice shouted.

Shannon's irritation increased. 'I didn't order a cab!'

'Yeah, you did, love. I've been stood here ten minutes.'

'You've got it wrong.' She spoke slowly, carefully, so the fool would understand. 'I did not order a cab.'

'*Yeah.* You phoned just after three.'

'Go away.' Shannon hung up. He immediately leaned on the buzzer again.

'Just let me in,' he shouted as she lifted the phone for the second time. 'Or come down here so we can sort this.'

'You must be joking,' she snapped, furious and fright-ened. 'There's nothing to sort. For the last time, I didn't order a cab! Get lost *now*. If you don't, I'll call the police.' She hung up and stood trembling in the dark, silent hall.

What the hell was going on? She ran into the sitting room and looked out of the windows. The street of Georgian buildings was quiet. Another car, a big, shiny, four-wheel-drive beast, cruised past. There was no sign of any cab.

Was this what a lone female in the mean city had to expect when she tried to get a decent night's sleep? Shannon's fear increased as she thought of the anonymous letter again. That word: *mortality.* She went into the kitchen, snapped on the pretty, built-in halogen spotlights and got the bottle of wine from the fridge. To hell with tea. She was gulping the chilled wine when the front door bell rang.

'Jesus!' she gasped. She froze, the glass to her lips. She put it down and walked slowly into the hall. The bell sounded again, three sharp rings. What was this, a murderer come calling? Oh God, Shannon thought, why didn't I let Nick stay? Or go home with him, like he wanted? He's right, I am stubborn. What the hell am I trying to prove to myself!

'Who's there?' she called, trying to give a *don't-mess-with-me-motherfucker!* edge to her voice.

'Hello? I live in the next apartment.' Another man's voice, this one soft and tired.

'What d'you want?'

'Sorry to bother you, but some guy's been buzzing me the last few minutes, telling me I'd ordered a cab and trying to get me to let him in. I wondered if he'd done the same with you? He might want to gain access to the building for some reason. I don't know if I should call the police.'

Shannon breathed again. She hadn't yet encountered any of her new neighbours, but supposed this was as good a time as any. She clicked on the hall light, walked to the door and peered through the spyhole. She caught a glimpse of dark hair and trimmed beard, but couldn't see the man's face properly because his head was lowered and he was rubbing his eyes as if dropping with sleep.

'Hang on a sec.' She dashed into the kitchen, grabbed her keys and sprinted back. She left the chain on as she unlocked and unbolted the door. He would surely understand she didn't want to let a stranger in at this time of night, even if he was a respectable, harmless neighbour and not a psycho. 'Yes, he tried it with me,' she said, opening the door as much as the chain permitted. 'I told him I'd call the police. I think he's gone now–'

Something crashed down on the chain, gripped it and cut it through, narrowly missing her hand. The door was shoved open with great force, throwing her backwards. Shannon staggered against the wall, tripped over a box of clothes and fell, landing painfully on her right shoulder. The man stepped inside, shut the door and dropped the large pair of pliers he'd used to break the chain. Pulled out a knife. She stared, frozen with terror. Seconds must have passed, but it felt like longer.

He hadn't had a beard last time they met, only stubble. And he wasn't wearing his hat or scarf. Shannon recognised the dark, hate-filled eyes, the acne-pitted complexion.

'Remember me?' he hissed.

'No!' She backed away. It was a face she would never forget.

'Yeah, you do. I can tell you do.'

Shannon felt suffocated, tried not to panic. 'Did you ... write me those letters?'

'What fucking letters? Dunno what you're on about.' He came closer. 'Tell me when you last saw me,' he ordered. 'That day you fucked things up for me. Go on. Or I'll cut you right now.'

'The Magistrates' Court,' she gasped. 'Keely Breeze. You slashed her throat.'

'That's right.' He smiled with satisfaction. 'Clever girl. Clever little lawyer.' He moved towards her, gripping the Stanley knife. 'And now it's your turn.'

Chapter Thirty-Three

'You do realise you're meant to have a permit from the Home Secretary for this sort of thing?' Curtis joked. 'Who d'you think you are, mate? Special Branch – MI5 or 6?'

'Yeah. Boyhood fantasy.' Finbar stared at the laptop screen with its map of the relevant part of Liverpool, the tiny flashing green dot that was Iain Blick's slowly moving Audi. 'They've circled The Village twice,' he said. 'They're stopping now.'

'Probably want to get a good look, check out the security.' Curtis stood up and stretched, glanced around Finbar's sitting room then looked out of the windows at the dark river. 'Still throwing it down,' he murmured. 'Bloody cold tonight too.' He turned. 'Mind if I help myself to a measure of your single malt?'

'While I'm paying for your time and expertise, yes, I do.'

'Chill out, Finbar, for Christ's sake! Everything's cool.'

'Not the word I'd use to describe my present circumstances.'

'Look, mate, I know you're in shit–'

'Yeah, that's the word.'

'But you won't tell and I won't ask. I just want to know what's happened to that laid-back, gently mocking Irish humour.'

'It got drowned on a rainy day in Limerick. What did you see when you drove around The Village earlier? What's it like?' Finbar didn't want to go there himself in case any patrolling member of Blick's gang clocked him. Or possibly the Branch. But no one would take any notice of Curtis – not unless they were a woman with a glad eye for the tall, good-looking black man. And there wouldn't be many women around there at this ungodly hour.

'Blue lights.' Curtis shrugged. 'Security guards. Some of them with doggies. Delivery lorries coming and going. There's a restaurant there called the River Room.' He yawned. 'Good place to have a drink and a bite once you and the girlfriend or missis have shopped 'til you dropped.'

'I'm not really interested in the facilities right now.' Finbar looked at the screen. 'They've started off again. They're probably heading back to Newsham Park.' He shut down the laptop. 'Let's get over there now.' He got up. 'We've got to be in place ready to remove the tracking device when they get back.'

Curtis grabbed his jacket. 'Ready when you are.'

Finbar did not dare leave the tracking device on Blick's Audi in case it was discovered. And now he was almost certain that their objective was The Village, one of the newest shopping complexes in the country. Getting a big build-up in the local and national press and on television, scheduled to open in just over a week's time. And close almost immediately if Blick had his way, thousands of lives lost amid a sea of spectacularly bloody carnage. Finbar could understand why Special Branch refused to bug Blick's flat or put a tracking device on one of the cars he used. They were right, it was risky. Too risky. But they weren't as desperate as he was. He pulled on his coat and looked at his watch. Three-forty a.m.

'We'll use your car,' he said to Curtis.

'Okay.' Curtis picked up his bag.

Curtis Bright was an old contact, an ex-army officer who now sold security products in his Manchester spy shop and over the Internet. His web page was crammed with a bewildering variety of goodies to satisfy even the most security-obsessed, paranoid saddo in existence. And Curtis didn't get much excitement these days. He didn't ask why Finbar needed to do this. The less he knew, the better, was Curtis' principle. He would take the money and keep his mouth shut. They went out and Finbar double-locked the apartment door.

'They've got the top flat, right?' Curtis asked as they drove towards the centre of town. He switched the window wipers to a higher speed.

'Yes, front of the house overlooking the park.' Finbar glanced at him. 'This microphone thing you told me about. Is it in the bag?'

'Sure is,' Curtis grinned. 'Take a look.'

Finbar unzipped the bag, took out the device and studied it. It was hand-held, looked like a shotgun. A small, plastic, umbrella-like dish fitted on to the end, and there was a pair of headphones. 'Tell me again.'

'It's a parabolic microphone,' Curtis explained. 'Bit like using a telephoto lens on a camera, except this picks up and amplifies sound instead of images. It's got an exceptionally high signal-to-noise ratio – that is, not much background noise – which makes it the mike of choice eighty percent of the time. Works on a nine-volt battery. It's directional. You'll have to hold it real steady, because I haven't brought a shock mount. This model's a laser version – it can pick up a conversation from a closed window in the line of sight.'

'Are there any legal uses for these things?' Finbar asked. 'I mean, apart from law enforcement – which of course doesn't necessarily mean legal either.'

Curtis laughed. 'I think some Swedish scientist originally developed parabolic microphones for listening to bird song.'

'No kidding.' Finbar wondered if Carl Mactire and his colleagues employed such devices. If they did, they were not necessarily going to tell him what they overheard. He needed to gather his own intelligence. He hesitated. 'Someone planted a bug in their flat,' he said. 'Well, not in the flat exactly, but in a briefcase that's in there. How big a risk is there of it being detected?'

'Mm. Depends.' Curtis moved the car off smoothly as the lights changed to green. He was driving along Upper Parliament Street in the direction of Smithdown Road, the orange-lit bulk of the Anglican cathedral to their left. 'Most commercially available bug detectors aren't that good, despite the hype. They can only detect very high or low frequencies – the kinds most used by amateurs, which are a bit of a giveaway. To do a really effective sweep you'd need a specialist firm. But with all the technology, the best bug-detecting method is still a pair of sharp eyes and experienced hands.'

'Right.' Finbar was sweating. He hoped Carl Mactire and his people were not amateurs.

The big Victorian house set in its own grounds was dark and quiet except for the lighted window on the top, right-hand side. Several cars were parked in the drive. Curtis stopped further down the road beneath one of the big chest-nut trees. They got out and retreated into the park. Curtis took his night-vision binoculars, trained them on the house then swept them up and down the road. There was nobody about; no joggers or dog walkers at this hour. Rain lashed the wide road and pavements. There were no sheltering leaves on the trees this early in the year. Finbar shivered and turned up his coat collar.

'Let me have a look.' Curtis handed him the binoculars. There were a couple of vans parked in the long line of cars along the road, one with a carpet firm's logo painted on the side, the other plain white. Could one of them contain a sur-veillance unit? Finbar gave the binoculars back.

'So now we wait,' Curtis whispered.

'Shouldn't be long. Unless they've gone somewhere else. But I doubt it.'

His thoughts turned to Nick, who had promised to phone after he had seen Shannon, and possibly found out what was in her latest anonymous letter. Unless she had decided to just give it to the police without opening it. Somehow Finbar did not think she would do that. But the afternoon and evening had passed without any call from Nick. Of course he might not have seen Shannon until quite late; she wasn't always easy to contact and sometimes forgot to switch her mobile back on.

What Nick had told him so far wasn't good. She was exhausted and very upset, had been sick with a terrible headache for part of the weekend after they'd split. But she was going to work as usual, putting a brave face on things. She would do that, Finbar thought, because Shannon had guts. But now it appeared the letter writer had murdered some young guy, just to prove they meant business. What the hell next? Shannon needed him and he hated the fact that he wasn't there for her, could not protect her. She thought he didn't care any more. Finbar flinched as cold rain dripped down inside his coat collar. He was soaked, shivering, looked like a drowned rodent. As did Curtis.

'They should be here any minute,' he whispered. 'Get that mike set up.'

Curtis quickly assembled the device. 'You put the headphones on and point it up at their window,' he explained. 'Don't forget, hold it steady like I said. It'll record everything.' He glanced to his right. 'This could be them now.'

A car was cruising along the road, its headlights dipped. It was the Audi. It didn't turn into the drive, but parked some distance from the house. Finbar peered through the binoculars again. There was the driver, Blick in the passenger seat and two men in the back. They stayed in the car for a minute then got out and ran back towards the house, pulling up their jacket collars against the rain. Finbar gave the binoculars back to Curtis once the men were inside and presumably going upstairs.

'Give them five minutes,' he whispered. 'Then you can get that thing off their car. Make sure you're not spotted – by anyone!' He didn't need to tell Curtis that, of course, but he was nervous. Curtis nodded and gave him the thumbs up.

Finbar put on the headphones and levelled the mike up at the lighted window. The sound was incredibly clear and close. A toilet flushed, rings popped on beer cans. Madonna sang about how it felt to be a girl.

'The security's so crap there you'd think it was an airport,' he heard Iain Blick laugh. 'It's going to be less of a challenge than I thought. All we need now is a nice, big lorry packed with the semtex our Irish friend has ordered for us.'

Finbar saw Curtis slip away, cross the road and walk slowly into the dark drive of a neighbouring house, as if he lived there and was returning from a night out.

'What about that arrest yesterday?' one of the men asked. 'Can it hurt us? I don't trust that self-important prick to keep his trap shut about anything.'

'Mr Montana can't hurt us,' Blick said, yawning. 'Old Blue Eyes only knows a tiny piece of a great big picture. You made sure of that all along.' A pause. 'Didn't you?'

Another pause. 'Yeah.'

Montana? Finbar frowned, remembering the guy Jan-Willem had warned him about. How was he involved with this bunch?

'It was a mistake to work with him in the first place,' Blick said. 'Your mistake. He turned out to be bloody useless. Not only that, a liability. We've had a lucky escape. Could be bad news for the lovely Ms Flinder, of course, helping to set up her client like that. Old Blue Eyes is going to want revenge. Can't do it himself, now that he's locked up. But maybe he knows someone who can.'

'We don't want anything happening to her yet,' someone said nervously. 'Linnell will freak.'

'Montana's got enough to worry about for the moment. He'll probably try to make a deal with the police. He won't do anything about the blonde just yet. And don't worry about our Finbar,' Blick said. 'He won't be a problem any longer after next Saturday afternoon around three. I'm going to kill the smartarse bastard. Turn that shit down,' he ordered. 'I'm off to bed. Might not be a bad idea for you lot to get some sleep too.' The music stopped.

Curtis appeared out of the darkness, startling Finbar.

Several minutes later they were back in the car, wet and shivering, the mike stowed in its bag. Finbar sat silent, staring at the wet road, his head full of Iain Blick's voice. So Montana had been a client of Shannon's! If only he'd known sooner. He could have warned her. And now she could be at risk from one of his contacts on the outside. He had to talk to Mactire immediately.

Curtis glanced at him. 'Hear anything interesting?'

'You could say that.' If hearing your own death sentence pronounced could be described as *interesting*. They turned on to the main road back to town. 'Stop if you see a phone box, okay? I left my mobile at home.'

'A phone box.' Curtis shook his head, amused. 'Now there's a challenge. They're getting as rare as high street banks and post offices. You can borrow my phone,' he offered.

'Better not. You don't want this call traced to you. Neither do I.'

There was a call box along Ullet Road, at the end of a row of shops. Finbar got out and ran to it, hoping the damn thing was working. It was. He dialled the special number Carl Mactire had given him. Seconds later Mactire's sleep-heavy, gravelly growl came on the line.

'Shannon Flinder's life is in danger,' Finbar said, his voice low and furious. '*More* danger, that is. Someone connected with Iain Blick – I don't know how, exactly – just got arrested, and he's trying to get someone on the outside to hurt her. His name's Demetrio Montana. Montana was on Death Row in the States and he murdered his girlfriend in the Netherlands. You better drag your arse out of bed right now and make sure Shannon Flinder's safe. Make damn sure she stays safe. Because if anything happens to her, I blow this whole sting thing and you're fucked. So am I, but I don't give a toss about that. Get it sorted,' he hissed. '*Now.*'

He crashed the phone down and ran back through the rain to the waiting car.

*

299

'Where's your money? *Money!*' he yelled, brandishing the knife.

So he wanted to rob her before he slaughtered her like a lamb, in true Biblical fashion. Insult added to fatal injury. Shannon backed further away. Fighting her terror, trying to think straight. She had nothing with which to defend herself, and couldn't imagine what she was going to do. If she screamed, would anyone hear? Would they bother to phone the police? Probably these new neighbours who she hadn't met and wasn't bloody likely to now would be very helpful to the police once she'd been murdered. They would want to get involved then, all right. Make statements about what they'd heard, pump the officers for gory details. She hated them already.

'In my wallet,' she gasped. She pointed to the row of hooks by the front door.

'Yeah, w*here?* There's loads of bloody coats here.'

'The pocket of that leather jacket.'

'Don't move,' he warned, waving the knife at her. He was more relaxed now, knowing he had her alone and at his mercy. He stretched out one hand, rooted in the jacket pockets and pulled out her wallet.

'Why did you want to murder Keely Breeze?' Shannon asked, playing for time. 'Did Demetrio Montana tell you to do it?'

'He didn't *tell* me to do nothing,' he spat. 'It was a favour. She was trouble. And I knew you could ID me, it was doing me head in. I wanted to find out who you were. But he wouldn't tell me. Said to lay off you, that you was cool and he'd sorted you. That there wasn't a problem. Lying bastard! I followed him, found out you were his lawyer. Saw you talking to some copper after they took him away.' He opened the wallet.

So that was what Demetrio Montana had meant when he'd said he was protecting her. 'I don't even know your name,' Shannon said wildly. 'Anything about you!' Except that he was a killer. 'Why do you want to kill me? I'm no threat.'

300

'You recognised me, didn't you? That's enough.'

'What's your association with Demetrio Montana?' Jesus! Shannon thought. Why am I talking like I'm in court?

'Shut up. What d'you think this is, a fucking quiz show? Now the soft bastard's gone and got himself banged up. With your help. All bullshit, that's what he was. And I'm not going down because of him – or you.' He shook the wallet at her. 'There's only a twenty in here, you miserable cow.'

'Take the two credit cards.'

'I will. Have a right laugh with them after I've done you. Least you won't have to worry about the bills.'

How bloody thoughtful. Shannon's breath slowed. She had to try and fight him. There was nothing to lose. She watched as he tried to ease the credit cards out of her wallet with one hand, while keeping the knife pointed at her with the other. Why bother to do that now instead of waiting until after he'd killed her? Did he think there might be so much blood on his hands that it would damage the cards' magnetic strips? Or was he, like the majority of sad souls Shannon encountered during her working hours, simply not bursting with intelligence? When his attention wandered for a couple of seconds she seized her chance. It was now or never.

She fled into the kitchen, slammed the door and wedged a chair beneath the handle, dragged the table against the chair. He pounded on the door, yelling and swearing. Her heart flipped with terror. She shoved the table in place, knowing it wouldn't keep him at bay for long. She glanced around, noted that the kettle was full of hot water, and switched it on. Grabbed her mobile. Her fingers were trembling so much she could hardly dial.

'Police,' she gasped. 'Yes, it's an emergency.' She kept her voice as calm as possible and jammed her hip against the table, trying to keep it in position. 'Someone's got into my apartment – they're trying to kill me! Hurry up.'

She was in such a state she almost gave Finbar's address. The man heaved himself at the door and managed to shove it open a few centimetres. How would the police get in when they arrived, Shannon wondered? They would have to break the door down. Would they be in time? 'Hurry up!' she repeated. The kettle came to a rolling boil and switched itself off. She dropped her mobile and tried to push the door shut again.

'I've called the police,' she yelled. 'They'll be here any minute.'

'What, in this city? Dream on. Not before I've done you, you fucking bitch!'

He was right, damn him. Shannon recalled her oh-so-funny joke to the copper in the Mags Court that day she got the first anonymous letter: *'Welcome to Merseyside Police. If you are being assaulted, press one'*. Which number for murder? She screamed as he shoved the door open further and managed to grope for the door handle and top of the chair. Shannon dragged off her robe belt and quickly looped it around his wrist and the door handle, pulled it tight and tied several clumsy knots. She grabbed his little finger and, cringing, bent it back until she heard a sickening snap. He yelped in agony.

'What the fuck? You've broken me fucking finger!'

'You're trying to kill me!' she screamed. 'What am I supposed to do, lie down and let you get on with it? Help!' she screamed again. 'Somebody help me!' Shannon pressed the switch on the kettle to bring it back to the boil, seized her abandoned glass of wine off the counter and smashed it over his trapped, tied hand.

'Oww! Jesus *Christ!*' A piece of glass stuck in his palm and blood trickled down. He shoved the door again, forced back the chair and table and burst in, lunged at her with the knife while he tried to wrench free his bound wrist. Shannon was ready. She flipped the kettle lid open and dashed the boiling water full in his face.

He started to scream, terrible, agonised screams. Dropped the knife and clutched his free hand to his burned face. Shannon kicked the knife across the kitchen floor out of his reach. Through his screams she heard the front door bell ring, and a male voice shouting.

'What the hell's going on in there? Some of us are trying to sleep, you know! If you don't turn it down I'll call the police.'

'Call them!' she screamed. 'Call them!' She was shaking, crying incoherently, her heart rate off the scale. She gripped the kettle and bashed him over the head with it twice. He sank groaning to his knees, groped blindly around the tiled floor. His wrist was still tied to the door handle. More blood dripped down. A wailing police siren grew louder, then stopped. The downstairs buzzer was pressed urgently.

Shannon pushed past him and raced into the hall, pressed the button to open the downstairs door. She ran to her front door, pulling the unbelted robe around her naked body. Time to go back to wearing nighties, now that she'd split with Finbar Linnell. Sobbing wildly, she opened the door and ran out on to the landing. An aggrieved-looking middle-aged man with dark hair and round spectacles stood there, hands in the pockets of his sad plaid dressing gown.

'What the hell's going on in there?' he repeated, his weasel features twisted with disapproval. He stepped forward and peered down the hall at the sobbing, groaning figure on the kitchen floor. 'What's wrong with him? What have you done?'

'Shut up, you moron!' Shannon screamed, pushing him out of her way. Her robe fell open and he stared like he'd never seen a woman's breasts before. 'He just tried to murder me!'

'What?' He turned pale and took a step back, watched as she pulled the robe around herself again and ran to the top of the stairs. Three uniformed police officers rushed up, followed by a stockily-built man with black hair and angry dark eyes.

'Ms Flinder? I'm Superintendant Carl Mactire–'

'In there,' she gasped, pointing. 'He got in, tried to kill me. He's connected with an ex-client of mine named Demetrio Montana, who was arrested for murder and attempted murder yesterday.'

303

They hesitated. 'Is he armed?'

'No gun. He had a knife, but I got that off him.' They went inside and Shannon turned to follow. Four-eyed, hairy legs from next door was still standing gawping. Useless bastard, she thought. She imagined him banging on the door and agitating about the noise she made screaming as she was knifed to death.

'Hi,' she said savagely. 'I'm Shannon, your new neighbour. Please accept my heartfelt apologies for disturbing your beauty sleep. Which you may now resume.' She glared at him. 'Sweet fucking dreams!'

Chapter Thirty-Four

'Why didn't you report these anonymous letters sooner?'
Cindy Nightingale looked at Shannon like the spider who'd
just seen the juicy bluebottle get trapped in its web. 'And
you've admitted you destroyed the first two you received.
Had something to hide, did you?'

'No, of course not. I thought they'd stop, so I ignored
them.' Shannon, still in shock after last night's attempt on
her life, tried to preserve her carefully constructed cool. 'I
thought it was some crank, I didn't take the letters seriously
at first. Any more than you lot would have done if I'd
reported them before Lucas Grant was murdered and that
note found on his body.'

'Everybody who gets in your way seems to come off
worst.' Cindy threw down her pen. 'Even the guy who broke
into your apartment last night. He could be scarred for life
after you chucked that boiling water in his face.'

'Well, I'm sure that's very regrettable.' Like hell. 'But the
possibility of getting more than he bargained for was a risk
he presumably accepted when he decided to break into my
home and try to murder me.' Bloody bitch.

'He's in agony now,' Cindy said. 'Needs morphine for the
pain. Word is he wants to press assault charges. He thinks
you used unreasonable force to defend yourself.'

She's winding me up, Shannon thought. Or trying to. 'He
had a Stanley knife, I had a kettle of hot water.' She kept her

voice neutral. 'I think it's clear who used unreasonable force. As I've just pointed out, he wanted to murder me. And don't forget what he did to Keely Breeze. Would you like to know how Keely's doing?' she asked. 'Her larynx is irreparably damaged. She'll have a transplant, but the doctors aren't sure it'll work.'

Cindy looked bored. 'Would you like to know what else we've found out about your client, Demetrio Montana?'

'Ex-client now. And no, I don't want to know.'

Shannon looked around the oppressive little interview room, wishing she could be out in the spring sunshine. She'd had more than enough of these places. She banished a sudden image of herself and Finbar still together, maybe living in that beautiful house in Ireland, bringing up the child they hadn't lost after all. Pain tended to strike at the most inconvenient of times.

'Montana was on Death Row in the States,' Cindy said. 'Texas of course, where else? Shot two social workers.' She grinned. 'His lawyer managed to get him off.'

'What?' Shannon sat up straight and smoothed her skirt. *'How?'*

'Don't know yet, but I imagine not being black helped. He left the States and spent the next few years in the Netherlands, living in some flat in Amsterdam. Long history there, culminating in the murder of his girlfriend. Then he came here. He's starting to open up to us more,' Cindy went on. 'Thinks he can strike a deal. Ha-ha. He told us he – and the guy who tried to kill you last night – were working for some terrorist group, who unfortunately he seems to know very little about. He says they wanted him to murder people and steal their identities, so some of their members could live undercover until they were needed for operations.'

'But why bother with that kind of thing nowadays?' Shannon asked, astonished. 'Surely those people can get access to any kind of false document?'

'Not necessarily. Depends who your contacts are. How

efficient you are. How psychopathic. It still happens a lot. Sometimes they even kill members of victims families too. Although they prefer people without families, of course. No family, no form.'

Shannon was silent. She couldn't take it all in.

'Anyway, Mr Montana says he screwed up by getting nicked and that this group, whoever they are, will try to kill him now. Wants twenty-four-seven protection, guards outside his cell, etcetera. He eventually told us about his little sidekick, Phelim, who tried to kill you last night. Thought that might give him some brownie points, make it look as if he'd tried to save your life.' Cindy paused. 'Even if he'd failed.'

'He warned you?' Shannon stiffened. 'When, exactly?'

'Not until late last night. He doesn't seem to wake up and want a chat until everyone else has gone to sleep.'

'I presume you intended to pass on that warning?'

'Well, at first we couldn't be sure he wasn't giving us a load of old baloney.' Cindy raised her eyebrows. 'But of course we would have warned you. What happened to you last night ties in with what he said.' She paused. 'That's how I know you weren't just trying to get someone else out of your way.'

'Look,' Shannon said, knowing where this was leading, 'I've been questioned about last night's attempt on my life and made a statement. I've also made a statement about the anonymous letters. Can we discuss those now, please? That's what I came here for.'

Cindy nodded and looked down at her papers. 'So you don't know Lucas Grant, you never have, and you can't think who's writing the letters or–' she smirked '–why anyone *else* would want to murder you?'

'Right. You'll have the letters forensically analysed?'

'Yeah. Dunno exactly how long that'll take.' Cindy smirked again. 'A few days, probably. Let's hope you stay safe in the meantime, eh?'

Shannon couldn't feel anger, couldn't feel any emotion

right now. She was drained, mentally and physically. 'Don't lose sleep over that, will you?'

'Not a chance. D'you think the letter writer knew your deceased Daddy-in-law?' Cindy eyed her speculatively. 'Knows you had him killed?'

Shannon stood up. 'If you're going to start making ridiculous allegations like that again, I'm out of here. Your biased suspicions proved unfounded, and the case was closed for lack of evidence.'

'It can always be re-opened. Should we get new evidence.'

'I can see this is pointless. You never give up, do you?' Shannon stared at her. 'It's about time you realised I'm not just another sad suspect you can intimidate. Don't you want to find Lucas Grant's murderer? Before they murder someone else?'

Cindy sneered. 'Afraid you'll be the next victim?'

'Maybe I'm not the only one who should be afraid.' Shannon picked up her bag. Her palms were wet. She was sweating one minute, shivering the next.

'And what the hell's that supposed to mean?'

'It *means* that if I was a police officer working on a murder inquiry and I knew there was a strong possibility that another person could be murdered but did nothing to prevent it, I'd be afraid,' Shannon said. 'Especially if the person at risk made an issue of it. Could put one great big dent in a beautifully blossoming career. You won't even get to squash your tits against the glass ceiling. Or are you one of those brisk, no-nonsense girls who like to pretend it doesn't exist?'

Cindy jumped up, glaring at her. 'Don't you threaten me, Flinder!'

'I never make threats.' Shannon forced a smile. 'Only promises. Now if I were you, I really would get on with being very much seen to be doing my job. Goodbye.'

She turned and walked out, glad she was able to do so. She remembered her traumatic night of interrogation in this same police station a few months ago, her terror that she was going to be charged with Bernard's murder and sent down for years. She had imagined her life ruined, her freedom taken away. Being separated from Finbar. She drove out of the police station car park, stopped in a nearby side street and covered her face with her hands.

The inside of the car was hot and stuffy and she was shaking again, sweating all over. Shannon longed to go home and sleep for hours, even if that sleep was filled with nightmares, even if she hated being alone in the apartment. But she had to go back to the office. Make phone calls, dictate letters, read statements, prepare cases. She hadn't told Mi-Hae and Khalida about last night because she couldn't face more questions and explanations, and didn't want to stretch their sympathy and understanding any further. They were in business together after all, running a law practice. She wanted to pull her weight, get on with the job. That was the best way. Shannon wished she hadn't told Nick about last night when he'd phoned her earlier, because now he was pestering her again about going to stay with him. One man had tried to murder her and was banged up. And there could be someone else out there who wanted her dead. Bizarre wasn't the word for her life right now.

'I can't do this,' Shannon groaned, tears filling her eyes. 'It's too hard. I can't cope any more.' She leaned over the steering wheel, crying loudly, then cursed as her mobile rang. Couldn't even have a whinge in peace. She saw that Rob was the caller. For God's sake. She didn't want to speak to him. Okay, he was upset. So was she! She wasn't his wife any more, and she certainly didn't feel like being the mother he'd never had in any except the biological sense. There were two messages from Nick and one from Helena. She called Helena.

'Keith Gould's been arrested for shoplifting again.'

'Oh, no!' Shannon groaned, wiping her eyes. 'Got any good news for me?'

'Your daffodils have come up.' Helena always said that if anyone was silly enough to ask such a question.

'I'll be back at the office in about twenty minutes.' That was because Shannon intended to drink one or two cups of the strongest, sweetest, most aromatic coffee she could find in Liverpool. And plug the aching hollowness in her stomach with a big slice of chocolate or lemon gateau, since she had gone without lunch. She drove off again, thinking about Keith Gould. Why had he gone and fucked things up for himself when he was in enough trouble already? Oh well. That was life, people fucking things up for themselves. Look at her.

She found the coffee and tangy lemon gateau at the Albert Dock, in a quiet café that looked on to the river. It was dangerously close to her previous address, but so what? Why should she avoid one of her favourite places because of Finbar? He wouldn't be around in the middle of the afternoon anyway. She sat outside, enjoying the sun's warmth and the breeze blowing off the river. The Liverpool Pilot boat sailed past, on its way out to meet some ship. The sky looked bigger here, deep blue with white clouds around the horizon, and she could smell the sea. There were a few tourists about, people visiting the nearby Maritime Museum. Shannon ate half the gateau, drank the hot coffee and ordered another cup. She slid down in the chair and closed her eyes, felt her body relax.

I won't let some scumbag little letter writer destroy me, she thought. I'll fight back. Like I did last night. Stay alive. Just to be bloody minded, if nothing else. One day this will be over and I can live my life again the way I want. She couldn't imagine what that life would be like. But it would be all right. Even without . . .

'Shannon,' a man's voice said.

The voice hit every nerve in her body like a high voltage electric shock. For a second she thought she had fallen asleep and was dreaming. Shannon opened her eyes and sat up. No, she wasn't dreaming.

It was Finbar.

*

'How are you?'

He expected an answer to that question? Shannon looked at him in disbelief, hands clenched in her lap. She couldn't move. The boy waiter brought her second cup of coffee and the bill. Finbar looked pale, she thought. Thinner. His green eyes were full of pain as he stared down at her. She didn't understand. Why did he look so unhappy, what was the problem? He'd dumped her, like he wanted. His life should be perfect now.

'I'm all right,' she managed to say. That was a lie now, but one day it wouldn't be. She wanted to jump up, hit him across the face, scream out the shock and hurt that was inside her. But she refused to give him the satisfaction. She would be cool if it killed her. And at this moment Shannon felt it just might. She had to get away.

'I saw you come in here,' he stammered.

'Did you? Well, now I'm leaving.' She stood up. Her heart was thudding and her legs felt weak. She picked up her brief-case, handbag and the bill, hoping she wouldn't stumble stupidly on the cobblestones as she walked away. Finbar stood in front of her, so close that she could smell his after-shave, his body, see the pulse in his throat. Startled, she involuntarily stepped back.

'Could we—' he swallowed '—can we talk for a minute? Please?'

Shannon glanced away to hide her confusion, her incredulity. What could he possibly want to talk about? 'I have to get back to work.' To her left the river glittered in the sunshine, and hungry seagulls cried overhead. The breeze ruffled her hair.

'Don't you want to drink your coffee? Finish that cream cake?'

'No, I've had enough.' She had to get past him. 'Excuse me,' she said politely, continuing to avoid his gaze. Finbar hesitated, then moved slowly aside.

'Look,' he began, his voice hoarse. 'I know I've got no right, but—'

311

'No,' she interrupted, her throat tightening ominously. 'You haven't. Goodbye.'

She walked off, went back inside the café and quickly paid her bill, praying he wouldn't follow. She didn't dare look round. Then she was out in the sunshine again, running for the safety of her car. She jumped in, locked the doors and drove off.

'Don't cry,' she muttered, swallowing and blinking back tears. 'Don't you dare cry, you wimped-out moron! You've done enough of that.' How many more days and nights from hell would she have to endure? What did he want to *talk* about? Forget it, she thought. Just bloody forget it. Her mobile rang again and she pulled over because she needed to wipe her eyes and blow her nose again. She hated to fall apart like this.

'Shannon, can I see you?' Rob asked.

'Go to hell!' She switched the phone off, felt like throwing the damn thing out of the window. She was angrier than ever at Rob since Finbar had dumped her. That wasn't fair or even logical, but so what? She drove off again, noticed that the two men in the small white van seemed to be staying behind her a long time. Just as she was about to start worrying, they turned down Stanley Street. Shannon got back to the office to find Helena in a strop, Mi-Hae moaning about fraud documents and two clients, young girls, waiting for her. One of them was flushed, reeking of alcohol and nasty perfume.

'Where's that magazine?' she asked Shannon, frowning. 'The one with the article about multiple orgasms? I was reading it last time I was here, but I never finished it.'

'That one was very popular,' Shannon replied. 'I don't know where it is – must have been nicked. Maybe I should have had photocopies made.' She opened the door and smiled at the girl. 'Like to come through?'

Work, she thought. Just what I need.

'So what did you expect Shannon to do?' Nick asked. 'Burst out crying and fling herself into your arms like the pop-up heroine of some fuckwit Hollywood movie?'

'I don't know what I expected.' Finbar looked up at the nearby Cunard Buildings. The clear sky was darkening. 'I was thinking about her,' he said. 'Couldn't believe what you told me, about that bastard trying to murder her! It freaked me, I wanted to ...' He stopped. 'I wished I could see her, speak to her. Then I saw her go into that café. I stood there for about five minutes, telling myself to leave it, just walk away. But I couldn't.' He turned towards the river, the Pier Head breeze strong in his face. It was cold now. 'I thought, this might be the last time I ever see her.'

'For Christ's sake, Finbar!' Nick pulled his overcoat around him. 'This is doing my head in. Can't you tell me what you're involved in, why you think you're in such danger that you have to talk about graves and worms and epitaphs?'

'I can't tell you anything. And you can't help. Just look after Shannon, that's what I want from you. I wrote her a letter,' he said. 'Explaining everything, begging her to forgive me. Then I tore it up and burned it.' He grimaced. 'Better she goes on thinking I'm a total arsehole, even after I'm—'

'What's Shannon supposed to make of a total arsehole who leaves her all his not inconsiderable worldly goods?'

'Too late to bother about that now.' Special Branch were giving Shannon protection at last, or as much as they could do without arousing her suspicions. 'What's happening with the investigation into the letter murderer?' Finbar asked. 'Any progress?'

'Shannon only talked to the police today. They're going to have the letters – that is, the one she had left to hand over – forensically analysed.'

Finbar frowned. 'That'll take time. And won't necessarily turn up anything.'

'Well, I'm sure they'll give it priority.' Nick's voice was grim. 'They don't want another murder on their hands.'

'Why won't Shannon stay with you? Or someone else?' Finbar felt helpless, furious that he couldn't do anything. 'She must be terrified after that bastard tried to kill her.'

'Won't run and hide, she says. Thinks there's no point.' Nick sighed. 'She may be right. I mean, take the guy who tried to kill her – he could have followed us to my place, broken in and murdered her there. I might not have been able to stop him. Or he could have got away to try again. You just don't know.' They were silent, gazing out over the river. The wind blew crumpled sweet wrappers and empty crisp packets across the concrete flags.

'Call me every day,' Finbar said. 'Or I'll call you. Keep me up to date.'

'Sure,' Nick promised. He hesitated. 'Finbar, when this – whatever the hell's going on with you – is over, and if you–'

'Survive?' Finbar prompted, a gleam in his eye.

'Okay. Yes. You'll try to get Shannon back, won't you?'

'I don't think so.' Finbar looked away. He shook his head. 'She's better off without me. Whatever happens.'

'But you love her! And I'm sure she still loves you.'

'It's not enough, Nick. Not when my dark past keeps catching us up.' Finbar did not mention Shannon's past, how she had been forced to have the evil headmaster killed before he ended up murdering her. That was an eternal secret between the two of them.

'Maybe it won't catch you up any more once this is over.'

'And maybe it will. I wanted the whole issue with Shannon, Nick. Marriage.' Finbar paused. 'One or two kids, if they came along. If not, it didn't matter. I just wanted her – for a lifetime. But it's not to be. I love her too much to try to get her back. I'm a selfish bastard, but not that selfish. She's talented, terrific, beautiful. Got everything going for her – although it might not look that way now. She'll meet someone else.'

'Yeah.' Nick's voice hardened. 'Someone like Rob, maybe.'

Finbar ignored that. He couldn't think about the man Shannon might meet, imagine her with someone else. 'I'll be just a bad memory,' he said. 'It's for the best.'

'Come on,' Nick argued. 'Look – me and Caroline. We've

been talking, trying to see if we can get back together. But it's no use. We're finished. I don't think we were ever really suited. We got married because neither of us could be bothered to split and start again with new partners – and because Caroline was pregnant! It seemed the right thing to do at the time. Of course we should have realised that was a recipe for disaster, although it doesn't always have to be. With us, getting married and having a kid just highlighted the problems. We did our best but the feeling, the commitment, just wasn't there. You and Shannon – that's totally different. You were made for each other.'

'Yeah, well. Are you trying to cheer me up, or what?' He couldn't talk about this any more. Finbar glanced at his watch. 'I've got to go,' he said. 'I'm late for a meeting.' The meeting was with Carl Mactire, and to get to it he had to follow a tedious series of elaborate, precautionary manoeuvres to lose anyone who might follow him. The thought of it bored and infuriated the hell out of him. He would go home and relax for a bit first. If he was late, fuck it.

'How long will you be?' Nick asked. 'D'you fancy having a bite to eat afterwards?' He grinned. 'Two sad single blokes together.'

'Unfortunately I don't know how long it'll take. Some other time. Tomorrow, maybe.' Finbar held out his hand. 'Thanks, Nick. For everything. Call me about Shannon, okay?'

'I will. Take care of yourself, Finbar.' Nick looked sombre. 'Let me know if there's anything else I can do.'

'Just be a friend to Shannon. See you.'

Back at the apartment Finbar poured himself a single malt and stood looking out over the darkening river. The violet sky was clear. It reminded him of the colour of Shannon's eyes. A pale half moon was rising. When did Blick plan to kill him, he wondered? Before or after the operation? Maybe he hadn't decided yet. He wasn't going to just kneel down and take the bullet. He had told Mactire the time and place. It was up to them now. And up to him to get himself out of danger, because no one else was going to do that for him. Mactire wanted to know all he'd found out about Demetrio Montana, but Finbar didn't have to tell the bastard everything. Any more than Mactire told him everything.

Finbar sipped his drink, savouring it. Did Shannon still love him, like Nick said? She had been admirably cool at their unexpected meeting, hadn't lost it. He was the one who'd nearly lost it. He was stupid to have followed her. What the hell had he thought he could say? It was just as well Shannon hadn't burst out crying and flung herself into his arms, because they would be in bed together right now – and she would be in terrible danger again. He tossed back his drink and went to shower.

Finbar changed into jeans and sweater, took his keys and jacket and left, feeling bored in advance. He couldn't use his car, but had to take several cabs. He walked out into the dusk, heading for Salthouse Dock and Strand Street. He turned as he heard a car drive up behind him. Shit! he thought, his heart sinking. It was the Audi. Iain Blick and two of his mates jumped out.

'And where are you off to this fine but chilly spring evening?' Blick smiled.

Finbar didn't flinch. 'Dinner with a friend.'

'How nice. But I'm afraid you'll have to cancel.'

He didn't expect this. What was going on? Had something happened? Did they suspect about the sting? If so, this was it. Prolonged torture, followed by blessed death. Finbar tensed, decided to make a run for it. He would worry about the consequences of that later. Before he could move though, something was jammed into his stomach. He looked down and saw the gun. Imagined the hole it could blow in him. His blood and insides spattering the concrete flags.

'I don't want to cancel,' he said calmly as they crowded around him. He hoped he didn't look as frightened as he felt. 'I want to see my friend. And I'm hungry.'

'What you want or don't want isn't the issue.' Blick stopped smiling. 'I had this really good idea,' he said.

'Decided to surprise you.'

'Well, that's nice. But I don't like surprises.'

'Oh, you'll love this one. You see, I thought you could come and stay with us. Call it protective custody, if you like. Starting tonight.' He gestured with the gun. 'Get in.'

'Can't I pack a bag first?' Finbar asked, stalling. 'The thought of wearing the same underpants for several days on the trot scares me more than whatever you fundamentalists have got planned.'

'I'm very weary of your backchat,' Blick said. 'Just get in the fucking car. Unless you want to die right here and now.'

'What would you recommend?'

'Move!'

They shoved him in and drove off. Sickened by fear, Finbar wondered if he would ever again stand in his living room sipping single malt while he watched the sun set over the river, and the moon and stars come out.

He wondered if he would ever see Shannon again.

PART FOUR

PARTFOUR

Chapter Thirty-Five

I've done it now. Announced my Big Intention. But there won't be any trauma, guilt or remorse in carrying this one out, oh no. Only pleasure, incredible satisfaction and release. Like I've never had before, and never expect to enjoy again.

Haven't seen our Shannon for a while. She's busy. Unavailable. In a partners' meeting, in court, instructing a barrister, in conference with a client. In conference, that's a laugh. Like any of those scroats she defends are capable of conferring. Ms Flinder's sorry but she can't accept any calls at present. Can I take a message, or would you like to try again later? So busy, so important, so much in demand. Of course I gave a false name and would have hung up immediately if I'd actually got through to the lady herself. I just wanted to know where she was, what she was doing. And I haven't called her apartment late at night again either. Why give her another chance to be a brave little girl?

The bitch seems to be talking her way out of trouble with the polizia, just as I feared. She must have talked her way out of it because she's still walking around as opposed to being locked in a cell. The Bridewell, maybe, where she's visited so many clients before representing them upstairs in the Mags Court. I'd have liked to see her shut up in there. Pleading that it was all a mistake, begging for a lawyer. Alone, without the Irish criminal to pull any strings for her, bribe or *blackmail people in high places. I still don't know what happened there, who dumped who. He might have got rid of her, it's possible. Maybe the beautiful Shannon became too much of a good thing, even for a man like that. She's too rich for any man's blood after a while. Must be like eating a gourmet dinner every evening. After a while you long for something simple, like a ham sandwich or a plate of chips.*

There doesn't seem to be any chance of the police re-opening the Case of the Splattered Headmaster. Oh well. I've given up on that now. It wouldn't have been enough anyway. At first I thought it would be enough for me to see the bitch humbled, brought down, publicly humiliated, her career and life destroyed. But it isn't. One thing's led to another, the situation has escalated. Now Shannon has to pay the ultimate price. For all her sins. Maybe I'll have to pay too. I don't care.

I'm making changes, winding down, tying up loose ends. Looking at things and people from a different perspective: the perspective of finality. It's sad. You think, why was I here, what did I do? What was the point of it all? There are no answers, not in this limited dimension of ours anyway. I hope there are answers somewhere. There bloody well better be. Then again, do I really want to know? The answers might be too terrible. On the whole, I think I prefer blessed, un-complicated oblivion. I was oblivious to the Big Bang and I'll be oblivious to the Big Crunch. Suits me!

Yes, it's sad. But there's a kind of relief too. No more pain, no more waste. No more longing for the unattainable, the unreachable. The untouchable. Just calm, acceptance. Resignation. Well, must get on. There's lots to do. Have another drink first. Why not? Won't kill me, after all. Ha ha.

Strange to think I won't be here much longer.

Neither will Shannon Flinder.

Chapter Thirty-Six

'I've got this really bad feeling about you, Finbar,' Iain Blick shouted. 'It's doing my head in.'

Finbar tried to turn his body and draw up his knees to protect himself from the blows. Not an easy thing to do when your hands were tied behind your back. They had taken his keys, wallet and mobile, stripped him and were now kicking the crap out of him. He wouldn't survive much longer if they didn't stop soon. Another kick landed in his stomach and he coughed and retched. He saw his own blood on the dusty floorboards.

'Okay, stop. For now.' Blick squatted beside him. Finbar could see his shoes: black, polished, expensive. A lover of the good things in life. Things paid for with blood money. 'You're sure you haven't told anyone our little secret?'

'No.' His body was one mass of throbbing pain. 'I swear.'

'Swear, do you?' Blick grabbed a handful of his hair and jerked his head up. 'Because it's like I said, I just got this really bad feeling.' His voice was calm now. 'And I thought you needed a lesson. It's your attitude, you see. The way you don't take anything seriously, act like it's all one bloody great big joke and you've got the last laugh. It really pisses me off. Maybe you think you're too clever for us. For anyone. Now why would you think that, I wonder?' He gestured to one of the men, who handed him a revolver.

Oh shit, Finbar thought. He wanted to close his eyes, but

didn't. He gagged as Blick pushed the gun barrel into his mouth.

'You're sure you haven't shared our little secret with anyone?' he repeated. 'If you have, tell me now. It'll be easier for you.'

He was choking, couldn't breathe, his eyes streaming. But Finbar tried to endure it and not panic. Because Blick was lying, and it wouldn't be easier for him. Better to be shot now than get tortured to death if he let slip about the sting. He tried to shake his head. Blick suddenly withdrew the gun barrel, wet with saliva, and handed it back. The man grunted with disgust, but took it.

'I didn't say anything,' Finbar gasped. 'Not to anyone. I didn't!' He couldn't go on. Blick let go of his hair. He retched again and vomited, narrowly missing Blick's posh shoes. Blick jumped to his feet and moved away.

'You'll clean that up, you dirty bastard!'

Finbar couldn't clean up anything because his head was spinning and he was unable to stand, even with help. He felt like throwing up again.

'Right,' Blick said. 'Lock the shit away for now.' He followed as they dragged Finbar to a small, dark room and heaved him on to the single, unmade bed, leaving his hands tied. The pain in his injured body was like nothing he'd ever experienced. He wondered when Mactire or Nick would realise he was missing. What would they do? Mactire would leave him to rot, he was pretty sure of that. And Nick couldn't do a damn thing to help him. He gasped and groaned as sharp pain suddenly stabbed him, wondered if the beating had cracked one of his ribs. He lay there shivering. Blick laughed.

'Cold? Dear me. Can't have that. Especially seeing as you haven't finished helping us yet.' He took a stale-smelling quilt and threw it over him. 'Let me tell you one thing before I say goodnight.' He paused, looking down at him. 'You won't have the last laugh. So you'd better cooperate fully from now on. And drop the bloody attitude because, as you can see, it's really not helping.'

324

He strode out, slammed the door and locked it, leaving Finbar alone in the dark with his pain and fear. And despair.

'Thanks, Shannon.' Keely Breeze could speak again at last after her larynx transplant, in a slow, hoarse, monotone whisper. 'You saved my life.'

'I just wish I'd made the connection between Kev Hoyle and Demetrio Montana sooner.'

'Not your fault.'

No? Shannon looked out of the window at the blue morning sky. It was a gorgeous day and Keely was safe now at last. But she was missing Finbar desperately. And neither she nor the police had any clue yet as to who was writing the anonymous letters, or who had made that phone call to her in the middle of the night. Lucas Grant's murderer was still out there.

'Better not call you "Blondie" any more, had I?' Keely whispered. 'How are you? You look rough.'

'Need more make-up, do I?' Shannon smiled. 'Never mind me. I had a word with the doctor before I came in. He said the op went very well.'

'Yeah. Once the swelling goes down, the voice'll get better. I won't sound so much like an alien with laryngitis.'

'And you'll be getting out of here soon?' Keely could also breathe without a tube again now.

'Saturday. Can't bloody wait.' Keely smiled. 'Good to swear again.'

'What's the first thing you'd like to do after you get out? Apart from swear.'

Keely leaned back on her pillows, pulling her blue cardigan around her shoulders. 'Go shopping. Don't worry,' she croaked, noticing Shannon's expression. 'With my own money.'

'Good.' Shannon pressed her hand. 'I don't want to see you back in court.'

'I suppose the coppers kept my Armani coat? I'll never see it again.' Keely had been agitating about the coat.

'You really want it back then?' Shannon asked. 'Doesn't it remind you too much of what happened?'

'Well, a bit. But I loved that coat. It was so cool.' Keely grimaced. 'Don't care that *he* gave it me. Least I got something good out of the bastard.'

'Well, in that case.' Shannon turned and picked up the carrier bag she'd laid on the chair. 'Here you are,' she said, pulling out the neatly folded, dry-cleaned garment. 'Good as new.'

Keely gasped and stared in delight. She reached out one hand, fingering the soft wool. Then she looked at Shannon, her eyes filling with tears. 'Stupid cow, aren't I?' she whispered. 'Could be dead! Thanks. You're a doll.'

'There's a message from Nick Forth,' Helena informed her when she got back, following her down the hall to her office. 'He wants you to call him.'

'Thanks.' Shannon sniffed. 'Helena, has some miracle occurred and you've got coffee made?'

Helena looked as if she was going to snap something sarcastic, but suddenly relaxed and smiled. *'Yes.'*

'Fantastic. Now I can have a lovely little private coffee break in my office instead of having to drink the muck at the Mags Court.' Shannon went into the tiny kitchen and poured herself a cup, got a chocolate biscuit to go with it. I suppose I'll just have to look for happiness in the small things, she thought. Back in her office she was just about to call Nick when the phone rang.

'Shannon, Nick here. How are you, or is that a stupid question?'

'It's a stupid question. Sorry, Nick, but I've only got about two minutes.'

'No worries. I just want to ask if we can have dinner tonight. I need to talk to you.'

'Okay. Dinner with a friend would be good. Normal, relaxing. Thanks, I'd like to.'

'I'll book a table at the French place near Rodney Street. Be there about eight?'

'Fine. I'll look forward to it. See you, Nick.'

He didn't sound very relaxed, but she had no time to ponder that now. She grabbed her briefcase and left for the Magistrates' Court. The blue sky had turned hazy, and the spring light was harsh.

The estate agent accused of assaulting two police officers was dishevelled and outraged after his long night in the Bridewell, protesting his innocence and swearing that the police had jumped him for no apparent reason when he'd tried to take a leak in an alley. The girl accused of jabbing her boyfriend in the face with a broken beer bottle during a row about who should stay in to look after the kids, hadn't turned up. Shannon got the innocent estate agent released, then hurried into the office and phoned the girl. Ring, ring. I'm out, bugger off. Got better things to do than turn up at court. She sighed and replaced the receiver.

'Good morning, Ms Flinder.' The clerk looked up at her and smiled. 'How are you?'

Why did people keep asking her that? Shannon supposed they meant to be nice and she ought to be grateful that they gave a toss. She smiled back. 'Fine, thanks. Bit rushed, as usual.'

'I think there's a thief around here,' he said, frowning.

Shannon looked out at the crowd of people in the lobby. 'Well, yes. Certainly more than one, I'd imagine.'

'I don't mean any of *them*. D'you remember seeing a notice about a Mont Blanc pen that got lost and was handed in?' She nodded. 'Well, it was in my desk, waiting for the owner to claim it. And now it's been nicked.'

'Oh, really?' Shannon looked at her watch.

'I've been trying to remember the other people who were in this office just before the pen got stolen a week last Friday. But there were only a few police officers and solicitors in here just before it was nicked. Including your husband.'

Shannon started. 'My *husband*?'

'Sorry. Ex-husband now, isn't it? Don't get me wrong, I'm not accusing him,' he explained hastily. 'Or the others. I just

327

wanted to ask if they'd noticed anything suspicious.' He grinned. 'And none of them are called Bernard.'

'What?'

'The pen was engraved. With the name Bernard. I suppose that's why it wasn't claimed. No one with that name works here. Must have been an outsider who lost it. But it's strange, because the Group 4 guy who handed it in said he'd found it in the corridor that leads to the Lawyers' Room. The public don't have access to that part of the building. I suppose someone could have wandered down there though.'

A Mont Blanc pen engraved with the name Bernard? And Rob hanging around just before it was stolen? The letters had been written in ink – except that a biro had been used to write the last one. She suspected the writer knew her, had some connection with the Mags Court. This all had to be nasty coincidence, of course. How many Mont Blanc pens were there, for God's sake? How many men named Bernard? It didn't mean anything. She was only getting a bad feeling because that name had a horrific association for her. Shannon wondered how Rob was. She hadn't answered his messages for days now, and he had stopped calling.

'Perhaps you could ask your ex if he noticed anything.' The clerk winked. 'That's if you're on friendly terms, of course. Armed détente and all that.'

She went out of the office and found a quiet spot in a corridor. She didn't want to go near the Lawyers' Room, had avoided it ever since the day she'd found her coat slashed up. Rob didn't answer his mobile, so she called his work number.

'Rob's on leave,' Lesley, one of his room mates, informed her. 'Inspector Nightingale's got the raving hump. But he needed it. He's in a right state.'

'About what?'

'Dunno. He won't talk to anyone. He seemed depressed, looked like he hadn't been getting much sleep. Wouldn't be amazed if he'd hit the sauce too.' A censorious note entered Lesley's voice. 'I don't think his divorce being finalised has

328

helped. I saw the papers on his desk. Rob kept them there for days, looked at them over and over. Maybe that's what's wrong with him.'

'Thanks.' Shannon hung up and called the Woolton house, Rob's parents' old home. She didn't know Katy's address or phone number, but she was pretty sure Rob wouldn't be with her any more, not unless there had been some miracle reconciliation. And even when miracle reconciliations happened, they did not tend to last.

No answer there either. She couldn't imagine Rob was out buying fresh food to cook himself healthy meals, or going for a brisk walk to enjoy the mild weather. When he was depressed he tended to sit around and brood. Let himself go. Drink. A lot. Shannon's heart sank as she remembered what *that* could be like. She switched the phone off and put it back in her briefcase.

'Where is he?' she whispered.

'Disappeared?' Shannon went cold. 'I don't believe it. Nick, are you sure?'

'Of course I'm bloody sure!' Nick's voice was low and fierce as he leaned towards her over the restaurant table. 'I haven't heard from Finbar, and neither has his office manager, his brother or anyone else. He's not at home or in Ireland. I can't reach him. It's been four days now.'

Shannon tried not to panic. It's okay, she told herself. Finbar's fine. Just stay cool, be detached. You have to look out for yourself now. She put down her wine glass and glanced out of the windows. Across the street was a derelict church surrounded by an ancient cemetery – how lovely, just the thing to chirp her up. In the middle of the cemetery was a strangely shaped grave, like a pyramid. Rumour was, some Victorian doctor who had had a pact with the Devil – didn't they all! – had insisted on being buried in a sitting position holding a handful of playing cards. Now he was supposed to haunt the place, a dark figure in cape and top hat.

'Finbar's probably gone off with some woman.' She tried

329

to smile, but failed pathetically. 'A romantic rendezvous at a secret, sun-soaked destination. And I don't mean Southport.'

'For Christ's sake, Shannon, this is serious!'

'Not to me it isn't,' she lied. 'Is this the important thing you wanted to talk to me about?' She was surprised at the anger and bitterness that gripped her. 'Should have known better than to think I could have a relaxing dinner with a friend, shouldn't I? A laugh, even – can't remember the last time *that* happened. Why did you pick a posh restaurant? Surely you'd realise the subject of Finbar Linnell would destroy my already fragile appetite?' She pushed away her plate of sole fillets and looked down at her smooth hands, the long shiny nails. Fidgeted with the sleeves of her dress. She could feel herself trembling.

Nick stared at her. 'Is that all you can say?'

'What do you expect me to say?' Tears pricked at her eyes. The staying cool and detached bit wasn't working. 'I'm trying to hold myself together here, Nick! It's not exactly easy. Someone tried to murder me a few nights ago, remember that?'

'Of course,' Nick said quietly. 'I'm sorry, Shannon. It's just–'

'I still can't discover who this bloody anonymous letter writer is,' she went on. 'The police aren't having much success either, despite their fab forensic analysis techniques. And now you tell me you think Finbar's disappeared.'

Nick's handsome face darkened again. 'I told you, I don't *think*. I know!'

'All right, you know. And I'm supposed to be interested because ... *what*?'

'Shannon – if there was a competition between you and the police as to who's displaying the greatest amount of contemptuous indifference here, let me tell you you'd be way out in front!'

'You're Finbar's friend and you're worried.' Shannon picked up her wine glass and took a big gulp of Riesling. 'But you're supposed to be my friend too. For God's sake,

Nick, how can you blame me for reacting this way? Finbar's got nothing to do with me any more. He dumped me – he doesn't want me, he's not interested! I could be dead, murdered, and what would he care? Why the hell should I give a toss about him now?' She jumped as a woman nearby laughed loudly.

Nick shook his head. 'You don't understand.'

'Oh yeah, I'm sure! And you know what? I don't care any more, because I've had enough. End of story. So get over it, Nick dear. I'm trying to, and you're not helping right now.' Shannon gulped the rest of her wine. 'Shall we get the bill?' She glanced around, looking for the waiter. 'Can't think why, but I've gone right off the idea of lemon pudding and double espresso.'

She wanted to get back to her apartment full of boxes. Her shiny, new, fast-boiling kettle. The coffee filter. New deadbolts, locks and chains. Friendly neighbours who appreciated you keeping the noise down as someone tried to rob you then knife you to death.

Nick reached over and grasped her hand. 'Hold up just one bloody minute here, Shannon!' His dark eyes glittered with anger. 'You should give a toss about Finbar because you love him. And because he loves you.'

'He doesn't!' She flinched and looked down, tried to pull her hand away. 'Nick, don't,' she begged. 'Please. I can't–'

His grip tightened. 'Finbar loves you,' he repeated. He hesitated. 'He didn't want to dump you. He's devastated about the break-up, he misses you like hell. He only did it to keep you safe.'

'Safe?' Knives and forks clattered on plates, glasses clinked. Shannon stared at him in shock. 'What do you mean? Safe from w*hat?'* she whispered.

'I don't bloody know. I only know he's in terrible danger, and that you would be too if you hadn't split. You've got enough trouble with this anonymous letter-writering-murderer.'

Shannon was silent for a minute. 'You're telling me

331

Finbar acted out of pure selflessness?' she said at last. 'To employ an overstretched cliché, that he was cruel to be kind?'

'He wanted you to think he was a bastard. So you'd hate him, get over it quicker. He's made a new will,' Nick said. 'Left everything to you.'

'*What?*'

'I'm the executor.' He let go of her hand. 'I've begged Finbar to tell me what's going on, but he won't. He told me to call him every day about you. Or he'd call me. But he hasn't. And like I said, I can't contact him.' Nick looked at her, distraught. 'He's gone, Shannon, and I don't know what the fuck to do. The police aren't interested. That's why I'm telling you. I thought maybe we could do something. Help him.' He shrugged. 'I don't know!'

'Finbar's always in danger,' she whispered, clenching her hands. 'I couldn't stand it. That's why I wanted to leave him.' A tear rolled down her cheek. 'But in the end I couldn't go through with it. That's when he ...' She thumped her fist on the table. 'I hate love! All it does is fuck you up big time.'

'Tell me about it. Let's get out of here,' Nick said.

Shannon was in a daze as she stood up and walked to the exit, waited for the hapless girl to find her coat. She remembered the look in Finbar's eyes the last time she'd seen him. Anguished, as if he still loved her. She hadn't understood. She did now. And it made everything worse. She wanted to go on believing he'd dumped her because he was a callous bastard and she was a stupid cow who'd got it all wrong. That was hard, of course. But to know Finbar still loved her, that he'd done it to keep her safe, that his life was in danger now and there was nothing she could do to help him – that was unbearable. All Shannon's fears, a great rush of love for him, came flooding back.

'When did you last call Finbar?' she asked as they crossed the street and headed for Nick's car. 'Or go round to his place?'

'Just before I came to meet you.' Nick stopped and looked down at her. 'I don't suppose you've got keys to his apartment? We could take a look round.'

'No. I gave them back when I left.' She remembered the keys lying on the table next to the glittering diamond engagement ring.

'Damn. Let's go there anyway,' Nick said. 'Maybe we can find a caretaker or someone who'll let us in. Or maybe there'll be a miracle and he'll be back. Maybe I'm freaking about nothing.'

A horrible thought occurred to Shannon. 'Finbar might have been home all the time,' she gasped. 'He could have collapsed, be lying unconscious.'

'Collapsed from what? A heart attack? Thirty-six is a bit young for that. Besides, he once told me he'd never been ill in his life except for the occasional cold.'

'When Finbar's club was blown up a few weeks ago he got thrown across the road head first into railings. He had a scan and they told him everything was okay, but you know what doctors can be like. Maybe it wasn't okay. They could have missed something. Blows to the head can cause subdural haematomas and–'

'What's that in English?'

'A blood clot on the brain. Sometimes it takes a few weeks before the person collapses. They get a terrible headache and. . .' Shannon clapped one hand to her mouth. 'Oh, God!'

Nick was grim faced. 'Let's get over there.'

The Albert Dock was quiet, water smacking gently against the quays. They stood outside the apartment building, looking at the row of names and door bells next to each resident's post box. Nick pressed Finbar's door bell twice. Shannon's heart was pounding and her legs felt weak. She'd left here in the middle of the night and hadn't thought she would ever come back. She shivered in the cold air.

'Nothing,' Nick said, disconsolate. 'Maybe we can–' He gasped as the door bell suddenly glowed red and there was a crackle as someone lifted the entry phone.

'Finbar?' he shouted, glancing incredulously at Shannon. 'For Christ's sake, where have you been? It's Nick. Let me in!' The buzzer sounded and the door swung open.

'I won't come with you.' Shannon hung back, trembling. She had tears in her eyes. 'He might not want to see me. It's okay now – I know he's all right.'

'Don't be daft, of course he wants to see you!' Nick grabbed her hand. 'Come on. Whatever it was must be over. I bet that's why he disappeared. Finbar got through it, he's okay.' His face was glowing.

They ran up the flights of stairs to the top floor. Finbar's front door was ajar and there was no sign of him. Shannon pulled her hand out of Nick's grasp.

'I don't like this,' she whispered. 'Something's wrong. Why isn't he at the door?'

'He's probably in the kitchen, cracking open a bottle of champagne.' Nick pushed the door wide and strode into the hall. 'Finbar?' he called. There was no answer.

'You didn't hear his voice over the intercom. You don't know if it was him who let us in. We could be walking into a trap!' It was no use; she had to know if Finbar was here or not. Shannon walked on past Nick and down the hall, looked into the empty kitchen. She reached the huge sitting room and stopped.

'My God!' she exclaimed, shocked. 'Someone's trashed the place.'

Nick came out of Finbar's bedroom. 'There's no sign of him. I don't understand!'

'Finbar's not here,' Shannon said. 'But someone is.'

They were suddenly surrounded by a group of silent men who grabbed the shocked, protesting Nick, handcuffed him and threw him on a sofa. Shannon didn't know why she wasn't shocked. She only felt drained, totally calm. Relieved that Finbar wasn't lying here unconscious or even dead. But if he wasn't here, where the hell was he?

One man detached himself from the group and approached her. Astonished and disbelieving, Shannon recognised his jowly face, the angry dark eyes. It was the Special Branch officer who had come to her apartment the night of the attempted murder. She couldn't remember his name or rank. Only that Special Branch dealt with terrorism.

'Who the hell's this?' Carl Mactire asked, gesturing at Nick. He glared at her. 'What are you doing here?'

She hated the sight of them, and was filled with rage. How dare they trample around and violate what had once been her and Finbar's private space! They acted as if they owned it now. She glanced around the wrecked sitting room. Had they trashed the apartment? She wanted to scream, yell at them to get out. She could either start crying or lose her temper. But she wasn't going to cry, not in front of these bastards.

Shannon faced him and glared back. 'I was just about to ask you that question!'

Chapter Thirty-Seven

'So the bomb's timer and power units are fixed.'

More music, if you could describe heavy metal as music, turned louder. Shouts, blaring car horns and screeching tyres from something on tv as well. No use, he could only hear snatches of what the men in the next room were saying. Finbar lay in the dark, slowly twisting and turning his bruised, beaten body, flexing his bound hands, in a fruitless effort to get comfortable. His arms and shoulders ached and his hands felt stiff. He remembered reading about a Chinese woman locked up by the Red Guards during the Cultural Revolution, who had spent weeks in a cell with her hands cuffed behind her back the whole time. That was a common form of torture, or 'persuasion' as the Red Guards preferred to describe it. He tried to stop himself groaning; not that they'd hear if he did. How could they stand the racket in there? Didn't they care about attracting attention from pissed off tenants in other parts of the house?

He shivered under the thin quilt, unable to get warm. He kept track of time by listening to the tv, tried to keep stretching his limbs so they wouldn't seize up. He got hardly anything to eat or drink and they wouldn't let him take a shower or get dressed, only untie his hands and let him stumble to the toilet a few times a day. Finbar couldn't think about Shannon. He had blocked her out of his mind, because that hurt almost as much as the beatings.

The worst was not knowing what they were going to do with him; or more to the point, exactly when they would kill him. What did they still want from him? Maybe nothing. It could be a ploy to make him think he had more time. What would Special Branch, namely Mactire, do now? Mactire would think he had been picked up and murdered, dumped somewhere. Or that he'd absconded, and was prepared to spend what time he had left on the run. Either way, Mactire would think the sting was blown. Unless he had ways and means of knowing it wasn't. Surely these bastards wouldn't kill him until after they'd perpetrated mass murder in the mall? Or would it be just before? One thing was certain; if they gave him another hammering he would be good for nothing except a quick bullet. He could hope for rescue, but not count on it. His best bet was to try to escape, although he didn't see how he could manage that right now.

Finbar flinched and tensed his injured, pain-racked body as the door was unlocked and flung open, the light snapped on. Two men came in. He was dragged up and dragged to the bathroom, his hands untied. He sat on the toilet, his heart pounding, feeling sick, dizzy and faint. One of the men shoved a towel at him.

'Take a shower. *Move*,' he shouted. Finbar took the towel and got slowly to his feet, crossed to the shower. They stood there, bored and impatient.

The feel of the hot water was so fantastic it almost made him cry. He lathered blue shower gel all over his bruised body. Flexed his stiffened fingers. They threw his clothes at him and let him get dressed, then took him back to the room and gave him crisps and ham sandwiches, a mug of strong, hot tea. Two other men with guns stood guard as he ate. Blick came in and sat on the edge of the bed.

'How are you feeling?'

Finbar nodded. 'Better.' He didn't trust himself to say much, in case whatever he came out with led to another kicking.

'Had enough to eat?' He nodded again as he swallowed

337

the last bite of sandwich. 'D'you know what day it is?' Blick asked. 'Or night?'

'Friday night.'

'Correct. Almost Saturday morning, actually. Okay. You've had a lovely hot shower and been fed. Now I want you to get a good night's sleep because you've got a busy day tomorrow. A busy day in which you do exactly what I say – or die.'

'What do I have to do?' There had been almost 200 truck bombings worldwide. It was a growing phenomenon. Was it his turn now to drive a stolen truck packed with semtex, park it in front of a shopping mall and pray he could get clear before it blew and scattered the bloody body parts of all those happy shoppers? He would need more than prayers to survive tomorrow.

'Guess what?' Blick smiled at him as if he knew what he was thinking. 'You've got the starring role. You're going to be our master bomber.'

Master martyr suicide bomber, more like. Finbar looked at him, wanting to smash the grin off his face.

No way, he thought. I'm not the martyr type.

'We suspect Finbar Linnell of involvement with a group of terrorists who are planning a major incident,' Carl Mactire said.

Shannon's heart sank. She had been here before. 'What incident? When?'

'That I can't tell you. We don't discuss operational details, and not with civilians.' He grimaced. 'Certainly not civilian criminal lawyers.'

Nick was looking at him incredulously. 'You're saying Finbar could be involved with terrorists? What bloody terrorists?'

'I can't discuss that.'

'I don't believe it. Where is Finbar? Is he safe?'

'That we don't know.' Mactire waved a hand. 'We didn't trash this place, someone else did. We don't know who. But

338

we have been searching for possible clues. And when some-one rang the door bell – well, we had to see who that was, didn't we?'

'What grounds have you got for suspecting Finbar's involvement in this incident ... whatever it is?' Shannon asked. I don't understand, she thought. He didn't want any more involvement with terrorists. He was determined about that, I know he was. She remembered his words, *'Maybe somebody wants something from me.'* What did they want? They must have threatened Finbar, forced him. 'What grounds?' she repeated.

'I told you, Ms Flinder, I won't discuss operational details.'

'That's not an operational detail,' she snapped. 'It's a per-fectly reasonable question, given that you've just accused him of being involved in some terrorist incident.' She glanced around the wrecked sitting room. 'You can't just enter premises and go through someone's personal belong-ings at your leisure! Have you got a search warrant?'

'We have. If that's any of your business.'

'Where is it?'

'I'm not required to show the search warrant to you. You don't live here. Any more.'

So he knew about her and Finbar. Shannon let that go, because there were more important things. 'Why did you turn up at my apartment the other night when I called the police about that man who got in and tried to murder me?' she demanded. 'That's hardly a Special Branch matter.'

'It can be when the complainant is the ex-girlfriend of a suspected terrorist.'

'Crap!' she snorted. 'Finbar Linnell isn't a terrorist.'

Mactire glared at her. 'Ms Flinder, do you know anything about the murder of the Defence Secretary that took place a few months ago?'

'Do *I* know anything? Why on earth are you asking me that?' Finbar had backed out, tried to stop the murder. Failed.

'Just answer the question, please.'

'I won't answer any of your damn questions!'

He shrugged. 'I just thought you might know something about it that we don't.'

'Like what, for instance?'

'Oh, you know.' His eyes bored into hers. 'Like who did it.'

She went cold. 'Get stuffed!'

'You see, it's the sort of company you've been in the habit of keeping. Makes me wonder. Why did you and Finbar Linnell split?'

'That's none of your fucking business,' Nick flashed before she could answer. 'Listen,' he said, 'I saw Finbar a few days ago and he was frightened for his life. He wouldn't tell me what was going on. Now he's gone missing. He's in danger. You should be trying to find him instead of harassing Shannon.'

'Oh, we'll find him, all right.' Mactire exchanged glances with the other men. 'Eventually. I'll have to ask you to leave now,' he said. 'And anything you've heard here is strictly confidential, of course. If you repeat one word of it to anyone you'll both be under arrest.'

'On what charges?' Shannon demanded.

'I'm sure I can think of something. Endangering national security, and that's just for starters.' He frowned. 'Please leave. Now. We've got things to do.'

'Oh yes. Operational details.' She stood her ground. 'What about Finbar?'

'There's nothing you can do. Forget you ever knew him, that's your best bet.'

Shannon bowed her head as tears flooded her eyes. Nick went to her and put one arm round her shoulders. 'Come on,' he said, hugging her. 'Let's get out of here. We can't do anything else tonight.'

'Not tonight, tomorrow or any other day,' Mactire snapped. 'Keep out of this. For your own safety.' He glared at them. 'You've been warned.'

'Terrorism!' Nick exclaimed as he fastened his seat belt

and stuck the key in the ignition. 'Jesus! D'you think it's true what they say about a possible incident?'

'I don't know.' Shannon wiped her eyes. 'But whoever or whatever Finbar's involved with, it's not from choice!'

He drove out of the car park into Strand Street. 'I wonder who they are?'

'Might be some disaffected paramilitary group,' Shannon said, thinking of what Finbar had said in the past. 'There's lots of them around and they pose a big danger. They're not all interested in changing the political process. Only bloody murder.'

'They must be threatening to kill him if he doesn't do whatever they want. And he obviously thought there was enough risk to you to—'

'Dump me.' Shannon wiped another tear. Nick stamped on the brakes and gasped as a Golf GTI coming from Mann Island shot red traffic lights and raced across the road they were on, narrowly missing them.

'Moron!' Nick shouted. 'Prat in a baseball cap – they're all the bloody same.' He glanced at her. 'You okay?'

'Yes.' She nodded, took a long, shaky breath. He drove on through the city centre.

'Shannon, I don't know about you, but I've had enough for one night. I'm knackered. I think we should both go home and try to get some sleep. I'll give you a call tomorrow morning.'

'All right.' He dropped her off outside her building and she quickly went in and ran up the stairs, experienced a frisson of fear as she unlocked her front door and walked into the hall. Shannon didn't bother to take off her coat. She poured herself a glass of white wine and sat in the kitchen, her mobile on the table in front of her. She drank half the wine then threw the glass and smashed it against the wall.

That was okay. It was her mess and she would clean it up. What can I do? Shannon thought despairingly. What the hell can I do now? I don't know where Finbar is, I can't help him. What will happen? She got down on her hands and knees, picking up pieces of broken glass. Cut her finger. Swore.

'Rob!' she whispered, staring at the wine-splashed wall.

He was in the CID, of course, not Special Branch. But he might know something about what was going on, have heard rumours of a terrorist incident. He wouldn't be gagging to help Finbar, of course, but she might be able to find out something. It was a long shot, but she had to try. She needed to talk to Rob anyway. And she couldn't sleep. She dialled his mobile, but there was no answer. Tried the house in Woolton. Same. He might be in and just didn't feel like picking up the phone. He wouldn't if he was depressed and drinking.

'I'll go over there,' she muttered. 'He'll still be up. It's only midnight.' If Rob wasn't home she would wait. What else could she do? Shannon got her car keys and hurried out. She was okay to drive, she'd only had a few sips of wine. Please let it be all right, she prayed as she ran downstairs. Let Finbar stay safe. He had got out of difficult situations before; she had to keep praying he would do it again.

The big Edwardian house in the tree-lined road in Woolton was dark and forbidding, and it didn't look like anyone was home. The road was so packed with cars she had to park some distance away. Shannon switched off the engine and sat there, remembering Bernard – Bernie the Bogeyman – and his depressed wife Margaret. Rob's alcoholic sister Melanie, abused by her father for years, a drug smuggler who ended up under a pile of coal in a derelict railway hut, a bullet through her head. Bernard, the headmaster, mutilating murderer of young girls. Who would have murdered her if she hadn't stopped him. Permanently. Shannon didn't want to get out of her warm car, press the bell and go in that house again. Face the son of that murderer, who was in a depressed state, and who might be drinking heavily. Rob turned into a different person when he was like that. The person who had betrayed her love and trust for him, raped her, destroyed their marriage.

Sitting there in the dark silence, all her bad feelings about Rob re-surfaced. What was he doing in the Magistrates' Court that day, the same day the missing Mont Blanc – engraved with the name *Bernard* – got stolen? He might have had some perfectly good reason, of course. But when he was there, normally the first thing he did was seek her out and start whingeing about something. Shannon thought of the anonymous letters, her slashed coat. Poor, murdered Lucas Grant. She had thought of Rob when she received the first letter, but dismissed her suspicions, especially after he'd been so helpful and friendly. Or appeared to be. And she was desperate, wasn't she? Vulnerable. Vulnerable meant open to attack.

I won't go in, she thought. I'll just speak to him on the doorstep. Assess his mood. Oh God, maybe I'm just crazy. Shannon got out of the car, crossed the road and walked back to the house, a feeling of dread in her heart as she entered the dark drive. Rob's car wasn't there. She hesitated, then rang the bell.

No answer. She crept further down the drive to the garage and peered in the dusty, cobwebbed window round the side. Rob's car wasn't in there. Damn. What now? Go in and wait for him? She turned and opened the wooden gate that led to the back garden. There was only the pale light of the spring moon to help her see her way and avoid falling over something. In the centre of the garden she could make out the headless stone statue of the young girl with a wreath of roses for knickers. Rob had knocked her head off during a drinking binge. He had also burned armfuls of his mother's beloved watercolours. Dreams of being an artist had kept Margaret going – along with wine, gin and Valium – insulated her from a bad marriage and all the other horrors she didn't want to see or think about.

The back door and French windows were locked. Shannon wondered if the spare back door key was still in its cunning little carved-out hiding place behind the loose brick in the wall around the corner. It was. A strong musty smell hit her when she crept into the dark kitchen and sitting room, as if no one had hoovered, cleaned or opened any windows in a long time. Well, Rob probably hadn't. He usually ignored things like that, unless it was to wonder why someone of the female persuasion didn't take the initiative. She didn't switch on any lights. The ponderous, carved, dining-room sideboard was covered with decanters, bottles and crystal tumblers. A pile of unopened post was spread over the dining table, along with more bottles and glasses. The smell in here was worse, Shannon thought, hurriedly backing out. Like stale sick. No way did she want to investigate *that*.

She went upstairs, frightened at being alone in this dark, silent house of ghosts. How could Rob stand to go on living here, even if he was having difficulty selling the place? It must get on his nerves, especially if he was depressed. It got on hers, and she'd only been here five minutes. The beds were stripped bare, except for the one in the large front bedroom that Rob occupied. The quilt was flung back and the pillow held a dip where his head had lain. Creased clothes lay everywhere.

Shannon went up another flight of stairs and opened the door of Bernard's old study. A faint smell of lavender polish lingered. Two empty wine bottles and a glass stood on the desk, which was covered with papers. A pen lay on top of an A4-size writing pad. She moved forward and clicked on the desk lamp. The pen was Bernard's Mont Blanc Le Grand, engraved with his name. Rob used it now, judging by the ink-stained tissues scattered over the desk. The writing pad was smooth, ivory, expensive paper. Identical to the paper used to write the poison pen letters. More coincidence. The bad feeling was getting worse. She opened a drawer and found matching envelopes. And a roll of pink satin ribbon.

'Oh, my God!' She spotted a large, hardbacked notebook, pulled it towards her and opened it, flipped through some pages. She froze.

'*. . . bitch criminal lawyer...didn't realise how much I'd* *enjoy cutting up her coat ... discovered my fountain pen was missing.'*

Shannon gasped again, ice cold, her body rigid with horror. 'Oh, Rob! *No.*' She turned over more pages, her hand shaking.

'*... anguished, rotten with guilt....Shannon, there's still time for you to be tied to the stake and smell your own burning flesh ... I'm a murderer ... I feel sick about what I've done, poor Lucas.*' She took a deep breath, flipped to the last page. '*I won't be here much longer. Neither will Shannon Flinder.*'

She was wrong. Rob did hate her that much. Shannon switched off the lamp, closed the notebook and clutched it to her. There was some stuff about how she'd hired a hit man to kill Bernard. So Rob did think she'd done it. He'd never mentioned it to her. The handwriting in this diary was Rob's, written with his father's pen. The ink was royal blue, so was the ink in the pen. He had disguised his handwriting for the letters, but now that Shannon looked she distinguished a vague resemblance, certain loops and the way some of the i's were not dotted. Rob had been writing her anonymous letters with his dead father's pen! Writing this diary of hate. And he had murdered Lucas Grant.

She was dry-mouthed and shivering with terror, could barely breathe. I have to get out of here, she thought. If he comes back...! She tried to turn, take a step. But her body refused to move.

Rob had changed when he had found out what his father was. She had tried to help him, save their marriage. But it wasn't to be. They'd got through the divorce and he'd been civilised, friendly even. More like the man she'd married. But Shannon was wrong, he was nothing like that man. All the time Rob had been building this crazy, twisted, terrifying narrative in his head, his growing feelings of isolation and impotence embedded in this hatred he now directed at her. She recalled his insane belief that the baby she and Finbar had lost was his. His indifference to Katy's pregnancy, then

345

his shock and grief when she had done what he apparently wanted and had a termination. Everything had combined to turn Rob into a murderer. In a horrific scenario written entirely by him. Literally written.

A chill draught swirled into the room, bringing with it a much worse smell, like something decaying. Shannon ran on to the landing and stopped, her heart thudding. The draught came from upstairs, from the attic that Margaret had called her studio, much to the scorn of Bernard and Josie Duffy, the cleaning lady. What was up there? Did she want to know? She climbed the stairs and stood still, straining her eyes in the darkness. No use. She clicked on the light.

The 100-watt bulb dangling from the centre beam illuminated the bare walls and the few blank canvases stacked against them. On the table were little dishes and tubes of dried, encrusted paint in blue, yellow, red, green and crimson. A jar of brushes from which dirty water had evaporated. The old black velvet sofa pushed against the far wall. Something lay on the sofa, covered by a dirty, paint-stained sheet.

'Oh, God!' Shannon whispered. The smell was stronger now, making her feel sick. Shivering uncontrollably, she moved forward, took one corner of the sheet between thumb and forefinger and pulled it down. She immediately dropped it and jumped back, stifling a scream of terror. The grotesquely swollen, purple-faced woman who lay there with a ligature knotted around her neck was Katy. Shannon backed further away, one hand clutched to her mouth to stop herself screaming. She switched off the light and ran down the stairs. She realised the groans and terrified gasps were her own. She was weak and breathless, as if she'd run a marathon. 'Get out,' she muttered. 'Get out *now*.'

Downstairs in the hall the front door slammed.

Chapter Thirty-Eight

Shannon stood on the dark landing, the diary clutched to her chest. Her breathing sounded horribly loud; she tried to calm it and slow her racing heartbeat. Rob locked the front door and slipped the chain in place, switched on lights and dropped his keys on the hall table. He grabbed the phone and made a call to someone who didn't seem to be home.

'Where are you, you fucking bitch?' he swore, banging the receiver down. If Rob meant her, Shannon thought, trembling, he didn't know how near she was! Bottles and glasses clinked in the dining room, then the television went on in the sitting room. She looked down. The old wooden stairs were treacherously creaky. How could she make it to the bottom without him hearing her, even with the loudness of the television? Hopefully he'd had a skinful. If he fell asleep on the sofa she could escape. But how long would that take? And what if he didn't?

Shannon crept back along the landing into the study, laid the diary on the desk and pulled out her mobile, dialled with clumsy fingers. Nothing happened. She gasped, her eyes filling with tears of frustration. The phone was down, dead. Why the bloody hell hadn't she thought to re-charge the battery earlier? *Thick.* Rob had a phone in his bedroom. She moved slowly in there, treading as lightly as possible, terrified that Rob might hear the floor creak even though he was in the sitting room at the back of the house. Saliva rushed

347

into her mouth and she gagged as the sickly sweet smell of Katy's rotting flesh hit her stomach again. Shannon swallowed, breathed, furiously willed herself not to throw up. How long did Rob intend to leave Katy's body lying in its paint-stained shroud on his mother's old attic sofa? God, this was crazy, she couldn't believe it was happening. It had to be all one bloody great big horrific nightmare from which she would wake up any second. Her mind wavered, teetering on the brink of screaming panic. Shannon forced herself to stay cool, concentrate on calling the police and getting the hell out of this house of death. She tiptoed around the bed, careful not to stumble over the trailing bathrobe belt and a pair of trainers. The faint light from the street lamp was just enough for her to dial by.

She had to speak in a hushed voice, almost a whisper, much to the annoyance of the woman and then the man on the other end.

'Your name's Shannon Flinder. And you say there's a body – a female, strangled? Evidence of another murder? And you're trapped in the house.' He sounded nervous now, getting the picture at last. 'Is your ex-husband armed?'

'Not as far as I know. But he's a police officer – in the CID – he could get access to firearms. It's a possibility you need to consider.'

'Okay. We'll get someone to you right away. Hang in there. Would you like to stay on the line or–'

'No, better not. Just hurry, *please.*' Hang in there. Shannon hoped she could. She gently replaced the receiver, picked it up and dialled Nick's number. Closed her eyes in despair as his phone rang and rang. He often unplugged it before going to sleep, especially on weekends. She left a message on his mobile.

'Nick, it's Shannon. It's after midnight and I'm stuck in Rob's parents' old house. It was Rob who wrote me the poison letters. I've called the police, they'll be here any minute.' Or so she hoped.

Nick wouldn't get the message until he woke up in seven

or eight hours' time. Where would she be then? At the police station? Wandering around her apartment in a state of shock, drinking a cup of coffee? Dead, purple-faced and strangled like Katy? Shannon forced down another wave of panic. She crawled on hands and knees back around the bed to the door. Got to her feet and crept out. Stood at the top of the stairs looking down into the hall. She could see the front door. The way to freedom.

Rob had left his keys on the hall table by the phone. Could she get down the stairs, unlock and unchain the door and get out before he heard anything? Or should she stay here until the police came? How long would they take, how long to scramble an armed response unit? If that's what they were doing. Maybe Rob would refuse to let them in. He had a dead body in the attic, for God's sake. So the police would have to break in. Rob might find her, murder her before they could rescue her. Take a chance, Shannon thought. Get out now.

She put one foot on the top stair, testing it. Went down a couple. *Creak*. Her heart jumped and she stopped, cringing, one hand gripping the banister. She was sweating now, her armpits and the space between her breasts wet with perspiration. She could smell her own terror. She went down another few stairs, into the light. More creaks. Dear God, don't let him find me, don't let him kill me! What bullshit fear brought out, how it shrank and reduced you. Pathetic. Laughing voices from the telly, not loud enough. Shannon focused on the hall table, the keys. She reached the foot of the stairs, crept forward, stretched out one hand to grab them.

Another voice. Not from the telly. Not laughing. She turned. Rob stood there, unshaven and dishevelled, his red-rimmed brown eyes narrowed with shock and anger. He wore jeans, a rumpled black sweatshirt. She recognised that look in his eyes. It was how he had looked when he'd found out about his father. How he'd looked when he had raped her, beaten her up. Told her he was a monster. She should

349

have listened instead of feeling sorry for him, thinking he didn't really mean to hurt her because he was freaked, had suffered a breakdown. How stupid was that? Shannon wasn't stupid now, not any more. But maybe it was too late for that to matter.

'Didn't you hear me?' Rob glared at her. 'I *said*, what the fuck are you doing here?'

She opened her mouth to form some sort of answer, but no words came out. She could only gape, stare. The blood didn't really drain from her face. It felt more like a flash. She prepared for flight or fight, hoping it wouldn't have to be the latter.

'I was worried,' she said at last. 'Haven't heard from you for a few days.'

'*What?*' He barked a laugh. 'You mean you wanted to?'

'Of course I did.' She swallowed. 'We're friends, aren't we?'

'Are we?' He came closer and she smelled whisky. And brimstone. 'Maybe. When it suits you.'

'Rob, that's not fair.' She backed away. 'I wanted to talk to you, see how you're doing, but you're not at work and you don't answer the phone. That's why I came round now. I was worried about you. I couldn't sleep.'

'Well, thanks for that. You've made my night. Sexy red dress,' he commented as her coat fell open. 'Nice. Is it for me, or did you go out tonight?'

'I had dinner with Nick.'

'Dinner with Nick,' he mocked. 'The steadfast tin soldier. Has he hit on you yet?'

'Nick wouldn't–'

'Shut up. I don't want to know. Have you been upstairs?'

'Just on the first floor landing,' she lied. 'I thought you might be asleep in bed.'

'Why didn't you come down when I got in?'

'Once I knew you were okay, I didn't want to disturb you any more. It's late. I decided it was best to just slip out and phone you – or come back – tomorrow.'

'Yeah, right. How did you get in?'

'The front door was open,' she lied again.

'It fucking wasn't.' He scowled. 'It was closed when I came in.'

'I know. I shut it.' She prayed he wouldn't remember about the spare back door key. Maybe she could slip past him, run out that way. Come on, come *on*, she thought. What was taking the police so long?

'There's something else I wanted to ask you,' she said, stalling, terrified he would get violent any second. 'It's about Finbar.'

'Did you dump him? Why?'

'No. He dumped me.'

'The Mad Mick criminal kicked you out of his bed?' Rob's smile was cruel. 'Bloody hell, now there's a thing! What can you possibly want to ask *me* about him?'

'Some officer from Special Branch visited, said Finbar was suspected of involvement in some terrorist incident being planned.' Shannon paused, biting her lip. 'I wondered if maybe you'd heard rumours of anything going on?'

'Still love him, do you?' Rob jeered. 'Want to help him, prove yourself indispensable so that he'll let you crawl back into his bed? Typical bloody woman. I wouldn't tell you anything if I knew every sodding detail.'

'Okay.' She shrugged. 'All right. I just thought you were bigger than that.'

'Don't patronise me, you arrogant bitch! I hope the bastard ends up dead. You wish that baby you lost had been his, don't you? Not mine.' Rob moved towards her. 'I'm going to teach you a lesson once and for all.'

'No! Don't touch me!'

He lunged at her and she gave a cry of fear as she dodged out of the way. But there wasn't much space for dodging about, and nothing with which to defend herself. Rob grabbed her and pinioned her against the wall. Shannon shut her eyes and turned her head to one side. 'You love him,' he yelled in her ear. 'You don't love me, you lying, evil bitch!

351

You never did. I'm going to kill you!' He dragged her into the sitting room and threw her on the sofa. She rolled over and tried to get up, but he hit her across the face and shoved her back again.

'The police are coming,' she gasped, dazed. 'Any second now. They know you wrote me those letters, they know you murdered Katy. And Lucas Grant. It's finished, Rob. Give it up.'

'It's not finished,' he shouted. 'Not until you've paid.' He reached behind him and grabbed something. Shannon saw with horror that it was a gun. She cringed as he levelled it at her.

'Do you know how much I hate you?'

'I think I've got a pretty good idea!' The gun looked like some kind of short pistol. 'Where did you get that thing?' Keep asking questions, try to delay.

'A mate of mine's a Firearms Officer. I told him I just wanted to play with it and he lent it me. He won't have a job any more after this weekend, but that's his problem.'

Shannon heard cars pull up outside, doors slam. 'Let me go, Rob. Now. Please.'

'I planned to kill you tonight. I was pissed off because I couldn't find you. And all the time you were right under my nose. It's fate. Do you believe in fate?'

'Not as such.'

'Cynical as usual. No wonder the Mad Mick dumped you. Stand up,' he ordered.

She slowly obeyed. 'Rob, this is really unclever.'

'Just keep it shut. Do what I tell you. Move.' She walked into the hall. 'Get upstairs. I've got a gun,' he yelled as someone pounded on the door. 'Stay out, or the bitch lawyer dies!' He grabbed her hair, pressed the gun to her left temple and propelled her up the stairs. On the landing the stink of decay hit her again. Shannon collapsed, her legs buckling under her.

'I need the loo,' she gasped. 'Going to be sick.'

'You do and I'll rub your face in it! *Move.*' He dragged her up and shoved her into the bedroom, now bright with lights shining in from outside. He forced her to the windows, smashed the glass with the gun butt and held her there, the gun pressed to her head. Shannon blinked in the strong light. Around the edges she could see police cars, dark figures moving purposefully, a crowd of the usual loathsome rubberneckers already gathering. They weren't even remotely ashamed of their thirst for vicarious violence, other people's tragedies. She felt dizzy, thought she might pass out. Rob shouted down at the police officers through the smashed glass.

'Stay out! Stay away, or I'll kill her. I killed the other bitch because she murdered my baby. I'll do it again. You come in here and she's dead before you get upstairs!'

A man's voice boomed at them through a loudhailer. 'Rob. Let Shannon come out, and then we can talk. Just let her go, now.'

'Fuck off!' he screamed. He turned and shoved her against a wall, then moved to the door and slammed it shut. Came back and stood in front of her, levelled the gun at her face.

'Rob, do what they say,' she gasped. 'This is pointless.'

'You destroyed me,' he said. 'If it hadn't been for you I'd never have killed Lucas. You made me feel evil. Tainted. You spread your stain all over me.' Shannon gave a terrified cry as he reached out and grabbed at her dress, ripping the neckline. 'Get your clothes off.'

'No!' Tears flooded her eyes. 'You won't do *that* to me again. I won't go along with whatever crazy shit you've got planned,' she sobbed, 'so you might as well shoot me now!'

Rob lowered the gun slightly and stood back, staring at her. 'Oh, I will,' he said, nodding. 'When I'm ready.'

'Rob, we were married. Happy. We loved each other. You're not going to murder me now, here in your bloody parents' house! Where all the trouble started.' She wiped her eyes on her sleeve.

'You had my father killed, didn't you?' he asked suddenly. He grinned, a twisted grin, the light slanting across his

353

cheekbone. 'Don't get me wrong, I don't care. He was a bastard and I hated him. He deserved to die. It's not what you did, it's the fact that you got away with it. That's what pisses me off. If I'd killed the shit I wouldn't be standing here with you in my sights. I'd be doing time.'

If this was her dying day she wouldn't admit it, and never to him. 'No.' Shannon shook her head. 'I didn't kill him. I don't know who did. There must have been more than enough people who hated him. I mean, where would you start? That's why your cop mates took the easy way out – or so they thought – and tried to fit me up.'

She had been desperate to save her own life. Save other lives. Stay free. But hadn't there been another emotion in there, muddying the purity of her motives? Revenge. Not joyful, not exultant. But hidden, ice cold, implacable. Oh yes.

'I didn't mean to kill Katy,' Rob said. 'She came round to collect some stuff she'd forgotten, and we had a row. I lost it. I didn't mean to hurt her.'

Shannon trembled. 'I know.'

'You fucking don't!' he shouted, angry again. 'How could you?'

'Because there's been enough hurt, Rob. You know that. You don't want any more.'

'No, you're right.' He went quiet. 'I've come to the end of the road.' He stepped back, lifted the gun and pressed it to his right temple.

Shannon squeezed her eyes shut and turned to the wall, hands covering her face. Go on, she thought, savage in her terror. Blow your stupid fucking brains out and don't bother me any more. Just get on with it. The phone started ringing.

'Don't answer that,' Rob warned. He lowered the gun.

'Why would I?' she cried. 'It's you they want to talk to.'

'Get away.' He menaced her with the gun again. 'Get in that corner by the window, sit down, put your hands on your head. Don't move a muscle.' She did as he said. He moved to the bedside table and grabbed the phone.

354

'I'm not talking to anybody,' he shouted. 'No negotiation. You come in, she dies. That's it.' He banged the receiver down, ripped out the cord and hurled the phone across the room, smashing it against the wall. 'Have you got a mobile?' he demanded. 'Give it to me.'

'It's not working.' Shannon pulled it out of her pocket and handed it to him. 'Battery's down.' She watched as he smashed it against the windowsill, then partially drew the curtains. 'I fucked Katy just before I strangled her,' he said, chillingly matter of fact. 'She might have been pregnant when she died.'

What a lovely thought. Shannon sat up straight, every nerve and muscle in her body straining. 'Rob, let me go,' she pleaded again, desperate to get through to him. 'Don't hurt me, don't hurt yourself. Just end this now. You can do it. I'll help you, I promise. I care about you.' She knew she was gabbling.

'You don't care. Shannon, shut up.' His face was in shadow. 'Don't talk any more.'

'I do care! It can be okay, Rob, it really can. But you've got to stop this now.' She paused. 'Look, won't you just let me go to the loo? And I'm cold, I'm tired. I need something to drink.'

'You don't need anything.' He stood over her, pointing the gun at her face.

'Don't hurt me,' Shannon gasped. '*Please*, Rob! Think what you're doing!'

'I have.' Rob's voice was suddenly calm, terrifyingly calm. 'I've been thinking about this for a long time. You get away with things,' he said. 'You always did. It makes me jealous – sicker than you feel right now. Well, all that ends here.'

'Rob, for God's sake!'

'Shut up.' He gripped the gun. 'You're going to die, Shannon.'

Chapter Thirty-Nine

'Shoot him!' Blick yelled as his men dragged the struggling lorry driver from his cab and kicked him to the ground. 'Hurry up. Go on, kill the bastard.'

'No!' Finbar sat handcuffed in the back of the transit van, watching through the open doors as they kicked and punched the helpless driver. 'Don't kill him, for Christ's sake,' he shouted, sickened. 'You don't have to do that! Just leave him here.'

Blick turned and glared at him. His smiling sense of humour was all gone now. 'Who d'you think you are, the fucking moral majority? No, don't hit him too hard,' he snapped as the man covering Finbar with the gun cuffed him across the head. 'He has to drive later.'

The deserted lorry park off the slip road beside the railway arches was flooded with spring sunshine. Finbar glanced at the blue sky. It seemed impossible that all this was happening. He winced and turned away as one of the men fired several shots into the by now unconscious lorry driver. The man's body jerked and lay still, bright blood forming a pool around his head.

'You're very sensitive all of a sudden,' Blick remarked. 'I mean, how many have you stiffed in your time? I suppose you'd say that was justified. Self-defence.'

Finbar wasn't going to argue. He sat still, trying to concentrate his energies, waiting for anything that might give him the chance to escape. Another man climbed into the van.

'Watch him,' Blick ordered. He was sweating. 'Don't take your eyes off him for a second.' He got out and slammed the doors. Finbar knew he was supervising the loading of the semtex into the lorry, which had been brought to the spot in another, larger van. They'd certainly been busy during the time they had kept him locked up in that box room in the flat. Minutes passed. Then Blick flung open the door again.

'Out!' They pushed him out and Finbar averted his eyes from the poor dead lorry driver. They were just going to leave him lying here in the sun, like carrion for vultures. Blick and another man took off his handcuffs and forced him at gunpoint into the lorry cab, into the driver's seat. Blick checked his watch. The radio was still playing, and there was a photograph of a smiling, dark-haired woman and two children, a girl and a boy, stuck on the dashboard. Finbar felt sick.

'Drive,' Blick ordered, holding the gun to his head. 'One wrong move, and you get what he got. Don't have an accident, or you'll be dead too. Once we're there we've got twenty minutes to get clear,' he said to the other man, who was nervous and sweating. 'No problem, it'll be fine. They put a biro in.'

'Biro' meant a dowel rod, which would hold the bomb's timer at a pre-set delay. It was an extra safeguard. The timing and power unit would contain a safety-to-arm switch and the timer, also the power necessary to trigger the detonator which would in turn detonate the device's main explosive charge. Even if he could get rid of these two bastards, stop the lorry and locate the timing and power unit, could he de-activate the bomb? He hardly knew anything about this stuff. Only what would happen when it went off; you didn't need to to be an explosives expert to get your head round that. Finbar's hands slid on the steering wheel; he drove as carefully as he could. He had a HGV licence, but hadn't driven a lorry in years. They knew about the licence, of course, so he hadn't been able to lie.

Sunny Saturday. People heading into the city centre, or to Southport with its prom and beaches. And shopping, of course, the main form of leisure activity. Finbar could see the dark-blue transit van with the other men inside trailing them in the stream of traffic. They drove out of town along the Dock Road, heading for The Village. Blick and his companion were silent, on edge. The cold gun barrel pressed Finbar's jugular vein. The brand-new shopping mall came into view, it's windows sparkling, a strip of river glittering in the background. The car parks were crowded, people everywhere.

'Two o'clock,' Blick said. He lowered the gun, digging it into Finbar's ribs. 'Follow the signs for the lorry parking bays. Don't try anything,' he warned again.

Finbar cleared his throat. 'No worries.' He wondered if shopaholic Paula was here with her boyfriend. And where was Shannon today, what was she doing? She hated shopping malls, so this wouldn't be her thing. Thank God. Shannon would be safe now, he thought. Hoped. Have a good, long life, he wished her silently. Be happy. I'm sorry for everything. I love you.

'Stop,' Blick snapped. 'Right here.'

Finbar glanced at him, startled. He was driving along a narrow road just past the mall's entrance, which curved around the building. The dark blue transit van was several metres behind them. 'But this isn't the lorry park yet.' He winced with pain as the gun was jammed into his ribs.

'I said, stop!' Blick shouted. 'Now.'

'All right.' He slowed the lorry and stopped, switched off the engine. Silence. Blick looked at him. He was pale, his eyes glittering.

'Time to say goodbye. This is where we get out.' He paused. 'But not you.'

'Hurry up!' the other man gasped, his frightened face shiny with sweat.

'Take it easy. Just cover him, all right? Do it!' The man levelled the gun again. His hands were shaking.

'I was going to kill you before we got out,' Blick said, pulling the handcuffs from his pocket. 'But then I decided it would be much more fun to leave you handcuffed to the wheel so that you'd have a bit of time to contemplate your impending demise. At least it'll be mercifully quick,' he said. 'A lot quicker than most people's.' He smiled. 'And actually you've got five minutes, not fifteen.' The man glanced at him, startled. That's news to him, Finbar thought.

'Well, you know what?' He looked calmly at Blick. Sweat prickled his body. 'It's a beautiful day. I'm not in the mood to sit here and contemplate my demise.'

Blick started to laugh. 'Never give it a rest, do you? You know, I'm almost sorry–'

Finbar grabbed Blick's arm that held the gun, wrenched it upwards and shoved him back against the other man. Startled, Blick fired. There was a shot and two deafening bangs. The shots went through the windows, splintering glass. The other man gasped in panic, kicked open the door and jumped out. Suddenly there were armed police racing towards them, surrounding the transit van, pounding on the back of the lorry. Finbar and Blick wrestled each other, grunting and gasping. The gun dropped on the floor. Finbar managed to grab the handcuffs and smashed them in Blick's face. He punched him several times. Blick slumped sideways across the seat, dazed. Finbar pulled the gun out of his hand.

'No,' Blick groaned, blood streaming from his nose. 'Don't kill me, please don't! Come on, you're a better person than I am.'

'Don't try to be witty, it doesn't suit you. But yeah.' Finbar levelled the gun. 'I am better than you – most people are. That's why I'm going to put you out of your misery, you fucking bastard.'

He fired twice. Blick crumpled, collapsed, his eyes blank and staring. Blood and brains spattered the inside of the cab.

Shaking uncontrollably, Finbar kicked open the door and half jumped, half fell out of the cab on to the rough concrete ground. He could hear raised voices, cries and screams in the background as people were shooed away. Armed police pulled him to his feet.

'Five minutes, maybe less,' he gasped. 'Before it blows!'

'No,' Carl Mactire's voice said. 'It's all right. We've de-activated the charge, the whole thing won't go off. There'll have to be a controlled explosion of the lorry after we've evacuated this place. Come on.'

Finbar pointed to the blood-spattered cab window. His clothes were covered in blood, and he could smell it. 'He was the leader. He tried to kill me.'

'Yeah. Okay. Whatever. You've saved the taxpayers the expense of his trial and life stretch. Not to mention your own.'

Finbar was bundled into a police car and driven away. From a safe distance they watched as the area was cleared and the lorry blown up. The explosion shook the ground, sent clouds of black smoke and leaping flame into the blue sky.

'Well,' some witty person commented. 'Opening Day certainly went with a bang, didn't it?'

Finbar turned to Mactire. He was dirty and sweating, drained. 'I'm going home.'

'You can't. Not yet. You'll have to come back with us and get debriefed.'

'Fuck that. It'll have to wait.' He was shivering suddenly, despite the sweat and heat of the day. 'I'm knackered,' he said. 'I've had enough. Get someone to drive me home. Now.'

'Okay, but we'll need you–'

'Yeah, whatever. Come on, hurry up.' Finbar suddenly felt like he might collapse if he didn't sit down soon.

A uniformed constable drove him home. He walked slowly into the silence and space of his wrecked apartment. It wasn't really wrecked, just stuff strewn everywhere.

Finbar poured himself a single malt, stripped off his clothes and put them in a bin bag. He never wanted to wear them again. He took a long, hot shower. He was still shivering, couldn't get warm. That was shock, of course. He put on a bathrobe, went back into the sitting room and poured himself another drink. Stood gulping it and staring out at the sparkling, sunlit river, trying to come to terms with the events of the past few days. He had survived. He was home. It was over, just like that. Well, not over in his head, of course. That was going to take time. What now?

Better let Nick know I'm alive, he thought. He went into his bedroom and collapsed on to the bed, pulling the quilt over him. Shannon's high-heeled shoe was still on the floor. Nick wasn't at home or at the office, so he tried his mobile.

'It's me,' he said. 'I'm alive.'

'Thank Christ for that!' Nick's voice was high, strained. 'What the hell happened? Are you hurt?'

'No, just knackered. In shock. I can't really talk now,' Finbar interrupted. 'I need a rest. I'll see you later and we'll–'

'No, Finbar, listen! I'm outside Rob Flinder's house – his parents' house in Woolton. The bastard's got Shannon inside at gunpoint. It's a siege, been going on since the early hours of this morning. He's threatening to kill her and himself. It was him who wrote her those bloody letters – and murdered that lad, Lucas Grant.'

Finbar sat up, gripping the phone. *'What?'*

361

Chapter Forty

'Shannon. *Shannon!* Open your eyes.'

She didn't want to. They felt too heavy to open. She stretched and groaned. How many hours now? The bedroom was getting warmer and more stuffy as the sun crept around to the front side of the house. The curtains were drawn. Had Rob hit her, knocked her out? Or had she just fallen into an exhausted doze? Shannon couldn't remember.

Why didn't the police hurry up and do something? Probably because this was the kind of situation they most dreaded, no matter if they were armed to the teeth. So-called 'domestics' where the man got violent. She had heard of many situations where they had been too late and the woman or even children had been murdered.

'*Shannon!*'

His voice was loud again, angry. She opened her eyes and looked at him, saw the gun still pointing at her face. Saw his rage. She couldn't believe she was still alive, still walled up here. Rob must be suffering from some kind of psychosis, she thought. And it had been coming on for a long time. She remembered some article she had read in a scientific magazine – or was it a psychology one? About how if a man's testosterone levels rose too high and the feel-good serotonin levels dropped low, it was supposed to be a fatal combination. Not for the man himself, of course, just for anyone unlucky enough to get entangled with him. Somebody

362

unlucky enough to get entangled with Rob – Katy – now lay strangled and decomposing in the attic over her head. Shannon took a breath and sat up straight, not too quickly. Adrenalin flooded back.

'Tell me,' Rob demanded, 'what it'll be like when we're back together. Go on.'

Oh God, not again. He'd been on about that all bloody night and she was fresh out of imagination. The police have to do something soon, she thought desperately. For Christ's sake, it's been hours! They were probably arguing amongst themselves, no one willing to make a decision or seize the initiative. And when they finally acted, what then? A big fuck-up? No doubt they had body bags as well as guns out there. Shannon imagined them lifting her into a body bag, trying to push all her hair in so that they could zip it up. Just one more casualty of violence, incompetence, indifference. That image suddenly made her furious.

'When we're back together it'll be wonderful.' She looked into his eyes and began to speak in a slow, dreamy voice. 'You'll have to sell this house, of course. It's got too many sad, bad memories. If you can't sell it you could always give it away. That would be a good gesture. Symbolic.'

He frowned. 'Symbolic of what?'

'It would mean you'd let go of the past. Put it all behind you.'

'Yeah. You're right.' Rob laughed suddenly. 'You know what? I'll give it to a family of asylum seekers. Freak the snobs around here.'

'Nice one,' Shannon said. 'Oh dear, there goes the neighbourhood. Property values bursting like champagne bubbles.' Fall asleep, you stubborn bastard, she thought, willing him. You must be more knackered than I am.

'And what about us?' Rob asked. 'Where will we live?'

'Well, we've got the money from our old house. Half each. We'll put that back together and buy a new place. But I'd like to get right away from here. Wouldn't you? Start afresh.'

363

'Yeah.' He nodded slowly. 'That'd be good. I've always fancied living in the Lake District.'

'Oh, I don't know. Too many tourists in summer.'

'Well, wherever. I don't really care.' His red-rimmed, bloodshot brown eyes bored into hers. 'And you'll get pregnant, of course. Soon as possible.'

Shannon felt a tightening in her stomach. 'Yes.'

'I want a girl,' he said. 'A daughter. I want her to look like you. She'll be ours, a part of us. Isn't that great? We'll love her, she'll love us. You'll make a fantastic mother.' He paused. 'We could have two, three kids.'

'It sounds wonderful,' Shannon lied, feeling chilled. She forced herself to smile. 'We'll be so happy.'

'I'm not fooling myself,' Rob said suddenly. 'I'd have to explain *that*.' He pointed the gun at the ceiling. 'But we'd get through it. You could help me, speak for me. I've treated you well, haven't I?' He looked at her again. 'Not hurt you or anything.'

'No. You didn't hurt me. You don't hurt someone you love.'

'Love? I thought I hated you,' he said, puzzled and frowning. 'I really did. I was going to kill you.' He lowered the gun, stared at it.

Shannon's heart raced. 'Rob, can I please go to the loo?' she asked, keeping her voice low and slow. 'I really need to. Otherwise I'll have to pee right here. It'll stink.' If she could only get out of this room and on to the landing, she had a chance.

He was silent for a few seconds. 'Okay. Do you promise you'll speak for me? Stick by me?'

'Of course I will. Like you said, we'll get through this together. Can you help me up?' she asked, stretching then tensing her adrenalin-flooded muscles. 'I'm stiff after so much sitting.'

'Sure. Give me your hand.' He sounded normal again now, reasonable. Shannon didn't know which was more terrifying. He could pull that trigger and kill her any second.

The fact that he hadn't yet done so didn't mean he wouldn't. She held out her hand and he took it, pulled her to her feet. They stood close together, looking into one another's eyes. I married this man, Shannon thought. I lived with him, loved him. I wanted to have his baby. How the hell did it all come to this? She was so exhausted, so drained with fear, that she could barely stand. A tear rolled down her cheek.

'What are you thinking?' Rob asked. He put up one hand and caught the tear with his index finger, looked at it for a second and let it drop. 'You've got beautiful eyes,' he said. 'I always loved the colour.'

Slowly, very slowly, Shannon reached up and slid her arms around his neck. He tensed, then gradually relaxed. Suddenly he dropped the gun and put his arms around her, holding her so tight she could hardly breathe. His body trembled, started to shake with huge, gulping sobs. She thought she heard stairs creak.

'I'm sorry,' he sobbed. 'I'm sorry, Shannon!'

'It's all right,' she whispered, hugging him. 'It's okay.' Where was the bloody gun? She slowly moved her left and then her right foot, feeling around for it. Her left toe touched the horrible object and she tried to edge it away under the bed. Rob stiffened.

'What are you doing?'

'Nothing,' she gasped. 'Sorry. Just dying to go to the loo, that's all.' *Dying.* Shit. Bad choice of word there.

He looked down at her, gripping her shoulders. His face was red, wet with tears. The look of rage was back in his eyes. 'No, you're not! You're trying to–'

'Get away from me!' she screamed, shoving him back. He started, then grabbed her again, his hands reaching for her throat. Shannon lashed out at him, struggling fiercely, desperate for her life. They fell on the bed. Rob got on top of her, pushed her legs apart, dragged her dress up over her thighs and hips.

'No!' Shannon screamed. *'No!'*

'Shut up!' His hands came up over her breasts, tried to

close around her throat. She thrashed around, screaming. He bent over her, bringing his face close to hers. She freed one hand and clawed at his eyes. He shouted in pain, tried to turn his head away.

'You fucking bitch!' Shannon brought up her right knee and thudded it into his groin. He gave a choked cry. She shoved him off, wriggled out from under him and scrambled off the bed, staggered to her feet. Crying in panic, she got to the door, wrenched it open and ran out on to the landing. Two armed police officers wearing bulky, bullet-proof vests were halfway up the stairs.

'Don't shoot me!' she screamed, terrified. They looked more shocked than her.

'Shannon, get back here!' Rob shouted. 'I'll–'

'Let me go,' she screamed, running down the stairs and shoving past the two officers. 'Let me go, let me get out of here!' She reached the foot of the stairs. The front door was open, more armed police grouped there. Shannon stopped and gasped as a single shot sounded from upstairs.

'Get the paramedics!' one of the officers shouted. 'He's shot himself.'

'Oh, no!' she whispered, tears flowing down her face. 'Oh, no. *Rob.*' People were pouring past her, rushing upstairs. 'Is he dead?' she called. What do you care? a contemptuous voice inside her asked. He held you hostage all night long, a gun stuck in your face. He would have killed you. But at this moment she did care.

'Come on, love.' A policewoman took her arm. 'Let's get you out of here.'

'Get off me.' Shannon pulled away. 'I'm all right.'

'But you'll need to see a doctor–'

'I *said,* get off me!' She wrenched her arm free. 'I don't need any bloody doctor.' She ran out of the house into a crowd of people and stopped again, bewildered. More police officers milled around and there were police cars and vans parked in the drive and outside on the grass verge. The wailing of an ambulance came closer as it turned into the road,

366

drew up and screeched to a halt, lights flashing. The paramedics jumped out and ran past her.

'Shannon!' a voice shouted. 'Shannon!'

She wiped her eyes and stared round. Finbar broke free from the cordon, followed by Nick, and ran towards her.

'Are you all right?' He grabbed her and swept her up in his arms, kissing her and stroking her hair. 'Are you okay?' He hugged her tight. 'I wanted to come in and get you, but those bastards back there stopped me.'

'Rob would have killed you,' she gasped, clinging to him.

'He nearly killed *you*.' His green eyes were brilliant with tears.

'Are you safe?' she asked. 'What happened to you?'

'Never mind about that now. Shannon, I'm sorry!' Finbar kissed her again. 'Sorry I hurt you so much. I thought you'd be safe without me, I thought–' He stopped, his voice choked. 'I love you.'

'I love you too.' She couldn't believe she was seeing him again. 'Don't let go of me.'

'I won't.' He hugged her tighter. 'I'll never bloody let go of you again!'

'Move back, please!' someone shouted.

'They're bringing him out,' Nick muttered. 'Jesus Christ ... Shannon, don't look.'

She clung tight to Finbar, her face hidden in his shoulder. 'Is Rob dead?'

'No,' Finbar said grimly. 'More's the pity. Looks like an intensive care job though. He might not make it.'

'Ms Flinder? Shannon.' The persistent policewoman touched her arm again. 'Would you like to come with me now, please?'

'No, she wouldn't.' Finbar turned on her. 'If it was down to you lot she'd still be stuck in there at the mercy of that nut job. Whatever you want, it'll have to bloody well wait. I'll look after her. Come on,' he said to Shannon. He smoothed back her hair, kissed her on the forehead and gently drew her away, his arms tight around her. 'We're out of here.'

Chapter Forty-One
Epilogue

'Did you sleep?' he asked her the next morning, coming into the bedroom with two cups of coffee. 'I didn't, or not much. I had to keep making sure you were still lying next to me.' He moved the closed blinds aside and looked out at the sunlit river, the cloud-streaked sky. 'Looks like being a good day.' Finbar didn't just mean the weather.

'No, I didn't get much sleep either.' Shannon rolled over, pulled the quilt up and propped herself on one elbow. Finbar sat on the bed and took her in his arms, hugging her. 'I had this horrible dream,' she said, leaning her head on his shoulder. 'I was living in a house with some hostile people I hardly knew. I went around turning on the taps and every time I did that, blood came gushing out. I told the others what was happening, but they wouldn't listen to me.'

'Hmm.' He frowned, stroking her hair and the nape of her neck, her smooth back. 'No, not very pleasant. It'll be tough for a while,' he murmured, loving the feel of her skin. 'For both of us. But we've got each other back and that's what matters.' His arms tightened around her. 'I can't believe how I nearly lost you! Shannon, I ... Who the fuck's that?' he muttered as the phone started to ring.

Shannon groaned. 'Can't they just let us have a peaceful

Sunday morning in bed, for God's sake! After all that's happened.'

'Apparently not.' Finbar picked up the phone. 'Yeah, who is this?' He listened, then cupped his hand over the receiver. 'It's the police,' he said, his voice grim. 'For you. If they want you to go down there today – or pay you a visit here – tell them to forget it. The doctor said you need complete rest and quiet for at least the next few days. That goes for me too.'

'No worries.' Shannon sat up in bed and took the phone. 'Okay,' she said after a minute. 'Thank you.' She handed the receiver back to him and he replaced it, reached down to pull out the plug.

'What did they want?' He passed her a cup of coffee.

'Rob's still in intensive care.' She shivered slightly. 'They say he'll make it. There's no brain damage. He missed putting the bullet in any vital areas.'

'That's a shame!'

'But it took a six-hour operation to get it out without causing any permanent damage. And he's lost a lot of blood.' She took a few sips of coffee then put the cup down and lay back on the pillows, her blue eyes sombre. 'They seemed to think I'd want to know that as soon as possible.'

'Bloody typical, isn't it?' Finbar felt furious. 'Bastard couldn't just top himself and leave you in peace!'

'You know, when Rob fired that bullet into his head yesterday ... I actually felt sorry for him. Wanted to help him. Even though he could have murdered me as well as Katy.' She frowned. 'How thick is *that*?'

'It's not thick. You loved the guy once, you were married to him.' Finbar hesitated. 'How d'you feel now?'

'Angry. At myself as well as him. And stupid. Why didn't I guess it was him writing those letters? Like you say, I was married to him once. You'd think I would have realised!'

'No,' he argued. 'You can never tell what someone will do, no matter how close you are – or were – or how well you think you know them.'

369

Shannon looked at him. 'I hope that doesn't go for us.'

'Of course it bloody doesn't.' He pulled her into his arms again. 'How long d'you reckon they'll put this twisted mass of neuroses away for? Once he's out of hospital and the trial's over. Should be at least several decades, don't you think?'

Shannon shrugged. 'Depends on the psychiatrists more than the judge. They rule. Despite their well-documented history of fatal mistakes. Fatal for other people, that is. But no. I don't think they'll let him out for a good few years to come. I did have bad feelings about Rob,' she said. 'He was obviously falling apart again. But I never thought he was capable of murder. All the time he seemed to care, wanted to help me. But when I found out he believed the baby we'd lost was his, I knew something was seriously wrong. I hadn't realised his head was so full of–'

'*Shit,*' Finbar finished briskly. 'Shall we try and forget him?' he asked. 'For now, anyway.'

'Yes,' she murmured. 'Let's do that.'

He stroked her shoulders then cupped one of her breasts in his hand, his palm slowly circling her hardening nipple. She gave a little gasp of pleasure.

'Big question,' he said, kissing her. 'When are you moving back in? It's bloody horrible here without you. We've got some lost time to make up for. And I think I'll get you a new engagement ring,' he grinned. 'New ring, new life. How about that?'

'Well–' Shannon hesitated, looked tense. 'I only just moved out, really, didn't I?'

'So?' Finbar stared down at her, shocked and anxious. 'Are you saying you don't want to move back in with me? Why not?' he asked. 'What's wrong?'

'Nothing's *wrong*. It's just that – I know what you did and everything – you thought it was best, you wanted to keep me safe because of what those terrorists threatened to do. But our break-up – and everything else that's happened – it all gave me a hell of a shock. It's been terrible for you as well. We could so easily have–' She glanced away.

'Exactly. That's why I want you to move back in right now.'

'I know. But I just think it's best if I stay where I am for a while,' Shannon said. 'Take some time, get my head together. I'm sorry, Finbar,' she whispered. 'But I don't think I'm ready to live with you again. Not just yet.'

'Right.' He nodded, and his handsome face darkened. 'Well, yeah.'

'It doesn't matter,' she said hastily, seeing his gloom. 'I mean, I'm only down the road. We can still see each other every day.' Shannon smiled and slid her arms around his neck. The quilt fell away from her naked body as she pressed herself against him. 'Every night.'

'I understand,' Finbar said, kissing her. 'At least I think I do. Can't pretend I'm happy about it. Suppose it serves me right though.'

'*No*. It's not like that. This is just temporary. I promise. I need time, that's all.'

'Take all the bloody time you want.' He smiled crookedly. His green eyes were wet. 'Just confirm one thing for me. We are friends again?'

'Oh yes.' Shannon sat astride him, pulled open his bathrobe and ran her hands over his broad, warm chest. 'Definitely,' she murmured.